THE RANDALL & CARVER SERIES

BOOKS 1 - 3

BLAIR HOWARD

Published Cleveland, TN 2026 Blair Howard Books

www.blairhowardbooks.com

blairhoward@blairhowardbooks.com

NEVER SAY DEAD

A RANDALL & CARVER MYSTERY BOOK 1

For Jo, as always.

1

Monday Evening

Mallory Carver leaned back against the bar counter and stared up at the water stains on the ceiling.

She didn't know how long they'd been there. She'd worked at The Saloon since... she specifically remembered the help wanted sign had appeared in October after she graduated high school, but she didn't apply until after Thanksgiving. And only then because she needed to get out of the house for a few hours each day. But the part-time job turned full-time, and...

Thirteen years later and I'm wondering if I can sell pictures of the ceiling for Rorschach tests, she thought.

She imagined a decade of drunks staring up at them, some seeing their mothers, others seeing their dogs. Maybe some saw a traumatic childhood event; *those would be the drunks that cried into their beer,* she thought.

She'd seen every kind of drunk you could imagine during her thirteen years at The Saloon.

Back in the day, when she was first hired, it had been the Old West Saloon and Cattle Grill. It was a nice place then—fun music, good, inexpensive beer, an attractive menu, and even some coin-op horses out front for the kids to ride. Then the owner died, and it became Mustang Sally's. Sally kept the entire staff, which had been a relief, and she'd been a good boss and had treated everyone well. But then she'd had an emergency and moved out of state. After that it became the Quick Draw, an apt name since people didn't stay long when they found out how much the drinks cost. And now it was The Saloon, where the drinks were cheap because they were cheap drinks. The speaker system was old, dating from Sally's time, but she and the live music were long gone. And Vinnie, who'd owned the place for the last six years, cared more about the pennies he pinched than he did complaining customers.

It's a hole. And I can't dig my way out, she thought gloomily.

She looked at the clock. It was a little before nine PM—what once was peak hour—but the only customers she had was a booth full of bikers drinking the most tasteless domestic beer they had on tap, and Art Peters ensconced at the end of the bar with his sleep apnea.

"If we don't have any business, I guess I might as well start cleaning up," she muttered, slipping an earbud under her long blond hair and starting her favorite podcast.

She felt that familiar thrill at the clanking sound of the clock tower and the bong of the hour as Devin Rudd began his podcast. "Not every terrible tale begins with a terrible event. Many times, the most mundane happenings can lead to the most horrific murders. This, then, is the story of a man who wished to be an art student, and what his desires wrought for those around him. This, then, is another... *Dark Tiding.*"

As the music began, she wondered who it was going to be this time. As Devin Rudd began to describe the idyllic setting in which the killer grew up, she stepped around the end of the bar, collected the bus bin and hauled it off to the dishwasher.

Where could she be? she wondered as she filled the dishwasher and pulled down the hatch. *It was just a routine hike.* As the water began sloshing around inside the washer, she tried to concentrate on the podcast. She'd missed the name of the killer—something mundane, someone she'd never heard of, which was unusual. She thought she knew them all; all those of any note, anyway.

The door buzzer jangled. She hurried back out to see who it was, but it was only the bikers leaving, a half-pitcher of warm beer on the table along with a ten-dollar bill. *At least I don't have to deal with them at closing time.*

Why hasn't she called her mom? It's been six days. Maybe she's lying hurt in a gully somewhere. She pushed the thought away. She had to work.

She grabbed another bus bin and walked over to clear the table, wrinkling her nose at the lingering smell of strong tobacco. *I don't mind the smell of tobacco, but that stuff reeks.* She waved a hand at the invisible odors, but they persisted. She hurriedly scraped the last of the paper trash into the bin and turned to flee the stink, but found herself facing Deputy Kal Cundiff.

"Evening, Mallory," Kal said.

She stopped, startled, the bus bin on her hip. Outside, the sound of motorcycles revving broke the silence.

"Oh, hi, Kal," she said, frowning. "I didn't hear you come in."

"That's because you're filling your ears with garbage," he said and smirked. "Who are you listening to tonight? Ed Gein? Ted Bundy? Or is it a five-part series on Charlie Manson?"

"It's not like that," she lied as she marched past him. But when she dropped the bin out back, she paused the podcast, slipped the bud out of her ear and into her pocket, and returned to her place behind the bar.

"All right," she said. "What brings you in here tonight? And in uniform? Don't tell me your dad has decided to take us seriously."

"Nah," Kal said and pulled a face, unable to look her in the eye. "The Sheriff's office has decided it doesn't qualify as a missing person's case."

"How can that be?" she insisted. "A person just has to be missing for more than forty-eight hours. Julie's been missing for *six days.*"

"Mal," he said plaintively, "this isn't one of those podcasts you listen to."

"Screw you, Kal," she snapped back. "Julie is a responsible young woman. She's an experienced hunting guide. She knows the trails like the back of her hand. Ever since Jared got hurt, she's been the dependable rock of the family. She wouldn't just… fly off and disappear without telling someone. It's not in her nature."

"Well, you know… sometimes the pressure builds up," Kal said in his best TV-cop voice. "All that responsibility, helping to run the business and all. And she decides to up and take a crazy vacation. It happens all the time. She'll be back. Mal, we never found her car, not at any of the trailheads. Not everything is some stupid criminal murder conspiracy."

"Is that what you think of me, Kal Cundiff? You think I'm bitching about my missing niece because I listened to a story?" She stepped around the end of the bar and stopped in front of him, using every inch of her five-foot-ten to loom over him. "My sister, Jennifer," she continued, "and my entire family is halfway to mourning because they think she might be lying dead up there in the forest somewhere, and all you can do is make sick remarks."

"Look, Mal, I'm sorry," Kal said, his face turning a rosy hue.

Mallory stepped back behind the bar and slammed down the hatch with a bang.

"Really?" she snapped. "You're sorry. Your dad is sorry. And my sister is at home crying over her missing daughter, and your department doesn't seem to care at all. Was there any other reason you stopped by to see me? If not, I have to close up, so you need to leave."

Kal reached around and pulled out a notebook from his hip pocket. "Okay. I was out of line, and I apologize. As it happens, I'm here to get a few details. Since you fancy yourself an amateur detective, you probably have them all memorized, right?"

She wanted to glare at him, slap the mocking smile off his face, but there was a sliver of hope: *Is he finally going to take it seriously?*

"Where do you want me to start?" she asked.

"You can gimme the basics first," he replied, his pen poised.

"Her name is Julie Romero. She's twenty-three, five-eight, slim, one-hundred-twenty-two pounds, with blonde, shoulder-length hair. She had her dog, Tobin, with her. Her parents have lived in Chattanooga for the last forty-four years. My sister, Jennifer, her mother, told me that she left last Tuesday morning for a hike on Red Grove Trail, off Highway 64; she didn't know which branch."

"Yeah, I heard," he said. "Red Grove. She oughta know better than to go into the forest up there by herself."

"And why not?" she asked, giving him an annoyed glare. "She's an experienced guide."

She knew that many of the locals had some wild ideas about the mountains and the Cherokee National Forest. And, while there were plenty of real-life dangers associated with walking through forests and mountains, centuries of Native American folklore and campfire stories had convinced half the population that the place was crawling with eldritch deities, dark forces commanded by witches, ghosts, territorial moonshiners, and cannabis and mandrake farmers. Most of it was bunk as far as she was concerned, but Kal didn't look too eager to check out the forbidding forest.

"Look, Julie isn't just some hiker," she said. "She's an experienced hunting guide. She works for her dad, Jared Romero, at his big hunting outlet off 64. She doesn't just get lost in her own backyard."

"Experienced hikers can and do get lost," Kal argued. "Happens all the time."

"Not Julie," she snapped. "If she was going to be late back, she'd have texted her father. What about her Bronco? That wouldn't just get lost, too, would it?"

"We've had an APB out for almost a week," Kal replied. "If nobody's found it, it means it's left the county. And with no evidence to the contrary, it looks like she drove it away."

Mallory opened her mouth to speak, but Kal beat her to it.

"Let me ask you something, Mal. Do you want to be here? In Chattanooga?"

Mallory paused.

"Because you just said she's lived here basically her whole life," he continued. "She's never been anywhere else. Never seen the big cities. Never tasted life outside of town or even outside her own family. How happy was she working for her dad?"

Mallory knew that Julie was frustrated with her dad at times. But she always smiled at everything... but was there pain behind that smile? Longing? Frustration?

How long had Mallory wanted to just pack up and leave? When exactly had *she* decided to stay? She had a sharp mind and a good education, with a 4.0 grade point average. Why did she stay? Why would Julie stay? *Because it's home. That's why.*

"See?" Kal said righteously when she didn't reply. "I knew you'd understand. Just give her another week and she'll come rolling back into town, apologize for being so thoughtless, and then brag about her big adventure in Nashville."

A part of Mallory wanted to believe him. It was an easy out, and it fulfilled all the criteria: Julie was safe. She was having a little reckless fun. Everything would be fine.

But it didn't answer the real questions, the ones her family kept asking. *Why* did she? *How* could she? *Where* is she? Why hasn't she called? And why is her phone off?

"We're not going to agree on this, Kal," Mallory said sadly. "I guess we just don't understand each other. It isn't personal. No one will listen to us, so Jennifer is going to do something about it herself."

Kal looked alarmed. "You don't mean she's going to go trekking up there her own self? That's insane. She does that, we'll have a real missing person's case on our hands."

"No, she's not going to do that. She's not stupid, Kal. She said she's going into the city tomorrow. Though, I suppose she might have lied to us and planned to run away into the woods instead."

"What's she gonna do, then?" Kal demanded.

"She's going to hire Tucker Randall," Mallory said.

"*What?* That overpriced PI who takes on, what, three or four cases a year? Your family is seriously going to put trust in that hack?"

"We haven't been seeing any results from your department so far, have we?" Mallory said.

"Tucker Randall is a publicity hound," Kal replied. "He'll suck you dry and leave you looking stupid while he parades around on TV."

"Better stupid than useless." Mallory saw that her jibe had hit its mark.

"Well, I've got to get going," Kal said and stuffed the notepad back in his pocket.

"Get it all down, did you?" Mallory asked, smirking, knowing he hadn't written a word.

Kal rolled his shoulders, adjusted his belt, looked at her and said, "Good luck with Randall, but I ain't holding my breath." As he opened the door, he threw one last shot. "If he even takes the case, which I sincerely doubt he will."

Mallory resisted the urge to throw something at the door. Instead, she stomped to the other end of the bar and gave Art a little shove. "Come on, Art. It's closing time. Do I need to call your brother?"

"What?" Art looked at her, then scrunched up his face as he tried to focus. "Nah-uh-uh. I'm good. I'll get home just fine."

I hope Julie gets home just fine, too.

2

Tuesday Morning 9am

IT WAS JUST BEFORE NINE AND A BEAUTIFUL MORNING, THOUGH TUCKER Randall ignored the sunlight streaming in through slats in the window blinds as he studied the open manila folders spread across his desk. His eyes flickered over forensic photos and police reports, but the file he was most interested in was the Nebraska case, the one he was tapping with the fingertips of his left hand. He was pretty certain it would be the most interesting of the six cases, but he wanted to make his decision with more than just a hunch and a fee.

He turned his attention to the case in Jacksonville, Oklahoma. *If I take this one, Nate will start bugging me to visit his kids again...*

The door opened, and his assistant poked her head inside and said, "Mr. Randall?"

"What is it, Debbie?" he asked, hoping she wasn't feeling chatty.

"You have a call on line one. It's your brother."

"Speak his name, and he shall appear," he muttered as he picked up the phone. "Nate," he said. "How's my favorite brother?"

"Your only brother. At least that's what Mom says," Nate replied.

"You know," Tucker said. "Technically, I'm not open yet. So I'm going to add an inconvenience charge to your bill, and—"

"Haha. Very funny," Nate replied. "I figured you'd still be in bed. I figured you'd be jet-lagged?"

"Nate, it was LA, not India. I lose more sleep than that on an average night."

"See, Tucker, this is what I'm talking about. You just throw yourself into these things with no regard for your health. Take a week off. Come out here to Tulsa. It's Ella's birthday on Saturday, and Laura's making a strawberry cake. The kids would love to see you."

"While I do enjoy Laura's cooking," Tucker replied, "I don't think I'll have time." He picked up the Jacksonville file and set it aside. "Besides, you're the family man, not me."

"You can say that again. Mom's losing hope on that one." Nate sighed—and a crackle of static burst in Tucker's ear. "So you won't come to Ella's party?"

"I'll be in Nebraska," Tucker replied. "It has everything I like in a case, and they still have snow up there."

"Why do you do this to yourself?" Nate asked, exasperated.

"Obviously, because I like it. Otherwise, I wouldn't," Tucker replied. "What are you talking about, exactly?"

"Your MO. This thing you have about taking only one case at a time. I'm a cop, and you and I both know it can take months to close a case. You're limiting yourself, Tucker, and you know you have more to offer, no matter whose hat you're wearing."

"I don't wear hats." Tucker paused. He could hear voices in the next room. Debbie was talking to someone. *A client? Arguing? No, two clients. Why are they raising their voices?*

"Tucker? You still there?" Nate asked.

"Yeah, I'm here. Just hold on a sec. Someone's in the outer office."

The arguing in the other room continued. *What the hell?*

His door opened, and two people burst in, a man and a woman.

"Tucker? Is this still about Marsha?"

"Sorry, Nate. I have to go. Clients. I'll call you later, okay?" And he hung up the phone before Nate could dredge up the past, again.

Whoever they are, they have a cosmic sense of timing.

"I'm sorry, Mr. Randall," Debbie said, flustered. "I tried to tell them you're not accepting new clients, but they wouldn't listen. They shoved past me. Do you want me to call the police?"

"No. Please don't call the police," the woman said, obviously distressed. "If you'll just hear us out. Give us five minutes, and then we'll leave. I promise."

He stood and looked at the couple. The first thing he realized was that the man was taller than he was. He had to be at least six-four. He towered over poor Debbie.

But that wasn't all. They both had that desperate look in their eyes, and there was also something about the woman. Something he couldn't quite place. She looked familiar. *I've seen her somewhere before, but where?*

"Please, have a seat," he said. "Thank you, Debbie. I don't think we'll need the police."

"I'm really sorry," the woman said as she sat down. "We're not normally this pushy. I mean, I've never—"

"There's no need to apologize," Tucker said. "Tell me about your problem, and I'll tell you if I can help."

She nodded, took a deep breath, and began, "I'm Jennifer Romero, and this is my husband, Jared. Our daughter, Julie, is missing. She went hiking, and she didn't return. We're hoping you can find her."

"Your daughter," Tucker said. "Is she an experienced hiker?"

"She's experienced," Jared said. "She works for me as a hunting and fishing guide. She knows the forest better than anyone I know. I own Romero's Outdoors out on 64, as you probably know. She's been hiking the trails since I carried her on my back when she was a kid."

By then, Tucker was only half listening to them. It was a missing person case, and he hated those. He'd spent more time during his years in the FBI chasing wayward kids than he cared to remember, and he was already regretting agreeing to listen to them.

In his mind, he was already setting up shop in a cabin in Northern Nebraska. He could smell the rich scent of crackling pine in the fireplace and taste the heat of strong black coffee on a cold morning.

He made a mental note to ask Debbie to check for the next available flight as he listened to Jared drone on about his daughter. Tucker told himself that as soon as they were done talking, he'd politely decline their business and refer them to another private investigator, but then he caught something Jennifer said that jerked him out of his reverie.

"...she went out to hike one of the trails, one that she's walked a hundred times, but she never came back. She didn't call. Her phone goes straight to voicemail. And her Bronco's disappeared. So has her dog, Tobin."

I could pitch this one to Billy, he thought. *He's nice, and he won't cheat them when the girl turns up in another day or two.*

"...and it's been a week now with no word."

"Wait," Tucker said. "A week? Why haven't you gone to the Sheriff's department? I'm just a private eye. They have far more resources than I do."

"We did," she said. "We filed a report, but they won't do anything. They won't even listen to us. They say there's no evidence and that she's probably just taken off for a few days."

He stared at her.

"They should be looking for her," Jennifer continued. "They really should, shouldn't they? But they aren't, and why would they? There are a lot of missing person cases in and around Chattanooga. It's a big city, and there are so many hiking trails around here, especially in the forests, and that just makes it worse. I guess they don't have time to investigate them all."

She was, he knew, referring to the Cherokee and Prentice Cooper forests, and many smaller ones besides. And he grimaced as he thought of the folklore and mystery that surrounded them, especially the Cherokee National Forest. It's vast, more than seven-hundred-thousand acres vast. Plenty of people had gone missing in the forest, never to be seen or heard from again.

"Exactly," Jared said. "I've talked to the county sheriff's office, several times, and the local police department. They won't even listen to us. They won't even acknowledge that she's missing."

Tucker raised an eyebrow and decided to play devil's advocate. "They could be right, you know."

Jennifer Romero stood up, slammed her hands down on the desk in front of him, leaned in and looked him in the eyes. And again, he was sure he'd seen her somewhere before.

"Julie would *never* leave," she said angrily. "Never! I know it. My husband knows it, and my sisters know it. All our friends know it. You have to believe us."

"We know something's wrong," Jared said quietly. "As Jen said, her phone goes straight to voicemail, and there's also been no activity on her bank account or her credit cards."

"You have access to her bank account?" Tucker asked.

"Yes. If she'd 'taken a vacation,' she'd need money, wouldn't she?"

"It was Mallory's idea," Jared said. "She's Jen's sister. She's a bit of a true-crime buff. She listens to podcasts about it all the time. Anyway, she insisted, so we keep all the important stuff, passwords, bank accounts and such in a folder."

A true crime nut. That's all I need, Tucker thought, resisting the urge to shake his head. It was a missing person case. He didn't do missing persons, and the mention of a possible amateur detective wanna-be drove the final nail into the proverbial coffin. So he dusted off the script he'd memorized for just such a situation.

"I'm really sorry," he began. "I understand how you feel, but I already have several commitments. And I just don't have the time to take on a new client. I can, however, refer you to my colleague, Will Preston. He is an excellent investigator, and he'll be happy to…"

He trailed off as Jennifer pushed a photo across the desk and said, "Look at her. It's my daughter, Julie. Look at her and tell me she's run away. Do it."

So he looked, and his breath caught in his throat. The photograph had been cropped, but the girl's face was a face from the past, a face that haunted his dreams. *Marsha! Marsha Cline?*

SIC David Lewis was seated at his desk, leaning back in his chair, his fingers steepled in front of him.

"Agent Randall... Tucker," he said, "I know this wasn't supposed to happen—"

"I did exactly what you told me to, David," Tucker said, interrupting him. "It was a done deal, you said. Marsha Cline's going to make it happen, you said. And all I had to do was to persuade her to make a statement. Which I did. She trusted *me, David. You were supposed to protect her."*

"There was an unforeseen—"

"Why, David?" Tucker shouted, leaning forward in his chair. "We're the Federal Bureau of Investigation, for God's sake."

"For what it's worth, Tucker, I really am sorry." He slid a glass across the desk. "Here. Have something."

Tucker took the glass, raised it to his lips, and felt the sting on his split lip where Lisa Cline had punched him in the mouth for breaking his promise to protect her daughter.

"You son of a bitch," he said, staring David in the eye and slowly shaking his head. "You had no intention—"

"It's not your fault, Tucker," David said easily. "It's not anybody's fault."

Tucker stood up, took a step forward and slammed the glass down on the desktop. It shattered with a sound like a gunshot.

The gunshot that had ended Marsha Cline's life.

He looked down at the scar in the palm of his hand. *If Marsha Cline had never met me, she'd still be alive,* he thought, then looked at the photo again. The resemblance was startling.

Julie Romero. Her eyes had that same overflowing joy for life as Marsha's once did. Her hair was a shade or two darker; her eyes were brown, while Marsha's were green. She was tanned, and there was a constellation of freckles spread across her smiling face.

Tucker could also see the resemblance in Jennifer Romero, and it pained him to look at her. If Marsha had been granted the chance to grow older, have a family, and live life to the full, Tucker was sure she'd look a lot like Jennifer.

He looked at her, nodded, sighed and said, "All right, I'll do it. I'll take your case."

"Oh, God. Thank you! Thank you."

And, as he looked into her eyes, glistening with tears, he wondered what the hell kind of a mess he'd just stepped into.

3

Tuesday 5pm

MALLORY REMOVED YET ANOTHER STACK OF PAPERS FROM HER HOME printer. This last batch was streaky, and she made a mental note to pick up more ink at Staples the following morning.

She thumbed through them, making sure she'd printed everything, then carefully placed the stack into a manila folder labeled "recent correspondences."

In anticipation of her meeting with Tucker Randall, she'd compiled as much information as she could. She'd spoken with everyone she knew who had contact with Julie and asked them to send her screenshots of their last text conversations. In addition, she'd marked Julie's usual hiking trails on a map and cross-referenced those areas with other missing persons cases she'd found in the news.

Mallory wasn't sure how much of this information was essential, but she figured every little bit counted. She was just sliding the folders into her messenger bag when her phone rang.

"Hey," Jennifer said. "We just got here. Are you on your way?"

"I'm leaving now. I'll be there in about twenty minutes. Is the PI there yet?"

"Not yet," Jennifer said. "We just got here. He isn't supposed to be here until five, and it's only… four-twenty-five. We'll go ahead and ask for a table in the back. I'll order coffee. See you soon, okay?"

Mallory said her goodbyes and then headed out to her car. Usually, she listened to the radio while she drove, but today she coasted along the back roads in silence, glancing now and again at the distant mountains.

The trail Julie was supposed to have taken was some forty-five minutes east of Collegedale, where she lived, off Highway 64, and Mallory couldn't help but imagine her niece up there somewhere, beyond the tree line, lying in a gully with a broken leg. *But where the hell is her Bronco? And why is her phone off?*

"We'll find you, Julie," she said under her breath. "I promise." And she prayed her obsession with true crime and mysteries would, just for once, come in handy. She hoped the vast amount of information she'd managed to compile would assist the PI and that he would find Julie as soon as possible. She was also aware, however, that much of what she had gathered was hearsay.

But maybe, she thought, *just maybe, it will help paint a more accurate picture of Julie's character and give him some insight as to what could have happened to her.*

It was ten minutes to five when she pulled into the parking lot at the Mountainside Café that afternoon. She parked as close to the entrance as possible, grabbed her messenger bag, opened the door, stepped out and closed and locked it behind her.

She looked around the parking lot, noting the preponderance of pickup trucks, shook her head and stepped inside, wondering why Jen had insisted on holding the meeting way out there.

Like many such places in the area—and there were quite a few, all of them dependent upon the seasonal outdoor population for their livelihood—the café had seen better days. The log exterior begged to be refurbished. The planters outside the front entrance lacked attention, and weeds filled the gutters. *Life always finds a way,* she thought as she pushed through the pair of foyer doors and into the restaurant.

Mallory could remember going there as a child, barely old enough to go to school. Jennifer was getting ready to graduate high school, and Katie had already met and was dating her husband-to-be. They would stop by for lunch after church most weeks. But it had been years since Mallory had last eaten there, and somehow, she felt a similar melancholy for the run-down restaurant as she did for The Saloon. Time had weathered both almost beyond recognition.

Julie, she thought as she pushed through the first set of doors into the foyer. As the youngest sibling, Mallory had taken to Jennifer's new baby. Eagerly, she'd taken on the role of big sister, and she stayed close to her through the years, mentoring her, supporting her, and showing her how to do… practically everything.

She pushed through the second set of doors, paused just inside, looked around and spotted her sister waving from a booth at the back.

"Hey, big sis, big bro," she said as she slid into the seat opposite them. "Any sign of Mr. Randall yet?"

"I got a text from him a few minutes ago," Jennifer said. "He's on his way. He should be here shortly."

"Good," Mallory said and dumped a folder on the table. "We have a few minutes to go over these, then."

"What's all that, Mallory?" Jennifer asked.

"A little bit of everything," Mallory replied as she rifled through the papers. "Just the most pertinent stuff to start with. I have copies of her emails, text messages and her last bank statement. I also have statements I took from some of her closest friends, you know, like Sarah and Jane, and compiled those as well. And these." She opened the manila folder labeled "Maps" and pushed it toward Jared.

"Do you mind looking those over to make sure I mapped out Julie's usual routes correctly? I used the info from your company website and also from Julie's personal notes, but I want to make sure I haven't missed anything."

Jennifer flipped through a few of the files, barely glancing at the contents. "How'd you get access to all this?"

"The family folder gave me a lot of what I needed, but I made some phone calls and went out and pounded the pavement a little."

"You pounded the pavement?" Jennifer scrunched up her face in disbelief. "Mallory, you sound like some kind of off-beat TV detective. The next thing you'll be telling us is that you canvassed the neighborhood or grilled some suspects. Please try to act like a normal person when Mr. Randall gets here."

Mallory pulled a face but smiled and shook her head. Jennifer had long since adopted the role as her second mother, which only got worse after their mother passed away. Regardless of Jennifer's good intentions, it sometimes got a little old.

Just once, I wish she'd give me a little credit, she thought, but then she took those feelings and pushed them aside. *Today is about Julie.*

"There he is," Jennifer said and waved.

Mallory turned and looked at him. He was tall. At least six-one. Well-built with brown hair.

"So that's him, is it?" Mallory said, unable to hide the fact that she was impressed.

Randall walked confidently across the restaurant toward them, weaving his way through the afternoon crowd.

"Mal, come and sit over here so we can all talk to him," Jennifer said.

"Oh, right, yes, of course," she stuttered as she scooped up the papers and stuffed them back into the folder, fumbling it so that it fell to the floor, spilling its contents.

Stupid, stupid, stupid, she scolded herself as she knelt to gather the wayward file.

"Here, let me help you," he said, bending down beside her.

"So you must be Mallory?" he asked quietly, as he helped her gather the contents of the file. "Jennifer told me about you. She said you were... organized, and I see that you are."

"O-o-oh. Um, thank you," Mallory said as she carefully stood up and sat down next to her sister.

Oh, for Pete's sake, just let me get through this without embarrassing myself even more.

"This looks... impressive and... thorough," Randall said, staring at the folder.

"This is my sister, Mallory Carver," Jennifer said. "And she is all about thorough. Ouch." Mallory had kicked her ankle.

"Hello, Mr. Randall," Mallory said sweetly, glancing at her sister. "I've put together some information I think you'll find helpful."

"Wow," Randall said as he flipped through the pages. "Well, Miss Carver, the more information I have, the better. Thank you."

"You're welcome," Mallory replied, and eager to prove that she wasn't an incompetent idiot, she took four more folders from her messenger bag and dumped them on the table in front of him. "That one you have there is just the summary folder. I have everything sorted and indexed in these."

4

Tuesday 5:30pm

When Tucker pulled into the Mountainside Café parking lot, he couldn't help but notice the dilapidated state of the building. *How can the owners let the place go like this?* he wondered. *Surely it can't be that hard to keep up with the routine maintenance.*

In the back of his mind, he could hear something his supervisor David once said to him. He couldn't remember the words exactly, but it was something about getting up every day, getting dressed, and then you realize that's all you have the energy for and that you're just going through the motions to get through the day.

Is that what you were doing with Marsha, David? Just going through the motions, damn you.

He couldn't understand how someone could become so hidebound as to miss the obvious on the way to the mundane, but he himself hadn't reached that stage yet. He still had time to ponder the secrets of life before they caught up with him.

He walked into the restaurant and spotted Jennifer Romero waving at him. She was with her husband and a blonde woman sitting opposite them. Jennifer said something to her and she rose to her feet, dropping a folder full of papers on the floor.

"Here, let me help," he offered and crouched down beside her. She turned her head to look at him, and he was astonished to see that she didn't look like her sister at all. This woman was... lovely, not that Jennifer wasn't. She was. But Mallory, if that's who she was, was different. She was taller than her sister, with large hazel eyes, and she looked fit as if she worked out.

The papers were now back in the folder, and she grabbed it from him and quickly scooted into the seat opposite him, close to her sister.

Tucker frowned to himself, thinking there must be quite an age gap between them.

Mallory said hello and handed him the file, saying something about helpful information.

He took it from her, opened it and flipped through the papers. *Sheesh,* he thought. *This is exactly what I expected. Reams of paper. Every kind of document imaginable.*

The folder also contained several trail maps, a dozen or more pages of texts and emails with highlights and hand-written notations, usually saying something like "Clearly not going on vacation" next to someone's text about what Julie was doing "next week," trail safety statistics with one dating back to 1975. Prevalence of animal attacks, broken down by category. There were even customer satisfaction ratings for the boots the girl was wearing and a recent doctor's physical for Julie.

"Wow," he said, trying not to sound condescending, and something to the effect that the more information he had, the better.

"You're welcome," she said and dumped four more files on the table in front of him.

He stared at the pile of paperwork for a moment, then looked up at her to say something about overreach, but he saw that she was watching him intently.

At first, because of the dropped folder, he'd assumed she was an easily flustered klutz. But suddenly, he wasn't so sure. Her jaw was jutted, her face set, and there was a formidable look of... a mixture of anger, confidence, vulnerability and even determination. This, he realized, was probably a girl who was told every day that she wasn't good enough, that she was wasting her time and energy. *Maybe,* he mused, *her family, and her sister in particular, gave her a hard time about her fascination with true crime, just as I did, even before I met her. But,* he thought with an inward sigh, *who listens to those things? People who want to be me. And who the hell would want to be me? If only they knew.*

He stared at the exhaustive stack of research, then looked at Mallory, smiled and said, "Thank you again." Thinking, *even if most of it is likely useless.*

"So, Mallory, what do you do for a living?" he asked as he flipped from one page to the next. "Do you work with Julie at the outlet?"

"No, I'm a bartender," she said in a challenging tone of voice. "And I have been for thirteen years."

He looked at her and nodded. She was tanned, but she didn't have the outdoorsy complexion her sister and brother-in-law shared. He also realized that he'd mistaken her age as well. Maybe it was just Julie on his mind, but he'd pegged her to be in her mid-twenties. But with thirteen years behind a bar, she had to be more than thirty. Not that he was going to ask her—being an investigator didn't remove as many social graces as one might think. *That's what background checks are for,* he thought, inwardly smiling to himself.

"And where do you work?" he asked, flipping through the pages.

"You probably passed it on the way here," she said, "It's… The Saloon."

Oh, that place? He recalled the shabby building. *Geez, if the Mountainside Café needs a refurbish, The Saloon needs… well, never mind. And this…* He gazed at the collection of pages of emails, text messages and colorful emojis. *None of it makes any sense.* There were actual words here and there, including one that caught his eye, "Can't wait until Music Fest next month," but the rest…

"Those are from Julie's best friend, Sarah Alexander," Mallory said. "They've been friends since middle school. They go everywhere together, and they tell each other everything. That file contains all of Julie's text conversations from the past month."

"Yes, yes. This should all be very enlightening," Tucker lied. "You must have worked very hard to put all of this…" *Whew, wow.* "…valuable information together. But I think it'll be better if I go over it alone, at my office. There are too many distractions here for me to do it justice." And he began to gather the paperwork.

"Oh, I completely understand," Jennifer said.

"But what if you have questions?" Mallory said. "I can help."

Tucker made a point not to look at her as he turned toward the Romeros. "I can always call you if something comes up, can't I?"

"Yes, of course," Jennifer replied. "Anytime."

"You have both of our cell numbers," Jared said. "Please don't hesitate to call."

Mallory frowned, not quite believing what was happening.

"Now," Tucker said as he stood up, throwing back his half-full mug of coffee as if it had been a shot. "I've got to get going. There's a lot for me to go through." He hefted the stack of folders and smiled. "I'll reach out to you as soon as I know something." Again, he spoke only to the Romeros. "And please, call me if you think of anything that might be helpful."

"But," Mallory said, "I could help."

"I'll keep that in mind," Tucker said, smiling politely. "It was nice to meet you, Mallory." Then he turned again to the Romeros and said, "I'm going to head back to my office now. If you need me, you know where to find me."

And with that, he wished them all a good evening and left, thinking he had a much better understanding of Jennifer's younger, true crime fanatic sister.

The entire meeting had lasted less than thirty minutes, and he was glad to be out of there, once again wondering what the hell he'd gotten himself into.

5

Tuesday evening 7:30pm

"Can you believe it?" Mallory asked for the third time. "The nerve of that guy. "

"Some nerve," Vinnie agreed.

"He completely shut me out! It was like I wasn't even there. Where does he get off doing that? Do you think he'll even bother to look at my files?"

She whipped her head around to look at her boss, Vinnie Mars. "I mean, he will, right? I put a lot of hours into them."

Her employer, the elderly man with the liver spots on his tanned bald head, was kneeling on the floor on the other side of the bar, tightening the screws at the base of one of the circular barstools.

"I would hope so," Vinnie replied, not bothering to look up at her.

"I know, right?" Mallory agreed. "I've spent the whole week compiling all that information. There's a lot of it. Sure, but some of it's got to be important, doesn't it?'

"Uh-huh," Vinnie responded.

"Of course it is," she said. "I mean, I mapped out Julie's hiking trails, didn't I? That should be useful, right? I worked really hard on that, making sure it was all laid out accurately, which was difficult because the Red Grove trail isn't even on some of the maps."

"Yeah," Vinnie responded.

"If that dumb PI doesn't even look through the files... You know, I probably would have been better off going to the police. Maybe I shouldn't have been so quick to dismiss Kal. If I'd have pressed him hard enough, I bet I could have made him listen to me."

"Probably," the old man mumbled, his shaking hands struggling to align the screwdriver with the slot.

"Now all that information is lost," she said. "Gone! It's all gone! I should have made a copy, but I didn't. Why was I so stupid to think Tucker Randall would listen to me? Nobody ever listens to me."

"Yeah, that's not good," Vinnie's lackluster voice intoned.

Mallory frowned at her boss. "Vinnie. Are *you* even listening to me?"

"Sounds good," he responded.

Her frown deepened, but she continued to talk. "You know, sir. I think I'll set fire to the place, starting with the contents of the office safe. What d'you think about that?"

"You know best," the man replied. His tongue was stuck out as he twisted the screwdriver.

Upset that she was once again being ignored, Mallory slammed the aluminum shaker she'd been cleaning down on the bar. The noise reverberated through the room, attracting the attention of just about everyone in the room.

"Is something wrong, Mallory?" Vinnie asked, squinting up at her through his steel-framed glasses.

"Oh, no. Nothing at all," Mallory said sarcastically. "Julie's missing. I've lost a whole week's work, and nobody ever listens to me."

Vinnie stood up and arched his back. "Ooh, that's... ow. My back! I need to go see a chiropractor," he complained, but after a few seconds, he looked at her and said, "So what're you going to do about it, then?"

Mallory sighed and rolled her eyes. "You know," she said thoughtfully. "I can't even start over. Not only was I stupid not to make copies, but I also gave Tucker all the login information. Why did I do that?"

"You want to know what I think?" Vinnie wheezed, holding his back. "I think you should take it as a sign, right?"

"How so?" she asked, hoping that maybe, just *maybe,* he had some advice to offer.

"A sign that you should get on with your job and let that city-slicker do his. That's what I think."

Mallory stared at him for a moment, then sighed and said, "Whatever you say, sir."

"Atta girl," he mumbled. "I gotta go sit down. M'back's killing me," he said as he stepped carefully around the bar and patted her shoulder. "You worry too much, my dear. I'm sure your niece is fine." He squeezed her shoulder and, with a hand on his back and the other sliding along the bar top, he walked slowly back to his office.

She heaved a sigh, grabbed her cloth and went to work on the rings on the bar top.

Damn it, she thought. *Why doesn't anybody ever listen to me? Not even Vinnie. Whew. Geez. I don't get it. Tucker Randall was supposed to fix everything. I gave him all that information, and he wouldn't even look at me. What is wrong with me? Why does he treat me like that? I hate this frickin' place. I've been stuck here ever since Mom died. I lost my scholarship to UTK... everything, and all because I was the only one who stepped up when she got ill. Me! No one else. And now they all treat me like I'm a moron. And now Julie. And this... this... Tucker Randall.*

"Hey, Mal. You gonna take the varnish right off."

Mallory jerked her head up to find Howie O'Neal standing at the bar with an empty glass in his hand.

"Oh, hey, Howie. Yeah, I have a lot on my mind. You need a refill?"

He shook his head. "Nah. It's about time for me to head on home. I just wanted a quick word with you before I go."

"Okay. What's up?" Mallory asked.

"Well," he began apprehensively, "I didn't mean to eavesdrop on y'all, but this place is awful quiet, and I caught the last part of your conversation with Vin about your cousin."

"Niece. Julie's my niece," she said.

"Right, right," Howie said. "Sorry. Did I hear you say somethin' about the girl being up near Red Grove when she went missing?"

Mallory nodded slowly. "Uh-huh. Yes, why?"

"Well. I'm sure y'already know I'm a bit of a mountain man m'self. Back before Jared's injury, we used to go huntin' up that way, two or three times a year; turkey and boar, up toward Banner Road. 'Course, that was a long time ago… Is that where she went?"

"Yes. Yes, it is," Mallory said. "She hikes up there all the time."

"Huh!" Howie pulled a face. "Ain't no good no more." He glanced at Mallory, frowning. "There's some unsavory characters up yonder. Squatters and 'shiners. Even wood witches, so some folk say."

"Are you saying Julie was kidnapped by moonshiners or witches?"

"What? No. 'Course not. But there's a little cabin out there. No one goes near it no more. They say the Burns boy is squattin' there."

"Burns… you mean Zach Burns? I thought he left town years ago."

"Yeah. Him," Howie said. "No. He still lives up there in the cabin. You know, I saw him take a deer with a bow once," Howie continued. "Big un it was… durndest thing I ever did see. Hell of a shot, so it was."

"You don't think he could have anything to do with Julie being missing, do you?"

Howie shrugged, pulled a face and said, "We've never had no trouble with him. Truth be told, I've only encountered him a handful of times. And he was just about as nice as you could want."

Mallory bit her fingernail as she considered this alarming new twist.

"Still," she muttered, staring down at Howie's empty glass.

"Yeah," Howie said, "I can't help but think about his poor mom, Wynona. He was only seventeen when he killed her. How could a kid like that kill his own mother? If he could do that as a boy, who knows what he's capable of doing now? Especially to a pretty young girl like Julie."

"He was never convicted, though, was he?" she said.

"Well, no," Howie replied. "I s'pose not. But I reckon everyone knows he done it. He was… what do they call it on TV? The prime suspect, the only suspect, really."

That's true, Mallory thought, then said, "As I remember it, there was no direct evidence. What they did have was all circumstantial, so they dropped the charges."

"Yeah, but the boy had injuries, didn't he?" Howie said. "He said he'd been fighting to save his mom but couldn't tell anyone who with or how he got 'em. I don't know how he got away scot-free like he did. Everyone in town knows he must have gotten those injuries from fightin' with his mom. It's hard to believe the cops and the judge believed all that blackout BS he was spouting."

"disassociative amnesia," Mallory said, nodding. *But if he did kill her, and if he's out there…*

"Anyway," Howie said, "just thought I'd mention it. Try not to worry about it. After all, it could've been one of the wood witches or 'shiners who nabbed her up. I'm off 'ome now. See you tomorrow."

"Thank you, Howie," she called over her shoulder as he walked out the door.

She turned her attention to the register, her head full of thoughts of Zach Burns. She'd known him in high school, sat next to him in math. He'd been a reclusive kid even then, *but he seemed nice enough. How could he become a murderer? Could he really have hurt Julie? Maybe somebody should do some poking around. Maybe I should call Kal. Huh, what a waste of time that would be. They never found her killer. As I remember it, they found Zach with her blood on his clothes, and that was it. They didn't bother to look any further. Typical! Jim Burns got her pregnant and married her right out of high school. The family was in an uproar.*

Mallory shook her head, trying to rid her mind of the graphic images it conjured of Wynona Burns' body. *But they never found it, did they? Just a whole lot of blood.*

She turned away from the register, looked around the room, grabbed a bus bin, rounded the end of the bar and bussed the empty tables, checking in on the half dozen patrons along the way.

She dumped the bin out back and returned to the bar.

Oh, dear God, she thought as she stared out across the dimly lit, dismal room. *How I hate this place.*

She sat down on a stool behind the bar and stared up at the stains, and inevitably, her thoughts returned to Julie.

Is she dead? Is she lying out there somewhere injured? Did someone take her? Was it criminals, or witches, or Zach Burns? Oh God, what if she's being held prisoner and...

It didn't bear thinking about. "This is ridiculous," she muttered. "Someone needs to do something. And I know who."

6

Tuesday Evening Late

By the time Tucker arrived back at his office that evening—a purpose-built extension to his home on East Brainerd Road—the clouds had rolled in and it had begun to rain.

He locked the door behind him and tossed the plastic bag containing Mallory Carver's files onto his desk, then stood for a second contemplating them.

"Geez," he muttered. "Really?"

And yet... he thought *it's entirely possible she's done some of my work for me.* While his experiences with amateur sleuths—and there had been several of them—hadn't been stellar, the one big difference with this one was that she *cared,* and she was determined to find her niece, and so was he.

He shook his head, made himself a cup of coffee, then stood once more before the intimidating stack of… what? He had no idea, and so, with a sigh, he sat down and picked up the first of the five folders, the one she'd claimed was the summary. Each of the documents was labeled with different colored inks. Snippets of information she deemed important were highlighted in different colors, denoting how important she considered them to be. And, of course, there was a helpful color key on a sticky note inside the folder, and he used it constantly as he sorted through the documents.

He hadn't been at it long before he realized he'd been wrong about her. The files contained a wealth of information, all in order and properly tabulated.

The summary folder contained a collection of excellent arguments against the sheriff's—and his own—statements that Julie had left of her own volition. There were copies of a number of text conversations with several of Julie's friends that indicated she'd had some very specific plans for the near future; a level of social planning that didn't mesh with the idea of an impulsive, last-minute fling. Even the emoji-laden conversation he'd spotted earlier had a helpful translation guide of sorts, and the actual text indicated that the two girls had planned for the upcoming music festival—Riverbend—for months. There was a credit card statement to back this up, showing the purchase of a 3-day VIP ticket from an online venue for the sum of $350—not something a frugal young woman would willingly toss away.

There were text, email and Facebook records that proved Julie had been in constant contact with friends and family right up to the day she disappeared. All of that stopped, seemingly on a dime, the morning she walked off into the Cherokee National Forest with her dog Tobin. None of it was rocket science. It was all available to a diligent police detective… *So why the hell didn't they do it?* he wondered, staring at the door. *If they had, they couldn't have come to any other conclusion other than something must have happened to her.*

He stared at the file and decided he would need to interview Julie's friends, but there were notes that hinted Mallory had already done so. Again, he wondered how far and by how much the young lady had jumped his investigation. He smiled at the thought, then set about locating the folder containing the interviews, with colored diagramming added. But he came across the folder with trail maps first.

Now this is some really solid work, he thought as he opened one of the maps.

Mallory had broken the trails down multiple ways: each trail had its own separate map with hand-written notes about the degree of difficulty. Each set of trails that intersected one another had a map, again with hand-written notes, and he was amazed how some trails came within speaking distance of each other, only to have sheer drop-offs or other geographical disadvantages to hikers, or hunters.

How could anyone know all this? Mallory must have walked every trail, many times. She must have an exceptional memory for detail. And the amount of work...

He sat back in his chair, linked his fingers together behind his neck and stared at the FBI vest hanging on the back of the door.

He sat for several minutes contemplating the maps spread across his desk, then leaned forward and picked up the map of the Red Grove trail.

The hiking difficulty of trails is determined by the National Parks Service by a series of scales numbered from 50-200. Anything under 50 is considered easy walking; 50-100 moderate; 100-150 moderately strenuous; 150-200 strenuous and a challenge; greater than 200 extremely strenuous only to be attempted by experienced, well-prepared hikers. Mallory had rated Red Grove 150, strenuous, and one of her and Julie's personal trail preferences. *So, she's a hiker, too. Interesting.*

There was also a note that, according to her sister, Jennifer, it was the trail Julie planned to hike the day she disappeared.

There were also notes that suggested the county sheriff's department had, so far, declined to search the areas. Their reason being that Julie's Bronco had not been found at either of the trailheads—there were two of them serving the eastern and western branches of the trail—and that indicated she'd left the area of her own volition and would no doubt return in due course.

There has to be a better reason than that, he thought and made a note to check in at the sheriff's office in the morning.

According to Carver's research, there's a high incidence of missing person cases in the area, and that makes me wonder if maybe there's a trafficking operation. That would be a whole other kettle of fish. And according to this, the purpose of her hike that day was work-related. She was supposed to be inspecting the trail. Hmm. If that's the case, why the blazes haven't the authorities searched the trail? It makes no sense; no sense at all.

For several hours he continued to work his way through Mallory's file until, at a little after eleven, a loud clap of thunder startled him, disrupting his concentration. He blinked, stood up and realized he was still wearing his Glock.

He slipped off his shoulder holster, walked over to the gun safe, and was just about to close the safe door and return to his desk when there was a frantic knock on the door.

What the hell? he thought as he glanced at his watch. *Who the blazes can that be?* He grabbed the Glock and stepped carefully to the window overlooking the office front step and peered out.

Standing there in the downpour, her hair plastered to her face, was Mallory Carver.

"Oh, for Pete's sake," he muttered and opened the door. "Well, don't just stand there. Come on in."

She stepped inside, her clothes and hair dripping wet.

"Thank you, thank you, thank you," she mumbled, stripping off her coat and handing it to him. "It's kind of..." she trailed off, looked at him for a second or two, then launched into a rapid-fire jumble of words.

"Okay. So I'm sorry to disturb you this late, but I had to talk to you. You see, I was at work, at The Saloon, and Vinnie—he's my boss—was being kind of a jerk, and I was trying to explain how nobody listens to me, only he wasn't listening to me either—"

"Hold on," Tucker said, interrupting her. "You're soaking wet. Let me get you some towels."

She nodded and continued, "...and I told him he was a jerk because he wasn't listening, but he told me I should just accept the fact that my niece was probably already dead. And then I talked to Howie, and he told me..."

He opened the adjoining door to his house, stepped into the bathroom, grabbed two large bath towels and handed them to her as she continued without a pause.

"... and Howie—he's a customer; comes in every night—told me there are a whole bunch of weirdos living up there around Red Grove, like moonshiners and pot farmers and maybe witches, too, who do crazy things at night. And then he reminded me of a guy who lives up there who everyone thinks killed his mother. He was charged with it, but he was never convicted, and he lives in a shack up on the mountain and hunts with a big bow. And Howie said maybe he killed my niece for some reason, but I don't know why he would and... and you..." She looked at him and, for the first time since he'd opened the door, she actually seemed to see him.

"And you aren't listening to me either, are you?"

He stepped closer to her, put a hand on each of her shoulders, and said, "Relax. Take it easy, okay?"

She bit her bottom lip, looked into his eyes, and he watched as a tear rolled down each of her cheeks.

"The bathroom's just through that door," he said gently. "Dry yourself off and then come and sit down."

She was gone no more than a few minutes, and when she returned, she stopped halfway across the room, stared at the papers spread across his desk and said, her voice catching, "Are those my files?"

He looked at them, then said, "Yes. I wanted to ask you about the interviews—"

"You read them?" she whispered.

"I... Yes, of course I read them... well, some of them. There's a lot here, and I have a way to go yet."

"You actually read my files," she said in disbelief.

"I read your files. Now, please sit down. You look as if you're about to collapse."

"I'm... I'm sorry, Mr. Randall," she said as she sat down in one of the two wingback chairs in front of his desk, the one so recently occupied by her sister. "Jennifer says nobody can understand me when I do that."

"Do what?" he asked, knowing the best way to get her to focus was to talk her down until she was calm.

"I get emotional and talk a mile a minute. Motormouth is what she calls me. I usually have more control, but Julie is like my sister, and it hurts all the time, and I don't know how to deal with it. She's… dead, isn't she?"

"Never say dead," he replied, then stared at her, not knowing what else to say. He wanted to reach out and take her hand and tell her everything was going to be all right, but instead, he said, "Can I get you something? Tea? Coffee?"

"Coffee, please," she replied.

He stood and went to the coffee maker.

"How do you—"

"Black please."

He nodded, scooped the beans into the grinder and ran it for a few seconds.

"You take your coffee seriously," she said. "I've never seen anyone grind their own beans before."

"You get a much better flavor that way," he said.

There was another awkward silence, then he said, "Okay. Well, let me grab a new notebook."

"Why do you need a notebook?" she asked.

"Don't you have some new information for me?" he asked.

She blinked as though she'd forgotten. "Oh. Right. Yes. Of course."

He took a notepad from his desk drawer, then went to the coffeemaker, poured some into a mug and handed it to her.

"Careful, it's…" Hot, he was going to say, but before he could finish, she grabbed the mug in both hands and took a sip.

"Oh, wow," she said. "This is so good. What kind of coffee is it? I know it's not the same as the stuff Vinnie serves."

"It's Jamaican," Tucker said. "I order it in. It's expensive, but it's worth it."

"It makes the stuff I usually drink taste like burned water."

"Exactly, which is why…" He paused, hesitated for a moment, then grabbed his notebook and pen, sat down beside her and said, "All right, down to business. So a bear came into The Saloon and told you about some witches? That was about all I was able to grasp from your… tirade." He smiled at her and nodded.

She looked at him over the rim of her mug, her eyes wide.

"Go ahead," he said, "fire away."

"Where d'you want me to begin?"

"At the beginning," he replied.

7

MALLORY SIPPED HER COFFEE AND BREATHED A SIGH OF RELIEF. *FINALLY, somebody wants to listen to me.*

It must have been twenty minutes or so later when she finished telling him about her conversation with Howie O'Neal, and by then she'd finished her coffee.

"...and that's about it," she said, looking at him expectantly. "What d'you think?"

He looked up from his notebook, nodded and said, "I think I'd like to know more about this Zach Burns."

"So Jim Burns, Zach's father," she began, "was, I dunno, eighteen? And he was a jerk; came from a wealthy family. He was a star football player, you know, who scored with all the girls. Well, he got one pregnant, Wynona Williams. Nobody knows for sure, but a lot of people think her daddy told him if he didn't make it right, he better not ever find him alone. So Jim married her, and they had a boy, Zach... Look, I only know this from what I've been told. Zach is the same age as me."

Tucker nodded but said nothing.

"So that was good," she continued, "but Jim and Wynona didn't get along. Then one day, something happened to Jim, and he died. Doc

Williams said that he fell and banged his head, but there was a lot of gossip. You know how that goes, right?"

Again, Tucker nodded, so she continued, "Wynona stayed on in the cabin on the mountain until one day she disappeared. They found a whole lot of blood in the cabin, but they didn't find her body or a weapon. What they did find was Zach lying semi-comatose, on the floor, inside the cabin with a huge knot on his head and Wynona's blood on his clothes. He was almost eighteen at the time. He was arrested and charged with Wynona's murder. But the charges were dropped for lack of evidence. After they dropped the charges, he just disappeared one day, and no one cared. Good riddance, most people around here thought. A lot of people said bad things about him, including my dad; he was kinda loud back then."

"And now he's back?" Tucker asked.

"So Howie says."

"And he's living in the cabin on the mountain?"

"Yup. That's what he said."

She fell silent. Tucker finished writing his notes, then he read through them.

"Well—" he began.

"Look, I'm sorry," she blurted. "Everything I said sounds like some kooky conspiracy theory, doesn't it?"

"No, it—"

"It does. It all sounds so stupid, but she's been gone a whole week, and every morning I wake up and grab my phone hoping there'll be a text from her… or even from Jennifer telling me she's okay. That she's been found."

She looked away and wiped at her eyes.

"I just feel like every little detail counts. I don't want to overlook anything. I want to provide you with the best possible shot at finding her."

He nodded, flipped through the pages of the notebook once more before closing it, then looked at her and said, "As much as I'd like to go through all of this information with you, it's getting late, and we need to get some sleep."

She looked at the clock on the wall. It was almost two in the morning.

"Oh, good Lord," she said and rose to her feet. "I'm so sorry. I didn't think… I didn't mean to keep you up so late."

"Comes with the business," he said. "I was already up when you got here. Besides, I wasn't finished going through your files. I probably wouldn't have called it a night until now, anyway. Um…" He hesitated. "I have a couch, and if you need a shower or something… Well, anyway, you can stay here if you need to." He looked uncomfortable, as if he didn't know what else to say.

"No, it's fine," she said. "I need to go home.

"Of course," he said, "I suppose you have someone waiting for you."

"Oh no, I'm single," she blurted out, then immediately regretted it. *Just sound lonely and desperate, why don't you, Mallory?*

"So you're going to see the police tomorrow morning?" she asked.

"Um…" He hesitated. "Yes, but it will be quite a busy day. After that, I'll be heading up 64 to take a look at the Red Grove trail."

Mallory cocked her head and narrowed her eyes. "Not by yourself, you're not. Red Grove is a seriously tough trail and not for amateurs, especially alone. I'll take you. I know it well. Julie and I hiked it together many times. I'll pack us some trail mix and some water, and I'll bring Annie—she's my dog—so don't worry about bringing anything. The sheriff's department opens at seven. Could we meet up at Hardee's on Shallowford at, say, seven-thirty?"

"Yes, that will work, I guess," he said hesitantly.

Mallory turned back to him. "I'm going to leave talking to the police to you, though, if that's okay. Most of the cops at the sheriff's department don't seem to like me. Can't think why." She shrugged and gifted him with a cheeky grin.

Tucker shook his head. "I can only imagine," he said wryly.

As Mallory drove home that morning, she tried to analyze everything she'd said and every response he'd made. She wanted to believe she'd been helpful but was having a hard time convincing herself.

She lived alone in a small community just outside the city limits, with only her Border Collie, Annie, for company. Home was a modest farmhouse on an acre of sloping land with a distant view of the mountains to the east, and it was some twenty minutes after leaving Tucker's office she pulled into the driveway. She stopped the car in front of the garage door, turned off the motor, set the parking brake, and then sighed and shook her head. She'd lived there for a little more than seven years, ever since her mom had passed away. She'd paid for it with her share of her mother's will and insurance money. She was one of those rare, debt-free individuals, and she was proud of it.

She stepped out of the car—the rain had stopped. The sky had cleared, and the half-moon, still fairly high in the western sky, every now and then dipped behind a fast-scudding cloud. She could hear the hooting call of an owl and the gentle sound of the night breeze passing through the trees. It was a peaceful moment, but she couldn't shake off the feeling that something wasn't quite right. She sighed, stared at the silhouette of the dark and distant mountains on the skyline, then shook her head and turned and walked around the garage to her back door, stepped up onto the deck and took her keys from her pocket.

As she opened the door, Annie ran out, her tail swishing back and forth excitedly.

Mallory bent down, petted the dog, then stepped aside and said, "Go on, girl. I'm sure you need to go. I meant to come straight home after work and let you out, but something came up; you know how it is, right?" Then she stepped inside and flipped on the porch light, feeling more than a little guilty about leaving the dog alone for so long.

"Hey, girl," she said as the dog rushed back inside several moments later. "Maybe I should get you a friend. You'd like that, huh?"

Annie wagged her tail.

"Yeah. That's what we'll do… not a boyfriend, though." She looked sternly at the dog. "Maybe a cute little Jack Russell. What d'you think about that?

The dog panted her approval, then ran to her bowl, turned her head and looked at her.

Mallory nodded and filled her bowl, then sat at the kitchen table and thought for a minute: *A shower,* she decided. *A hot shower is exactly what I need.*

Carefully, she locked the back door, checked the front door and drew the curtains and shades. Only then did she strip down and head upstairs to the bathroom.

The almost scalding water felt wonderful on her chilly skin. She reveled in the warmth until, finally, with the water cooling, she shut it off, stepped out and toweled herself off.

She'd just drawn her robe tight around her and was on her way to her bedroom when… she heard something downstairs.

What was that? She stood still, listening; nothing. *It's just my imagination... Oh, m'God. There it is again.*

She looked at Annie. The dog was on the alert, her ears pricked. She looked up at her.

"It sounds like there's someone on the back porch, Annie."

Thump! Thump!

Footsteps! Those are definitely footsteps.

She ran downstairs.

"Oh, dear God. Where did I leave my phone?"

She ran to the heap of damp clothes she'd left on the floor of the utility room, fumbled the phone out of the back pocket of her jeans and punched in 9-1-1, and then she paused. The sounds had stopped. Outside, she could hear the wind picking up, the branches of the Japanese maple slapping against the wood siding.

It's just the wind. I must be turning paranoid. She cleared the phone and set it down on the table, then walked into the kitchen.

Thump! Thump! Scrape! Scrape! There it was again, only this time it was accompanied by growling.

Annie barked, bared her teeth and growled.

Oh God, what is it? A bear? She ran to the mantle and grabbed the keys to the gun case, ran to it, unlocked it, grabbed her father's double-barreled shotgun, slid two shells into the chambers and snapped it closed.

Then, listening intently, she crept toward the back door. The growling had stopped. Now all she could hear was something whining, and it sounded familiar. She paused, frowning. She waited. The whining stopped, and then, there was… nothing.

She took a deep breath, unlocked the door and pulled it open.

"Tobin?"

She snapped on the porch light. Julie's dog was lying flat out on the deck, gasping.

"Tobe. Tobe, come here," she whispered and laid the gun down on the floor. The dog crawled toward her. On her knees now, she grabbed him and pulled him into her arms. He whined and licked her face.

"Good boy, Tobe. You came home. You… you came home," she stammered, nuzzling and kissing his cheek. She leaned back and looked at him. He was filthy and thin, much thinner than she'd ever seen him; she could feel his ribs. His fur was matted with what Mallory prayed was mud and not dried blood. "Where's Julie, Tobe?" she muttered. "Where is she?"

8

Wednesday morning

Late as it was when he went to bed, sleep didn't come easy. Details of the Romero case kept circling through his mind, and he couldn't shake the nagging feeling that he was missing something, something important.

Barely had he fallen asleep, so it seemed, when he was awakened by his office doorbell. He'd texted Debbie before Mallory had arrived that evening, asking her to come in early. He looked at the bedside clock. It was seven-twenty-five.

"Damn," he muttered as he scrambled out of bed.

With no time to shower, he washed and dressed quickly, ran down the stairs, told Debbie good morning and what needed to be done, and then headed out.

It was almost eight-fifteen when Tucker pulled into the Hardee's parking lot that morning. He was late, something he'd rarely tolerate in others.

It wasn't until he saw his reflection in the restaurant's glass door that he realized he'd forgotten to shave. He hesitated for a moment, considering whether or not to drive to the drugstore to buy an electric razor. But he was already late, and even though he'd not seen Mallory's pickup in the parking lot, she *was* a client, and for him not to be there when she arrived would be unprofessional. So he sighed, pushed through the door and ordered a coffee and a sausage and egg biscuit.

He briefly considered ordering something for Mallory, but not knowing what she'd like to eat, he decided against it. He paid for his order and sat down at a table near the front window, where he had a view of Amnicola Highway and the Chattanooga Police Department.

He watched the early morning commuters making their way into the city. *Where the hell is she?* he wondered, glancing at his watch. It was almost eight-thirty. What little was left of his coffee had gone cold, and his biscuit was long since gone. He took out his phone and checked to see if he had any messages, but then realized they'd not exchanged phone numbers and the only way to get in touch with her was to call her sister, Jennifer, something he didn't want to do.

I guess she overslept, he thought. *She looked like she was running on fumes last night... this morning.*

But he wasn't upset. He'd already gleaned what useful information he could from her files and last night's conversation. And he liked to work alone anyway.

As he sat there, absently staring out the window, watching for her car, he noticed a cherry red Camaro turn into the PD front entrance and park in one of the visitor's spots. He couldn't tell exactly what year the car was, but it appeared to be an 80s model, and even from across the highway he could see it had been fully restored. *Must be worth a tidy sum. I wonder who it belongs to?*

He smiled and nodded as the man he recognized as Sheriff Cundiff stepped out of the car. *He's way out of his jurisdiction. What's he doing here, I wonder.*

Cundiff, an older man, tall with white hair, a heavy gut and a military bearing, closed the car door, locked it and then walked purposefully into the PD, ignoring the ragtag gathering of people and uniformed officers loitering around outside the building. *Impressive.*

The man has an imposing presence. I wonder what he's doing here? Only one way to find out, he thought.

Amnicola at nine-fifteen on a weekday morning can be something of a nightmare, but fortunately, there's a traffic light at the corner of Amnicola and Wisdom.

He waited for the red light, then dashed across Amnicola, then Wisdom, into the PD parking lot and up the front steps, through the doors and into the foyer where the female duty sergeant—who reminded him a bit of Debbie—was smiling down at her computer, which indicated—to him anyway—that she was looking at something other than work.

"Excuse me," he said. "I'd like to speak with Sheriff Cundiff. I saw him come in a few minutes ago."

The sergeant looked up at him, narrowed her eyes, and said, "He's in with Chief Johnston. Does he know you?"

Tucker shook his head. "No, but it's kind of important. Please tell him that it's Tucker Randall and that I'd like to talk to him about the Julie Romero case."

She frowned at him but picked up the phone and, after a short, one-sided conversation, looked at him and said, "If you'll take a seat, sir. Sheriff Cundiff will be with you shortly."

Tucker nodded, stepped away from the desk, sat down near the window and glanced out across the road, briefly wondering if Mallory was awake yet.

He hadn't been seated for more than a few minutes when Sheriff Cundiff appeared in the doorway.

"All right, boy," he said. "You want to see me. Here I am."

Tucker, mildly annoyed that the sheriff addressed him in such a dismissive, diminutive tone, rose to his feet and strode purposefully toward the man, his expression blank.

"It's nice to meet you, Sheriff," Tucker said, offering his hand. "I'm Tucker Randall."

"I know who you are," he snapped, gripping his hand firmly. "What d'you want?"

Tucker, realizing this was going to be a public, stand-up meeting, looked Cundiff in the eye and said, "The Romero family has hired me to find their daughter, Julie. As you already know, she's been missing for more than a week."

"You're here for the Romero girl?" Cundiff raised his eyebrows.

"I am, and I was hoping I could get a look at the file," Tucker said bluntly. "I'm thinking that maybe we could collaborate and find the kid sooner rather than later."

"There is no case file," the sheriff snapped, "and if there was, it would be in my office in Benton. But see, there's no reason to think she's missing. You're wasting your time, son." He glared sternly at Tucker, then continued. "Not to mention wasting police time and the people's hard-earned money. Now see here, you just dragged me out of a meeting with the chief—"

"Then how do you explain Julie's disappearance?" Tucker said, interrupting him.

"Now lookie here, Randall. You know as well as I do that Chattanooga ain't exactly the place young folks want to be anymore, and my boys haven't been able to locate that Bronco of hers, so the consensus is that she just up and left."

"Oh, come on, Sheriff," Tucker replied. "Surely, you're not buying into that. What about the forest, the trails? Why haven't they been searched?"

"Because there was nothing to indicate she was ever out there," Cundiff replied, a little uneasily. "No car. No-thing!"

"You're wrong, Sheriff," he said, anger slowly building inside him. "I've read her journal, and it puts her right there, on Red Grove trail."

"She's twenty-three, son!" Cundiff replied. "Kids are fickle at that age, and like I said, my boys didn't find her Bronco. It wasn't in the lot at either of the two trailheads. She was never there."

"The fact that you didn't find her car doesn't mean a damn thing, and you know it," Tucker snapped. "How do you know she wasn't kidnapped? Someone could easily have taken her and her car. It's been eight days, for God's sake. Why the hell aren't you out there looking for her?"

As soon as he raised his voice, two uniformed officers stepped up.

"You got a problem here, Sheriff?" one of them asked.

"Boys," Cundiff said with a slight smile on his lips, "I think our friend, Mr. Randall, here, needs some fresh air. Kindly escort him out of the building, would you?"

A strong hand gripped his shoulder. Tucker shrugged it off. "I can take myself out."

He looked Cundiff in the eye and said, "Thank you for taking the time and for the conversation, Sheriff. As enlightening as it was, I think I'll need to speak with the police chief in Benton and then head up there and take a look at the Red Grove trail myself."

The sheriff laughed and shook his head. "I'm telling you, Randall," he said. "The kid just took off. There's no case. And… if you do go poking around up there, good luck to you."

Tucker nodded, turned and walked across the foyer to the door, opened it, then turned and looked back at the sheriff.

"I'm warning you, Randall. Stay out of the forest. If not, you'd best be careful. There's been plenty of folks who've gone up there and never come back."

Was that a threat? he wondered. *Are you kidding me?*

Tucker cocked his head, smiled at him, and walked out of the building. He'd lived in Tennessee all his life and he knew there were some weird goings on up there in the mountains, but he also knew that most of it was folklore, tall tales, urban legend. He also knew that that kind of garbage didn't make experienced woodsmen go missing. Julie *knew* the forest, and he knew deep in his gut that she was still out there somewhere, and he was more determined than ever to find her.

He was halfway across the street when his phone buzzed. He took it from his pocket and glanced at the screen. It was Jennifer Romero. He accepted the call.

At first, he couldn't understand a word she was saying because she was talking so fast.

"Slow down, Jennifer," Tucker said gently. "Tell me what's wrong?'

"Please," she said. "You have to get over here now."

"What's going on, Jennifer?" Tucker asked, a sinking feeling in his gut. *Oh, geez. Please don't tell me they've found her body.*

"It's... It's... Please. Just come. I'm at Mallory's house. She's found Julie's dog, Tobin."

He froze for a moment until someone honked at him. He was still in the middle of the street.

He strode to his car. "I'm on my way," he said as he started the car. "Give me the address."

9

Wednesday 9:30am

MALLORY WAS SEATED AT THE KITCHEN ISLAND, ELBOWS RESTING ON THE quartz surface, face buried in her hands, desperately searching for a hopeful scenario—one where her niece was alive and well and Tobin's appearance wasn't an indication of… what, she didn't know. And, for the first time in her life, she felt sure she had a real connection with her sister.

Jennifer and Jared were huddled together on Mallory's living room floor with Tobin.

Julie would never abandon Tobin, she thought. *Maybe she's hurt? It's possible, right? She could have fallen while out on the trail... broken a bone or twisted her ankle. If she couldn't walk, maybe she sent Tobin to find help? He might be able to lead us right to her.*

Despite the holes in such a scenario, Mallory clung to the hope that Julie would soon be found and all would be well.

But if she's injured, why doesn't she call? Bad service? No; there are cell towers all along the top of the mountain. Maybe her phone died? No. Julie carries two backup chargers, but what if both died? No. That can't happen. Why haven't the forest rangers found her? They travel those trails every day, and Red Grove isn't exactly a secluded spot... What if she slipped and tumbled into a gully and dropped her phone? That's possible, right? But she wouldn't have her phone turned off, would she? So why is it going straight to voice mail and where is her car? How do we know she isn't dead?

Before she could come up with a reasonable answer to that one, however, there was a knock at the door.

She slid off the stool, saying, "I'll get it. It must be Mr. Randall."

If Jennifer heard her, she made no sign. Jared looked up and nodded as she went to the front door and opened it.

"Hey. Sorry I let you down," she said, "but... Well, you'll see. Come on in."

"Your sister called me, and—"

"Yeah, I know," she said as he stepped inside. "They're both here, Jennifer and Jared, but they're in a bit of a state. I'm not sure they'll want to talk to you right now. My sister's hardly said a word since she called you, but, well, we'll see. You want some coffee? It won't be like you make it, but I like it."

Tucker nodded. "Sure. That would be nice. Thank you."

"Good. Follow me. We'll go through to the kitchen."

She was worried he was going to ask her how *she* was doing, something she would have appreciated at any other time, but not then. She was barely holding it together, and she knew if he asked, she'd break down and cry, and that wasn't an option.

But, he didn't. Instead, he merely nodded and said, "Where are they?"

"In the living room; this way."

"Jennifer, Jared," she said. "Mr. Randall's here."

Jennifer looked up at them, her face white, tear-stained, holding Tobin tight against her chest.

"I'm sorry, Mr. Randall," Jared said. "We... that is I... can you give us a moment, please?"

"Of course," Tucker said. "Take as long as you need." Then he looked at Mallory, his eyebrows raised.

"This way," she said and led him into the kitchen.

"Please, sit down. How d'you like your coffee?" she asked.

"Better than what I had this morning, I hope," he replied, smiling, then added, "Black will be fine, thank you."

He took a seat at the kitchen table. She poured two cups, set one down in front of him, then sat down opposite him.

There followed a moment of awkward silence while she waited for him to say something, but he didn't. He just looked around her kitchen.

Finally, unable to bear the silence any longer, she picked up a salt-shaker and said, "I found this at a yard sale a couple of years back. I paid ten dollars for it."

He took it from her, smiled and said, "It looks like a baby Elvis that ate a pound of bacon. So go on. Tell me. How much is it really worth?"

She smiled. "That's the thing about antiques. You never really know what you're getting. An Elvis buff would look at it and see a tchotchke. A collector might recognize it as a rarity. It was made in 1956, and it is quite rare. Depending on who's at the auction house, anywhere between fifty and five hundred."

"So," he said. "You're an antiques collector. I didn't expect that."

Not sure if the comment was a jab or a compliment, Mallory smiled at him and said, "Oh, I'm just full of surprises."

I bet you are, he thought.

He pointed to the centerpiece and said, "And that? Where did you get it?"

"That's a Fenton Art Glass bowl," she replied. "I paid fifty dollars for it two years ago at an estate sale. It's worth more than three hundred."

"Really?" He sounded surprised and not a little impressed.

"Really," she said.

And so it continued for some twenty minutes more until finally Jared poked his head through the door and beckoned them and said, "Jen's feeling a little better, if you'd like to join us."

Jennifer was still sitting on the floor with Tobin beside her, his head resting on her thigh, his eyes closed, twitching restlessly as if he was having a nightmare, while Jennifer slowly, gently stroked his head.

Tucker looked down at the dog, grimaced, then he turned to Mallory and said, "Have you reported this to the police?"

She shook her head. "No, I haven't. I doubt it would do any good. They'll just say Julie dumped him and left the state... or something."

"We'll have to tell them," he said. "We need to organize a search party, and they have the resources; we don't."

Mallory frowned. "What are you smoking?" she asked. "They're not going to do that. The cops are... They won't go into the woods. They're scared... They're scared of the moonshiners and boogie men who're supposed to live up there."

Jared snorted, laughed harshly and said, "In all my years in the business, I've never seen any of that crap." He paused reflectively, then continued, "That being said, I do know there are moonshiners operating up there, and pot and ginseng growers, but they're harmless enough, as long as you don't mess with them or their grow. But Julie knows better than to interfere or get tangled up with them; and most of them know her anyway. They wouldn't harm her. Though I have heard rumors about a trail they're supposed to run all the way up through the Appalachians into Virginia, but it's off the maps and probably just hearsay."

"Hmmm..." Tucker said, almost to himself. "That's interesting."

Mallory could almost hear the gears turning inside his head as he considered it.

But didn't Jared just say that it was all hearsay? she thought. *What could he possibly be thinking that would cause him to frown like that?*

She reached out, touched his arm and said, "Hey, what are you thinking?"

He turned his head, looked at her and said, "I... nothing. It was nothing. Look, as interesting as all this is, right now my concerns are with Tobin." He nodded toward the sleeping dog. "We have to report it to Sheriff Cundiff because, at the end of the day, he's the one who'll organize the search. And we need to take Tobin to the vet, poor thing."

Jared looked upset but didn't argue.

Jennifer nodded firmly in agreement. "They'll have to listen to us now, won't they?" she asked. "Hopefully, it isn't..."

She didn't finish, but Mallory knew what she was thinking. *Hopefully, she's wrong.*

"Good," Tucker said. "So, now that's decided, I have a couple of questions. Are you up to it?"

Jennifer and Jared nodded.

"Of course," Mallory said. "Whatever you say. We'll do everything we can to help."

"Geographically speaking," Tucker said, looking at Jared, "is there any reason why Tobin came here instead of going home?"

"I don't know why he would. It's not much closer," Jared replied. "Not in terms of distance, anyway."

Mallory nodded. "He's smart. He wouldn't have gone into the city because he'd be afraid of the traffic. I don't know how he could have made it all the way here. It must be forty miles, or more, from the Red Grove trailhead to here."

"You're sure that's where she went?" Tucker said.

"That was the plan," Jared replied. "She was going to inspect the trail. We have outings planned from now through the end of September."

"Julie and I take the dogs up there all the time and let them run off-leash," Mallory said. "Tobin knows the trails and the area about as well as Annie does."

"Annie?" Tucker asked.

"Oh. Yes," Mallory said, realizing she hadn't introduced her yet. "She's my dog. I put her in my room because she kept worrying Tobin and whining. I can bring her out to meet you... if you like."

But Tucker was already thinking ahead. "I want to take a look at that trail myself, but first, we must notify the police."

Jared frowned. "I wish I could help. But between the limp and the arthritis... Well, I'd just slow you down."

Mallory could see tears glistening in his eyes. Jennifer grasped his hand and squeezed it. Mallory swallowed hard, wanting to say something comforting, but she feared she would only make matters worse if she tried.

"I'll take you," she said. "I know those trails almost as well as Julie. We'll take Annie with us."

Tucker nodded.

"We really do need to get Tobin to the vet," Jennifer said. "We'll call Sheriff Cundiff. That way, you two can get started. You won't want to waste any daylight."

"Good," Tucker said. "We'll call you if we find anything, so don't worry."

Mallory helped Jennifer load Tobin into a crate and then waved as they backed down the short driveway. She watched as they turned onto the highway, and then, already feeling a little better, she returned to the living room.

"You ready?" she asked. "It's already after eleven. We need to go. My stuff's already in my car. You can leave yours here."

10

Wednesday 11:45am

The sun was shining brightly, the birds were singing in the treetops and golden beams of sunlight bounced off the moist pine needles that blanketed the forest floor. Verdant green foliage decorated both sides of the Red Grove trail, while a handful of butterflies drifted by on gossamer wings. It was indeed a beautiful day to be out in the forest, but Tucker saw little of that. All he could think about, given Tobin's condition, was what they *might* find.

Having seen the dog, he had no doubt that the poor girl had never left the forest. *Not willingly, anyway,* he thought, breathing hard.

The trail was indeed difficult, and he was finding it hard going.

Mallory, however, was a hiking machine. Her breathing never changed as she strode onward and upward as Annie, her Border Collie, trotted along beside her, dodging this way and that, sometimes running off into the trees only to return to her side a moment later.

Any thoughts he might have had about Mallory's fitness for the task were dispelled, and it was clear she was every bit the trail guide Julie was. *So why doesn't she pursue it?* he wondered.

Unable to think of a reason, he turned his attention back to the trail, looking for anything that appeared to be out of the ordinary, anything that might offer a clue as to what had happened to the missing girl. But by then, he'd already come to the conclusion that she was probably dead.

Never say dead, Tucker, he thought. *Never say dead.*

Mallory's mood, he noted, had greatly improved, but he was worried she might have caught on to what he was thinking. For some reason that he couldn't fathom, however, she seemed almost alarmingly optimistic, and he silently prayed he hadn't raised her hopes, especially when his gut was telling him things would only get darker from here on in.

Tobin looked like he'd been out here alone for the full eight days, he thought. *And if we do find Julie—and it's a big if—I doubt she survived. And even if she did, if she had an accident, a fall, she'd have been easy prey for the wild animals.*

He shook his head and tried to rid himself of the thought, but it lingered and morphed into a scenario he didn't want to contemplate.

Damn it! he thought as he stumbled over a gnarled tree root. *This was a terrible idea. What the hell was I thinking? What will it do to Mallory if we do find Julie? What if she's... Geez, it doesn't bear thinking about.*

For a moment, he considered sending her home, but he could tell from the pep in her step and the way she kept chattering that it would be useless to even suggest it. *There's no way she'll listen to me... no matter what I say.*

He sighed and marched onward, struggling to keep up with her as she strode confidently ahead, still talking. By then, she was some twenty yards ahead of him and he couldn't hear much of what she was saying. Something about Julie and a blackberry bush? And soon he became lost again in a world of his own, thinking about the case, Sheriff Cundiff, and why they hadn't organized a thorough search of the forest and the trails, especially the Red Grove trail. And his gut was telling him that something just wasn't adding up.

His mind was awhirl with dozens of disconnected images: Tobin's muddy fur. Julie's messages about the Riverbend festival. Sheriff Cundiff's expensive car. A rumored trail run by moonshiners. There were so many odd details about the case and, try as he might, Tucker couldn't piece them together in a way that made any sense. Something was missing, but what? The answers were there. He was sure of it. *All I need is the trigger...* he thought as he struggled on over the rough terrain.

A few minutes later, Annie appeared seemingly out of nowhere and slowed to lope alongside him, looking up at him with watery, dark brown eyes.

"Hey, girl," he said and reached down and gently scratched behind her ears while Mallory, now some dozen yards or so ahead, slowed and waited for him to catch up a little, then continued on again, saying something about him trying to keep up. But by then, she'd opened the gap between them again, and Tucker, too busy trying to stay on his feet, heard little of what she was saying.

When he'd first suggested they check out the trail, he'd assumed it would be a well-defined path, like the hiking trails he was accustomed to in and around Chattanooga, well-traveled and easily navigated, but this "trail"... Well, it was hardly that. It was undulating, narrow at times with room for only one person at a time, sometimes densely overgrown, often dark, and everywhere littered with trip and fall hazards. But worst of all were the insects and, for at least the tenth time, he wished he had brought some bug spray with him. *The last thing I need is to contract Lyme disease.*

As he walked, he couldn't help but think about the case he'd turned down in Nebraska and imagined what it might have been like had he made the more intelligent decision. *Smart Tucker,* he thought, *would still be in the preliminary stages of a challenging but interesting murder investigation. Smart Tucker wouldn't have to worry about black widow spiders, brown recluses, ticks, two-hundred-pound wild boar, or four-hundred-pound black bears on the hunt for an easy mark like Stupid Tucker. But no. Here I am, knee-deep in bug-infested grass looking for... something useful.*

But it had rained the day before, and he had serious doubts they were going to find anything. Any tracks there might have been would certainly be long gone. *Maybe she dropped something. Maybe her abductor dropped something.* He stopped walking and looked around, taking in the terrain, the dense undergrowth, the trees. *Even if they did, I doubt we'd be able to spot anything in this—*

"Yo, city boy!" Mallory called to him, snapping him out of his thoughts.

She'd stopped, turned around, and was staring back down the trail at him. "Never been hiking before?"

Tucker frowned. "Of course I've been hiking before. On actual trails, not this… this wilderness."

Mallory laughed, a light tinkling sound that echoed through the spring air as gentle and pervasive as windchimes. "So, by that, I assume you mean you've been to the Greenway?"

"Keep smiling," Tucker said as he stopped walking and leaned forward, his head down, hands on his knees.

He lifted his head and looked at her. "This is not your average hiking trail. It's tough, and it's damn dangerous. One wrong step, and you could end up in a copperhead nest."

Mallory rolled her eyes and, laughing, walked easily back down the trail to join him. He straightened up and watched her approach, as sure-footed as a mountain goat.

She stood before him, feet apart, one hand on her hip, the other on the strap of her backpack, and said, "It's not so bad, Mr. Randall. Not if you're used to it, which you're obviously not. I told you, Julie and me, we bring Annie and Tobin up here all the time. I've hiked this trail… I was going to say a hundred times, but that wouldn't be true. It's like… forty or fifty, I guess. Anyway, if their scent isn't enough to keep the snakes away, then you can bet that Annie would at least bark and let us know if there was anything dangerous nearby. She's such a good girl." She bent down and petted her dog affectionately. "Isn't that right, baby?"

Tucker rolled his eyes and said, "At least someone's looking out for me. And please, call me Tucker. Mr. Randall's so… formal."

He bent down to pet Annie; she licked his hand.

"Okay. Tucker it is," she said. "You know, she really likes you. She doesn't usually take to strangers. She's very protective of me. She didn't like *me* that much when I first adopted her."

"Maybe it's the beef jerky I hid in my pocket," he said with a laugh.

"Oh, you have some? Gimme," she demanded, holding out her hand.

"I was kidding," he said, smiling.

He stared up into the canopy. The sun was still high. He looked at his watch—almost ten after one.

"How much further?" he asked. "We've been up here almost two hours, and I don't want to be caught out here at night."

Again, Mallory smiled at him. "Oh come on, softy. Don't tell me the cops have rubbed off on you. Surely, you're not afraid of spending a relaxing night under the stars with little old me?"

He almost choked. "Are you serious? Unless I'm mistaken, there's a cold front moving in, and the lows for tonight are supposed to be in the upper forties. We're not exactly prepared to brave the weather, now are we? And about those stars; have you looked up there? God only knows what's creeping about up there in the treetops."

She looked up, then back at him and said, "Maybe you're right. Come on. We've a way to go yet," and she turned and started back up the trail.

"So how much farther?" he asked again.

She stopped, turned around and looked at him.

"Hmmm... Well, we're almost halfway there now. It's nearly six miles from the trailhead that Julie should've been on that morning. So... a little more than three miles?"

Tucker tried not to think about what three more miles through the forest would be like, desperately hoping that this narrow "trail" would feed into a larger, more traveled path. "Does anyone else hike up this way? Any of the neighbors, perhaps?"

Mallory shook her head as she once again took the lead. "Not really. Most of the people who live out this way are older. They know the trail, but it's been a while since I've seen anyone else on it."

"The farther out you go, though," she continued, "the more likely you are to encounter people. The Clearwater subdivision is a couple of miles or so to the east. It's not very big, but I've seen a few of those kids out here in the woods, but they don't usually stray too far from their homes. The only trouble we've ever had out of them was when an older boy was caught trying to set off firecrackers during the dry season. It could have been disastrous if he hadn't been caught. Forest fires can be devastating, you know."

"Yes, I know," he said dryly, and realizing that Mallory was starting to ramble again, he began once again to pay less attention to her words and more to their surroundings.

"What d'you think happened to Julie?" Mallory asked quietly.

"She could have had an accident," he replied carefully. "She could have fallen…"

"Yeah," Mallory snapped, "or she could have been abducted. Or…"

Or met an unfortunate fate at the claws of a hungry animal? Tucker thought. It was all possible, but his gut was telling him it was unlikely. Julie was an experienced hiker, a hunting guide, and there was something about how Tobin had trekked through the woods, smart enough to make it to Mallory's house, that made Tucker sure the dog would have tried to protect Julie from an animal attack, no matter how big said animal might be. And, as far as Tucker could tell, the dog didn't have a scratch on him.

And then there's always the possibility that Julie disappeared of her own volition. She loved nature and, God forbid, if she'd decided to end her life, wouldn't she do it in a place she felt connected to? It was a remote possibility; Julie didn't seem the type to take her own life, and Tucker knew better than to suggest it to Mallory. And besides, he was confident the girl wouldn't have abandoned her dog. So with accident and suicide out of the picture, what did that leave?

Foul play.

Tucker might not yet know how the pieces of the puzzle fit together, but whatever had happened to Julie, he was now certain a third party was involved… "Argh!"

Had he been watching his footing, he might have seen the rusty barbed wire, but he wasn't, and he didn't. He tripped and hit the ground hard, his left side taking the brunt of the impact.

"Tucker!" Mallory yelled. "Are you okay?"

Before he could assess the damage, she was already beside him, hauling him to his feet; her strength amazed him.

"I'm fine," Tucker replied automatically.

"No, you're not. You're bleeding," Mallory cried, pulling his arm towards her. "Oh, my God. It's really deep! You're going to need stitches."

"What the hell is barbed wire doing way out here?" he said.

"Old-timey moonshiners, probably," Mallory said. "They used it to protect their stills from intruders, but that was a long time ago. They don't do that anymore."

"I know just what to do," she continued as she dropped her backpack, opened it, and took out a small first aid kit and a pocketknife.

"Wait… you're going to stitch me? Out here in the woods?" Tucker blurted.

"No, silly. Of course not," she said. "I'll bandage it up and then we'll go see the doctor." She pulled her shirt tail out of her shorts and tore a strip off the hem.

"It's just a scratch, Mallory," he said, "and I'd rather go to the ER."

"Uh-uh!" she shook her head. "The ER will take forever. I know a good doctor. Just let me help you, okay?"

Against his better judgment, Tucker agreed.

"Good. Now you hold still a minute." And she took a piece of gauze from the kit and neatly bandaged his arm.

"There you go," she said, taking a step back. "We'll have you good as new in no time at all, but first we have to get back down off this mountain."

11

Wednesday 4pm

It was almost four o'clock when they exited the trailhead onto Highway 64. The drive back to Mallory's house took another thirty minutes, and by the time they arrived, it was already four-thirty.

Mallory let Annie into the house, made sure she had fresh water and something to eat, then ran back out to the car, jumped in, started the motor, put it into reverse and hurtled out onto the highway.

"Look," Tucker said, hanging onto the strap with his right hand, "I think you should take me to the ER—"

"Nonsense," she snapped, interrupting him. "The ER will be packed solid. It always is. Where I'm taking you is closer and you won't have to wait forever."

He shook his head and closed his eyes, not arguing further. "Okay… If you say so, but don't we have to have an appointment?"

"No. It's a walk-in clinic," she said as she rounded a bend, tires squealing.

The first part of the journey passed for the most part in silence as Mallory focused her attention on the road, glancing only now and then at Tucker to see how he was doing. It wasn't good. She could see the bandage was soaked through with blood.

"What's that buzzing?" she asked as they stopped at a red light.

"It's my phone," he replied, taking it gingerly from his pocket. "It's my brother, Nate. I swear he's got supernatural instincts," he said as he declined the call.

"Shouldn't you have answered?" she asked as the light turned green.

Tucker shook his head. "He likes to talk, and if I tell him I'm on my way to get stitches because I had an accident in the woods, he'll pitch a fit, so no, I don't want to talk to him right now."

Mallory chuckled. "You know, I think your brother would get along well with Jennifer. I'm sure she's OCD. Is Nate older than you?"

"By a year," he replied.

"Oh wow. You guys must be close, then. That must have been so cool, growing up together. Is he your only sibling?"

Tucker nodded. "Yes. Thankfully. I don't know if I could have handled more than one Nate."

"Is he a detective, too?" she asked.

"No, but he is a cop, a lieutenant," he replied. "He graduated top of his class at the academy and could have done well, but he just wanted to be a regular state trooper."

He fell silent for a moment. "By the way, I spoke to Sheriff Cundiff this morning. It didn't go well. I'll tell you about it later when this mess is cleaned up," he said, looking at his bandaged arm.

She nodded. "So, how about you? How come you're a PI?"

"I haven't always been a PI," he replied. "I was with the FBI, but that didn't work out so well, so here I am."

"The FBI?" she said, glancing at him. "I'm impressed. What happened?"

"That's… not something I want to talk about," he said, staring straight ahead. He was quiet for a moment, then asked, "So, where exactly are you taking me?"

"I'm taking you to Dr. Wilson," she replied. "He runs a small private practice. Maybe you've heard of him? Everyone around here knows him. He and his wife are very much involved in the local community."

Randall shook his head. "Chattanooga's a big city."

"I guess." She sighed.

She drove on in silence. *Yes,* she thought. *I suppose it is a big city by Tennessee standards, anyway.*

Chattanooga, population one hundred eighty-two thousand, and that many more in Hamilton County, was the fourth largest city in the state. Mallory had lived there all her life, and she knew it inside and out, but she could count on the fingers of one hand how many times she'd traveled further than Nashville or Atlanta. And she often wondered what it would be like to wake up in the morning and look out upon a new horizon.

"Do you have family here?" she asked, breaking the silence.

"Nope. My parents moved to Florida when they retired," he replied. "They live in Panama City. Nate moved to Tulsa. His wife's family lives there."

"And… There's no one else?"

"Not really. Just a few cousins here and there."

"You have a lot of friends, though, right?"

"Really?" he asked, looking at her. "You're beginning to sound like Nate. Yes, I have friends. Not a lot. But quality over quantity, right?"

"I'm sorry," she said. "I didn't mean to pry. So, this is it," she said as she pulled into the parking lot. "It's a small practice, but Doctor Wilson is well-respected and *very* good at his job."

"Hah! I hope you're right," Tucker said, "since I'm about to let him sew me up,"

"You'll be fine," she said as she turned off the engine. "Come on."

And, reluctantly, he followed her into the small white building.

"You're sure about this?" he whispered.

"Oh, don't be such a baby," she replied.

"I'm not," he said, frowning.

A few minutes later, a nurse appeared in one of the doorways and took them through to one of the patient rooms, where they waited in silence until finally, the door opened and the doctor and his nurse stepped inside.

"Hello, Mallory," he said. "What can we do for you today?"

"Nothing for me, Doctor. It's my… friend here. He fell and cut his arm."

Wilson frowned, looking down over the top of his glasses at Tucker's blood-soaked bandage. "So I see," he said.

"I tripped and fell on some rusty barbed wire," Tucker said.

"Well, let's take a look at it," he said as he snapped on a pair of purple latex gloves. "Hold up your arm… Good. Hold it right there."

He glanced at Mallory as he started removing the bloody bandage. "So, what were you two doing that caused this?"

"We were looking for my niece, in the forest," Mallory said. "She's been missing for more than a week. Mr. Randall is a private investigator."

"Is he now?" Wilson said. "How interesting. And where exactly were you looking?"

"Red Grove," Mallory replied. "D'you know it?"

He shook his head and said to Tucker, "No, but I'd stay out of those woods if I were you. There's no telling what or who you might run into." Then he glanced at Mallory and said, "As a child, this one was in and out of my office with all sorts of little injuries—jumping out of trees, falling off her bike, fighting with the boys. She was a rare one."

"I've matured," Mallory said, embarrassed.

The doctor rolled his eyes and smiled, "That you have, my dear."

"Don't you live up that way somewhere?" she asked.

"No, but I do have a small vacation cabin just outside Archville, on Kimsey Mountain Road," he said as he gently finished removing the blood-soaked gauze. "Hmm. This is deep. I'll have to stitch it. You'll also need an antibiotic."

"I know Kimsey," she said. "It goes all the way up to Highway 68, north of Ducktown."

Wilson didn't answer. Instead, he turned to his nurse and said, "If you'll take him back and prep him for me, please, Mandy. Thank you. In the meantime, Mallory, you can come with me."

Mallory followed him back to the window in the reception area.

"Linda," Wilson said to the receptionist. "If you would, please give Miss Carver the paperwork. I'll be in my surgery with Mr. Randall."

"Of course, Doctor," Linda replied as he walked away. She smiled at Mallory and handed her a sheaf of papers on a clipboard. "There you are, dear. Let me know if you have any questions."

Mallory stared at the top sheet and said, "I'm sorry. I can't answer any of these questions."

"Oh... I thought—"

"He's just a friend," Mallory said.

"Of course. I'm sorry," Linda said, smiling. "Well, never mind. You can help him fill them out when Dr. Wilson's finished with him."

"Thanks," Mallory said, then turned away from the window, sat down and picked up a magazine.

Why would Dr. Wilson embarrass me like that in front of Tucker? she wondered.

Mallory was still absently flipping through an old copy of *Vogue* when, some twenty minutes later, the doctor returned with Tucker, who was several shades paler and clearly in pain.

She stood and took several steps forward. "Would you like me to help you fill this out?" Mallory asked, holding up the clipboard. "I can write for you... if you like."

"Oh no," Dr. Wilson interrupted. "That won't be necessary. Take them home. You can bring them with you when you come back next week. But get this prescription filled *today,* and make sure you take them all. That's a nasty gash you have there, and if it goes septic... well, we won't talk about that. Now, Linda will take your payment. Your credit card will be fine. Good day to you both, what's left of it."

"Thanks for your help, Doctor," Mallory said. "We appreciate it."

Then she turned to Tucker and said, "Come on. I'll take you back to your car... I have a pizza in the freezer. You want to share?"

He looked at her, hesitated, then smiled and said, "Sure. Why not?"

12

Wednesday 7:45pm

TUCKER WAS IN A RARE MOOD AS HE DROVE BACK TO HIS OFFICE EARLY that evening. His arm was stiff and aching like the devil. He was annoyed with himself for letting Mallory drive him to the doctor's office. He'd enjoyed their conversation, but he knew he'd been over-friendly. He also knew he shouldn't have gone to a private physician—not when working on an assignment that could potentially turn high profile.

Nor did he miss the inference that Dr. Wilson wasn't too impressed with Mallory. At first, he thought he was just kidding around with her, but by the end of the visit, he was sure the doctor was actually a little annoyed with her.

Had she really been that much of a handful in her youth, or was he just annoyed that she'd taken him there instead of the ER?

The drive back to her house where he'd left his car had been… to say the least, entertaining. The pizza was good for store-bought, and so was the cabernet. And, though he was reluctant to admit it, so was the company.

It was almost seven-forty-five when he arrived at his office to find that Debbie had left him a note asking him to call Jennifer Romero.

Bracing himself for the worst, he picked up the phone and made the call.

"Mr. Randall, great news," she said. "I thought you ought to know; they're *finally* going to organize a search."

"That *is* good news," Tucker replied. "So when—"

"Mr. Randall. This is Sheriff Cundiff. We're on speaker. You're more than welcome to join us, but you should know the case is now officially under the jurisdiction of my department, and I expect you to be forthcoming about any information you've gathered so far."

"As long as you promise to do the same," Tucker replied.

He heard the sheriff click his tongue, then say, "Of course. All we want is to find Julie. I have my son, Deputy Kal, here with me. He just came back from the vet's office. Apparently, the dog's not in bad shape so… Hold on a minute, Mr. Randall." He heard him say something to Jennifer, and then he said, "Hold on. I'm going outside."

There was a brief interlude, then Cundiff said, "Okay, it's just you and me now. I have her phone, but they can't hear. I've asked the Romeros not to join the search party. I'm sure I don't have to explain why."

"Of course," Tucker replied, nodding to himself. It was clear the sheriff had the same gut feeling as he did.

"You think she's dead," he said.

"I wouldn't go that far, not yet," Cundiff replied. "There's still a chance she's taken off, but… Well, time will tell. In the meantime, I was wondering if you could talk to them. I know they want to be at the front of the search, but… Well, I would appreciate it."

"Of course," Tucker replied. "I totally understand. I'll talk to them and Mallory. Anything else?"

"Not that I can think of. Well, only that I'm going to have Kal text Mallory to let her know what's happening, but if you could handle her and the rest of the family for me, we'll be good."

"Of course," Tucker said. "I take it you'll get back to me with the details?"

"Tomorrow morning," Cundiff said. "Six o'clock at the ranger cabin on sixty-four. You know where that is?"

"I can find it," Tucker replied.

"Good. Come prepared for a long day. See you tomorrow, Randall." And with that, he hung up.

So, he thought, *I have to convince the Romeros. That's not going to be an easy conversation. And Mallory? That's going to be impossible.*

13

Thursday 6am

TUCKER HADN'T BEEN GONE MORE THAN THIRTY MINUTES WHEN Mallory's phone rang.

Jared? she thought. *He never calls me...* She flipped the screen and took the call.

"Jared. What—"

"Mal, where are you?" he asked. "I called your work, but Vinnie said you'd called in. Are you all right?"

"Yes, I'm fine. I'm at home. Is something wrong?"

"No. It's all good. They're organizing a search party. They want to start at first light. There are a lot of volunteers. They're going to search all the trails. We'll work the Red Grove. You up for it?"

"Oh, that's wonderful," she replied. "Of course I'm up for it. Where do we meet and what time do I need to be there?"

"At the ranger cabin on sixty-four at six," he said. "They're rounding up volunteers now. Sheriff Cundiff says they're going to search every trail within ten miles of Red Grove. How did you and Randall do today?"

"We hiked the eastern branch of Red Grove, just partway, though, but we found nothing. Tucker fell and cut his arm and... Oh, never mind. I'll tell you about it later. Is Jen there. Can I talk to her?"

"She's talking to the sheriff," Jared replied. "How is he? Is it bad?"

"Bad enough," she replied. "I had to take him to Doctor Wilson for stitches. He just left—"

"Hey," Jared said, interrupting her. "It looks like Jen has wrapped things up with the sheriff and I need to talk to her. See you in the morning, then?"

"I'll be there!" she replied and hung up.

Finally, she thought. *Something's going to go right! I can feel it.*

IT WAS fifteen minutes to six when Mallory drove into the parking area at the ranger cabin the following morning. The cabin, set back off the road in a small clearing, was some seventy yards east of the western branch of the Red Grove trailhead, which pleased her; the going would be easier than the branch they'd hiked the day before, though not much.

She parked her car in front of the cabin, put Annie on her leash, stepped out and looked around. The only indication of life was a green pickup belonging to one of the forest rangers, the open cabin door, and the overpowering smell of...

Coffee! she thought and went up the steps and into the cabin.

"Hey, Bert, Matt," she said to the two rangers. "What's up?"

She knew them both from hiking in the forest and from The Saloon, where they were both regulars.

"I smell coffee," she said. "Any chance I could have some, please?"

"Sure can," Matt replied. "In the kitchen, he'p yourself. You're here for the search, Mal?"

"Yup!" she replied as she walked through to the kitchen. She grabbed a mug from the sink, washed it out, then filled it with some of the strongest coffee she'd ever tasted.

"You want some?" she yelled.

But before the two rangers could answer, she heard the sound of multiple vehicles entering the clearing.

Coffee in hand, she joined Bert and Matt at the door and watched as another forest green pickup truck pulled up in front of the cabin.

"That's Captain Sweet," Bert said from his desk. "Time to look busy."

Captain David Sweet, the head ranger for the district, climbed out of the truck and said, "Hi, Mallory. It's been a while. Nice to see you again."

"It has," Mallory replied. She and Dave had dated for a while in high school. After they broke up, he dated and then married her friend Sandra Fisher. "How's Sandra?"

He scratched the back of his head. "She's fine, I guess."

Uh, oh, she thought. *That doesn't sound good.*

"I hope all this..." He waved a hand in the direction of the gathering crowd, which now included three sheriff's cruisers and more than a dozen assorted private vehicles. "...works out for you."

He looked at the mug in her hand. "I could use some of that. You want to do the honors while I get this lot sorted?"

"Of course," she replied. "Black?"

"As your hat," he said as he walked away.

Annie pushed up against her leg, tail wagging. Mallory wasn't sure if the dog was just nervous or excited at the prospect of chasing squirrels. "Good girl," she said absently as she reached down and scratched behind her ears. "I don't see Tucker yet, do you?"

It was at that moment her phone rang. She took it from her pocket and glanced at the screen. It was her sister, Jennifer.

"Hi, Jen," she said. "What's up? You're on the way, then? Good. How long will you be? I'm sorry. What did you say? He said what? Are you kidding me? And you agreed? No. That's not going to happen. Leave it with me. See you in a few minutes then."

We'll see about that, she thought with a huff.

By six-fifteen, the lot was full. The numbers had grown to more than seventy-five, by Mallory's count, and included five mounted rangers and four K-9 sheriff's deputies, and by six-forty-five, they were ready to disperse to the various trailheads.

"All right, everybody," Sweet shouted.

"Wait—" she tried to interrupt him, but Deputy Kal Cundiff grabbed her arm.

"Now, Mal," he said, "there's no need for you to be bothering the captain. He's just setting everyone up."

"Yes, I know," she said, jerking her arm away. "I talked to Jen just a few minutes ago, and they want me to stay back with her and Jared. That's not going to happen. We need to be up front."

"No way," Kal said. "We can't have her or you up front. What happens if we find their little girl up there dead? She ain't going to look pretty after all this time, now is she? Not after more than a week."

"Wow, you really are something else, Kal," she snapped. "Maybe if your dad had listened to us and organized it a week ago, we could have been spared all of this. Well, it might be okay with them to stay at the rear, but not me. I'll be with the Red Grove West party, and I'll be at the front because neither your dad, you, nor any of his deputies know the trail better than me. And short of arresting me, there's nothing you can do about it."

"Well, I guess, but Dad—I mean the sheriff—ain't gonna like it."

"Then he can bite me," Mallory snapped and then turned away and marched off to find Sheriff Cundiff and tell him exactly what she planned to do.

She found him on the far side of the clearing, talking to Tucker Randall.

Oh, so he's here? That's good.

"Good morning, Sheriff," she said. "I know my sister has already thanked you, but I'd like to do so, too." She looked around and continued, "This is amazing. There must be almost a hundred people here. Thank you, Sheriff."

Cundiff made a dismissive gesture with his hand. "You don't need to thank me, Mallory. I barely lifted a finger. The county really came through for us, didn't they?"

"They did, but thanks anyway," Mallory said. "Are you going to be leading the search, Sheriff?" She glanced at Tucker. He was looking at his phone.

Cundiff shook his head. "No, I'll be somewhere towards the middle of the Red Grove West group handling communications… Looks like we're about ready to go." He started to turn away.

"Just a minute, please, Sheriff," she said. "I want you to know that I'll be taking a lead position on Red Grove West today. I know that trail better than anyone, and I'll be taking my dog, Annie, with me."

Cundiff stared at her for a moment, his lips clamped together, then he turned to Tucker and said, "I thought you said you were going to deal with this, Randall?" Cundiff snapped.

"I'm sorry, Sheriff, but I think she's right. She does know the trails, and so does her dog. I think they should be out front."

Cundiff frowned, removed his cap, ran his fingers through his thinning red hair, turned to Mallory and said, "No, ma'am. It ain't happening. The best thing you can do right now is stay back and support your sister. She needs you."

"With all due respect, sir," Mallory snapped, "my sister doesn't need anyone, and I'm sure Jared can provide all the support she needs… I need to be up front. And that's where I'm going to be."

After a long moment, the sheriff sighed, scratched his head, replaced his cap, and caved. "Well, I suppose I can't stop you. But you do understand why I want you at the rear with your sister?" He trailed off, giving Mallory a meaningful look.

Her first instinct was to look away, but she managed to hold his gaze. "I do. You think she's dead, don't you, Sheriff?"

"I didn't say that," he snapped. "Aw, hell. Just… do what you want. I can't stop you. Geez, you're one stubborn…" He paused, shook his head and said, "Sheeit!" He turned on his heel and headed toward the rangers.

It was on the tip of her tongue to ask him who'd told him she was stubborn, but she didn't because she already knew the answer, and it was walking toward her, mug in hand, a happy smile on its face.

"Hey, Mal. You talked to my… the sheriff?"

"Yes, Kal. I did," she said resignedly, glancing at Tucker.

He looked up from his phone and smiled.

"What did he say?" Kal asked.

"He said we need to get moving."

Sheriff Cundiff walked back to their little group and said, "Kal, you know what to do. Mal… Geez, you go with Kal and do as he says and don't get in the way. You understand?"

It was all she could do to refrain from giving him a smart answer, but instead she said, "Yes, sir."

"Tucker, you can join me whenever you're ready."

Tucker nodded. "Thank you, Sheriff, but I think I'll go with Deputy Cundiff and Mallory."

"Suit yourself," Cundiff said. "Kal, you keep a sharp eye on them, you hear?"

Kal nodded at his father, closed in on Mallory, and suddenly he was standing just a little too close and she took a step back, her hands in the air. "Hey. He said to keep an eye on me, Kal, not smother me. Just keep your distance, okay?"

"I thought you were going to go with the sheriff?" Kal said to Tucker, frowning.

"I changed my mind," Tucker said, smiling at him.

"Yeah, well, okay then," Kal said and turned to face his group of twenty-four people. "Okay, everybody, listen up," he shouted. "We're going to search the western branch of the Red Grove. I'm going to take the lead and stick to the trail. I want you guys to split into two groups of twelve. The first group will take the lead with me and will spread out six on either side of the trail. Try to stay about six to ten feet apart. The second group will follow the first group twenty yards or so behind and do the same. The sheriff and his party will follow on behind. Any questions?"

There were none.

"Now I know it's going to be rough going," he continued, "but we need to do this right, okay? We're looking for anything out of the ordinary. You find anything, anything at all, you stop, stand still, raise your hand and shout, 'Here.' You do *not* touch anything. You got me?"

There was a chorus of yesses.

"All righty, then. Let's go." He looked at Mallory, then at Tucker. "You two are with me then. Follow me and stay close. Understood?"

Mallory gifted him with a withering look. Tucker grinned at her and winked.

"Hey," he whispered as Kal stepped off toward the trailhead. "I enjoyed the pizza last night."

"Me, too," she said. "It was fun. How's the arm?"

"I really don't know," he said. "It hurts a bit, but that's to be expected, I suppose."

"It will be fine," she said, not really knowing what else to say. "Doctor Wilson's a good…"

"Doctor?" he completed the sentence for her, smiling.

"Yes, that," she said. "I'm glad you're here, Tucker. Thank you."

He glanced at her. She was striding along, head down, her eyes on the trail, Annie at her side.

She looked up at him and said, "Hey, eyes on the ground. Watch where you're walking. We don't want a repetition of what happened yesterday."

By then they were some several hundred yards into the trees, and the group had fanned out on each side where the going over the inches-deep carpet of pine needles and rotting leaves was soft, not exactly tough, but it was slow. And Mallory, as experienced as she was, was glad Kal had insisted that she and Tucker stick to the trail.

The deeper into the forest they went, the deeper the shadows became and the lower the temperature dropped, and Mallory suddenly had an attack of the shivers. She'd known what being at the front meant, and while she thought she was ready to face anything, she knew she could never be fully prepared for…

Oh, heavens, she prayed. *Please don't let us find her dead.*

14

Thursday 6:45am – 8:30pm

TUCKER BEGAN THE SEARCH WITH ENERGY AND DRIVE, AND FOR THE first hour, he marched steadily onward, his eyes on the ground. Fortunately, the going was easier than it had been the day before.

A half a mile in, the pace slowed as the search intensified. Kal Cundiff and Mallory were several yards ahead of him; Kal searched the trail in front and to the left, Mallory to the right, while Annie bounded every which way and back and forth.

An hour in and his legs and feet had begun to ache. The going and having to test each step for trip and fall hazards were beginning to take their toll. By noon, his legs were on fire, but as far as he could tell, Mallory and even Kal seemed to be coping just fine.

By three, with the terrain steepening, he could go no further, so he called a halt and sat down on a fallen tree trunk.

Mallory, who'd said little to him for the last several hours, turned, came back and said, "You okay, Tucker?"

He shook his head and said, "No, not really. I'm sorry. I thought I was in good shape, but I'm just not used to this… to this. My legs are about to give out. If you don't mind, I'm going to sit here for a while. How far have we come?"

"Two and a half miles, maybe a bit more," she replied. "It's been slow going because of the search. D'you want to go back? The sheriff's party can't be far behind."

"We've been out here almost nine hours, Mallory," he said. "And we haven't found anything; no sign she was ever here. It's as if she disappeared off the planet."

Mallory nodded and sat down beside him. "You're right," she said. "I don't get it. I thought Annie would find something, but she hasn't. Not today or yesterday. Julie must have taken some other trail… I guess."

"Hey. Everything okay?" Kal asked. "We need to keep moving."

"You two go on," Tucker said. "You need to maintain the search. I'll sit—"

Kal's radio chirped. "This is Sheriff Cundiff, folks," he announced. "It's getting on for four, so I'm calling it a day. We'll pick up where we left off tomorrow, so group leaders, mark your spot and then make your way back to the trailhead, where there'll be some refreshments. Over and out."

Kal looked down at them and said, "You ready to go?"

"Give me a minute to get my breath, Deputy," Tucker said. "You go on ahead. I'll follow in a minute."

"I'll stay with him," Mallory said. "See you back at the cabin?"

Kal didn't look happy, but he nodded and said, "Be careful." Then he turned and walked away down the trail.

They sat there in silence for a moment until, unable to stay quiet any longer, Mallory said, "What d'you think happened to her, Tucker? Be honest with me, okay?"

He took a deep breath, turned his head to look into her eyes and said, "I don't know, Mallory. I don't believe she fell off the trail into a gully. She's much too experienced to have done that, and I don't believe she took off either. There's something else in play. Either she was kidnapped, or…"

"Or she's dead," Mallory finished for him. "You think she's dead, too, don't you?"

He looked into her watery eyes and said, "That's what the odds are, I'm afraid. She's been gone nine days now… Look, there's a good chance she's been kidnapped. If so, we'll find her."

"Come on," Mallory said, standing up. "We've a long way to go. Here, let me help you up." She offered him her hand.

He was tempted to ignore it, but then, not wanting her to think he was being an ass, he reached up and took it, and she pulled him up. And, once again, he was impressed by her strength.

The trek back to the cabin was indeed long and, in the dim light, fraught with trip and fall hazards. But it was all downhill, and with Mallory leading the way, they made good time, though it was nearly eight-thirty and almost dark when they made it back to the ranger cabin. The cars and trucks were all gone, and the lot stood empty except for Mallory's car, Tucker's SUV, a single sheriff's cruiser and three ranger pickups.

"Let's sit a minute, shall we?" Mallory said.

She'd said little during the trek down the mountain. Tucker had assumed it was because she was concentrating on the trail, but little as he knew her, it seemed out of character. So, when she asked him to sit, he did. He sat down on the porch steps beside her. Annie jumped up, sat down beside him and pushed her head under his arm. He smiled and scratched her ears.

He glanced sideways at Mallory. She looked… defeated.

"…see you guys tomorrow," Kal said over his shoulder as he stepped out of the cabin. "Oh, hey, Mal, Mr. Randall. You made it then?"

She said nothing.

"Well," he said and paused for a second before continuing, "we didn't find anything, but that's a good thing, right?"

"Go away, Kal," she mumbled. Annie perked her head up and gave a little *yip*.

The deputy looked at Tucker and shrugged as if to say, *What can ya do?*

"You have a nice evening," he said, then walked down the steps and across the lot to his cruiser. And they watched as he drove out of the lot.

"You guys want some coffee?" Bert called from the open cabin door.

"Not me, thank you," Tucker said.

Mallory just shook her head.

"There was an awful lot of people turned up," she said, breaking the silence. "I was really surprised."

Tucker nodded. "Yeah, me too. It was a good effort."

"Can I be honest with you?" Mallory asked after a moment and then continued without waiting for an answer. "I don't know how I feel about today."

"What do you mean?" he asked.

She leaned back, pulled the scrunchie from her hair, shook her head and her blonde hair cascaded down around her shoulders.

"I'm frustrated, Tucker, and disappointed." She turned her head to look at him. "We didn't find anything. All those people… dogs, horses, and cops… nothing."

"I know. I'm sorry," Tucker said quietly.

"But at the same time," she continued, "I'm relieved. You know? When the search began, I told myself I would be okay with whatever we found because at least I'd know. But as it progressed, and we got deeper into the woods, I kept thinking about it, and I… I began to pray we wouldn't find anything. How awful is that?" she asked.

Annie nudged him. He stroked her head.

"No, it's not awful. It's quite natural to feel that way," he replied. "Don't be so hard on yourself."

Mallory laughed, looked away and shook her head.

"What's so funny?" Tucker asked.

She turned her head and looked him in the eye. "Nothing," she said. "It's just that I can't believe you said that. I mean… People in glass houses."

Tucker frowned at her. "What's that supposed to mean?"

She rolled her eyes. "You're always so reserved," she said. "All that 'I work alone' stuff. I don't get it. Someone must have hurt you pretty badly."

"You've got to be kidding me," he said.

"Nope," she said. "I'm a pretty good judge of character. I haven't worked thirteen years in a bar for nothing. You want to talk about it?"

Tucker looked at his watch. It was just after nine. He looked up. The sky was a field of stars. He looked to the east. In the glow of the lights of Cleveland, Tennessee, some thirty-five miles away to the west, he could see what looked like gathering storm clouds, though it wasn't supposed to rain again for several days.

He glanced at her. She was still staring at him. And suddenly, he felt uncomfortable.

"That's not a good idea," he answered eventually. "It's getting late and..."

She nodded. "I have a question. You don't have to answer if you don't want to, but when I was talking to Sheriff Cundiff, you were looking at your phone. What was that all about? Were you avoiding me? Why would you do that?"

Tucker took a deep breath, not quite knowing how to answer.

"This is your big chance, Agent Randall," David Lewis said. "SAIC isn't a fancy title. It's the real thing, and you earned it. And the Clines are old friends. I'd hate for anything to happen. But I really think you're ready for this."

"I am, sir!" Tucker replied. "I won't let you down."

"And I have every confidence in you," David said.

Marsha Cline had been working as a waitress—a temporary job between semesters in college—when one of her customers forgot to take their credit card. She'd rushed out to find the woman but had heard sounds of a struggle in the alley beside the restaurant. As she went to investigate, a man came running out, bumped into her, looked her in the eyes, and then shoved her aside and bolted. Marsha looked down the alley and saw a man lying on the ground. She ran to him. She was going to help him to his feet, but he'd been stabbed several times. She called 911, but by the time the ambulance arrived, he'd bled out and was dead.

Marsha had witnessed a murder, the latest in a line of unsolved stabbings. She was the only witness who could identify the killer.

Two days later, the restaurant was broken into, and the employee files stolen. The next day, two of the restaurant employees were stabbed to death. So the Clines had sought out David Lewis, and he had appointed Tucker to watch the young woman.

He sighed and said, "I wasn't avoiding you, Mallory. I found an old picture on my phone, one I thought I'd deleted a long time ago. It's the picture of a young woman I was assigned to protect… It ended badly."

He took out his phone and found the picture of himself with David Lewis standing next to an older couple. And between the couple…

"Oh… my God. That looks like Julie!" Mallory gasped.

"I know," Tucker said. "That's Marsha Cline. That's who I was supposed to protect. She was a witness in the biggest case in my FBI career five years ago. She was frightened, but between me and her parents… We, that is I, persuaded her to testify against a murderer."

She bit her bottom lip as she looked at him, wide-eyed.

"My boss," he continued, "assured me, and her, that she'd be safe, that she'd be protected, but…" His voice broke.

"You don't have to go on," Mallory said.

Tucker continued anyway, "But he was wrong. I persuaded her. I took her statement. She described the killer perfectly. But…" He let out a sigh. "It turned out the case was bigger than we all thought. What she saw was a mob execution, and the police had busted a major drug operation. Less than twenty-four hours after she'd identified the killer, she was dead."

"That was not your fault," Mallory said firmly. "You can't blame yourself."

He looked sideways at her, smiled grimly and said, "Who else is to blame? The killer? My boss? Her parents? No. I was the one who handled it wrong, and she paid for it with her life." *That she did, Tucker* —it was an angry whisper at the back of his mind—*and I'm never going to let you forget it.*

"When your sister and Jared arrived in my office," he continued, "I'd already made up my mind to take a case in Nebraska. I was… I was just humoring them, but then Jennifer showed me a photo of Julie and I thought I was seeing a ghost."

"Tucker," Mallory said. "I'm sorry. I had no idea."

Tucker, feeling embarrassed that he'd confessed so much to a woman he hardly knew, stood up to leave. But Mallory stood too, placing herself in front of him, her eyes filled with tears.

"Thank you for taking our case. I know how hard it must have been for you. I wonder if… But shouldn't we get going?"

He smiled at her and said, "Yes, we should. We have another long day tomorrow."

"You're right," she said. "Of course, you are. I'll see you tomorrow then. Have a good night, Tucker." And she turned and walked to her car.

"Mallory," he called after her.

She turned, her hand on the handle of her car door and looked at him, "Yes?"

"What did you want to ask me?"

She paused, frowned, thought for a moment, then said, "I don't remember. It couldn't have been important. Goodnight, Tucker."

She turned to her car, opened the door for Annie to jump in, climbed in after her and drove away into the night.

"Goodnight, Mallory," he muttered as he watched her go.

15

Friday through Monday

Mallory, unhappy with the way the search the previous day had turned out, decided to organize her own search party: Jennifer and Jared, with Jacqueline—Julie's elder sister. They would be taking Jared's Gator 4x4. Sarah Alexander—Julie's best friend—was also joining them with a handful of their former classmates. But not Tucker Randall.

It had been around five-thirty that morning when she called him.

"Hey," she said when he answered. "You still in bed?"

"No, I woke early. I'm in the kitchen making coffee… Look, Mallory, I hope you'll forgive me, but I'm not going to be able to make it today. My legs and hips have stiffened up, and I can barely walk. I should have known better. So, I'll just stay in my office today. I have plenty of research and investigating on Julie's case to do. And you have to admit that I wasn't much help yesterday."

"Oh, I wouldn't say that," she replied, "but I do understand, and, yes, you should stay home and rest for at least a couple of days. I've organized a search party of my own. We're going to search the Ridge Trail, which is probably a waste of time. I don't see her going all the way up there, but you never know, and it will keep me away from Kal's groping fingers."

"Well, you know where I am," he said. "Please let me know if you find anything."

"You bet. You rest up, okay? Talk to you later, Tucker." And she hung up, feeling a little disappointed he wasn't going to join her.

The next three days passed slowly and fruitlessly.

On day one, they found nothing at all. The second day, they found the remains of a campsite—a stone fire ring, some scraps of fabric perhaps from a tent, some empty food cans, beer cans, bottles, and other trash. On the third day, they found a small cabin. There was no one there, but there were signs of recent habitation: cans of food, bottles of water, some pieces of paper—notes, sketches, doodles—ashes in the fireplace, and an iron bed with a mattress and a couple of blankets. Other than that, nothing.

The sheriff's department sent a CSI unit to investigate both sites, but neither one yielded any indication Julie had ever been there.

And so it went on to the point where Mallory found herself praying that Julie was dead, because if she wasn't, if she was alive, what would it mean? *If she's been abducted? What horrible things are they doing to her?*

On day four of the search—now without most of Julie's former classmates or Jared because of his limitations—Mallory was wondering why they hadn't seen anything of Zach Burns. Howie O'Neal said he lived up that way in an old cabin, and she wondered if it was the one they'd found. She knew, of course, there were several more cabins scattered around the forest, but it was possible. *But where is he? He has to be somewhere, right?*

She'd talked to Tucker on the phone several times during the four days, but he'd had nothing constructive to say. And, truth be told, neither had she.

Mallory had also been talking back and forth with Julie's friends, trying to figure out what they were missing, because there had to be something. But they had nothing helpful to add, and she felt as if she'd run into a brick wall.

She also had a feeling that if she and Tucker could put their heads together, maybe they could figure out what it was she was missing.

As she was getting ready to go to work that Monday afternoon, Mallory couldn't help but think of some of the more perplexing true crime cases that she'd heard about. She wondered how the smooth voice of Dark Tidings would handle Julie's tale…

Tragedy struck the small, upscale community just beyond the city limits of Chattanooga when a young woman seemingly disappeared, vanished without a trace. Julie Romero—twenty-three—a sociable young woman whose smile could light up any room, was an experienced hunting guide who loved the outdoors until... a routine hiking trip in the Cherokee National Forest turned into what appears to be an unsolvable mystery. No evidence as to how or why she disappeared has ever been—

Mallory shook her head and forced herself to focus on the task at hand, but then, *No,* she thought, *that's not going to happen. The police may have ended the search, but they haven't closed the case. And Tucker is still here, and I know he's cracked tougher cases than this one.*

"Vinnie, I'm here," she called as she walked into The Saloon.

She felt nauseous. She was tired. No, she was worn out and wished to hell she could take some time off, but she needed the money; it was the only thing keeping her afloat, both financially and mentally. And it was the single constant in the ever-evolving catastrophe that had suddenly become her life.

Maybe you wouldn't be so tired and nauseous if you ate properly, a voice in the back of her head said, a ghostly version of Jennifer's nagging rhetoric. She pursed her lips, knowing it was true. She hadn't eaten a proper meal since the pizza she'd enjoyed with Tucker.

Vinnie called over from the jukebox, "You wanna try fixing this piece of junk? I been at it all day."

"Sure, Vinnie," she said and sighed.

"And while you're doing it, don't forget to mind the bar," he added.

"Sure, Vinnie," she repeated, too tired to argue.

"What? Is there an echo in here?" Vinnie said as he shuffled off to his office.

For several minutes, she tried to figure out what was wrong with the ancient jukebox but gave up in frustration. *The poor thing has run its course,* she thought. *We should take it out back and shoot it, put it out of its misery.*

She went behind the bar and began to clean up Vinnie's mess and, out of habit, she stuck an earbud into her left ear, covered it with her hair, and turned on a Dark Tidings podcast. But after a few minutes of listening to Devin Rudd talk about how Lawrence Bittaker abducted one of his victims, she shut it off. Every word sounded like a description of what might have happened to Julie, and she just couldn't stomach it anymore.

Her stomach was churning, reminding her she'd eaten only a slice of toast and apple all day. She looked around the bar. There were only six customers and, of course, Art Peters, who was in his usual spot propping up the end of the bar. Everyone's glasses or bottles seemed to be full so, after a final glance at the old machine—*he could replace it for a hundred bucks,* she fumed—she went to the back room and turned on the air fryer.

Vinnie didn't have much of a selection. The only reason he'd bought the machine was an attempt to compete with an Applebee's-wannabe just up the road. His selection of overpriced appetizers was scraped from the bottom shelf of a convenience store freezer section he'd picked up at a sale.

She sighed and set a fish filet, chicken nuggets and some mozzarella sticks to cook for fifteen minutes and then went back out to "mind the bar."

In the forty-five minutes since she'd been at work, no one had entered, and only one person had left.

As she waited for her food to cook, she looked out over the bar at the five patrons scattered around the room, three in one booth, one in another, and another at a table, plus Art at the end of the bar, but he didn't count. He was a fixture.

Why do they come here to drink alone? she wondered.

The timer in the back room dinged, and she went back to find her food burned on one side. *Idiot!* she chided herself. *You were supposed to flip them halfway.* She started rummaging through the freezer for more, but Vinnie poked his head out of the office.

"Hey, what you doing?"

"I burned my food," she explained. "I'm going to make another plate."

"You make another plate, you're going to pay for it, right?"

"Oh, come on, Vinnie, look at this?" She showed him her fish filet. "I can't eat that."

"You should pay more attention. You get one meal a shift, and you're lucky I give you that. You think I'm made of money?"

"And I hardly ever take it!" she said. "So, you're saying you'll charge me for cooking tomorrow's meal?"

"Not if you make it tomorrow!" he said and pulled his head back into the office.

I should just throw this crap at him, she thought as she turned everything over and ran the air fryer for a few more minutes. *That's the way to do it. Scrape off the black and use lots of sauce... What a dickhead.*

After a long and boring shift of filling the glasses of the few customers she had, she looked at the clock to find it was still only ten o'clock. Art had gone home early for a change, and the last customer had walked out fifteen minutes earlier, and she doubted there'd be anyone else coming in, so she went back to the office.

"Vinnie, it's been dead all night," she said. "There's no one out there, not even Art, so is it okay if I leave early?"

"What you want to leave for?" he asked. "Your shift is to eleven. You can stand out there and get paid for doing nothing, right? Put on your scary stories and ride my dime."

"Oh, come on, Vinnie, I'm exhausted. I've spent almost two weeks trying to do something about Julie."

"Yeah," he agreed. "You get up stupid early, run around all morning, then come in tired and complain about it. I noticed."

She resisted the urge to slap him for his lack of empathy. "Well, I want to go home and go to bed. Get some rest, and come in fresh tomorrow." Every word was a lie, but she expected he knew that.

"Whatever." He waved a hand dismissively at her. "I wouldn't do this for Roger or Patty. But you're my best bartender. Go on. Piss off and get some rest." And with that, he turned back to his ancient computer.

AND SO MALLORY DROVE HOME. The ride was uneventful, but try as she might, she couldn't get Julie out of her mind.

Fifteen minutes after she left The Saloon, she entered her house, let Annie out the back door and poured herself a large glass of red. That done, she picked up her flashlight and wandered out into the dark, down the paved path to the fence at the end of her backyard.

It was a moonless night, the air humid, the sky a vast field of stars, though storm clouds were gathering to the west and she could feel rain in the air.

She stood at the fence and stared at the silhouette of the distant mountains to the east, dark against the indigo sky, and her heart went out to Julie. *Where are you, Jules? Where the hell are you?*

She heard something snap. In the quiet of the night, it sounded like a gunshot. She looked to her left but could see only the outline of the tall trees that separated her lot from the one next door.

Snap!

Oh, m'God. There it is again. A gun. Her heart hammered in her chest. *I should have brought a gun. Why didn't I bring a gun? I have a gun! Why didn't I bring a gun!*

Another snap, this one much closer.

"Annie," she whispered. "Where are you?" But Annie wasn't there. She was off somewhere, out in the field beyond the fence, *schnauzing for rabbits, no doubt,* she thought.

She spun around, terrified that she was about to come face to face with... what? She didn't know. She waved her flashlight this way and that, and then... she found herself looking into the bearded face of a man.

Shocked, she stumbled backward into the fence, almost falling, but before she could hit the ground, the man reached out, grabbed her arm and, without saying a word, pulled her to her feet.

"Julie?" The voice was deep, dry, questioning.

"What? Who are you? What do you know about Julie?" she whispered, her voice shaking.

The shadowy figure cocked his head to one side. All she could see under his hood were his eyes, glinting darkly. "Mallory?" the voice sounded somehow less frightening and... familiar.

"Who are you?" she said, her voice rising in volume. "What d'you know about Julie? Tell me, please."

But instead of answering, the man backed away, then turned and ran.

"Please," she yelled. "Don't go. Tell me about Julie. Come back. I need to know!"

But all was still and quiet as the tears rolled down her cheeks. She bent down, picked up the flashlight, and started back along the path to her back deck, where she sat down, her empty, forgotten glass in one hand, her flashlight in the other, and began to cry loudly.

Five minutes later, Annie came bounding along the path and up onto the deck.

"Where've you been, you little monster?" she said, reaching out to fondle the dog's head. "Fat lot of good you are. I could have been murdered and you wouldn't have known."

16

Friday evening 11pm

Tucker had spent the four days at his office, at the police department, the local sheriff's office and even the Hamilton County sheriff's department digging through old files and folders. To say he'd worn out his welcome would be the understatement of the century; to the point where Sheriff Cundiff was tempted to throw him out.

He searched through every file box he could find, every case file on the departmental computers, anything to do with missing persons, smuggling and forest-related crimes.

He'd visited the library and used their microfiche reader—*Microfiche! Really?*—to search old newspapers for any hints or clues, even speculations about any series of related crimes in the area. He'd even attempted to interview some of the older folks in Benton, Copper Hill and Ducktown, but no one would talk, especially when they realized he was looking into local crime.

So, that Monday afternoon, Tucker was mentally exhausted and reduced to sitting at his desk staring up at the ceiling.

"I just don't understand it, Debbie," he said, though he suspected it wasn't the first time he'd said it. "Why did the dog get left behind?"

"I don't know, sir," Debbie replied.

"I mean, Tobin was Julie's dog, right? If she was planning to do a runner, she wouldn't have left him behind, would she?"

"No, sir. Did she always take the dog with her?" Debbie asked.

"As far as I know, yes. So, if she left the dog, she didn't leave town, and something bad must have happened to her."

The vet had given Tobin the all-clear, and he was back with the Romeros. *Maybe Mallory's idea about taking him up the trail is a good one.*

And then there's the missing Ford Bronco. Hah! Scrapyards. That's another lead that hasn't been followed up on. He did a quick search online and found no less than a dozen salvage yards in Hamilton County alone. Five in Bradley County and several dozen more spread out over a dozen Southeast Tennessee counties.

"Hey, Debbie," he said, "I need you to do something for me. I need—"

"Mr. Randall?" she said. "It's almost seven o'clock."

He blinked twice, then looked at his watch. It was indeed almost seven.

"I'm really sorry, sir," she said. "I know you like me to stay late sometimes, but I really do need to get home tonight. Ben made a roast today, and he's expecting me."

"Of course, Debbie," he said. "I'm sorry. I wasn't paying attention to the time. Go on home and enjoy your dinner. What I need will wait until tomorrow. We'll talk about it in the morning."

"Thank you, Mr. Randall," she said and collected her things. "See you in the morning, then. D'you want me to come in early?"

"No. Eight-thirty will be fine."

She closed the door and Tucker leaned back in his chair, linked his fingers behind his head and closed his eyes. It was quiet; too quiet.

"Maybe I should get myself a dog," he mused. "Someone to talk to when it gets lonely in here."

He looked at his watch again. It was fifteen after seven; too late to call the salvage yards, so he buried himself in copies of crime reports going back over the last twenty years. *If I don't get a break soon, I'm going to have to refund the Romeros. Okay, so where's the Bronco? If we can find it, it would be a solid lead.*

At a little after nine, he tossed the fruitless crime reports aside and turned to Mallory's maps and compared them to copies of the maps they'd used during the searches. There were some slight differences between them, but he ascribed that to different hands tracing them out. He looked at copies of the notes Sheriff Cundiff had made. Comparing those to the maps, he was pretty sure most of the trails over a ten-mile radius had been well-explored. Yes, there were several spidery-looking, unexplored squiggles on Mallory's map which he thought might be worth a look, but—

And that was the last he remembered until he was awakened by a mighty banging on the front door that startled him awake. His chin cupped in his palm, he jerked but caught himself and rubbed his face. *What time is it? Five after eleven! Geez. How long have I been asleep?*

He looked down at his desk. He'd switched from Mallory's maps to Julie's bank statements and then to her text messages, hoping to find any connection.

The banging continued. *What the hell?* He rose to his feet, went to the door and opened it to find a rain-soaked Mallory Carver.

She pushed past him into the room and turned to face him, her arms thrust down by her sides. "I know that this isn't the best time, but I've been attacked. Well, not actually attacked, but I was at the bottom of my yard and there was a man. He had a beard and... Tucker, he *scared* me, and I fell, and he grabbed me and then—"

"Whoa, stop," he interrupted. "Is he still there?" *Stupid question. Of course he isn't.*

She paused, shook her head and said, "No."

"Well just hold on. You're soaking wet. I'll get you some towels." He went into the house and returned a moment later with several bath towels and handed them to her.

"When did it start raining?" he asked.

"I don't know. Not long ago. Twenty minutes, maybe?"

"Get yourself dried off," he said. "I'll go get some blankets." She nodded.

"Feel better now?" he asked after she'd wrapped herself up and sat down on the couch.

Again, she nodded, staring at him.

"So," he said, "are you going to tell me about it?"

She looked up at him and said, "I'm sorry. I didn't know what else to do."

"Tell me what happened."

"Well, Vinnie let me off work early, and I went home and let Annie out, then I went to get some air. I walked to the fence at the end of my property to look at the mountains and..."

"You said someone grabbed you," Tucker said. "Who was it?"

"I... I don't know for sure," she replied. "But I think it might have been Zach Burns."

"What?" Tucker frowned. "You mean the kid who killed his mother?"

"I don't know. It was dark. He was wearing a hoodie and he had a beard. He only said two words. 'Julie?' a question, as if he thought I was her. Then he recognized me and said 'Mallory.' It was when he said my name that I thought I recognized his voice."

"And he didn't say anything else?" Tucker said thoughtfully.

"No. I asked him what he knew about her, but he didn't answer. He just backed away, then turned and ran. He was big, Tucker; huge."

She paused for a second, then said, "Maybe I am making too much of this. What could have—"

"No, no," Tucker interrupted. "This could be the break we've been looking for. We need to find this guy. If he's who you think he is and he thought you were Julie, it means he didn't kill her. This guy O'Neal you told me about. He said Burns was living in a cabin somewhere up there in the forest. D'you know where it is?"

"No," she replied, "but I do know where Howie lives. First thing in the morning, I'll go there and ask him."

"I think I'll join you," Tucker said. "I was going to start looking for the Bronco at the salvage yards, but my assistant can start researching that for me. Are you hungry? Would you like something to eat?"

"No… Well, maybe a little? I burned my dinner at Vinnie's place. It was awful."

"Hang tight, then. I'll go make you something hot."

"That would be wonderful. Thank you," she replied.

When he returned less than ten minutes later with a plate of lasagna, he found her stretched out on the couch, fast asleep.

17

Saturday morning 7am

MALLORY WOKE WITH A START, SAT UP AND LOOKED AROUND. *OH MY God,* she thought. *I'm in Tucker's office. Oh crap. This is terrible. What was I thinking? I have to get out of here before—*

"Oh, you're up. Would you like some coffee?"

Crap! she thought as she turned her head to look at him.

He was standing in the doorway, leaning against the frame with his arms folded, smiling down at her.

Inwardly, she shook her head, sighed and accepted the situation for what it was; bad.

"Yes. Please," she said. "But first, I need to go out to my car and grab my purse."

"If there's anything you need to clean up or whatever, you only have to just ask," he replied.

"I appreciate the gesture," she said, "but I'm pretty sure you don't have anything a woman carries in her purse." And she immediately regretted her choice of words. *Damn! Now I sound like I'm— Oh hell, what does it matter? I must look like hell.*

"Tucker," she said. "I need to go home. I need a shower, a change of clothes, and, and I need that coffee, please."

"By all means," he replied easily. "You can take a shower here. You can… borrow one of my T-shirts. We can eat some breakfast, and then we'll go to your place. You can change clothes, and then we'll head out to see this Howie guy. Okay?"

"I guess," she said, "but coffee first."

"Yes, ma'am," he replied. "Right this way, if you please."

And she stood and followed him into the kitchen.

IT WAS JUST after nine that morning when Tucker turned off Tennessee 30 in Greasy Creek onto the dirt road that led to the log house where Howie O'Neal lived alone with three coonhounds.

He parked the car next to Howie's pickup, and he and Mallory stepped out to be immediately surrounded by the three friendly dogs, all woofing excitedly and wagging their tails.

The day was warm, but with a slight breeze wafting through the trees. Howie's cabin—a modern, polished log build set on two acres of woodland—was not quite next door to another, much older cabin surrounded by a couple of dozen vehicles in various stages of disrepair: some on blocks, some on flat tires, some almost swallowed by long grass and creepers, and all dated earlier than 1970. The lot was a veritable graveyard: the place where unloved classic cars go to die.

"What's with that one?" Tucker asked, nodding at the dilapidated cabin.

"It's an old homesteading thing," Mallory replied. "It belongs to Howie, too. Dates back to the early nineteen hundreds. You find a spot, chop down a few trees, build yourself a cabin, then, many years later, when you've had time to build a decent house, you turn the old homestead into a handy outbuilding. Smoke meats, store vegetables, cure tobacco, keep animals, whatever your fancy. That one looks to be about… I dunno. Maybe sixty years or so old? It's… kinda nostalgic, don't you think?"

She pointed a little further away. "See that bald patch of ground over there? That looks like the location of the original cabin. That pile of rocks looks like it might have been the chimney or maybe a burn spot. Or maybe it was a garden. It's hard to say anymore. They would have used what was left of the structure as firewood to heat the new cabin in winter."

She glanced at Tucker and saw him nodding, putting it together in his mind.

"You really know this stuff, don't you?" he asked.

She smiled at him but said nothing.

"Hey, little girl, whatchu think you're doin' sneaking about on my property?" Howie O'Neal said from the front porch.

"Sneaking?" she replied. "A bear makes less noise chasing down a deer."

"Ain't that the truth," he grumbled. "I heard ya comin' from more'n a quarter mile away."

"As intended," Mallory said. "Everyone knows you don't sneak onto a man's property around here. That will get you shot in a hurry."

"Ain't that the truth?" Howie repeated. "So watcha doin' here?"

"Mr. O'Neal, I'd like to ask you a few questions, if I may—" Tucker began.

"Nope! Ya may not." Howie turned to Mallory. "But the lady has my attention."

"You mentioned Zach Burns the last time we spoke," Mallory said, inwardly smiling. "You said he lives in a cabin somewhere up here. D'you know where, exactly?"

"Sure do," he replied.

"Oh good," Mallory said, taking her map from her pocket. "Could you show me where it is on this map?"

"Gimme that thing." He held out his hand and she stepped forward and handed it to him.

"So it's right around here somewhere… just above this ridge right here," Howie said, pointing to a spot on the map.

"Is there an easy way to get there?" she asked. "Can we drive?"

"Sure, sure," he replied. "You need to drive on up this road right here"—he traced the route with his finger—"for maybe two-and-half miles, then you make another right here and drive on for maybe another mile, and it'll be on your right. The number's one-oh-five, if I remember c'rectly. There's a mailbox at the entrance to a dirt driveway. Drive on up there to the cabin. It's quite a way..." He paused for a moment, looked her in the eyes and continued, "Now, you take care up there, missy. It's wild country, and that boy ain't quite right in the head, if you know what I mean."

"Thank you, Howie," she said. "You're a treasure." And she leaned in and kissed him on the cheek.

"Well, I'll be," he said, putting his hand to his cheek. "You get on outa here, you young hussy," he said, smiling.

Ten minutes later, deep in the forest, Mallory, glad she wasn't alone, stopped the car in front of a dilapidated mailbox upon which she could barely make out the number 105; the paint weathered and faint.

"This is it, Tucker," she said. "Howie was right when he said it was a dirt road," she continued as she gazed at the overgrown entrance to the driveway. Had she not been looking for it, she would undoubtedly have passed it by without even knowing it was there.

She backed up a little, turned into the driveway and drove on up the hill, the overhanging branches brushing the sides and roof of the car.

After what had to have been several hundred yards, she broke out into a small clearing in the middle of which was a long, low log-built cabin surrounded by a wraparound porch. The house itself was surrounded by a lawn, surprisingly well-manicured.

She drove on up to the house and parked beside a dilapidated 1970s Ford F-150.

She sat for a moment, staring up at the front door. Despite her confidence and knowing that she had Tucker with her, she felt infinitely nervous about confronting the man who had frightened her so badly only a few hours earlier.

"Mallory, are you okay?" Tucker asked, and for a moment, she wanted to tell him she wasn't.

"I can do this," he said. "You don't need to…"

Oh no. It's on, now, she thought and, seizing upon a rush of bravado, she unbuckled her seat belt, saying, "Nope, I'm going to do this. Besides, if he hurt you, I'd never forgive myself."

"Him? Hurt me?" Tucker said, grinning as he pulled his jacket open to reveal the Glock 17 in its holster under his left arm. "They don't call me 'Quick Draw McGraw' for nothing. I'm ex-FBI, remember?"

"Geez," she said, shaking her head. "All right. Let's do this." And she pushed the door open and stepped out of the car. She was about to mount the steps when she heard something behind her.

"What're you doing here?" a voice snarled. "Don't you know you're trespassin'?"

Mallory jumped, startled, and whirled around.

Tucker, half out the passenger door, true to his word, in one smooth action, swept his right hand under his jacket and pulled the Glock. *Oh, m'God. How did he do that?* she wondered.

Twenty yards away, on the edge of the trees, stood a bearded man aiming a compound hunting bow at them, the bowstring pulled taut.

"Put the bow down, Zach," Tucker said quietly, just loud enough for the man to hear.

"I said, what're you doing here? This is private property," the large man shouted.

"We've come to talk to you, Zach," Mallory said calmly, though she was on the verge of panic. "It's me, Mallory. You came to my house last night. You knew who I was then."

The large man held the bow steady but didn't reply.

"Tucker, put the gun away. I can handle him," she said quietly, trying not to tremble.

"Mallory, we—"

"—are trespassing," she finished for him.

Tucker did as he was asked and holstered the weapon.

"Zach," Mallory said, "You came to my house last night. You were looking for Julie. Please, can we talk about it?"

Slowly, the bearded man lowered the bow and slackened the string.

"You're Zach Burns," she said. "We were at school together. Don't you remember?"

He nodded. "I remember. Why're you here?"

"You thought I was Julie… Zach, could we sit down somewhere to talk?" she asked.

Burns thought about it for a moment, then walked over to them, the bow at his side in his right hand.

He marched past them, up the steps, took a keyring from his left pants pocket and unlocked the door. Then turned and said, "Come on." And he disappeared inside.

Tucker looked at Mallory and said, "Well, you did say he was big."

18

Saturday morning 11am

AND ZACH BURNS WAS INDEED A BIG MAN. TUCKER ESTIMATED HE HAD to be at least six-four. At six-one and broad-shouldered, and with his FBI training, Tucker had always figured he was a match for just about anyone; but this guy? He was a bear of a man.

They followed him inside and watched as he hung the bow over the fireplace.

He turned to face them, looked at them and said, “Don’t entertain much. You want some tea?”

Tucker was about to decline, but he saw Mallory give him a look, so he changed his mind and said, “Sure. Please. Thank you.”

“Me too, please, Zach,” Mallory said.

Zach Burns went to the refrigerator and returned with a jug of golden-green liquid and poured some of it into two skinny tumblers.

That’s a pitcher and two bar glasses! she thought.

“I make it myself,” he said as he placed them on the table. “The leaves grow on the south side of the mountain. There’s an old cottage there. Nobody goes there anymore, only me. Sit down, why don’t ya?”

They sat down at the table. Burns remained standing.

Tucker picked up his glass and took a sip, then looked at Burns in surprise. "This is excellent," he said. "What is it?"

"It's tea with some herbs from the old cottage garden."

"It's wonderful," Mallory said. "Zach, you should sell this."

"Hah! No one would buy from me," Zach said. "All they can think about is my momma."

After that there was a moment of strained silence until, finally, Tucker said, "We're here to talk about Julie Romero, Zach. She's been missing for two weeks. We think she got lost somewhere in the forest. We were hoping you might know something or may even have heard something."

"Julie?" The name rolled off his tongue. "You know better than that, Mallory," he said as he sat down at the table. "Julie would never get lost around here."

"Well, do you have any idea what might have happened to her?" Tucker asked.

He shook his head. "I know she's nice," he said. "She comes around here most weeks. Sometimes she stops and we talk."

"She went missing on the thirteenth," Tucker persisted. "D'you know anything about that, Zach?"

The big man's eyes narrowed. He looked angry. "What are you sayin'? You think I had somethin' to do with it? No! I don't know what happened to her. I was looking for her last night. I thought you were her," he said, looking at Mallory.

Tucker was about to say something more, but Mallory cut in and said, "What about her dog, Zach? What about Tobin? Did you see him?"

"Yeah, I've seen him, Toby. In the woods with Julie. Then he was here, by himself, all alone. I tried to give him some food, but he just growled at me and ran away. That's why I was lookin' for Julie last night. I knew something was wrong." He looked down at the table, utterly downcast.

"So, when was the last time you saw him without Julie?"

Zach was silent, then looked down and away to his left, a sure sign he was about to lie, but he didn't; he looked up at them and didn't answer.

"All right," Tucker said, changing the subject. "You seem to know the woods pretty well. Have you any idea where she might have gone? Is there anywhere, any trail that the search parties might have missed?"

"Search parties?" Zach looked confused at first. "Oh, yeah. I saw them stumbling around out there."

"And," Tucker kept his tone neutral. "Did they miss anything, d'you think?"

Zach laughed. It sounded weird, like a cross between a dog bark and a seagull cawing.

"They kept to the main trails; missed more'n half the branches, the small trails. I did see you out there a couple of times, Mallory. You walked some of them, but the police and the Feds… they don't know these woods as well as they'd like you to believe. They didn't go nowhere near the trails Julie walks."

"What about the other people who live on the mountain?" Mallory asked, "The 'shiners, the pot farmers. Heck, even the pagans. D'you think Julie might have upset any of them?"

"No." He shook his head. "Most of them stay away from the townies, and as for the witches, they only come by in spring an' fall. All they do is dance an' stuff, an' drink themselves stupid. They make fires. The forest service keeps an eye on them and shuts them down during fire season. They're harmless."

Tucker frowned. None of what he was hearing came together, considering what he'd heard said about this man. *He's been living alone too long, but he's as sane as I am,* he thought. *Mallory said there's a rumor he killed his mother but was never convicted. I'm not seeing it.*

"When was the last time you talked to Julie, Zach?" he asked.

"Huh." Zach was quiet for a few moments, then frowned and said, "Must have been the day before I saw Toby wanderin' around on his own. Didn't get to talk to her much. She was with her friend."

"With her friend?" Mallory said, raising her voice. "What friend? Are you talking about Sarah?"

"Sarah. Yeah. She wanted Sarah to meet me. She talked about it a lot before she brought her. She said it was important. I don't think she liked me."

Mallory was about to speak, but before she could, Tucker held up a hand, stopped her, and said, "Why was it important, Zach?"

Burns looked at him but didn't say anything.

"Zach! Why did Julie say it was important?" Mallory demanded.

Again he looked away to the left, then said, "I'm not gonna say," he replied sullenly.

"Tell me what she said," Mallory said angrily.

"I'm not supposed to tell anyone," Zach said, his brow furrowed. "You need to go now."

"Oh no," she snapped. "That's not how it works, Zach. You're going to tell me what you know, and you're going to tell me now."

Burns stood up, his face red with anger. "Get outta my house," he growled. "And don't come back."

Tucker stood, grabbed Mallory by her arm and pulled her to her feet. "Come on. We need to go." Then he turned to Burns, held up both of his hands and said, "It's okay, Zach. Just calm down. We're leaving."

"But—" Mallory said as he grabbed her arm again and steered her across the room.

"Shush," Tucker said as he opened the door.

Once inside the truck, Mallory sat still, staring up at the door, a single tear rolling down her cheek.

"Hey, hey," Tucker said. "It's okay."

"I'm sorry," she said and wiped her cheek with the back of her hand. "I really screwed that up, didn't I? Now he'll never talk to us again. What if he's the only person who can help?"

Tucker, trying not to think about that, said, "Well, we now know a lot more than we did. We know Julie was friendly with Burns, and we know she introduced him to her friend Sarah. I know you must have talked to her. She was part of your search party, wasn't she? Did she mention meeting Burns?"

Mallory slowly shook her head. "No. She didn't. But you're right," she said. "He said he saw Julie and Sarah the day before he saw Tobin alone. That means—"

"—that Sarah could have been the last person to see Julie alive," Tucker finished for her.

Mallory's face hardened. She grabbed a tissue from the center console and wiped her eyes. "I've read their texts, and I talked to her myself," she muttered. "And she never said a thing. We need to talk to her."

She flashed her keys at him. "And I know exactly where the pony princess is going to be today."

She stuffed the key into the ignition, turned it, the engine fired, and Mallory reversed away from Zach's front porch, made a turn and drove back down the long, narrow driveway.

Five minutes later, they were back on Tennessee 30 heading for Highway 64 with Tucker holding onto the strap above his door as Mallory drove the pickup over the bumps and potholes. Finally, she made a hard right onto Highway 64, and Tucker heaved a sigh of relief and let go of the strap. He glanced at her several times as they headed back toward Chattanooga, but her eyes remained focused straight ahead until they hit APD 40 and then I-75 south. Only then did Mallory let up and relax a little.

"The Alexanders are one of the wealthiest families in Hamilton County," Mallory said, finally breaking the silence as she hurtled up Whiteoak Mountain at eighty miles an hour. "No one knows who owns more land around here, them or the Burns family; Zach's folks. Old man Alexander owns CKD Chemicals. It's old money."

"Where do the Burns get their money?" Tucker asked.

"Real estate," she replied. "They own half of downtown... Well, not half, but a lot. Anyway, Sarah's always been into horses. She plays polo, you know."

"She doesn't sound much like Julie at all," Tucker said. "Strange bedfellows. How come they're so close?"

Mallory laughed and shook her head. "They've been buddies since... I don't know when. They were the two chirpiest kindergartners you ever did see. They latched on to each other from the outset and never let go."

She drove on in silence for the next several minutes, then took the Ooltewah exit and said, "We're almost there. How are we going to handle it?"

"There's no getting around it," Tucker said. "She has some answering to do. There's no point in trying to sugarcoat it. We'll just dive right in and ask the questions."

"Right," Mallory said, nodding. "Right," she muttered, more to herself than to Tucker.

Five minutes later, she pulled off the road and onto a paved drive bounded by an avenue of neatly trimmed trees that gave way to a vast open area at the far end of which was a huge, three-story mansion flanked on one side by a six-car garage and on the other by a matching atrium. To the rear and to the right, Tucker could see a horse barn that was almost as big as the house, surrounded by what he knew to be horse training rings—some with jumps, some without. The complex portrayed the image of wealth on a grand scale, and Tucker could only gawk at the layout in amazement.

Beyond the barn, in one of the rings, several people were watching a rider putting a beautiful black horse through its paces, leaping over one jump after another until finally, it galloped like a wild thing for the gate while the watchers stood and clapped.

"That's Sarah," Mallory said. "They say she could have made the US Olympic Equestrian Team but didn't have the b... But she backed out during the trials. She's pretty damn good though," she finished a little wistfully.

By then they were at the barn and out of the car, and the rider noticed them and waved, then she turned, leaned down and said something to several of the watchers who turned and looked at them, and then she rode across the field to join them.

"That's a black Friesian," Mallory said as the horse and rider approached. "They're not great jumpers, but they are beautiful. Must have cost them a fortune."

"How d'you know that?" Tucker asked. "D'you ride?"

"Me? Hell no. I could never afford it. No, I'm just a mine of worthless information, as they say."

Tucker stared at the horse's rippling muscles, its gleaming coat, and its easy gait in awe. It looked as if it had leapt off the cover of a book.

"You're right," he said. "It's beautiful."

"Hi, Mallory," Sarah said. "How are you holding up?"

"As well as can be expected, I guess," she replied. "This is Tucker Randall. He's the private investigator Jennifer hired to find Julie. Tucker, this is Sarah Alexander."

"Nice to meet you," Sarah said.

"Likewise," Tucker replied. "That's a beautiful horse."

She leaned forward and patted the animal's neck. The horse tossed its head, shook it, and then whinnied.

"Thank you," Sarah said.

"Good jumper?" Tucker asked.

She smiled and said, "He does his best. So, is there any news, Mallory?"

"No," she replied. "Which is why we're here. I was hoping we could have a word?"

"Um, sure. Of course." Sarah looked back at the others on the field. "I'm almost done with my afternoon practice. If you'd like to drive over to the oak trees over there beside the barn," she said, turning in the saddle and pointing to the trees, "there are a couple of tables and some benches. I'll take him in and meet you there."

"Fine," Mallory said. "See you in a minute, then."

Sarah nodded, wheeled the big horse around, touched him with her heels and cantered back to where the small group of spectators was waiting for her.

"So, these people are nice, are they?" Tucker asked.

"Of course," Mallory replied. "Why wouldn't they be?"

"I dunno," Tucker said. "I've run into people like these before, and I can't say it was ever a rewarding experience."

"What do you mean, 'people like these'?" she asked, frowning. "They're nice. I've known Sarah since she was in kindergarten."

"Oh... nothing." Tucker shook his head. "It's just that... Oh forget it. I was just trying to get your feel for these people, is all. Money, vast amounts of money, so I've found, can change people."

"The Alexanders have always been very nice to me," she said as she parked next to the small stand of oak trees. "Which, if you consider I'm just a barkeep in a clip joint, says a lot, don't you think?"

Tucker sighed. "I think..." Tucker began, then hesitated before continuing. "I think you tend to put yourself down. I also think you think you know someone, but you really don't. You never really know anyone."

"That's... a horrible outlook to have," she replied, twisting in her seat to look at him. "What you're really saying is that you don't trust *anyone.*"

He shrugged. "That's not... exactly true, but in this case, you say you've known Sarah since she was a child, that she's Julie's best friend. But here we are. Julie's missing, and she was perhaps the last person to see her, and she's never bothered to tell you? Why not? Does she know something? Is she hiding something?"

"Let's find out, shall we?" Mallory said, opening the car door and sliding out.

Tucker smiled grimly and did the same. During his years as an FBI agent and, lately, a PI, he'd met a long list of so-called "nice" wealthy people.

Oh, he was just the nicest boy...

She was always so quiet...

And one in particular, *He wouldn't hurt a fly. Why I've seen him rescue bugs from the pool.*

That one murdered two teenage hookers. It was only down to luck that they caught him before he murdered a third.

And now, he thought, *but they were best friends. Geez.*

19

Saturday afternoon 2pm

MALLORY COULD HARDLY BELIEVE HE'D SAID THAT. *YOU NEVER REALLY know anyone? What's that about, for Pete's sake? I barely know you, Tucker...* But before she could finish the thought—

"Hey, you two," Sarah said as she joined them and sat down at the picnic table opposite them. "Nellie, my groom, is currying Buckeye for me, so I have a few minutes. What did you want to talk about?"

Tucker opened his mouth to speak. His intention was to put her at ease, but before he could, Mallory jumped in.

"Sarah," she said, staring her in the eyes, "we know you were with Julie just before she disappeared that morning. Why didn't you tell me?"

Whatever Sarah had been expecting Mallory to say, that clearly wasn't it.

"*What?* What are you saying, Mallory?" she snapped. "Are you implying that I had something to do with it? If you are, you're crazy."

"I'm not accusing you of anything," Mallory snapped back. "But you were there that morning. You should have said something. Why wouldn't you, knowing she was missing?"

"I did," she said, now on the defensive. "I told the sheriff, and I told Kal Cundiff, and he acted like it was no big deal. I told him that Julie and I arranged to meet at the trailhead at seven. We usually drove up there together, but I told him we took two cars because I had to get back to meet my dad at the vet at noon, and that we hiked back to the trailhead together. I left her there at a little after eleven. What she did after I left, I have no idea. She certainly didn't tell me, and when I told Kal about it, he said something like, 'It doesn't matter who she was with at eight if she disappeared at twelve' or something like that. And now you come here accusing me… I can't believe you'd do that, Mallory. I mean… We're friends."

Mallory glanced at Tucker. He was taking notes.

"She took you to meet Zach Burns that morning, didn't she?" Mallory asked. "So what was the big secret? Why did she want you to meet him?"

Tucker looked at Sarah. The question had obviously made her uncomfortable.

She knows something, he thought, watching her struggle to come up with an answer.

"Well, she didn't exactly tell me," Sarah said, "but I figured it out. She was waiting for me at the trailhead—"

"Which one?" Mallory asked.

Sarah frowned. "Does it matter?" she said. "Red Grove East. Anyway," she continued, "before we started out on the hike that morning, she said she had something she wanted to tell me. But she didn't. And when I told her she'd promised to tell me, she said something like, 'Oh, it was nothing important. Forget it.' Well, whatever. Anyway, I'm pretty sure it was something to do with Kal Cundiff."

"What about Kal Cundiff?" Mallory asked.

"Well, they were dating for a while. You knew that, right?" Sarah said.

Tucker looked at Mallory. She looked stunned.

"Uh, uh… No! You can't be serious," Mallory stuttered.

"Oh, but I am," Sarah replied. "They were on and off for months."

She looked at Mallory, then at Tucker, then at Mallory again and said, "She once told me that Kal was up to his britches in crap and wading in deeper. That was around the time she broke it off. But I know Julie, and she's been acting all squirrelly again like she does when she likes a guy. And Kal said he'd been talking to her—that was when I was at the sheriff's department—and he said he hadn't heard from her. I think she was getting ready to tell everyone they were a couple."

"But why didn't she tell any of us?" Mallory demanded.

"Well, Mal, you know..." Sarah hesitated.

"What do I know?"

"I mean, she knows how you listen to all those true crime things on the internet," Sarah said. "And well, Kal... If he really is into something—and from what she told me, he probably is—she wouldn't want to say anything because she figured you'd make a big fuss about it... and Kal."

"I don't believe what I'm hearing," Mallory said, shaking her head. "What the hell could Kal be doing that I would make a fuss... about? Oh no. You're not telling me he's a bent cop, are you?"

Sarah nodded slowly and said, "The rumor is that Kal has ties to the moonshiners."

Mallory stared at her, her mouth hanging open. She gulped, looked at Tucker, then at Sarah. She was speechless. She felt numb, and all she could think of was the words Tucker had spoken a few minutes ago, "You never really know anyone." *What else didn't I know?*

She listened to Tucker ask Sarah questions about their hike that morning and how Julie had wanted her to meet Zach Burns, "a ridiculously big man with a black beard," which she did, but wasn't impressed. She said he smelled like one of her horses, and while she loved that smell, it wasn't something she was looking for in a man, and that Zach could have been Grizzly Adams' twin, "Ugh!"

And for once, during the entire conversation, Mallory couldn't help but agree with her. The thought of being in the arms of such a gorilla of a man made her shudder.

And so Tucker continued to question her for several more

minutes, but she, Mallory, at least, learned nothing new. What she did know, however, was that Kal Cundiff knew a lot more than he was telling—shifty little son-of-a—and that if Julie had stumbled onto, or into, something she shouldn't... Well, after listening to all those podcasts, she could come up with only one solution, and it was something she didn't want to even contemplate.

And what good was all that listening? she thought. *Hours and hours, and I have to find out from Sarah fricking Alexander that Kal Cundiff is bent, taking bribes? Why the hell didn't I figure that out? Creepy little... If he—*

The thought was interrupted when Sarah suddenly got up out of the seat, walked around the table, sat down beside her and gave her a big hug.

Mallory was shocked but returned the hug, cheeks together, arms wrapped around each other.

"I'm sorry, Mal," Sarah whispered in her ear. "I mean, if I messed up... I'm so sorry."

"It's okay," Mallory said without feeling and without knowing what else to say. "It's not your fault."

"Thanks," Sarah said. "It... It means a lot to hear you say that." Then she kissed Mallory on the cheek, stood up and walked away without a backward look until she reached the barn, where she stopped, turned and gave them a little wave.

"What a load of grade-A *crap*," Tucker said.

Mallory looked at him. "What? What are you talking about, Tucker? She—"

"No, not her," he said. "The crap the sheriff's office has been feeding me."

"I'm sorry, Tucker," Mallory murmured.

"Don't be," he replied. "It was my choice, but I need to talk to Kal Cundiff now. The problem is, I just can't go barging in there. He'll know something's up. I need to make an appointment..." he said thoughtfully. "I need an excuse. Any ideas?"

"No. None. Why don't you let me talk to him? I'll give him something to think about," she said, then added, "Oh dear. Oh—"

"Mallory? Are you all right?"

She blinked, nodded and said, "Yes… I just—"

"Here, give me your keys," he said. "I'll drive you home, okay?"

The thought of "never-clutched" Tucker Randall tearing up her gearbox was just enough to snap Mallory out of whatever fugue she'd been in. She laughed and said, "In your dreams, big fellah. I'm not going to sit there and listen to you grinding my gears all the way home. Get in. I'm all right. I promise."

Despite his dour look and her unsettled stomach, she managed a tiny smile at his obvious discomfort at the idea of her taking the wheel again, especially after the wild ride from Zach Burns' cabin.

The drive home was… silent, at least as far as Mallory was concerned, which was more than a little uncharacteristic. Tucker, however, more than made up for her lack of conversation: making comments about Kal Cundiff, how to make an appointment without tipping him off, and even about the big black horse.

Ten minutes out from her home, she looked at him and said wearily, "You can come in if you like. I'll make some coffee. I just need a few minutes to get ready."

"Get ready? Get ready for what?" he asked.

"For work, of course," she replied. "I have to be at work by five o'clock. It's almost four now. So I can drop you off at your car before I go to work."

"What are you talking about, Mallory? My car's at your place, remember? Are you sure you're all right?" he asked.

"Oh, yeah. Right… You came to my place this morning, didn't you? Yes, of course I am. I'm fine."

Ten minutes later, she parked her truck in the driveway next to Tucker's SUV, mounted the steps to the front door, unlocked it, stepped inside and tripped over an ecstatic Annie and suddenly found herself on her knees on the carpet.

"It's okay," she said as Tucker rushed to her side. "I'm fine. I… Oh, come on, Tucker. I said I'm fine," she said as he helped her to her feet.

"I know you are," he said skeptically, "but why don't you sit down on the couch for a minute and get your breath back?"

"I have to let Annie out."

"I can do that," he said. "You sit still for a minute and take it easy. You've had a rough two weeks. I'll make the coffee."

He stood back and looked down at her. She looked pathetic, staring up at him.

"Stay there," he repeated. "Come on, Annie."

IT WAS ALMOST ten o'clock when Mallory woke up with a start from her nightmare. Not just any nightmare; *the* nightmare, the one she'd been having ever since Julie had disappeared. *What happened?* she thought as she fumbled around in the dark. *Why is it so dark? Where am I? Oh, my God. What time is it? I'm supposed to be at work.*

But she was on top of her bed, still in her hiking clothes. She swung her legs off the bed and sat up, feeling gritty and grungy, and badly in need of a shower.

The phone in her pocket buzzed. She took it out and looked at it. It was just a missed call from an unfamiliar number. "Probably spam," she muttered as she noted the time. It was five after ten. "Geez. Vinnie will be furious. He'll fire me for sure."

She made her way slowly downstairs and found Tucker and Annie sleeping soundly together on the couch.

Now when we came home, he told me to sit on the couch, so how come I was on the bed and he's on the couch? Geez, he must have carried me upstairs. Who does *that?*

"Hey, macho man," she said, shaking him awake. "What the hell happened? I'm supposed to be at work, and you're supposed to be at home."

He looked up at her and said, "You know, you need to turn the heat up. You could hang meat in here."

"I like to sleep in the cold," she replied. "I'm hungry. I need food. Do you need food?"

"Yes, I could eat something," he said, pushing Annie to one side—

who rolled onto her back and stuck all four legs in the air—and he sat up and rubbed his eyes. "You were out of it," he said, "so I thought I'd stay for a while, just in case."

"In case of what?" she asked, looking down at him, smiling, her hands on her hips,

"I dunno," he snapped. "Just in case, okay? What've you got to eat?"

"I'll find something," she said, "but first I need to call Vinnie and apologize for not turning up. It will probably be the end of my illustrious career as head barkeep and bottle washer."

"He already called," Tucker said. "I told him you were exhausted and had gone to bed. To say he wasn't pleased… Well, you may be right."

Shit! she thought. *I really need my job. Oh well, I'll just have to schmooze him a little. In the meantime…*

"Come on," she said. "Let's go to the kitchen. I'll put the heat up a little, pansy boy."

She adjusted the thermostat up two degrees and then went to the refrigerator. "It won't be much, I'm afraid," she said, looking at the remains of a three-day-old Chinese takeout, a half-empty quart of milk, and four eggs. "I need to go grocery shopping. Pancakes be okay?"

"Pancakes? At eleven o'clock at night? Sure, that sounds good. Anything I can do?"

"No. They'll only take a minute," she replied.

"I can't remember the last time someone cooked pancakes for me," Tucker said some five minutes later as she set a short stack down in front of him. "Well, except for IHOP, that is."

"I hope you like them," she said. "I don't do cooking anymore. When Mom got sick, I had to take over the cooking for the family. I'm not good at it, and I hated it. When Mom and then Dad passed, I basically quit."

For several moments they ate in silence, then Tucker said, "By the way, I made an appointment to see Kal Cundiff tomorrow."

"That's good," she replied. "You want me to come with you?"

He shook his head. "No. If he has history with Julie, he'll not be too inclined to talk in front of you."

She looked at him and frowned. "I suppose…" she said, seemingly unconvinced.

"It'll be okay," Tucker said. "What d'you know about his father?"

"Not much. Only that Kevin Cundiff is a gnarled old oak," Mallory said, slowly shaking her head. "He won't bend, Tucker, and I don't think Kal will talk to you. He might talk to me though."

Again, Tucker shook his head. "He'll talk. I'll make him. It's what I do, remember? I was thinking they—the police—were just negligent, but now…" He paused and shook his head, staring down at what was left of his pancakes, then looked up at her and said, "No, I don't think they were negligent. I think their reluctance to investigate Julie's disappearance was a deliberate attempt to cover up whatever it is they're doing. And we need to find out what that is."

"But you don't think Kal could have had something to do with Julie's disappearance, do you?" Mallory asked.

"I don't know," Tucker replied. "I've known a lot of crooked cops, and in my experience, a bad cop is capable of just about anything."

"Yes, but Kal? I've known him forever."

"Yes, well," he said, "you think you know someone, but—"

"—but you really don't," Mallory interrupted and finished for him. "I know, I know, but I still can't believe Kal would hurt Julie."

"Yes, well," he repeated, pushing his empty plate away. "We've had a tough couple of weeks and it's getting late. I need to go home and get some sleep, and so do you."

"Yes," she said halfheartedly. "But you could stay here if you like… on the couch."

Tucker smiled at her and said, "Thanks, but that wouldn't be a good idea, now would it? What would the neighbors say? And besides, if I stay here, I'll still have to go home in the morning. So, I'll bid you goodnight and see you tomorrow after I've talked to the deputy?"

"Umm, yes, I guess," she said.

He nodded, stood up and said, "Get some sleep, Mallory. And try not to worry about things you can't change."

She rose to her feet and walked him to the door.

"Thanks for all you do, Tucker," she said as he opened the door. "I really do appreciate it."

"My pleasure," he said and winked at her. Then he walked quickly down the steps to his car and drove away into the night, leaving her standing just inside the open door staring after him.

20

Sunday morning 10am

It was getting on for ten o'clock that Sunday morning when Tucker parked in a visitor's spot outside the sheriff's office.

He sat for a moment staring at the glass front entrance, getting his thoughts together. This was not, he knew, going to be a friendly meeting; more of a confrontation.

Finally, he took a deep breath and exited the vehicle. The perky desk sergeant he was used to dealing with was nowhere to be seen, but Sheriff Cundiff was.

"He's not here," Cundiff said when Tucker asked to see the deputy. "What d'you want him for?"

"I have an appointment with him at ten," Tucker replied, looking at his watch. "It's almost ten now. Where is he?"

"I told you. He's not here. He has a scheduled patrol this morning," Cundiff explained. "You sure you got the right day? It is Sunday, you know?"

"Yes, I have the right day. I talked to him at around seven yesterday evening. He said ten o'clock, and here I am."

"Well, Randall, you drove all this way for nothing, didn't you?" he said and began to turn away.

"I don't think so, Sheriff," Tucker said easily. "What I need to talk to him about is important, so why don't you get on the radio and have him come on in?"

Cundiff turned to face him again, a look of disdain on his face.

"You're not a Fed anymore, Randall. You can't…" he began, then caught the look on Tucker's face and changed his mind. "Ah, what the hell," he continued, "but it better be important."

He keyed his radio and said, "You forget your appointment this morning, boy? Get your ass in here now."

Less than fifteen minutes later, Kal Cundiff, looking flustered and more than a little wary, walked into the department and looked around.

"Good morning, Deputy," Tucker said, stepping up behind him. "I thought we had an appointment?"

"Yeah. I forgot. Sorry. What d'you want to talk to me about?"

"You want to do this out here, in the lobby, where everyone can hear?" Tucker asked quietly.

Cundiff frowned, looked around at the several deputies who were chatting together, then muttered something Tucker couldn't hear. He assumed it wasn't a compliment.

"This way," Kal said, pushing open the door to a small conference room. "We can talk in here."

Tucker nodded and stepped inside, then turned to look at the deputy.

"Siddown, why don't ya?" Kal Cundiff said, glaring at him.

Tucker smiled, shook his head, sat down at the table, and said, "Who kicked your cat this morning, Kal?"

Cundiff sat down opposite him, leaned on the table, narrowed his eyes, and said, "What's this all about, Randall? You're about to get me into trouble, havin' the sheriff drag me in off patrol like you did. What is it you want? Spit it out. I ain't got all day."

"I'm here to talk to you about Julie Romero," Tucker said. "Any comment?"

"Comment?" he said. "Why would I have any comment? No, I don't have no comment."

"You didn't talk to her that day she went missing?" Tucker asked. "Think about it, Kal. It was a Wednesday."

"No. I didn't."

"That's not quite true, is it, Kal?" Tucker asked.

"What're you trying to say, dickhead? That I had somethin' to do with Julie's disappearance? Well I didn't, see? So you can quit barking up that tree."

"I didn't say you did," Tucker said quietly. "I was just wondering if you spoke to her, that's all."

"Didn't say a word to her," Cundiff snapped. "We done here?" He started to get up.

"No, we're not done here, Kal. Far from it. Sit down. You say you didn't talk to her?" He stared Cundiff in the eye and inwardly smiled when he saw his eyes flicker and look away to the left.

"That's what I said," he replied.

"So, if I were to look through the impressive stack of text messages Mallory downloaded from Julie's phone, I wouldn't find anything there?"

Kal frowned, looked away, just for a second, then stared at Tucker and said, "I don't text Julie's phone." And Tucker, for once, didn't think the deputy was lying. But there was something else there; he wasn't lying, but…

I don't text Julie's phone! Hmm. So, if he wasn't lying, does that mean he texts to something else, a computer, maybe?

"But you were seeing her, weren't you?" Tucker said.

"What? No, well not—" He was angry. "Oh, I get it. You're trying to pin it on me. Well it won't work. Yeah, I was seeing her; nothin' serious. We just dated a little, back a few months ago. But she broke up with me. Who you bin talkin' to, Randall? I bet it was that stuck-up little heifer, Sarah Alexander. Sneaky little cow, she is. I never could understand why Julie hung around that little gossip."

"I haven't spoken to her," Tucker lied. "I just listened to what people were saying. It wasn't much of a secret, was it? And, from what

I was able to piece together, it seems you two have … let's say, some unresolved issues?"

"Bullcrap," Cundiff snapped.

Tucker nodded and smiled at him. "No problem. I know a guy who does excellent work on phones… and computers," Tucker said. "I'll just hand her devices over to him and see what he comes up with. But… you need to know, my friend, if I find anything of yours, you're going to have some serious explaining to do." And with that, Tucker stood up and turned toward the door.

"All right! All right," Kal said and swore loudly. "Sit down, damn it. Okay, so we… we use an app. It's supposed to be for discreet chats. It's called Significant, or Syllable, or something like that. I know it begins with an S. Even after she broke up with me, she'd talk to me sometimes. I always thought…" His forehead wrinkled. His eyes closed to mere slits. "I always thought we'd get back together, but then she told me she was seeing someone else."

Now it was Tucker's turn to frown. "You sure? Did she say who it was?" he asked.

Cundiff shook his head. "Yeah, I'm sure. She flat-out told me. No, she never said who it was."

"But do *you* know who it is?"

Cundiff looked at him and said, "No… I don't."

Tucker nodded and changed direction. "Where were you that morning, Kal? Tell me, and if it checks out, I'll go look somewhere else."

Kal froze, his eyes wide. "Hey. I'm a frickin' deputy," he said. "You're not a cop anymore, so I don't have to tell you nothin'."

Tucker nodded, stood up again, walked to the door, then turned and said, "That's right, Kal. You don't. But if you have nothing to hide, you'd talk to me, which leads me to believe two things. One, you do have something to hide, and I'm pretty sure I know what that is. And two, you don't have an alibi for that morning, and you know what happened to her. I think it's time we brought the state police into this." He turned again and pulled the door open.

Kal leapt out of his chair, charged around the table, shoved the door shut with a bang, and stood with his nose almost touching Tucker's, his face twisted with rage.

"You jumped-up son of a bitch," he shouted. "What the hell d'you think you're doin'?"

"I'm doing my job, Kal," Tucker replied quietly. "While you seem to be a disgrace to yours."

Kal drew back his fist, just as Tucker had expected.

Too slow, he thought as Kal swung at his face. He leaned a little to his right. The punch slid by. Tucker grabbed his wrist, snapped it behind his back, and slammed the deputy face-first against the wall.

"Tut, tut," he whispered in Kal's ear. "One of the first things the FBI teaches new recruits is how to dodge a lousy punch," he whispered as he increased the pressure, and Kal's heels lifted off the floor.

"Now stop embarrassing yourself and your father," Tucker said, "and tell me where you were so I can move on."

Kal struggled in his grip, puffed for breath, then yelped, "Okay, okay. Lemme go," he gasped. "I'll tell ya."

Tucker released him and Kal stumbled forward, then turned to face him, his face red, his teeth bared, his hand on his weapon.

"You're going to shoot me here, knowing I'm unarmed? How d'you think that will go down, Kal?" Tucker taunted him. "Even your daddy couldn't get you out of that one."

Kal's face twisted with rage, but his hand dropped away from his gun.

"Look," he said, "the Cundiffs have been here since we moved from Virginia back in the seventeen fifties. We know these mountains, the forest and the trails, and we used them to move… trade goods. We smuggled supplies past the British, and we stole Union gold and delivered it to Jefferson Davis. In the thirties, we moved shine, and then weed startin' in the fifties. It's what we do; always have done. People still pay well for good moonshine, and ours is the best."

"Marijuana, you say?" Tucker asked. "It's legal in most states now."

Cundiff scoffed. "Hahaha. Yeah, that regulated medicinal crap. But anything worth smoking has to be farmed proper, like. Not that I do that," he added quickly. "Our main still is not far from the trail that

Julie liked to walk. It's on Cundiff land, not that anyone notices, or even cares."

"You still haven't answered my question," Tucker said. "Where were you between eleven and five the afternoon she disappeared?"

"I was on the other side of the county, almost to Etowah, taking care of official business. We had a problem with one of our, um, transports. You can check the duty logs on that. And I already told everyone in the family that she was off limits and they was to leave her alone. If someone in the family had done something to her, I'd've been told."

Maybe you'd like to think that, Tucker thought, watching Cundiff stare belligerently at him. *But I'm not sure you think at all.*

"So, are we good now?" Cundiff asked. "Cause if we are, and you're done askin' your questions, you can kindly shove off and let me get on with my day." His eyes narrowed. The corners of his lips turned upward to form what might have been a humorless smile. "Or maybe I should ask a few of my family members to pay you a visit. You don't wanna meet them, I promise."

"Kal," Tucker said, "you're about as smart as a one-eyed donkey. That camera up there behind you has been on the whole time we've been talking."

He spun around, looked up at the camera and was about to speak when the door opened and two deputies rushed in.

"You okay, Kal?" one of them said, his hand on his gun.

"Yeah. I'm good," he snapped. "*Mr.* Randall was just leaving. See him out, will you?"

Well now, that was interesting, Tucker thought as he made his way down the steps to his car. *That was quite an information dump he dropped in my lap.*

Tucker fished the micro recorder from his pocket and turned it off, grinning to himself. *Not that it would be admissible, but it certainly would be useful to an outside investigator.*

Five minutes later he was on sixty-four heading back toward Chattanooga, singing along with George Jones on Willie's Roadhouse. "He stopped loving her today…"

Tucker was on I-75 heading south past the Ooltewah exit when he called Mallory.

"Tucker," she said. "What's up?"

"Here's a silly question," he replied. "Does Julie have a computer?"

"Yes, of course. Who doesn't? Why d'you ask?"

"She and Kal Cundiff have been communicating through some kind of secret app. I want to know what they've been talking about. Where is it?"

"It's at Jennifer's. We could take a look at it."

"Has anyone else looked at it? The law, for instance?"

"Well, yes. Kal stopped by and looked at it. He said there's nothing on it."

Of course he did. He would, wouldn't he?

"When did he look at it?" he asked.

"I don't know, not for sure. More than a week ago. I guess we could find out."

"I'm on my way back now. I'll pick you up in say… ten minutes? We'll grab a quick sandwich and then go see what we can see."

"I have to be at work at five," she said. "That gives me at least a couple of hours. I can't be late, though. I missed work yesterday. I can't understand why Vinnie hasn't called me."

"Mallory, I told you. He called last night," Tucker said.

"Yeah," she said. "I remember. I also remember I said I was going to give him a piece of my mind when I get there tonight. Still, I thought he would have called today. He'd need to know if he needed to get someone to cover for me."

"You don't have to go, you know."

"Oh, you don't think I'm gonna pass up the opportunity to gut the little creep like a fish, do you?" He thought he could hear her teeth grinding. "But we have a couple hours yet. What dirt did you manage to dig up on Kal?"

"You can listen to it on the way to Jennifer's. I'll be there in just a few minutes."

21

Sunday afternoon 2pm

It was a little after two o'clock when they arrived at the Romero home. Jennifer opened the front door, her eyes red and swollen. "Oh. Hi, Mallory," she said before catching a glimpse of Tucker behind her. "Oh, and you, Mr. Randall! Do you have any news for us?"

Before he could answer, however, Mallory said, "Jen, I tried to call you three times to tell you we were on the way, but your phone went straight to voice mail. Have you turned it off? Is everything okay? You don't look well."

"I'm fine," she said, taking the phone from her pocket. "I'm just tired, is all. Oh dear. It's dead. I guess I forgot to charge it again. I can't seem to remember anything these days." She put the phone back in her pocket. "You'd better come in. You have news, right?"

"Nothing new. Sorry," Mallory replied as they followed her into the kitchen. "But we do need to look at Julie's computer, Jen. Is that okay?"

"Why d'you need to do that?" Jen asked. "The police already looked at it."

"Kal Cundiff, right?" Mallory asked.

Jen nodded.

"That's why we need to look at it," Mallory said dryly. "In her bedroom?"

"Yes, but what did you mean about Kal? He's a deputy."

"It's a long story," Tucker said. "And we need to confirm it."

"Of course, of course," Jennifer said. "Upstairs, second on the… Why am I telling you, Mal? You know where it is. Go on up. I'll be down here if you need me."

Mallory paused outside Julie's bedroom door, looked at Tucker, nodded and pushed the door open.

The room was neat and tidy, the bed made, the dresser and bedside table tops neatly ordered, and the few papers and notebooks on the small desk under the window arranged neatly around a MacBook Air laptop.

"I don't even want to be in here," Mallory said. "Too many memories. Painting each other's nails, watching the silly shows on her little TV, and helping her choose photos to make collages next to the mirror. Hmm, the mirror's been moved, and the pictures are different. The little TV's been replaced by a flatscreen. The bookcase is new. So is the Xbox. When did she start playing that, I wonder?"

She stood for a moment while Tucker went to the laptop.

Wow, how little I know her since she's grown up, Mallory thought as she looked at the photographs.

"It's still plugged in," Tucker said as he sat down and lifted the lid and tapped the spacebar. "No password. We're in," he said, looking at the crowded desktop display. "I'm surprised."

"I'm not," she replied. "Julie was always careless about stuff like that. Same with her phone."

"I guess she trusted her mom and dad, then," Tucker said as he scrolled through her files.

"Oh, they wouldn't touch her stuff… Heck, I don't think they'd know how to. If she didn't take it anywhere, she wouldn't see the need." Mallory sighed. "I told her she needs to use a password to keep hackers and malware out, but all she said was, 'why would anyone want to hack little old me?'"

Tucker frowned, barely listening to her. He picked up a small black object from the top of a pile of notebooks. "Hey, see this?" He held it up for her to see. It looked like a cell phone, except instead of a screen, the face was a display of tiny photo cells.

"Looks like a phone," Mallory said. "I didn't know she has two."

"It's not a phone," Tucker said. "It's a solar power cell. You use it for charging cell phones. I saw one just like it on the sideboard in Zach Burns' cabin," he said.

"So Burns has a cell phone, then," Mallory said. "Interesting, but not surprising. Everybody has one. Even mountain men like Zach Burns. I wonder if he has a computer as well?"

"What did Kal say the program was called?" Tucker asked.

"Syllable, I think. Or something like it," she replied.

"There's nothing like that here," Tucker said.

"Let me try," Mallory said.

Tucker pushed the chair back and stood up. Mallory sat down, looked at the screen and said, "You're right. Let's try this." And she clicked the Launchpad icon.

"There," she said. "Look at that. SeaMonkey, Spacejock, Spybot, Stardock, Startup folder… STD? Oh, STDUtility, some kind of PDF viewer. Stellarium, and SUPERAntiSpyware. Nothing."

"Go back to the other screen," Tucker said. "Let's see what we… there." He pointed. "Open that folder, the one labeled TAHC."

Mallory opened the folder and found icons for a dozen more programs. "AOL Instant Messenger?" she asked. "Is she even old enough to know about AOL? Googlechat, MSN chat, Sibilant, Trillian—"

"Sibilant," Tucker said. "Try that one."

Mallory clicked the icon and up popped up a long list of chat histories.

"Clever girl," Tucker said. "TAHC is chat spelled backwards."

"Sneaky, more like," Mallory muttered. "I still think a password would be better… Geez, there are a lot of chats here. I wonder if she uses the same account for her phone too. Can we get her phone records?"

"The sheriff's department should have done that, but they didn't," Tucker said. "I suggested they do so to Sheriff Cundiff, and he said he'd need to get a warrant. Click on the last one. The one dated the thirteenth."

She did and up popped:

DeputyDawg: *09:30*
i was thinking we could go on a hike
tomorrow for old times sake

Makelikeatree: *09:34*
I wish you would stop this, Kal
I told you I'm not interested

DeputyDawg: *09:35*
we had something good before babe
no reason we can't make it work
this other guy don't have what I can offer

Makelikeatree: *09:37*
I'm trying to enjoy time with my friend
If you have to talk, at least wait until
after lunch

DeputyDawg: *09:38*
what you out with sarah again
dunno why you hang with her
she's just an airhead

Makelikeatree: *10:03*
Didn't you ever hear the song?
If you wanna be my lover, you gotta get

with my friends
Insulting my best friend is a stupid way
to convince me that you're interested

DeputyDawg: *10:05*
whats it take for you to say yes again
DeputyDawg: *10:45*
Julie when will you say yes again
DeputyDawg: *11:08*
gotta go out to the county border
someone pulled over the wrong car and now
i gotta deal with it
cant trust anyone

Makelikeatree: *11:55*
I'm about to say yes, Kal
Just not to you

DeputyDawg: *12:24*
who the crap you keep talkin' about
DeputyDawg: *12:39*
come on babe talk to me
DeputyDawg: *12:57*
Julie why you gotta be like this

"WHY DOES she still have this program if all she does is argue with Kal?" Mallory asked. "And who is she seeing?"

"Go back to the list… Yep… Good… Click on that one labeled Ogre."

Mallory clicked, then narrowed her eyes and said, "Ogre? Who the hell is Ogre?"

"There," Tucker said. "Open the last chat marked the eleventh."

AintNoMountain: *19:12*
I'm really looking forward to
introducing you to Sarah
She's been my best friend for years

Ogre: *19:23*
I don't know if this is a good idea
I'm not that kind of guy

AintNoMountain: *19:25*
No, everything is going to be fine.
I promise
Sarah is really nice

Mallory looked at Tucker and said, "Ogre's Zach Burns."

"Yup," Tucker said, smiling.

Ogre: *19:31*
Nice people don't like me.
Whoops. I spelled that wrong. People

AintNoMountain: *19:32*
If they don't like you, then they
can't be very nice, can they?

Ogre: *19:40*
Why are you so nice to me, Julie?
Nobody else is
You're an angel
you're

AintNoMountain: *19:42*
I like to be nice to everyone
I'm an angel?

Why did you change your name to Ogre?

Ogre: *19:54*
I feel like an ogre

AintNoMountain: *19:55*
You're not an ogre
You're the sweetest and most gentle man I've ever met
And I'm sure Sarah will think the same

"Well, that didn't happen, did it?" Tucker said. "Sarah said she thought he smelled funny."

But Mallory didn't hear him, or if she did, she didn't reply. She just sat there staring at the screen. *'You are the sweetest and most gentle man I've ever met.' If she said that,* Mallory thought, *she meant it, but then, Julie always thinks the best of everyone.*

Then Tucker's words sank in. "Yes, she said he smelled like one of her horses. Can't say I noticed anything like that, but then, I didn't get that close to him."

"Mallory, this is two days before Sarah went on the hike with Julie," Tucker said. "Ogre is Zach Burns." He tossed the charger in the air and caught it. "I guess our mountain man needs a phone to talk to the ladies."

"Makes sense," Mallory said thoughtfully.

"We need to document everything," Tucker said. "We need to download and print everything."

Mallory looked at the time, then turned to look at him and said, "It's after three. I want to go in to work early. I need to talk to Vinnie, so I need to go home and get ready. I'll ask Jen if I can take the computer with us." She traced the cord to the wall and pulled it free.

It was almost four o'clock when Mallory pushed through the front entrance of The Saloon to a round of wolf whistles from the gathered gentry seated at the bar and in the booths.

She ignored them and walked quickly to the bar where Roger was busy cleaning a glass.

"Roger, *where* is Vinnie?" she asked angrily.

"Last I saw, he was in his office." Roger gave her a strange look. "I don't think you're… He asked me to cover for you tonight. He said he didn't think your new friend would be letting you out."

"Did he now?" Mallory snapped. "Son of a bitch," she muttered as she rounded the end of the bar, pushed past Roger, marched to Vinnie's office door and shoved it open so hard the knob slammed against the wall.

"Vinnie! What the hell have you been telling everybody?" she shouted.

He looked up from counting cash. "Ah. There you are. I figured you'd be takin' another night off, so I asked Roger to fill in for you. Good night last night?" he asked, a nasty little smile on his lips.

"You're an evil little man, you know that?" she yelled. "You know what I've been going through ever since my niece went missing, and you just don't give a damn, do you? Why did you say all those horrible things about me?"

"How could anybody forget?" He shrugged as he laid the handful of bills down. "You never shut up about it."

"You told everyone I was having sex with Tucker Randall last night. Didn't you? I wasn't. I wouldn't. I hardly know him. I was exhausted. I passed out at three in the afternoon after hiking over half the damn mountain."

"And he picked up the phone when I called," Vinnie said. "How'm I supposed to know you weren't—"

"You insensitive little son of a bitch. How dare you make up this kind of garbage?"

"Seemed legit to me," he said, grinning at her. "If he'd done the job right, you wouldn't be in here screaming at me."

She stared at him, unable to believe what she was hearing. "You nasty, nasty little man. You think that? Very well, then, I'll give you something to smile about." And she turned on her heel and walked out.

"Wait!" Vinnie shouted as she pushed past Roger again and stopped at the "high-end" rack. She turned the spotlights on, took out her phone and took three photos making sure her camera recorded the details of each and every bottle. Then she swept each and every bottle off of the shelves, jumping back as she cleared each shelf and the bottles crashed down onto the floor, shattering, sending an explosion of broken glass and booze almost from one end of the bar to the other, prompting another round of cheering and hooting from the assembled drinkers.

Vinnie finally caught up to her, shook his fist in her face, and yelled, "You're gonna pay for that."

"Sure I will," she retorted. "Bill me," she taunted. "I took pictures of everything you had up there. It was nothing but a collection of nearly empty bottles. If you get five hundred for the entire mess, it'll be too generous."

"You can't do that!" Vinnie insisted. "What kinda person are you?"

"What kind of person tells a room full of people that his 'best bartender'"—she made quotes with her fingers—"is getting laid while she's out looking for a missing family member, you insensitive little shit? And I can guarantee you this, if you even try to get me for the booze, I will hit you for slander, defamation, loss of public standing, and I'll call the Public Health office and tell them exactly what kind of dump you're running here. They'll close you down for good." She turned to leave.

"You know what? You're fired!" Vinnie yelled after her.

"Too late, you gormless little sloth," she shouted over her shoulder. "I already quit. Come on, Tucker. Let's get the hell out of this hell hole."

Tucker, who'd followed her into the bar, had been sitting calmly in one of the booths talking to two of Vinnie's customers and recording their versions of what Vinnie had told them the night before.

"You know that's not going to be admissible in court," she said as they settled into her truck.

"Oh, but it will. They consented to be recorded, and your lawyer can call them as witnesses. Airtight."

"I can't afford a lawyer," she replied, "and besides, I did do a little property damage."

"That you did," Tucker said. "Much to the delight of the patronage. I doubt he'll do anything about it, though."

"Well, if he does, I'll just sue him for the deed to the place, right?" Mallory asked.

Tucker raised an eyebrow. "I think you need to find yourself some courtroom podcasts. Or at least watch some *Law & Order.*"

"And why wouldn't I?" she replied lightly. "I'm going to have a whole lot of free time from now on… Okay, so what now, Sherlock?"

"And that makes you Dr. Watson?" he asked, smiling at her.

"I'd rather be Irene Adler," she said with a grin.

"Scandalous," Tucker replied with a smirk.

"Bohemian," Mallory retorted.

But the moment faded along with Mallory's adrenaline when the gravity of what she'd done began to sink in: she was out of a job with no prospects, and Julie was still missing.

"Hmm," Tucker said. "I think the next step will be to take a deeper look at Zach Burns. After all, if the rumors about him are true, the man's an unconvicted killer, and he obviously knew and was friendly with Julie. If he… and she…" He didn't finish either sentence. Instead, he continued his thought, "I'll pay another visit to the sheriff's office and see if they'll let me take a look at his file."

"I can give you a summary," Mallory said. "His mother died. She was brutally murdered. They never found her body or the murder weapon, but they did find a lot of blood. The DNA test established it was hers. There was so much she couldn't possibly have survived. It's kind of what got me interested in true crime. They found Zach in the house, semi-comatose, with her blood on his clothes. And he claims he remembered nothing, not what happened, how the blood got there, nothing. He was arrested on suspicion of murder, but they had to let him go due to lack of evidence. And then he just disappeared into the wilderness."

"Thanks for that," Tucker said. "It'll help me get through the file faster."

"No problem."

"Well, it's only… four-fifteen," Tucker said, looking at his watch. "How about you take me back to your place to get my car and I leave the laptop with you? You can go through those messages, download and print them while I head over to the sheriff's office and see if I can get a peek at Zach's files."

"Sounds like teamwork," she said. "Glad to be on the team."

He gave her a smile. "Yeah, me too," he said dryly.

22

Sunday afternoon, 4:40pm

For the second time that day, Tucker walked briskly into the sheriff's department lobby, confident that, with it being Sunday, both the Cundiffs would be long gone.

"Something I can do for you, Randall?" Sheriff Cundiff said from behind the front desk.

"Er… Yes. That is…" For a moment Tucker was lost for words. *What the hell's he doing here? And why's he at the front desk.*

The sheriff glared at him, his eyes narrowed.

"Well? Come on. Out with it. I don't got all night. Why are you back here again for the second time today?"

"I came to talk to you about Zach Burns. D'you have a minute?"

At first, Cundiff looked surprised, then pleased. "Ah-ha! So, you found our very own 'Boy Who Lived,' complete with scar. Why d'you want to dig up that seedy part of our past?"

Tucker frowned. The sheriff's reaction wasn't quite what he'd expected.

"Just curious," Tucker said cautiously. "He has quite a reputation, and I seem to have run out of leads. If he's a killer, he could at least be a person of interest."

"Well now, I haven't seen that boy in years," Cundiff replied. "Lives somewhere up there in the forest, so they say." He paused, looked at Tucker and, not receiving a reply, he nodded and continued. "Sure, you can look at the file. There's not much to it, though. Come on around this side and watch the desk in case someone comes in, and I'll go get it. Might take a minute, though."

Now there's a surprise, Tucker thought as he watched the sheriff walk away. *Why's he being so cooperative? He must be up to something, but what?*

Then he remembered the younger Cundiff's parting words: "Maybe I should ask a few of my family members to pay you a visit. You don't wanna meet them."

"I guess you were surprised to see me here," Cundiff said as he returned and placed a box on the desk in front of Tucker.

Tucker looked at the box, then at the sheriff, but didn't reply.

"Well, I had paperwork to do," Cundiff continued, "so I sent everyone home." He smiled a strange smile as if he knew something Tucker didn't. But all Tucker said was "Thanks," then opened the box and took out the first folder, flipped it open and glanced at the first page.

"Geez," he said when he turned to the second page, an eight-by-ten photograph of a young boy, his entire midsection covered in blood. His hands and face all had copious amounts of blood on them. "This is Zach Burns?" he asked, looking up at the sheriff.

"Yup! That's him. That was taken the day Wynona Burns died in her home, alone with her 'little boy.'" Cundiff made quotes with his fingers.

Tucker looked again at the photo of a much younger Zach Burns than the one he'd met in the cabin. He was a tall, heavy-set, clean-shaven man and, but for the blood, a good-looking young man. *What the hell is wrong with this picture?* he thought.

He looked up at the sheriff. He was smiling.

"Hmm," Tucker said. "So, either Zach Burns killed his mother or he knows who did."

"That's about the size of it," Cundiff replied with a smirk. "See, he was found sitting there, in the house, totally out of it; semi-comatose was how the doctor described it." He tilted his head to one side, narrowed his eyes and continued, "He told the detectives, when we finally got him to talk, that he didn't remember anything. He had a nasty wound to the side of his head and a concussion, and he was covered in Wynona Burns' blood, along with some of his own, as you can see." He nodded at the photograph still in Tucker's hand.

"It would have been a slam dunk," Cundiff continued, "except there was no body and no weapon. Oh, we detained him, held him for forty-eight hours, questioned him, but we got no more out of him than he couldn't remember anything." He stared Tucker in the eye for a moment, then said, "We had to let him go, but we haven't closed the books on Wynona's murder, not yet."

"And there was nothing at the crime scene to—"

"No," the sheriff snapped, interrupting him. "Other than Wynona's blood, the place was clean: no prints, other than hers and the boy's, nothing. As I said, had it not been for the absence of the body and the murder weapon, that boy would be in jail to this day."

"So, from what you're telling, it's clear he didn't hack his mother to death?" Tucker asked. "Because if he did, he must have somehow gotten rid of the body and the weapon, then come back all covered in blood and waited for someone to find him. That makes no sense, Sheriff."

"You think?" Cundiff asked, smiling. "He could have done just that. Let me tell you something, Randall. By the time that boy was twelve, he was as tall as me. He was sixteen years old when his mother died. And, like you, nobody thought he could have done it. But as he got older, he started gettin' a little rough with people. And when he threw a punch at his football coach, people started wondering; if a big, strong fella like Zach Burns could throw a punch at his coach, maybe he did kill his momma.

"Wynona was a slip of a woman; couldn't have weighed more than a hundred-ten. When she died, the boy was six foot tall and was playing linebacker. It would've been a cinch for him to do just as you said: haul her body out of there, dump it in the truck bed and then haul it off somewhere."

"You checked his truck, right?" Tucker asked and immediately regretted it.

"What d'you think we are out here, Randall?" the sheriff snapped. "Of course we checked the damn truck. It was clean."

"He could have wrapped her in a tarp… Okay, okay. I get it. What little you have is circumstantial," Tucker said. "You have no body and no murder weapon. Sure, he took a blow to his head, but it's more likely he could have gotten that trying to protect her rather than fighting with her. And if he did kill her, where did he take the body?"

Cundiff shrugged. "As I said, he was a big fella, even then. I mean really big. He could have carried her off and buried her somewhere. He knows the forest better than anyone."

"Better than you, Sheriff?"

Again the sheriff shrugged, but he said nothing.

"So," Tucker said, "what you're saying is that Burns fought with his mother, killed her, carried her body off into the forest, buried her, *then calmly walked back to the house* and sat down and waited for your people to come and arrest him. I don't buy it."

"Like I said; he's a big fella," Cundiff said for the third time. "And he had a head injury. He could have done it and buried the knife along with her."

"Cadaver dogs?" Tucker asked, already knowing the answer.

"Of course, but have you any idea at all of just how big the forest is? It's more than seven-hundred-thousand acres big. That's how big it is, and as I said, he knows it better than anyone."

Tucker heaved a sigh and shook his head.

Cundiff looked at him and said dryly, "Yeah, right. That's exactly how we all felt. Still do." He paused and then continued, "They sent him off to Memorial for his head, and they treated him. I don't have those records, though. But I likely couldn't show 'em to you anyway, on account of HIPPO."

"You mean HIPAA?" Tucker said dryly as he opened the medical report. "Ah-ha, here's a psych evaluation—"

He saw little more than the name "Dr. John Wilson" before Sheriff Cundiff snatched it away.

"Oops. Forgot that was in there. Yep, HIPAA. Can't be lettin' you see that."

"And you have no other suspects, persons of interest?" Tucker asked, looking the sheriff right in the eye.

Cundiff didn't flinch. He stared right back, then said, slowly, "No. No, sir. Not a one. The Wynona Burns case is cold as the grave, in more ways than one. Now, if we're done. I've got paperwork I need to finish."

Tucker could tell from the look on Cundiff's face that he was through talking; that he'd gotten all he was going to get. So he returned the file to the box, stood up and said, "Thank you, Sheriff. You've been most helpful."

"Glad to be of service, son. You be safe out there. You heah? Oh, and by the way, Kal told me how you ran him around the block earlier today, so let me make this clear, Randall. You keep your nose out of our business. You have no idea what you're messing with."

"I have no interest in your illegal operation, Sheriff," Tucker said. "All I'm interested in is finding Julie Romero, and I think you know more about that than you're willing to let on. I also think you slow-walked the case because it might have interfered with the family business. But that is what it is, and if anyone decides to come after you, it will be because of your own negligence or malfeasance. All I want to do is find the girl."

"You arrogant, know-it-all son of a bitch. Get the hell out of my department, and don't come back. When you find that girl, she's gonna be dead. That's what happens to careless people around here."

"That sounds almost like a threat, Sheriff," Tucker said as he shoved the box back across the desk at him, "or an admission. So! If I were you, I'd try to remember that the least said, the better."

And then, showing far more boldness and confidence than he felt, he walked around the massive desk and strode out the front door.

Well now, that went well, he thought as he opened his car door and slid in behind the wheel. *Smart Tucker wouldn't have riled up a bootlegging sheriff like that. Smart Tucker would have schmoozed him instead.*

But he had learned something new. That quick glimpse of the ME's report had triggered a thought—and a new question.

Why would a GP be doing a psych evaluation on what possibly could have been a mentally deranged teenage boy? It makes no sense... No sense at all.

23

Sunday evening 5:30pm

ON A WHIM, AND FOR NO GOOD REASON HE COULD THINK OF, TUCKER decided to drive by Dr. Wilson's office. Not that he expected anybody to be there; it was, after all, almost five-thirty on a Sunday evening, and if you were to ask him why he did it, he probably wouldn't be able to tell you, other than it was indeed, just... a whim.

So, it was no little surprise to see not one but two cars parked outside the front entrance to the doctor's office: an expensive Cadillac SUV and an inexpensive, aging Honda Civic.

He parked next to the Civic, noting that the lights were on inside the clinic, and then sat there for a moment wondering if he should go and knock on the door.

"Nothing ventured..." he muttered as he pushed open the car door, stepped out and walked quickly to the entrance. The sign on the inside told him, "Open 8AM to 6PM Mon-Fri. 8AM to 12PM Sat. Closed Sunday."

"Strange." He glanced back at the two vehicles, frowned and then he smiled. "Methinks the good doctor is entertaining."

He looked at his watch. It was five-thirty-five. He raised his hand to knock on the door… then changed his mind, grabbed the handle and pushed and, low and behold, the door opened and he stepped inside.

"Excuse me," a voice said from behind the sliding glass window. "You can't come in here. It's Sunday. We're closed. You need to leave so I can lock the door. We open at eight—"

"I apologize for the intrusion," Tucker said, smiling, "but I saw the cars outside. I was here a couple of days ago, and this…" He pulled back his sleeve enough to show her the bandage. "And I just wanted to ask the good doctor a few questions."

"But we're closed."

"And I only need a few minutes of his time," Tucker insisted with an edge to his voice.

The receptionist looked confused. She obviously didn't know what to do. Tucker looked at her and smiled, and raised his eyebrows in question, then waited for her to speak.

"Very well," she said, picking up the phone. "He's doing… his paperwork. I'll let him know you're here, but he won't be pleased, I can assure you."

She tapped a button, listened for a minute until the doctor picked up, then said, "Doctor Wilson, there's a man here demanding to speak to you. I told him we were closed, but he's insisting. Can you come up here, please? What? Call the p…" She glanced up at Tucker and then whispered into the phone, "No! Absolutely not. You know I can't do that. You come up here and deal with him yourself." And she hung up.

Tucker stepped closer to the window and looked down at her desk. There was a small makeup kit—open—and a name badge. It was facing away from him, but he had no trouble reading it upside down. "Linda Warner."

Linda Warner, if that's who she was, glared at him, stood up, flounced out of the office and disappeared into the depths of the dragon's lair, leaving Tucker smiling hugely in the waiting room.

"Naughty, naughty," he muttered, smiling to himself.

She came back a few moments later, followed by Dr. Wilson.

"Mr. Randall," he said, frowning. "Linda tells me you're having problems with your stitches. Couldn't it have waited until tomorrow morning? I'm in the middle of paperwork... Well, never mind. You're here now, so let's take a look at it, shall we?"

"The stitches are fine—"

"But Linda said—" the doctor interrupted him.

"Yes, I know," Tucker said, interrupting the doctor. "The truth is, I was passing by and I saw your cars parked outside, and I thought perhaps you might take a moment to answer a few questions about the case I'm working on. I mentioned it while you were stitching me up. I'm looking into the disappearance of Julie Romero?"

Wilson stared at him, narrowed his eyes, frowned, then smiled and said, "Of course. Mallory Carver's niece. But... I don't see how I can help. Julie's a patient here, but I've seen her only... well, no more than once a year for the past..." He glanced at Linda through the glass. She was staring at him. "...four years?"

He raised his eyebrows in question. She tapped rapidly on her computer, then nodded and said, "Yes, four years."

"So," he said, looking again at Tucker. "As I said, I hardly know the lady, and I certainly can't reveal any of her medical information. That would be a violation of HIPAA. I could lose my license."

"It's not Julie I want to talk to you about," Tucker said. "It's Zach Burns."

"Excuse me?" The doctor frowned.

"I looked at the medical records associated with Wynona Burns' death," Tucker said. "You were asked to give Zach Burns a psychological evaluation after his mother died, and I was wondering why a GP would be asked to provide such an evaluation."

"For one thing, I was Zach Burns' primary physician," he replied. "For another, I wasn't always a GP, as you call it. I was... well, that's in the past. Ask your questions, Mr. Randall. I'll answer them if I can."

Tucker glanced at Linda. She obviously wasn't happy. "Is there somewhere we can talk in private?" he asked.

"Of course. We'll go to my office. If you'll follow me?"

"Please, sit down," Wilson said when they entered his office. "It's not very grand, I'm afraid, but it serves my needs."

Tucker glanced at the piles of paper on his desk. *So, he really is doing paperwork. Maybe I read it wrong... Nah. Those two have something going. I'm sure of it.*

"So, how can I help you?" Wilson said, clasping his hands together on the desk.

"What can *you* tell me about Zach Burns?" Tucker asked.

Wilson frowned. "Off the top of my head, and after all these years, not much, I'm afraid. Let's see…" He leaned back in his chair and stared up at the ceiling. "Zach Burns? Hmm. He was in the house the night his mother was brutally murdered. He received a blow to the head and was in a state of semi-consciousness when he was found. He spent a day at Memorial, then was taken into custody and questioned, but he was unable to provide any answers other than he couldn't remember anything. That was when Sheriff Cundiff asked me to take a look at him, which I did."

"So what you're telling me is that he lost his memory?" Tucker asked.

"In a nutshell, yes and no. Dissociative amnesia," Wilson replied. "At first, everyone, like you, believed that he'd 'lost his memory,'" he said with a smile. "He didn't. That's a terrible misunderstanding of the problem. Dissociative amnesia occurs when a person blocks out certain events, often associated with stress or trauma, leaving the person unable to remember important personal information; the memory, however, but for the odd gaps, such as the several hours during which Burns either murdered his mother or watched it happen, remains intact. That's the layman's definition."

He paused for a moment before continuing, "Zach had one or more heavy blows to the head, and I think he probably watched his mother being… murdered. It's likely he blacked out from the physical trauma and then willed himself to forget the terrible events he witnessed. Other than the gap, his memory is as it always was, intact."

"What happened after he was released?" Tucker asked.

"Wynona's sister, Angela Sidenham, I believe her name was, took him in. He lived with her until he graduated high school—a little more than two years—during which I saw him twice, I think, but his condition hadn't changed, and it probably never will. Anyway, as I said, he graduated high school, and less than three months later, he disappeared into the forest—that would have been... thirteen years ago?—and little has been seen of him since."

"The rumors are that there was no second person," Tucker said. "That he killed his mother and received his injuries in the process."

The doctor shook his head. "No. I don't think so. I'm afraid some of the local folks started that rumor. But after the incident with his football coach, it became a full-blown truth, if you know what I mean." Wilson steepled his fingers and looked at him across his desk. "I tend to go with the evidence, and, by all accounts, there was none."

"Yes, I heard about the incident with his coach," Tucker replied. "I'm surprised he wasn't expelled."

"He probably would have been had the coach not taken up for him and admitted he pushed him a little too hard."

Tucker tried not to think of Burns' size, his quickness, or his ability to disappear into the forest. But like the doctor, he believed in the evidence, and the lack of a body or murder weapon were pretty conclusive. *Zach Burns did not kill his mother.*

"So, is Zach Burns considered a suspect?" Wilson asked.

"More a person of interest," Tucker said.

"I understand," Wilson said. "Well, I hope I was able to answer your questions, Mr. Randall. But I really do need to get back to my paperwork." He spread his arms as if to encompass the stacks of paper on his desk. "If not, I'll be here all night. So, if there's nothing else."

"Of course," Tucker replied. "Thank you for taking the time and for allowing me to barge in here like I did. I don't think Ms. Warner was too happy about it, though."

"She's very protective of me," Wilson said as he walked him back to the reception area. "Show Mr. Randall out, please, Mrs. Warner. And you can lock up and go yourself."

"Yes, Doctor," she replied, rising from her seat and gathering her things.

Mrs. Warner, Tucker thought. *No wonder she didn't want to call the police.*

"One more thing, Mr. Randall," Wilson said as he was about to step outside. "I still need your paperwork."

"Yes, I'm sorry," Tucker replied. "I guess it slipped my mind. I'll get it to you ASAP. Goodnight, Doctor."

Wilson nodded, turned away and disappeared back into the labyrinth.

24

Sunday evening 6:15pm

Mallory was in one of those moods when she arrived home a little before five that Sunday afternoon. She was tired, elated, and disappointed, all at the same time. Tired for obvious reasons, elated because Tucker had "welcomed her to the team," and disappointed that he hadn't taken her with him to the sheriff's department.

So, when she arrived home loaded up with groceries and Julie's laptop, she let Annie out and quickly loaded the groceries into the refrigerator. Then she poured herself a huge glass of red, took a big gulp, closed her eyes, swallowed, shuddered, then opened the door to let Annie back in.

She stood for a moment at the open door, looking out toward the distant mountains, and again she shuddered; this time thinking about her encounter with Zach Burns and then at the thought of what might have happened to Julie.

Finally, she stepped back inside and closed the door, picked up the laptop and, glass in hand, carried it into the living room, sat down in her recliner, put up her feet, set the laptop on her knees and opened it.

Then, having set her glass down on the side table, she put her head back and closed her eyes.

An hour and a half later, she opened her eyes again with a start, looked at the dark computer screen, then around the room. *Oh Lord,* she thought. *I must have fallen asleep again.* And then she realized she was hungry. So she set the computer aside, struggled out of the recliner, and went to the kitchen.

For a moment, she wondered what Tucker was doing and whether to invite him over for something to eat—but decided against it.

So, she thought, *I'm on the team. I wonder what that means... exactly? Hah. Not a whole lot, if I'm honest with myself. I'm out of a job, have just enough money set aside to carry me through the next three months... and no prospects. Damn. Oh well, I do have the laptop, and I can look through the messages by myself. Phew.* She blew out a huge breath and sat down at the kitchen table. *I've been feeling so tired lately, and I've been eating nothing but garbage. I need to do better. I must have put on five or ten pounds, and I look like hell. I need to get back on my diet and burn off the fat.*

She turned her head and looked at the fridge, grinned and muttered, "I'll start tomorrow."

Annie looked up at her, head tilted to one side.

"Oh, don't look at me like that," she said to the dog. "I'll start tomorrow. I promise."

"Errrr, woof."

"Oh shut up, Annie," she said, getting up from the table and going to the fridge.

She opened the freezer section and stared inside without enthusiasm. For a moment, she considered ordering a pizza but decided she couldn't wait. So she grabbed a bag of Orange Chicken from Trader Joe's and some microwavable Jasmine rice, and less than fifteen minutes later, she and Annie were enjoying the pseudo-Chinese delight.

Now, she thought, having rinsed off her plate and Annie's dish and put them in the dishwasher, *let's take a look at those messages.*

She set the laptop on the kitchen table, plugged it in, and opened the Sibilant program.

The early messages to Kal had been flirty and fun, and Julie obviously enjoyed talking to him.

MakeLikeATree: *18:32*
I love that you're out
there watching over us.
It makes me feel safe.

DeputyDawg: *18:37*
You know it babe.

But the dialogue soon became strained.

Messages from Julie, for example: *I can't believe you did that,* and *Why did you lie to me?* received responses like *sorry babe you know how dad is,* or *look its confidential you know,* and *can we just talk about it?*

But then it seemed as if some messages were missing altogether, or perhaps the conversations had continued off-screen. And Mallory began to think she was missing key information. And then the messages stopped for several months until Julie had a minor car accident, a fender-bender that Julie had never mentioned, not to her or her mother because Jennifer would have told her about it. It was then that the messaging resumed.

MakeLikeATree: *19:54*
Look, I just don't want my parents
finding out, ok?
I wasn't supposed to be out there
tonight

DeputyDawg: *19:57*
sure babe you know i can do
anything for you
can we let the past be past?

Just go out with me again ok

MakeLikeATree: *20:01*
I can't change the fact that you do
what you do
and I can't forget about it

DeputyDawg: *20:03*
im not saying you have to forget
but you dotn need to make
a big deal out of it
its nothing

MakeLikeATree: *20:05*
You're a cop and you're
breaking the law, Kal.
What kind of person are you
Doing that kind of stuff?
It's wrong, and I can't be
involved. It's not right.

DeputyDawg: *20:06*
Oh come Jules aint you been
asking me to break the law
a little? You know im
protecting you give me
another chance please

MakeLikeATree: *20:08*
Fine. I'll go out with you,
just for a drink. Nothing more
But you have to stop.

DeputyDawg: *20:12*

great. but change your screen name
pick something nice again

Ariel: *20:16*
How's this?

DeputyDawg: *20:19*
awesome. like the mermaid
you gonna wear any seashells for ne?

Ariel: *20:20*
Only if a storm strands us on a deserted island

DeputyDawg: *20:21*
thats ok
i like how you look without
anything on anyway

"Oh… my God," Mallory muttered, shuddering at the thought of Kal and Julie naked together. "That totally creeps me out. Whatever was she thinking?" *And what was she thinking, going back to him after… whatever it was? I guess she must have found out that Kal was involved with the moonshiners. What was it Tucker said?* "You think you know someone, but you really don't," she muttered. *Geez, did I ever really know Julie? And how weird is it that she found Zach, who thought of himself as an ogre—*

Her phone beeped, startling her.

"What the heck?" she said as she picked it up and looked at the screen. It was a text.

Oil Points Bulletin *18:25*
Have you checked your mileage lately?
Be sure to stop into your local Oil Baron—

"Geez, like I needed a panic attack," Mallory muttered as she marked it spam.

"Pheeew," she said and made a noise with her lips. "Oil Points Bulletin…" *Didn't Kal say they put one of those out for Julie's Bronco? Not oil, though,* all *points bulletin. Crap.* She shook her head. *You've got to stop this, Mallory. Not everything has to be about the case, does it? Geez, it seems as if Julie's occupying your every waking thought. Of course she would. You love her. Why wouldn't she?*

But Mallory was tired, really tired. She'd been fighting the system for more than two weeks. Between work and the searching and the digging, she'd barely slept a wink, and on top of all that, she'd been neglecting her health, lost her job, and was probably looking at a lawsuit. She just wanted it to be over.

But it won't ever be over. Not unless we prove that she went missing, or she ran away, or she's dead. We'll always wonder.

But the thought of the All Points Bulletin nagged at her. *When did the sheriff's department post the APB? How far out did that range? Ten miles? Twenty? Fifty? A hundred? Lordy, that's a big area.*

"I wonder if they still have the APB active?" she muttered. "I bet they don't. They weren't interested in looking for her right from the start. I wonder if they heard anything, and if they did, did they follow up on it? I bet they didn't. Damn that Kal Cundiff. I wish I could…"

Okay, so let's take the positive approach, she thought. *I can do some checking myself, but where? Hmm, I know. Tucker mentioned salvage yards. That's a good place to start.*

She Googled "salvage and scrap yards near me." That brought up more than a dozen listings in the Chattanooga area alone.

She opened a Notepad document and copied and pasted the names of the businesses into a document. She stared at it for a moment, then had another thought: *I need to widen the search. Suppose I stole a car in Ocoee. Where would I take it? Probably not Chattanooga. Hmm. Okay, so how about East Tennessee?*

She Googled "auto salvage and scrap yards in east Tennessee." That brought up a single business in East Memphis. *Hmm. I'll just have to do it by county. That will take all night. Okay, so let's narrow it down, then.*

Thirty minutes later, she had listings in ten counties, including two in North Carolina.

She looked at the clock. "It's seven-forty… and Sunday. I'll have to start in the morning."

She looked at Annie, who was asleep in her bed. "Come on, girl. I'll take you out, then we'll make it an early night."

Annie jumped up and ran to the back door.

Mallory stepped out onto the back deck and sat down in an Adirondack chair to watch Annie do her stuff.

You know, she thought as she watched the dog disappear into the long grass at the far end of the garden, *it probably doesn't matter if I call them tonight. I mean, I could leave messages and they could call me back in the morning. That might even be better. I could get them all done tonight instead of talking to each and every one; that would save a lot of time.*

She stood up. "Annie," she called. "Come on. We have work to do." And the dog came running up the garden path.

"Good girl," Mallory said, bending down and making a fuss of her. "You want a treat?" Annie wagged her tail furiously. "Of course you do. Come on then."

She gave the dog a Meaty Bone, then settled down in her recliner and looked at her Notepad document. "That's not going to work," she said and took five minutes to transfer the information into a spreadsheet. Then she took a deep breath and called the first name on the list. It rang twice before the voicemail picked up. She waited until the over-friendly spiel ended, then for the beep, and then she began.

"Hi, my name is Mallory Carver, and this is an urgent request as part of a homicide investigation." *Oh, dear God. I hope it isn't.* "We're looking for a missing nineteen-ninety-two Ford Bronco, tan and brown, with a crumpled passenger side front fender. It also has a lot of stickers on the tailgate. The tag number is XLT941. If you've seen this vehicle within the last three weeks, please contact me direct at this number. Thank you." She gave the number, hung up and marked it off on the spreadsheet.

That should do it, she thought as she dialed the next number on the list.

By ten after ten, she was done. She'd left messages at ninety-three businesses. She was exhausted and could barely keep her eyes open.

She'd made calls to businesses in Athens, Decatur, Evensville, Pikeville and most of east Tennessee as far north as Knoxville. She'd called companies in Georgia as far as Dalton, Ringgold, Chatsworth, Mineral Bluff, Ellijay, and even Chickamauga.

"I'm done," she mumbled. "I need to go to bed." She yawned and looked at Annie. The dog was asleep in her bed, on her back, all four legs in the air.

"Come on, Annie," she said. "One last pee-pee and we'll go night-night."

Monday morning 9:10am

Mallory woke late the next morning, Monday, when, at just after nine o'clock, her cell phone rang, or rather buzzed on the nightstand. At first she thought it was part of her dream and ignored it, and it wasn't until it fell off onto the floor that she decided she needed to answer it.

Vision bleary, body aching, head aching, she leaned over the edge of the bed, groping for the errant phone. Finally, she found it, grabbed it and looked at the time. "Oh… m'God," she gasped as she flung herself back onto the pillow. "It's ten after nine. How did I sleep that long?"

The call ended before she could answer it. She held the phone up so she could see it and saw there were dozens of missed calls; messages. She opened her voicemail and found thirty-five new messages. "Oh shit."

"Come on, Annie," she snapped as she leaped out of bed and almost fell. "Whoops, come on, girl. You need to go out." And together, they ran down the stairs to the back door.

She turned the dog loose, then all but ran back up the stairs to the bathroom, took a quick shower, and dressed quickly in a pair of old jeans and a white T-shirt. She ran back to the bathroom, brushed her hair. Then, feeling *almost* like a new person, she ran back downstairs, peeked out the glass pane in the back door to make sure Annie was okay, then she turned and tapped the switch on the coffee maker.

That done, she took her phone from her pocket, grabbed a paper and pen, and started playing the messages.

"Hi, this is Susie at Bucks for Trucks. I just wanted to let you know that we haven't seen any vehicles matching your description in the last three months. Hope your search goes well."

She wrote *BFTrucks — no.*

She played the next message. "Hi, this is Eric from Olympic Towing. Haven't seen anything like that. Sorry."

She wrote *Olympic — no.*

She heard Annie scratching at the door to come in. She let her in, refreshed her coffee, then went back to work.

She played the next message, the next, and the next, all with similar messages. No one had seen the Bronco.

Diligently, she listened to each and every call until, by ten o'clock, she'd finished, feeling utterly defeated and realizing the flaw in her reasoning the night before. *What about the ones that didn't call back? Now I have to call them all again. Damn it.*

"Geez, thirty-five and nothing," she mumbled. "That leaves… fifty-eight that I have to call again." Her phone buzzed. "Please, please, please," she muttered as she accepted the call.

"Hello," she said.

"Is this Ms. Carver?"

"It is," she replied carefully, having been the victim of more spam calls than any human being deserved.

"Oh, good. Good morning. This is Derrick from B&L Salvage returning your call. That Bronco you're looking for? We got it. It ain't in good shape, though."

"Oh, my Lord, thank you, Derrick," she replied. "How long have you had it?"

"It came in about a week ago. It's been stripped. Had to be hauled in. It's scheduled for crushing, but—"

"Oh, please, don't do that," Mallory said, her heart thudding. "It's evidence in a possible murder case. Can you send me a picture of it? Just to be sure? I need to see it."

"Sure. Give me a second—" It wasn't thirty seconds later that she received a message. She opened the file to see a picture of a computer screen on which was a photograph of Julie's Bronco: the familiar front grill and headlights, the minor crumple on the passenger side fender. *Oh, my God. That's it,* she thought. *That's Julie's Bronco.*

"That's it," she said, unable to contain her excitement. "Does it have stickers all over the tailgate?"

"Not that I know of," Derrick replied, "but to be honest, I didn't look. You sure this is the one you're looking for?"

"Yes. I'm sure," she replied. "What's the tag number?"

"No Tag. Plate's missing. Sorry."

"Okay. Not a problem. I'm coming to look at it. Please don't do anything to it. Where's your shop, or yard, or... Where are you?"

"Like I said, lady, it ain't in the best con—"

"It doesn't matter. Where are you, sir?"

"We're in Maryville"—he pronounced it Murvul—"off of Highway 411."

"Could you give me the address, please, for my GPS?" she asked.

"Sure," he said and gave her the address.

"Hold on, please," she said.

She went to her laptop on the kitchen table, brought up Google Maps and tapped in the address.

"You still there, Derrick?" she asked.

"Sure am."

"It's about a two-hour drive from where I am," she said. "I'll start out as soon as I can. Will you be there around... It's almost twenty after ten now. We should be there around one, give or take. Will you be there?"

"Yup. I go to lunch around twelve, so yeah. Come at one."

Her phone buzzed in her ear, but she ignored it.

"I'm on my way," she said.

25

Monday morning 9:30am

At nine-fifteen that morning, Tucker was seated in his car a half block down the street from Dr. Wilson's clinic, wondering if he'd missed her and whether or not he should go inside. He'd been there since seven-forty-five, hoping to catch Linda Warner on her way in to work.

Why? Because he had a hunch, a gut feeling that something wasn't quite right about the so-called good doctor. Was it something the man had said to him or the way he'd said it? Or the way he'd spoken to Mallory? He didn't know. What he did know was that the feeling wouldn't go away until he'd figured out what it was that was bothering him.

Tucker was a seasoned investigator taught his craft by the best in the business, and he'd long ago learned to trust his feelings; thus, he listened to his hunches, and he wasn't alone. There was something indefinable about a hunch, and every lawman in any capacity learned early on to "trust their gut."

And Tucker Randall's gut was telling him there was something decidedly iffy going on at Dr. Wilson's little clinic.

Dr. Wilson had been more than willing to talk about Mallory while he was stitching Tucker's arm, weaving a subtle tale of a girl always on the lookout for adventure, getting into trouble and not always telling the truth. *Sure, Mallory comes across as excitable sometimes,* he thought and slowly shook his head. *But she's not a liar.*

His gut told him that much, and she'd proved herself a meticulous, though occasionally emotional, temporary partner. *And why wouldn't she be emotional about her missing niece?*

Then he'd asked Wilson about Zach Burns, and the doctor's readiness to talk about him in spite of the HIPAA laws—which had been the first thing he'd mentioned when he told him he wanted to ask him some questions—was just one more twitch in his gut. A twitch that had grown and festered after he, the doctor, had painted a portrait of a gruff and brutal teenager who'd turned to violence, and perhaps even murder, matricide. *But bitter and violent men, and especially murderers, don't serve tea to trespassers. And it sure as hell didn't take much persuasion to get the doctor to talk about him, regardless of his supposed fear of the aforementioned HIPAA laws... But above all, I just don't like the man. He's one snide, arrogant...*

He dismissed the thought from his mind. His personal feelings about the doctor were irrelevant. He'd seen the doctor arrive at eight, followed a moment later by his nurse, but of Linda Warner, there had been no sign. *So,* he thought. *I've either missed her or she's not at work today... Nope, that's her red Honda Civic over there in the corner of the lot, so she must have come in early. Oh well. Can't sit around here all day. Let's go talk to her, Tucker.*

He was reaching for the starter button when he saw the clinic door open. Expecting it to be a patient, he started the engine and was about to put the car in drive when Linda Warner scurried out. He touched the button again and turned off the engine. Then he checked the dashboard clock. It was nine-thirty exactly.

"A little early for lunch," Tucker muttered, "but hey, I'll take what I can get."

He stepped out of the car and headed in Linda's direction. She was almost to the street corner when he caught up with her.

"Linda. Is that you? I was just on my way to the clinic. Have you got a minute?"

She stopped walking, turned and saw who it was, and she wasn't pleased. "Mr. Randall?" she said angrily. "No. I don't want to talk to you." And she turned again and began to walk quickly away.

He quickened his pace and caught up with her again. "Wait, Linda. Just hold on a minute, please?" he said, hoping the familiarity of his use of her first name would give her pause. "I just want to ask a few questions… about a missing girl—"

"I know what you want," she said furiously, interrupting him. And without slowing her pace, she continued, "And I told you I don't want to talk to you. Now go away and leave me alone. D'you hear?"

Tucker followed her around another corner. "Listen to me, please? I just want to ask you about Julie Romero. She's missing, and her family is distraught. She was Doctor Wilson's patient. I just want to find the girl."

"Then why are you bothering the doctor?" she demanded, still marching onward, her head down, eyes staring straight ahead.

"I really don't know the answer to that, Linda. Julie was his patient. I'm just looking for a little insight into the girl's… I don't know… character? I want to find her and put her parents' minds at rest. If you'll just give me a minute and answer a few questions, I promise I'll leave both you and the good doctor alone. How does that sound?"

Linda slowed to a walk, then to a stop, turned around, looked him in the eye and said, "D'you mean that? Because Doctor John says you're just looking for a camera opportunity and some dirty laundry to air."

"He said what?" Tucker asked, stunned by the revelation. "I promise you, that's the last thing I want to do."

He watched her features soften, then, "Now you listen to me, Mr. Randall." She lowered her head and stared up at him through her lashes while wagging a finger at him. "John Wilson is a wonderful man."

"I'm sure he is—" Tucker replied.

"He does a lot for this community," she said, cutting him off again, "and I'm not going to let you ruin him."

"I understand, and that's not my intention," Tucker replied.

"And his wife is a harridan, a shrew. I don't care what anyone else thinks about the Burns family." She drew herself up.

What? Where the hell did that come from?

"Stasia doesn't appreciate him, hasn't for years. But he's trapped in a prenup that would destroy him. Ever since the misunderstanding that got him dismissed from Erlanger, he's been completely dependent on his wife for money."

What the hell is she talking about?

"He's married to a member of the Burns family?" Tucker asked, stunned.

"Yes, Stasia Burns," she replied. "She pays for almost everything."

"But, what about his practice? Surely—"

Again, she cut him off. "Oh, his clinic hardly makes enough money to stay open. And he's a very generous man, you know. He donates to all sorts of good causes, helps troubled families in the community. He even gives free therapy sessions at night." She was obviously upset.

"Linda, what did I do last night to upset you?" he asked gently.

"Why, you... You came in and disturbed him while he was doing his essential paperwork. Sunday is the only time he can do it. And I really should have locked the door, but as usual, he'd agreed to see Mrs. Adams for an unscheduled therapy session. That's the kind of man he is. I was afraid he'd—"

"Be angry with you for letting me in?" Tucker asked.

"No. Not angry," she said, looking around to see if anyone was nearby. "It was... I... That is, we... I didn't want him to be upset."

Tucker looked at her. Her eyes were watering. "You two... You're..." He didn't want to say it, but on the other hand, he wanted to know.

Linda lowered her head and her voice. "My husband, you see, Walter, passed away five years ago. It's been very difficult for me. He was a good man and I miss him, but..." She looked up at him and shrugged. "Well, you know."

Wow, Tucker thought. *What do I say to that?* "Yes, of course. I understand—"

And, yet again, she cut him off. "I'm fifty-three, Mr. Randall. No one wants to… It's hard to find…" She bit her lip. "No one wants to date a fifty-three-year-old secretary, and he… Well, sometimes after work… he and I, we… Oh, my God. You know what I mean. So when you burst in and he got upset and told me to leave… yes. I was pissed off. I'd been looking forward to… some time alone with him."

"I'm sorry," Tucker said. "I didn't know. Here, let me give you my card. If you think of anything about Julie, anything at all, really, please let me know."

Linda took the card from him, glanced at it, then slipped it into her purse. "I have to go now. I have to get the doctor something to eat. It's going to be a busy day. Goodbye, Mr. Randall." And she walked away, her head held high.

Tucker watched her go, walked toward his car, then turned again and watched her go into the sandwich shop. He shook his head. *Unbelievable,* he thought as he opened his car door and slid in behind the wheel.

He sat for a moment thinking, wondering what to do next. He frowned. *Strange,* he thought. *I haven't heard from Mallory. That's not like her.*

He took out his phone and called her. It went directly to voicemail.

"Hi. I'm not available right now. Leave a message—"

He ended the call, frustrated. *Damn it! What the hell is she doing?*

He dropped the phone onto the passenger seat and reached for the starter button, and the phone rang. He glanced at it. *Hah! It's Mallory.*

"Hey. I just called you."

"Yeah. I know. Sorry. I was—Oh, never mind. You need to get over here right away. We've got to go."

"Go? What are you talking about? Go where?" Tucker asked.

"I found Julie's Bronco," she yelped.

"Geez," he replied, pushing the starter. "How did you do that? Where is it?"

"I made some calls. It's in Maryville. It's about two hours away, so come on."

Some thirty minutes later, after a heated argument about who would drive—which Tucker lost decisively—they were on I-75 driving north in Mallory's Dodge Ram pickup.

Why do I get the feeling that she could have solved this case all by herself? he wondered as they rocketed through the I-75/I-24 split. *She's like a dog with a bone; never gives up.*

But he also remembered the rack of destroyed wine bottles at The Saloon and the way she yelled at Zach Burns, a man twice her size. *And a frickin' big dog, at that, and I sometimes wonder if she's not all...*

"So, what did you find out this morning?" Mallory asked, breaking into his thoughts without taking her eyes from the road, and as she reached out to adjust the radio to a classic country music station.

"D'you mind?" Tucker said, changing it to a soft rock station. "I'm not a fan of country music."

She glanced at him and frowned. "Really?"

"Yes, really," he replied. "It's all... 'my girl left me, my momma died, someone stole my truck.' It's depressing, a mood killer."

"Hah!" she said and shook her head. "So, are you going to tell me or not?" she asked.

"I found... Look, I'm not sure it's worth sharing."

"What do you mean?" Mallory said. "You haven't had a problem sharing anything else."

"I just mean... I'm not sure it means anything. And... Oh hell. Doctor Wilson is having an affair with his secretary, Linda Warner."

"What?" She whipped her head around to look at him, and the truck veered violently to the right onto the edge of the hard shoulder.

"See?" he said as she eased the big vehicle back onto the pavement. "That's exactly the reaction I expected. I told you. It doesn't mean anything. Now keep your eyes on the road, *please.*"

Mallory was sullenly silent for a while, and Tucker couldn't help but wonder, *What's going on in that pretty little head of yours?* But he settled back in his seat, closed his eyes and said nothing.

"You know, it's going to be a really boring ride if all I have to talk about is the number of phone calls I made last night." Mallory shifted in her seat. "So what else can we talk about?"

"You seem to be obsessed with your true-crime podcasts and talk about them all the time, so I'm told," Tucker said. "Why do you listen to that crap? It's beyond depressing… and it's unhealthy."

"That's enthusiasm, not obsession," she countered. "And where was this hesitance to speak when Cundiff told you about his smuggling operation?"

"That pertained to the case, and I was hoping to learn something," Tucker said, then paused and continued. "And what about that shouting match you had with your boss? And the stunt you pulled with the liquor rack?"

"Former boss," she said, smiling. "He's a horse's ass and I have no regrets. Hell, I enjoyed it." She paused, then continued quietly, "Maybe the booze thing was a little over the top."

"Thank you," Tucker said, closing his eyes again. "I should have left you behind and done this myself. Now stop being so annoying and concentrate on your driving."

"You couldn't have left me behind because I'm the only one who can identify her Bronco."

"Really?" he said. "Nineteen-ninety-two model, tan and brown, crumpled passenger side front fender, stickers all over the tailgate. How many of those can there be in East Tennessee?"

"Geez," she muttered. "All right. You win. Satisfied?"

Tucker smiled but didn't answer.

Mallory drove on in silence until they reached Athens and then said, "You said you were in the FBI, and then you quit after the girl died, right?" Mallory asked quietly. "So why did you become a private investigator?"

Tucker pursed his lips, looked at her and said, "It wasn't just the Marsha Cline case. She was just the beginning of the end. I've never quite gotten over her; probably never will… Okay, so it wasn't long after she died when a little boy went missing.

"I told David, my boss, I could do the job. I wanted to prove to myself—and maybe to David, too—that I was still the agent I should be. Anyway, I approached the family and discovered the boy had an uncle. To cut a long story short, it turned out the uncle's friend was the perp. I tracked him down, arrested him, found where he had the kid locked up, and then made the mistake of talking to the media. Then I was handed another missing person case—are you beginning to see a pattern here? It turned out that she, the mother, had ditched her family and run off with another guy. It took a while, but I found her and again, I ended up on TV."

He sighed. "And one case followed another, all missing persons, kidnappings, murders, six more cases, and I just got fed up with the interviews and the publicity. And all the time, Marsha was there, haunting me, playing with my mind. And then, one day, I bumped into the Clines in the mall, and Jim Cline told me in no uncertain terms that I was a grandstanding jerk, bragging about how many cases I'd solved. That was it. That was all it took. I quit the FBI, applied for a PI license, and swore I'd never take another missing person case as long as I lived."

"But you took our case," Mallory said. "Why?"

He shrugged. "I think I told you before, your sister shoved that photo of Julie under my nose. I thought for a minute it was Marsha. So, I took it as a sign from above that maybe I could make amends for my past failures. It's not going too well, is it?"

He lapsed into silence, leaned his head back against the rest, hands on his knees and closed his eyes.

It was no more than a moment later when he felt Mallory's hand close over his. She gave it a gentle squeeze and then took her hand away and put it back on the wheel, and said, "It will be all right, Tucker. We'll find her. I know we will."

But he didn't know if she'd be alive when they did.

26

Monday afternoon 6pm

MALLORY SPENT THE REST OF THE RIDE TO MARYVILLE TRYING TO decide what to say to Tucker, but she could never find the right words.

And none of the things I've done over the last ten years, and in particular the last three weeks, have been any help at all.

Five long days searching the trail had turned up nothing.

Her dives into Julie's phone records had missed Sarah's involvement.

She'd had no idea Julie was dating Kal Cundiff.

She'd had no idea the Cundiffs were running an illegal smuggling operation.

She'd missed the importance of Julie's laptop entirely.

She'd not known that Julie was involved with Zach Burns.

Yes, she had managed to find the Bronco, but any competent police search would have found it two weeks ago.

"This is it," Tucker said, jerking her out of her reverie. "There. Hey, Mallory. You've passed it."

She braked, looked around and saw the sign go by to the left.

"Whoops. Sorry. I was... Oh never mind. Hang on," she said as she checked her mirrors. Then she made an illegal U-turn, drove back several hundred yards, made a right into the yard and parked outside the converted container that served as the office.

She jumped out of the truck, suddenly feeling quite nervous—not something she experienced very often. But this really was the moment.

"Let's do this, Tucker," she said and took a deep breath and marched into the office. "Hi," she said brightly. "Are you Derrick?"

He looked up at her, did a double take, then rose to his feet and said, "No, I'm Gus. Derrick's out in the yard. What can I do ya for?"

"I called earlier about a tan and brown Bronco. Derrick said—"

"Oh, yeah," Gus said. "That one. He told me about it."

Mallory waited for him to say something else.

"We got it," he said, finally.

"Can we see it?" Mallory asked.

"I guess," he replied. "Dunno why you'd want to, though. It's in pretty bad shape—"

"Gus," Tucker interrupted, "that Bronco may be the missing piece in a police investigation. We need to see it."

"Nah," he said, shaking his head. "The police already investigated it."

"That would have been the local police," Mallory said, her impatience mounting. "It's the subject of a police investigation. Now. Can we see it, please?"

"Whatever. It's barely salvage now," Gus muttered. He pointed to a crudely drawn map on the wall. "We're here," he said. "You wanna follow along to right here, and when you get to the Jeeps—"

"Can you just show us, please? We've had a really long drive," Mallory said, pleading.

The man gave her a dismissive shrug. She drew herself up to her full height and glared at him.

He rolled his eyes and then said, "Sheesh, women! Okay, I got a few minutes. Follow me." And he led them out into the semi-chaotic structure of what turned out to be a major salvage yard, a maze of pathways bounded by stacks of scrap and crushed vehicles. They followed him as he made turn after turn following a set of landmarks that could only have made sense to him.

"Here it is," he said finally. "They found it in the parking lot at the rear of an abandoned strip mall about five miles from here. Is it yours?"

"It was my niece's," Mallory said.

"Well," Gus said, "you sure this here's the one?"

The Bronco was, indeed, Julie's. But not even Gus' previous warnings had prepared her for what she saw.

The Bronco was on its axles. The wheels were missing, and so was the license plate. The outside of the body was pretty much as Mallory remembered it, but the interior had been completely stripped, picked clean. But it was the tailgate that upset her the most.

Julie had been an avid sticker collector. Wherever she went, she would buy a sticker for her tailgate. Mallory had helped her put the first ones on when she was only sixteen. Jared had bought the car for her sixteenth birthday, and by the time she was twenty-three, the tailgate was entirely covered. To look at it from behind, you couldn't tell what color it was.

But now, all the stickers were gone. Someone had taken the time to remove them all. Not a trace of Julie remained. And she realized that any hope she might have had that Julie was alive, this deliberate attempt to erase her presence from the Bronco, made it clear that someone had wanted her to disappear.

"I need to get the VIN number," Tucker said. "You said it was found at the rear of a strip mall," he continued. "It was taken from a parking area at a trailhead off of Highway 64 in the Cherokee National Forest more than two weeks ago. That's quite a haul from here. And it was brought in… when, exactly?"

Gus frowned, narrowed his eyes, thought for a moment, then said, "Not sure exactly when. Not without checking the log, but I'm thinking… it was a week ago Friday, late afternoon, as I remember it. Tow guy said the cops had called it in. Chased some kids away from it.

You're lucky it's still here. It was scheduled for the crusher this morning."

So convenient, Mallory thought. *Just some kids playing in an abandoned car. No wonder the cops didn't bother with it.*

Tucker turned to Mallory and said, "We need to call this in to Sheriff Cundiff. I wonder where it was the week before it was found? Someone went to a lot of trouble to make sure it couldn't be identified. Several of the VIN numbers have been removed, even the one on the engine, but whoever it was missed the one on the inside of the tailgate. I've made a note of it. I'll call it in when we're done here."

Mallory said nothing. She could only stare at the ruined vehicle.

"I need the address where the Bronco was found," Tucker said to Gus. "Maybe we can get some camera footage."

"Again, I'll need to check the log," Gus replied. "We can do that now. I need to go back to the office anyway. You done here, miss?"

"I'll be a minute," she replied. "I need to take some photos. You go on. I'll catch up."

"Don't be long," Tucker said. "We have a long drive back."

She nodded, took her phone from her pocket and took as many photos as she could of the interior, front, back, and driver's side. She couldn't get to the passenger side because the car was pushed up against a stack of crushed vehicles more than two stories high.

That done, she walked back to the office, wondering how she was going to tell Jen and Jared that Julie was almost certainly dead. It was a thought that almost made her throw up.

Is this what Tucker felt like? she wondered. *If he did... if he does, I can understand why. This is the worst moment of my life, and it's not even over.*

By the time she reached the office, she could barely hold back the tears. She arrived just in time to hear Tucker hand over his phone to a man she didn't recognize standing next to Gus. He turned out to be the elusive Derrick, the yard manager.

"Sheriff Cundiff would like to talk to you," Tucker said as he handed Derrick his phone.

"This is Derrick Sims," he said.

There was a pause while he listened.

"Yes, sir, Sheriff. I'll get right on it." He nodded his head.

"Yes, sir. I'll need a warrant." He put his hand over the phone and whispered to Gus. "Go rope that Bronco off and put a sign on it. It's not to be touched." He waved for Gus to go right away.

"Sorry," Derrick said into the phone. "I was just telling my foreman to rope it off. You need me to organize transport for you?"

He winced when he heard what could only have been a negative response.

"Okay, okay," he said. "I got it. It's not to be touched. So when—" Derrick stopped talking abruptly and listened, his mouth hanging open.

"We close at six," he said, shaking his head.

"Yeah. Yeah. No... Fine, but somebody's going to have to pay for my time. Yeah. Uh, uh, no. Okay. By ten o'clock... Yeah. Yeah. And goodbye to you, too, Sheriff." Derrick let out a low whistle.

"Geez," he said as he handed the phone back to Tucker. "Is he always like that?"

Tucker grinned at him. "The guy doesn't take no for an answer."

"You can say that again," Derrick replied. "He's sending a flatbed from the Chattanooga forensic department. Said he'll call me back with a definite time. I told him by ten. That didn't go down well." He sighed and shook his head. "I promised I'd stay here and help them load it. Good thing we have good lighting. Oh well."

Tucker looked at Mallory, saw the state she was in and said, "Let's get you home, Mallory."

She nodded, thanked Derrick for calling her back and for agreeing to stay for the forensic team, and then she numbly followed him out to her truck.

"You want me to drive?" he asked.

She almost said yes, but then realized he wasn't a stick shift driver and smiled and shook her head.

"No. I'm fine," she said. "It's just... I was wondering what and how I was going to tell Jen, and it upset me, is all."

It was a long and quiet drive back home. Neither one of them had much to say, and Mallory was glad of the quiet, but when she pulled into her driveway, Tucker looked at her and said, "Look, I don't want to come off as pushy, but I know this is a tough moment. So would you like me to call your sister for you, or is there a friend you could invite over? I'm not sure you should be alone right now."

"No. Thank you, Tucker," she replied wearily. "I'm okay. It's just that... Everything in my life is a shambles. I feel like such a total failure," she said. "Julie's gone, and I know deep in my heart that she's dead. And I don't know what to do. It's like... where do I go from here?"

Tucker let out a deep breath. "I'm so sorry, Mallory," he said, reaching out to touch her hand briefly. "Under the circumstances, I don't know what else we could have done, but I want you to understand something. Can you look at me for a second?"

She turned her head and looked at him.

"You did everything you possibly could," he said gently. "For five days, you searched the forest. You found Julie's Bronco. You found and organized all the information that we used to get us to this point. You... are amazing."

"And what good was it all?" she asked, turning her head away.

"If it wasn't for you," he insisted, "we wouldn't be where we are now. Julie disappeared without a trace. I mean... *without a trace!*"

"And now it's too late to do anything," she muttered.

"No. You're wrong," he said.

She looked back at him. His face was set.

"*I'm* not going to quit," he said. "I didn't start this, but I sure as hell am going to finish it." He hesitated for a second, then continued, "And you've been a huge help. Will you work with me a little longer?"

She shrugged. "I don't know, Tucker. I need to sleep on it. Maybe in the morning... I don't know," she repeated. "I'll need to think about it. Julie's dead. I knew that more than a week ago, but I ignored it. I knew Julie didn't run away."

She opened the car door and paused. "But thanks for all you've done and for your kind words. You're…" She closed her eyes and shook her head. "You're the first person to take me seriously in a very long time." And, not knowing what else to say, she closed the door and walked up onto her porch, hesitated at the screen, then turned and watched Tucker go to his car and drive away. She didn't notice the dilapidated pickup parked at the side of her house. Neither did Tucker.

She heaved a sigh, turned again to the screen door, opened it and heard barking in the kitchen.

"Annie," she called. "It's me. I'm home. What is it? Why are you barking?" she said as she walked into the kitchen to find the dog at the back door.

"What the…" She pushed open the back door. Annie rushed past her. She flipped on the outside light and saw Zach Burns lying face down on the deck.

"Help me," he slurred.

"Oh, my God. What happened?" she shouted as she dropped to her knees beside him. "Annie. Get away. Go on, move. Go!" Then she looked down at Zach and saw all the blood.

"Wait, wait, wait," she cried as she jumped to her feet and ran into the house to get some towels. *No, not towels!* she thought. *Too absorbent. They'll suck the blood out.* She rummaged around in her utility room, found some clean rags and grabbed a roll of packing tape. It was all she could think of.

She ran back outside, dropped to her knees beside him and said, "Zach. I need you to sit up, okay?" as she tried to lift the big man. Somehow—she never did know how—she managed to get him upright. As he leaned back against the deck rail, she opened his shirt and covered the wounds—five tiny punctures to the chest—with a pad made from the rags.

"Zach," she said, "I need you to hold it in place, tightly, while I tape it, okay?"

He placed his enormous hand over the rags as she fought to get the packing tape to unroll, then she reached around him—he was so big she could barely make it—grabbed the end of the tape with one hand

and unrolled it with the other, taping his shirt and the pad of rags in place.

"Take your hand away," she said.

Weakly, he pulled his hand out from under his shirt and let it drop to his side.

"Hold up your hands, both of them, up, up. That's it. Now then," she said, as she wrapped the entire roll around his massive chest.

"Now, we need to call an ambulance and get you to a hospital—" she began.

"No" he shouted. Mallory, startled, took two steps back. "No hospital," he whispered.

"Zach, you're hurt bad," she said. "You've lost a lot of blood. We need to get you help."

"No… hospitals," he gasped. "No… hospitals."

Oh, my God. What am I going to do?

Maybe I could drive him to the ER at Erlanger, pretending that... No, that won't work. If he sees something he doesn't like, he might try to fight me while I'm driving, or jump out and run away.

"Okay, no hospitals," she agreed. "But I know someone who can help. Can I take you somewhere to get help?"

"Who to?" Zach asked.

"Someone I know. I trust him." She looked at her watch. It was almost five. "There's still time," she muttered to herself. "Come on," she said and grabbed his arm and lifted, trying to support him. "You're going to have to help me, Zach. You're too big for me to lift."

His face flickered through a series of emotions, none of which Mallory could decipher, until finally he nodded and said, "Okay." He gasped. "Julie likes you. She said she trusts you."

Somehow, she managed to get him through the house, down the porch steps and into the passenger seat. Then she ran around the truck and hopped in behind the wheel. It was only then that she noticed her white top was covered in blood.

Oh, my God, she thought for the umpteenth time as she turned the key, fired up the motor, rammed the gearshift into reverse and careened backward out onto the highway. *What the hell could have happened to him?*

"Zach," she said, glancing at him as she drove west on East Brainerd Road. "Look at me. What happened? Who shot you?"

"Don't know," he replied. "Poacher in the woods, maybe. I was looking for turkey. I didn't see him. He just shot me. I fell down. Got up. Ran. Came to find you. Only one I trust."

She thought about the blood on her back deck and shuddered. "What did he shoot you with, a shotgun?"

He was silent for a few moments, sucking in air, then he said, "Yeah. I think so. He only got me a little. I'll be alright."

She glanced sideways at him. He didn't look alright.

Ten minutes later, she swerved into Dr. Wilson's parking lot. It was almost six o'clock, and the lot was clear except for the doctor's Cadillac and a little Honda.

"Wait here, Zach," she said and leaped out of the truck and dashed inside.

The receptionist's desk was empty. *Where's Linda?* But she had no time to ponder that.

"Dr. Wilson," she called as she leaned just past the lobby threshold. "Dr. Wilson, help! I need some help, please."

She heard some shuffling beyond the closed door, and a clang as if something had fallen to the ground, and then the door opened and a harried-looking Dr. Wilson came out into the reception area.

"Mallory," he snapped. "I might have known. What is it you want?" he demanded, his face flushed.

"Someone's badly hurt," she said. "In my truck." She almost told him it was Zach, but knowing the prejudice that surrounded him, she thought better of it. "He's in my truck," she repeated.

The doctor paused, stared at her, and then his lips curled into a slight smile and his eyes seemed to brighten. He nodded and said, "I'll be right out. Let me just grab my..." And he turned on his heel and disappeared back the way he'd come.

She ran back out to her truck. "It's going to be okay, Zach," she said through the open window. "The doctor's on his way."

Zach merely groaned in pain. His eyes remained shut.

"Zach?" she said, grabbing his arm through the window. "Zach. Wake up. I want you to know something, all right? Tucker and I, we found Julie's Bronco today. It… it was… Julie's dead, Zach. I just know she is. Whatever you and she had… I'm glad she found someone she cared about."

The sound of a car starting caught her attention. *Is that the doctor leaving?* she wondered, turning to look at his car. *Why would he...* But it wasn't the doctor's car. It was the little red Honda.

"And I'm sorry I yelled at you," she continued, hoping that this wasn't the last time she would be able to say the things she needed to get off her chest. "I've just been so upset about not finding Julie. And you were really helpful. I hope… I hope that—"

"You know what I hope," a voice said behind her. "I hope this love fest isn't going to take much longer. I have things to do and places to be."

Mallory turned and found herself staring into the barrel of a pistol, and behind the pistol stood a smiling Dr. John Wilson.

"I was hoping for Tucker Randall," he said with a laugh. "But hah! You brought Zach to me instead. Hopefully, the third time will, indeed, be the charm."

27

Monday afternoon 6pm

It was around five-thirty that afternoon when Tucker left Mallory at her home. She'd had little to say to him during the drive home from Maryville, and she had said only a little more to him other than goodbye when he left her, but he understood. And, as he drove back to his office, despite his promise to Mallory to stay on the job until the end, he somehow couldn't help but feel that he'd failed, again.

How did I fail? he thought. *You were supposed to find her, that's how, and you haven't, is how.* He shook his head. *There wasn't even a ten-percent chance, ever, that we'd find her alive. I knew that. And even Mallory said she knew that. So yeah, you failed, Tucker. Damn missing person cases; never again.*

Maybe Mallory and her supreme optimism had affected him a little. Maybe her professed certainty that she would find her niece and that everything would turn out well had persuaded him to believe it, too, at least a little.

It wouldn't take much. You wanted in the worst way to find this Marsha Cline lookalike, hale and hearty.

He finally made it back to his office, got out of his car and walked inside, feeling a little like a stranger in his own space. *I don't really want to be here, do I?* he thought, looking around. *Mallory's all torn up. Everything in her life has been ripped apart, her world turned upside down, and here I am, home alone. Screw it. I'm going for a drink.*

He turned around to leave again, but then he heard the all-too-familiar voice. "Mr. Randall?"

"Oh, hey, Debbie," he said as he turned back around. "I'm sorry. I didn't expect you to be here. Have I had any calls today?"

"Just one. But I need to tell you something. My Ben had a really bad fall yesterday."

"Oh, Debbie. I'm sorry to hear that," Tucker said. He'd met Ben several times. He was a hearty, smiling, and garrulous man who, given half a chance, would talk your ear off about whatever he'd been watching on the History Channel.

"I had to call the ambulance, and he's been at Erlanger since last night."

"But why didn't you tell me this… oh," Tucker said. "I left before you got here this morning, didn't I? But you could have called if you needed some time off."

"No, sir. I need to take more than just some time off. I need to leave, Mr. Randall. I'm sorry, but I have to resign… and I was hoping you'd let me leave at the end of the week. I'll tidy up all the loose ends and—"

"You want to resign? Because you need to take care of Ben," he said. "It must have been a really bad fall."

"They don't know if he can complete the physical therapy once the bones heal," she said.

"Oh… Debbie, I don't know what to say," he said. "Of course, I'll do whatever I can to help. You've been with me for too long for me to… Look, if there's anything you need, anything I can do."

"I appreciate that, Mr. Randall," she said with a tiny smile. "And I know you mean it, but I won't ask for anything unless it's absolutely necessary."

"I understand." *And that's why she didn't call me. Because she's the kind of woman who likes to deal with her problems herself. I'm going to miss her.*

"Well, visiting hours are until eight tonight," Debbie said, "and I promised I would come by. I'll see you in the morning, Mr. Randall," she said as she walked out the door.

He sighed and began to shuffle some of the papers on his desk. He was about to leave again to go for the drink he'd promised himself when his phone rang. He took it out of his pocket, looked at the screen. The number was unfamiliar. He was about to decline it when something told him not to. He frowned. *Who is this?*

"Hello, Tucker Randall speaking," he said.

"Mr. Randall?" the voice was female and somewhat familiar, but not one he recognized. "You said to call you if I thought…" the woman continued. "If I thought there was anything you should know. Well, there is."

"I'm sorry. Who am I speaking to?"

"It's Linda Warner," the voice whispered.

"Oh, yes. My apologies. It's been a long day," he said. *And she sounds very different. Where's the spunky, defensive woman I met earlier today?*

"Look," she said, "I know I was… a little upset before. And… Well, we didn't have any appointments late in the day today. And I was supposed to lock the door, and I didn't… you see?"

"Um… Mrs. Warner?" Tucker said. "I don't mean to rush you, but—"

"Fine," Linda huffed. "But I thought you ought to know that your friend Mallory Carver came in a few minutes ago, before we'd… finished, and she was raving about someone being hurt. And John rushed out, then came back, grabbed something from his desk drawer and just told me to leave; to get my clothes on and leave."

But I just left Mallory less than forty-five minutes ago. What the hell? Who the hell, and… why didn't she call me for help?

"Thank you for calling me, Linda," Tucker said. "But why do I need to know about this?"

"Well, I was going over the new company credit card statement today," she said, "and two Saturdays ago, John used the clinic credit card to pay for an Uber. It was expensive; almost two hundred dollars. One hundred ninety-seven, to be precise."

"Why is that unusual?" Tucker asked, frowning, something at the back of his mind already tickling him.

"Because he always drives his car," she said. "He has a Cadillac. So when I asked him why he'd put it on the clinic card, he said he'd needed a ride for a couple of hours and got his cards mixed up and that I shouldn't worry about it. But I do. It's my job to worry about things like that."

And then it clicked, and Tucker suddenly realized the Bronco had been abandoned two hours away, in Maryville, and Gus at the scrapyard said it had been towed in more than a week ago.

"Where's Dr. Wilson now?" Tucker asked casually, not wanting to spook her.

"Well, I don't know. He's not at the clinic. I went back because, in my hurry to get out of there, I left my purse in the examination room. His car was there, but he wasn't. I guess he's working with Mallory and that gentleman who was in her truck," Linda replied.

"Did you see the man?" Tucker asked. "What did he look like?"

"I don't really know," she replied. "All I could see was that he looked... well, big? He was a big man."

Zach Burns? Has to be. But why did she take Zach Burns to—never mind.

"Linda, I hope you'll bear with me, but I need to ask you a very personal question," Tucker said. "Did the doctor ever take you somewhere... secluded? Somewhere where you two could be alone together?"

There was a moment of silence, and then, "Um... well... there were several different times—I don't remember exactly how many—when Stasia went on vacation without him," she said. "Well, anyway, that's when he first took me up to this little vacation cabin they have, the Burns family, that is. It's kind of small, so nobody ever uses it, at least that's what John told me. We've had some very nice weekends up there. And he seemed so happy, as if he'd spent his childhood there or something. I don't know. But that's where we went. Why d'you ask?"

"Linda, I need you to tell me exactly where that cabin is," Tucker said.

"But why—"

"Because the doctor's life might depend on me getting there in a hurry," he lied.

28

Monday evening 7:30pm

MALLORY COULDN'T STOP STARING AT THE GUN POINTING AT HER HEAD.

"Why are you doing this, Doctor Wilson?" she asked. "Why are you threatening Zach and me?"

"You? Because you're a nosy little busybody, Mallory Carver," Wilson snapped. "You always were a nasty little tyke. Him? I only ever meant to threaten him. He was the one who could unravel my life. If he'd just kept his mouth shut, none of this would ever have happened."

"Kept his mouth shut about what?" Mallory asked, her eyes wide with fear.

"There you go again," he snapped, glaring at her. "Just shut the hell up and... be quiet, or I'll shoot you both right here," He raised himself up, took his eyes off her for a moment, peered into the truck bed, then said, "Get that string stuff out and tie Burns' wrists together, tightly, and don't think I won't check."

He glanced around to make sure no one was watching.

"Come on, come on," he snapped. "Get him out of the truck and be quick about it."

Mallory did as she was told, helping Zach to slide out of the passenger seat. Then she took the baling twine from the truck bed and began wrapping it around Zach's wrists.

"Tightly now," Wilson snapped. "I'll be checking. I'm not one of those cartoon villains you see on TV. Tie it properly, tighter, yes, like that."

Oh, my God, Mallory thought. *He's flipped out. He's crazy.*

Mallory, not knowing what else to do, fearfully obeyed and did as she was told and tied Zach's wrists.

"Get out of the way," Wilson snapped and stepped forward and tugged at the bindings.

Seemingly satisfied, he nodded and said, "Now, you filthy animal, get in the back."

"What?" Mallory said. "He can't. He's injured. Can't you see?"

"Shut your mouth and help him. Do it *now!*" he snarled, waving the gun in her face.

"Oh dear," she muttered, taking Zach by the arm. "Come on, Zach. We have to do as he says."

Zach could barely stand, even with Mallory's help. He slipped as he tried to climb up and almost fell, but somehow she managed to get him seated on the tailgate and then watched him wriggle and squirm his way onto the truck bed where he lay breathing heavily, his shirt soaked with blood.

Wilson thrust the gun closer to Mallory's face and said, "Don't think I won't shoot you right in that pretty face. Now climb up there and tie his feet and be quick about it."

Again, Mallory did as she was told, wondering when, or if, she'd get a chance to make a grab for his gun. She was pretty sure she could take him, but she knew that one small slip and it could cost her her life—and Zach's. So she climbed up into the truck and tied his ankles.

"I'm sorry, Zach," she whispered. "It's going to be all right."

"Shut up," Wilson snapped. "Get back down here. Come on. Quickly now."

She'd been around guns most of her life, but this was the first time she'd ever had one pointed at her, and it unnerved her. She knew the slightest pressure on the trigger could end her life, and that if she was going to make a move, she had to be sure.

"Close the tailgate," Wilson said as he pointed the weapon at her.

Seven, maybe eight feet, she thought. *Too far to jump him and too close for him to miss.*

"Good," he said, the corners of his mouth turned down in a nasty grimace. "Now walk slowly around and get in. You're going to drive. Don't try anything or try to run. If you do, I'll shoot you dead."

He watched her every move until she'd climbed in behind the wheel, then he stepped up to the still-open passenger side door and said, "Good girl. Now put your hands on the wheel while I get in."

Mallory gripped the wheel tightly with both hands, trying to analyze his movements, watching for an opportunity to grab the gun.

"Good girl," he said as he closed the passenger door. Now," he continued, half turned in his seat so that he was facing her, the gun in his lap pointing at her, his finger on the trigger. "I want you to drive. If you cooperate, maybe I'll give you a little reward. And don't worry, I won't keep you up too late." His suggestive leer made her shiver.

"Why do you think I would cooperate with you?" she snapped. *Oh, my God. He is. He's off his rocker. What am I going to do? My phone...*

"I need your phone, Mallory," he said as if reading her mind. "Hand it over."

"Why? Why d'you want my phone?"

"Mallory," he said gently. Then, "*Hand it over!*" he shouted.

She jumped, startled, then took out her phone and handed it across to him.

"That's a good girl," he said as he powered it off.

Hah, they can still track it, you crazy bastard.

"Now drive," he said. "Take I-75 north to Exit 20. Do *not* exceed the speed limit, and don't do any sudden braking. Go."

Mallory took a deep breath, put the truck in reverse, made a left turn, drove to Lee High, turned north to Bonnyoaks, made a right and took the ramp onto I-75 going north.

"Why did Zach need to keep his mouth shut?" she asked.

"What?" Wilson said as if waking from a dream.

"Why did he need to keep his mouth shut?"

"Why?" He glanced sideways at her. "Because I killed his mother," he said with a smile. "Sad, really," he continued reflectively. "I really enjoyed Jim Burns' little harpy. Never could understand why he knocked her up in the first place."

It was then Mallory knew he intended to kill them both. She bit her lip, and the truck sped up. *Oh, Lord. I have to do something—*

"Slow down," he snapped. "You're doing seventy-seven."

"But if you didn't like her, why sleep with her?" Mallory asked.

"Oh, don't dignify it with a word like sleep," Wilson scoffed. "I made her a deal. I cover up the fact that she brained her husband to death with a cast iron skillet, and she let me visit her whenever I… needed to, at her place. It's what we now call the 'family cabin,' though nobody ever goes there now, except for me—whenever I… needed to. It wasn't like Jim didn't deserve it anyway. He was a wicked little shit. And that nasty look she gave me every time…" He grinned at Mallory. "Boy, that was fun. I enjoyed having her bent around my little finger."

"But why did you kill her?" Mallory asked, trying to keep him talking while she tried to figure out a way to… *To what?* she thought. *He's a frickin' maniac. A total whack job.*

"It was her fault," he replied reflectively. "The silly bitch allowed herself to get *pregnant!*" Wilson shouted.

Mallory flinched, glanced at him and saw that, for some strange reason, he was smiling.

"She claimed it was some other man," Wilson continued, staring out through the windshield, and for a moment, Mallory considered making a grab for the gun. But then he looked at her and said, "But I knew better, you see. And if there was ever a paternity test that pointed to me, Stasia would ruin me. I'd be left with nothing." He shrugged and then continued.

"So I killed her. I cut her throat. Zach was outside in the woods, but he came back. I hit him over the head with a brass candlestick. He went down like a sack of shit. I hit him again. I thought he was dead.

So I dragged Wynona's body out into the backyard, then came back for Zach. But he was gone. He must have run off into the woods. Head like a rock, that boy..."

He paused for a moment, then said, "Take Exit 20 and drive to Highway 64 and head east—"

"You're taking us to the forest," she said, interrupting him.

"I'm taking you to the family cabin," he replied. "You'll like it there. It's nice. Nobody ever goes there now, except for me." He paused again. Mallory glanced at him as she drove up the ramp and turned east onto APD-40.

"I never knew why anyone showed up out there the next day and found Zach semi-conscious. That was a puzzle I never did solve. Hmm."

What the hell am I going to do? Mallory was getting desperate. She knew if she didn't do something soon, she was going to die, or worse, be raped and then die. But somehow, she wasn't scared; just desperately trying to figure out how to get the gun away from him.

"Why didn't you kill Zach while he was still at school?" she asked, trying to keep him talking.

"Oh, I was going to, first chance I got. But you see, I was a psychiatrist back then—I have two medical degrees, you know—and, being as I was already treating him for depression, they asked me to do a psychological assessment. It was then I realized he was suffering from disassociative amnesia and—"

"And you could hardly kill him while he was in custody, could you?" Mallory asked sarcastically.

"See? You get it," he replied. "Ah, but you're disgusted. I like that... You know, my current... partner is a little lacking, shall we say? I don't suppose... No, I didn't think so. Oh well, never mind. It was just a thought."

Mallory refused to dignify that with a response. "So why didn't you kill Zach? You must have had plenty of chances over the years."

"You're right," he replied. "I really should have taken care of him a decade ago. But he never said anything until a few months ago; back before Christmas, it was. I thought he'd forgotten all about it, but I was out walking one of the trails and I heard someone shout, 'You killed my mother.' I looked around and saw him. I went after him, but he disappeared into the woods; good thing too, because if I'd caught him, he probably would have killed me. After that, I always carried my twelve-gauge shotgun with me."

"Then what happened?" Mallory asked. "Why now?"

"The second time I saw him, I heard a sneeze and then an arrow hit the tree next to my head. My turn to run," he said with a grin. "I caught sight of him a couple of times after that, but he always managed to get away, until yesterday afternoon, that is. I ran across him on the Cross Creek trail. I fired, and I hit him. I know because he staggered and then ran off. I reloaded, but he was gone. I thought he'd crawled away and died, but obviously, he didn't. Looking at him, though, he should have… a smaller man would have… But never mind," he said brightly. "No harm, no foul. I have him now, and I can finish the job."

How long had he been lying on my porch, I wonder?

"You killed Julie, didn't you?" she whispered.

He sucked in a breath through his teeth, making a hissing sound. "That was unfortunate," he said. "Your niece was a tall girl. I saw her at the Red Grove North trailhead, not far from my cabin. She was wearing the same jacket Zach was wearing when he shouted at me. It was overcast, dark under the trees. I thought she was him. I had this with me." He lifted the pistol from his lap and then let it rest on his knee again.

She said she was going to hike Red Grove East, Mallory thought. *Why did she change her mind?*

"I couldn't believe how lucky I was," he continued. "There was no one around. The place was deserted, as it usually is. I shot her three times. Then I saw the dog. I shot at it, but I missed and it ran away. Then I realized what I'd done. It was a stupid mistake, but…" He shrugged. "What can you do? I shoved her body in the Bronco and drove to the cabin and—"

"And you buried her body and drove her Bronco to Maryville, where you dumped it behind a strip mall," Mallory finished for him.

"Well, we found it this morning at a scrap yard, and the sheriff's sent a truck to recover it. They'll know it was you. They'll find something; they always do."

"Hah! Good luck with that," Wilson said, smiling. "I wore gloves, and even if they do, Cundiff will have to cover for me. He owes me big time."

"You mean," she said as she suddenly realized, "you know about the sheriff and his—"

"Who do you think subsidizes his family operations?" Wilson laughed. "Not me personally, of course. But the Burns family, the Alexanders, the Lawrys; they all have their fingers in all sorts of pies around here. Cundiff might make money moving things, but he works for Carmichael Burns."

No wonder Cundiff didn't want to investigate Julie's disappearance, Mallory thought. *Somehow I've got to get out of this mess.*

"Well, here we are," Wilson said. "Take a right at the mailbox and stop in front of the cabin."

Mallory pulled the truck gently to a stop so as to not spook the man with the gun.

"Now get out slowly," he said. "And leave the door open."

She did as she was instructed, knowing that this was the moment she might be able to make a break for it and lose the doctor in the woods.

But I can't leave Zach behind to die.

No, she wouldn't do that. She decided to bide her time and hope she could find an opportunity to save them both. Unfortunately, that decision was made for her.

Wilson opened his door and slid out carefully. "You've done fine so far, Mallory," he said. "Last chance. I'd love to keep you around a little longer," he continued as he walked slowly around the back of the truck, the gun pointed at Zach. "What do you say? You want to stay and play. I'd make it worth your while and, of course… you'd live," he finished with an evil smile.

She had no idea how to answer him. She knew she had to try to persuade him she wouldn't try to kill him the first chance she got. But then...

"Hmm," he said and sucked in a breath through his teeth, shaking his head. "Too late, Mallory. Even in the dark, the look on your face tells me everything. Oh, well. Never mind."

He glanced into the pickup bed, aimed, and pulled the trigger.

"NOOOO!" Mallory screamed.

29

Monday evening 8pm

TUCKER RANDALL MADE GOOD TIME UNTIL HE MADE THE TURN OFF Highway 64 and headed toward Greasy Creek and then Kimsey Mountain Highway.

"Highway," he muttered as he negotiated the narrow, heavily forested, two-lane up the mountain. "What a frickin' joke that is."

It was the first time he'd driven this route, and he didn't know the area. He didn't know if there were deer on the road. And, even though it was only just after eight o'clock, and it was still light, he had to have his headlights on. It was a thirty-mile-an-hour road and he was doing sixty, and he'd had his teeth gritted all the way, so much so his jaw was aching. He took the bends too fast, almost losing control twice. He even passed a red car on one of the bends, gritting his teeth and half-closing his eyes as he did so. *How far ahead can they be?* he wondered as he fishtailed another tight bend. *Whoa! There it is... I think.*

He almost missed the turn. He slammed on the brakes and went skidding to a stop, tires screeching.

He backed up a little and checked the mailbox. *Yes! This is it,* he thought as he hauled down hard on the wheel and made a right onto the narrow dirt track.

Come on... come on, come on, he thought savagely as he negotiated the track and the overhanging tree limbs, branches brushing both sides of his SUV. And all the while, just one thought was running through his mind. *Please let me get there before he kills her,* over and over.

He crested a rise, entered a small clearing, and there it was, Mallory's pickup, directly in front of him. He hit the brakes and skidded to a stop just as a gunshot rang out. "No!" he shouted as he pushed the car door open and jumped out—just in time to hear a second gunshot. Without pausing to think, he yanked the Glock from his shoulder holster and ran forward.

"Well, lookie here," he heard a voice call out. "By all the luck in the stars. Tucker Randall. How fortuitous."

"It's all over, doctor," Tucker called back. "I know what you did."

"Hah. You do, huh? No one will believe you." Wilson laughed. "I'm a lauded member of the community. I'm a generous doctor with a rich family. And the sheriff's covering for me. And you, you're just a two-bit hack who likes seeing himself on television—"

"And you're a frickin' psycho. Let, me, go, you monster," he heard Mallory shout.

Tucker blew out a breath to steady himself. *Whew! Thank God. She's still alive. The sheriff? What the hell?*

"I called the state police," Tucker shouted. "They're on their way," Tucker lied.

"You're full of shit, Randall," Wilson shouted. "I don't believe you. Now, if you want this little bitch to live, step forward, slowly."

"I have a gun, and it's pointed right at you," Tucker shouted. "Let her go and give yourself up."

"That's not going to happen. I also have a gun, and it's pointed at her pretty little head. Now step forward where I can see you or I'll blow her brains out."

"Shoot him, Tucker," Mallory yelled. "Shoot the crazy son of a bitch."

"Now, now, Mallory," Wilson said mildly. "There's no need for that kind of language. I said come forward, Randall. If you don't, I swear I'll shoot her in the head."

Cautiously, Tucker walked slowly forward until he could see Wilson with Mallory in front of him, his arm around her neck and a gun at her ear.

"Drop your gun, Randall."

"So you can shoot me?" Randall replied, his Glock aimed at what little he could see of the doctor. "I don't think so. No matter what you do next, you're done. You're not going to get away with it."

"You think?" he snapped. "With you two out of the way, who's to know?"

"I told you, the state troopers are on their way," Tucker lied, waiting for an opening. "I told them where the bodies are buried."

Wilson frowned, looked worried for a moment, then said, "Bullshit! As I said, I don't believe you. Now drop the gun or—"

He was interrupted by the sound of an engine. Tucker resisted the urge to turn, but then headlights cut through the dusk, lighting up Mallory's truck and the two figures in front of it.

"Who's that?" Wilson yelled. "Who did you bring with you?"

"I didn't bring anybody," Tucker replied.

The car pulled up beside his SUV. He glanced to his left. It was red, a red Honda Civic. *That's the car I passed on the way up here. It's Linda. What the hell?*

The car door opened, and she stepped out and shouted, "John? John, what are you doing? Have you gone mad?"

"Linnie? What the hell are you doing here?" Wilson shouted. "Go away."

"John, why are you doing this?" she asked. "And where did you get that gun?"

Wilson took the gun away from Mallory's ear and swept it back and forth, pointing it first at Linda, then at Tucker.

Tucker decided enough was enough. He fired a shot low and to the left, hoping to distract Wilson.

Mallory's driver's side front tire exploded. Wilson jerked, startled by the unexpected bang just to his right, and Mallory exploded into action. She grabbed Wilson's wrist with both hands, ripped it away from her throat, spun around, whipped his arm up and over her head, spun around again and slammed her forearm down on the back of the doctor's left elbow as hard as she could. Even in the echoes of the gunshot, Tucker heard the crunch of broken bone. He couldn't believe how quickly Mallory had moved.

Wilson dropped his gun and screamed. "AAAHHH. Oh crap oh crap oh crap. You broke my arm. You stupid bitch. You broke my fricking arm. Ugh!" He gasped as Mallory landed a vicious kick to his ribs, and he crumpled forward and fell to the ground.

"Mallory, stop!" Tucker yelled as she reared back for another kick. "We need him alive."

"No, we don't," she yelled as her foot slammed into the doctor's chest again.

Tucker holstered his weapon, ran forward, and grabbed her before she could land another blow. "Mallory, it's over. We did it," he said.

"We didn't do anything, Tucker," she snapped. He could see the tears rolling down her cheeks. "He killed Julie. He killed Zach. He killed Zach's mother."

Tucker pulled her close as she began to sob uncontrollably. "I know, Mallory. I know."

He looked around and saw Linda Warner on her knees beside Wilson.

"Why did you do this, John?" she asked as he moaned in pain. "Why did you kidnap that girl? How could you? You're a doctor."

"Just covering other people's mistakes," he mumbled. "Can't trust anyone anymore."

"But I thought you trusted me," she whispered. "I thought you loved me."

The doctor half choked, half laughed, and then gasped. "Are you serious, you stupid… OW," he yelped as she punched his broken elbow.

Tucker heaved a deep breath, kicked Wilson's gun under Mallory's truck, then took out his phone and called 911.

"9-1-1, what's your emergency?"

"This is Tucker Randall," he said. "I'm a private investigator. I'm at a house on Kimsey Mountain Road. I need an ambulance, the state police—not the sheriff's department—and a cadaver dog unit." He gave her the full address and then waited for her response.

"You have a victim in need of medical attention. You also need the state police and a K-9 unit. Please confirm."

"No, not a victim," Tucker corrected. "A criminal."

"Message received and understood. Dispatching units to your location. Please stay on the line."

"He was right," Mallory said. "You didn't call the state police, did you?"

"Nope. I didn't," he said as he steered her toward the cabin. "Where's Zach Burns? I heard you say Wilson killed him."

"He's in the back of the truck," she replied, her voice breaking. "Wilson shot him just as you arrived."

"Are you sure he's dead?" Tucker asked.

"I think so. I think he shot him in the head."

"I'd better take a look," Tucker said. "Stay here."

He was back almost immediately. "Yes. He's dead. There's a bullet wound in his forehead. I'm sorry you had to witness that."

"I would have tried to get the gun away from him sooner, but I just didn't have an opportunity." Mallory sniffed. "Julie's dead, Tucker. He told me he killed her. I think she's here somewhere."

"If she is, they'll find her," Tucker said.

His phone crackled. "Are you there, Mr. Randall?"

"Yes, I'm here."

"The state police are on their way. ETA, seventeen minutes. How are things where you are?"

"Under control," Tucker replied.

"Thank you. Stay on the line please."

"Why did you blow out my tire?" Mallory said.

"Sorry," Tucker said. "I was trying to distract him."

"Well, you did. Thank you."

Tucker looked around the door of the cabin for a spare key but couldn't find one.

"Linda," he called. "Is there a key anywhere?"

"I'll get it," she said as she stood up and left the doctor's side.

She reached up and felt along the top of the picture window and found the key to a lock on a small garden shed. She went inside and retrieved the house key from under an old gas can.

Once inside the cabin, Mallory began pacing back and forth, a bundle of nervous energy.

"I'm really sorry, Mallory—" Tucker began.

But she waved him off. "I'm glad it's over," was all she said. And then continued pacing, her arms wrapped around herself, staring off into space.

Tucker inwardly shook his head. It had been a terrible ordeal with an explosive climax, literally. And he was dreading making the call to Jennifer and Jared Romero. At least they'd found Julie… or soon would. Mallory, he knew, would insist on being present for the removal of Julie's remains, and the pain would tear her apart.

Tucker sat down on the couch in the living room to wait for the state police. He was quietly content, knowing that he'd arrived just in time to save Mallory, though unfortunately not Zach; but, as he looked around, he frowned. Something was bothering him. He had the feeling he'd been in the room before, but he knew he hadn't. He looked around again, then stood up, looked around again, and then it clicked. He pursed his lips, looked down at the rug, dropped to one knee and pulled back the corner of the rug to reveal a large, dark stain on the wood floor.

"What is that?" Mallory asked as she stepped to his side, her arms folded over her chest. "That's weird," she said. "It looks like… is that blood?"

"I think it must be where Wynona Burns was killed," he said. "I recognize the room from the crime scene photos; the rug, the pictures."

"He cut her throat," Mallory said. "He told me about it. She got pregnant. He didn't want that."

"I wish… I wish I could have done something more," Tucker said with a sigh as he dropped the rug back in place and stood up. “I feel like I haven’t accomplished… anything.”

“There’s nothing more you could have done. Julie was already dead when Jen hired you. Now we know where she is. Without you, we wouldn’t be here now. You saved my life, Tucker. I’m still here only because of you. Thank you.”

“You don’t need to thank me,” Tucker replied.

He looked around the room again, then said, “This isn’t just where he brought his dates. It’s where he brought his victims: Wynona, Zach, Julie and… you, and… maybe they’ll find more bodies out there.” He stared out the window and then continued, “He brought you and Zach here to kill you… You know, Linda said he seemed happy here.”

“Maybe this was the only place he ever felt fully in control,” Mallory whispered. “Bad marriage, endless patient problems…”

“A failing practice,” Tucker added, “one affair after another.” He sighed. “But this isn’t how I thought it would end.”

“They’re coming,” Mallory said. “I can hear the sirens.”

“I hear them, too,” Tucker said. “It’s time. Come on. Let’s go.”

And they stepped out into the flashing lights.

EPILOGUE

Six months later

MALLORY CARVER WAS SEATED IN THE FRONT ROW OF THE COURTROOM alongside her sister Jennifer, Jared, their daughter Katie, and her husband. Their son Justin and his wife Jackie were seated in the row behind. Tucker Randall and Linda Warner were seated together two rows back.

It had been a while since Mallory had last seen Tucker, and it made her happy to see him now, even if it was under such stressful circumstances.

Judge Andrew Grayson, something of a fixture in the local judiciary system, was a tough, no-nonsense old bird known for his harsh sentences. The trial was over, and all that was left was the sentencing.

The judge nodded to the bailiff, then fixed his beady eyes on the defense table.

"The defendant will rise," the bailiff called.

The doctor and his defense team rose to their feet.

"John Robert Wilson, having been found guilty on all charges. On count one, that you did willfully murder Wynona Iris Burns, I hereby sentence you to prison for the rest of your life. On count two..." and so it went on until the doctor had accrued three life sentences plus fifty years, all to run consecutively and without the possibility of parole.

And for the first time in seven months, Mallory breathed her first truly free breath. "It's really over, isn't it?" she asked Jen.

Jen smiled at her and said, "Yes, it's over."

"I should have figured it out sooner," Mallory said. "I could have—"

"You did everything you could. More than I ever thought possible," Jen said, wrapping her arms around her. "It's not your fault. You... You and Mr. Randall, you found her, and that's all that matters. We were able to bring her home. Thank you, Mallory."

But the truth was, Mallory Carver couldn't get over the fact that she didn't notice Julie drifting away from her or how, knowing Kal Cundiff as well as she did, she never knew about the Cundiff family's nefarious operations.

Neither Kal nor his father, nor any member of the family had been charged with anything. The only evidence against them was the stories Tucker and Mallory told the state police, but as Tucker had known all along, it was all hearsay, and the powerful Burns, Alexander and Lawry families closed ranks, and the stories were officially deemed the stuff of urban legend. In other words, they got away with it.

So, Mallory thought, *I guess I'll just have to believe that we did everything we could.*

Finally, after the court cleared, Mallory wished her sister well and walked slowly out into the lobby, where she bumped into Tucker, who was talking to Linda Warner.

"So, *Mr. Randall,* Mrs. Warner. How are you both?" she asked. "How's the latest case going? How d'you like working for Tucker?"

"Hah!" Tucker said. "You haven't changed a bit, Mallory. Still with the questions." He smiled at her, stepped forward and gave her a quick hug. "It's so nice to see you again. How've you been?"

"I asked first," Mallory said. "How are you two getting along?"

Linda rolled her eyes. "He's fine. He misses you. Talks about you all the time."

"No, I don't," he snapped.

"Yes, you do. Why only yest—"

"That's enough, Linda," he said, smiling.

"As to your query, yes, I'm fine… except for my back. I think I need to see a chiropractor and—"

"Oh, I know someone," Mallory said. "Jemma Moon, occupational injury and massage therapist. Do you want her card?"

Tucker looked uncomfortable. "Um… Mallory. No! After what happened last time. No thank you. No offense, but I think I'll find one for myself if you don't mind."

"Oh, come on," Mallory retorted. "That was—"

"Yes, I know," Tucker said, interrupting her. "Well, it was nice to see you again. I, that is we, need to be going. Linda?"

"Just a minute, sir," Linda said. "I need a quick word with Mallory."

"I'll be outside. Look after yourself, Mallory. Call me if you need me," Tucker said, then turned and walked away.

"He really is spooked, isn't he?" Mallory asked.

"Not as much as he puts on, I think," Linda said with a smile. "Well, are you ready for tomorrow?"

Mallory couldn't hide her smirk. "You bet I am."

By eight-thirty the following morning, Tucker was in his office, ready to peruse his list of potential cases.

He'd taken a long, hot shower, dressed in tan pants and a white shirt—open neck, no tie—eaten a light breakfast of two scrambled eggs on toast, drank two cups of coffee and then went to his office to find Linda was already there, as she had been for the last five months. *She's been a miracle,* Tucker thought.

When Debbie left, he didn't think he'd find anybody to replace her, not so quickly, anyway. But there Linda was, no job, highly experienced and needing work, so he'd hired her on the spot.

He spent a half-hour looking at the half-dozen files Linda had left for him the day before. *A missing show dog in Indiana worth $15,000? Hmm, interesting. A stolen Mercedes; pass. A possible affair in Ohio; well, he's worth enough, and if she wins...*

Linda popped her head in the doorway. "Mr. Randall? D'you have a minute, please?"

"Sure, come on in. Sit down. What's up?"

"I'm afraid I'm going to have to leave you."

"What?" he said, his head snapping up to look at her. "Oh no. Look, if you need a vacation or something—"

"Uh-uh," she said, shaking her head. "I was happy to help out for a little while," she explained, "but this isn't what I want to be doing anymore. It reminds me of… well, you know."

I know all too well! "Wow, this is… sudden. Are you giving me a two-week notice? I suppose I'd better put out an ad or something."

"Oh, I already did that, sir. And I've already interviewed my replacement. She's a real go-getter, very organized, and likes to be involved. I think you'll find she's just what you're looking for."

"You did, huh?" Tucker replied skeptically, and then it began to dawn on him. "Now wait a—"

"I've already explained the job to her in detail," Linda continued, "and I'm certain you'll find her to be well-qualified."

"You must think I'm—" The door opened. "Oh no," he said.

Mallory stepped into the office, smiling widely, and sat down next to Linda. She was wearing a blouse and skirt, and her hair was piled up on top of her head in a way he hadn't seen before.

Tucker heaved a huge sigh, leaned back in his chair, shook his head, and gave up. He knew when he was beaten.

"Good morning, *Ms. Carver,*" he said dryly, thinking she was so dressed up she barely looked like herself.

"Mornin', *Tuck,*" she said with an impish smile. "How's my timing, Linda?"

"About ten seconds late, but acceptable," Linda replied.

"So you two cooked this thing up between you?" Tucker asked. "But why? All you had to do was ask for the job."

The two women shared a glance and smirked. "And I'm sure you mean that, sir," Linda said. "And I'm really pleased, for the both of you, but no. No notice. Ms. Carver, as you call her, can start today. I do have something waiting for me. I have a date at noon."

"Ooh, with who?" Mallory asked. "Or should I say, whom?" she asked, lifting her chin and smiling at Tucker.

"Excuse me?" Tucker said. "Aren't we forgetting that you two conspired to cut me out of the hiring decision for my own business?"

"And can you think of a single reason why you shouldn't hire me?" Mallory asked.

"Oh, I can think of several reasons—" he retorted. But then he looked at her. She had a new confidence about her, and her eyes were smiling at him.

"Oh, hell," he said. "Okay, but I can't have you going around dressed like that. You'll scare the clients to death. The top's fine, but if you're going to accompany me out in the field, you'll need to wear pants and not those damn skinny things."

Mallory cocked an eyebrow. "Out in the field, *sir?* I thought I was going to be your secretary."

"Oh come on, Mallory," he said. "If you think, that I think, that you're going to sit in here while I'm out in the field, then you must also think that I'm as stupid as I look."

Linda laughed. "Well, on that note," Linda said and stood up, "if you'll excuse me, I need to head home and put on something entirely inappropriate. I want to see if I can make Howard O'Neal's eyes pop out."

"Howard O—" Mallory looked confused for a moment and then, "Wait! You mean *Howie?*"

"What can I say?" Linda shrugged. "I met him at that horrible bar where you used to work. He's been lonely a long time. And we… sort of clicked." She tossed her head and said, "Well, ta-ta, then. Don't you two do anything I wouldn't do… Oh no. Ignore that. There's nothing I wouldn't do." And with a big smile, Linda swept out of the office.

Tucker sighed. "Geez," he said, shaking his head. "So when did you two get together to cook this up?"

"Actually, about five months ago," Mallory said. "I would have started earlier, but I needed to take care of a few things first. I had to make arrangements for my house and generally help Jen through the worst time of her life. But I'm ready now."

"What do you mean, arrangements for your house?" Tucker asked.

"Katie's pregnant, and she wanted to move back here. And since I was taking this fabulous new job, I sublet my house to her."

Tucker frowned. "Why not just let her live there?"

"Would *you* do anything like that without getting it in writing? Which reminds me, here's my application."

She handed over the forms Linda had supplied. They were neatly filled out and impressive. Tucker nodded his head from side to side as he glanced through them, then put them away in his desk drawer.

"I can file those for you if you like," she said with that same impish smile on her lips and in her eyes.

"Later," Tucker said dryly. "You can do it later. Right now, we have work to do. If I'm going to be able to pay you, I need to find our next case… By the way, how much did Linda offer you?"

She opened her clutch, took out a piece of paper and slid it across the desk to him.

He glanced at it, then at her, and said, "Wow, you'd better be worth it."

"Oh, I am," she replied. "Now, about *our* next case," Mallory said with a smile. "I think you should skip to the bottom of the pile and look at the one about the coal mine sabotage in West Virginia."

"Why would I want to go to West Virginia?" Tucker asked.

"Take a look," Mallory insisted.

And as Tucker read the file, he realized it was just the kind of case he liked, a real David versus Goliath story, a large corporation trying to squeeze a competitor out.

"Okay," he said. "I'll give you a try. We'll see how you work out."

"I usually begin my workout with a five-mile run, then a couple of dozen seventy-pound bench presses, followed by a dozen fifty-pound squats," Mallory replied.

Tucker couldn't help but laugh. *Oh, this is going to change everything,* he thought. *But maybe change is exactly what I need.*

"Very well. Go ahead and give West Virginia a call," he said, smiling at her, "and tell them Randall and Carver are on the case."

THANK you so much for reading, ***Never Say Dead***, the first book in the Randall & Carver Mysteries series. I hope you enjoyed it! Keep reading with ***Happily Never After***.

HAPPILY NEVER AFTER

A RANDALL & CARVER MYSTERY BOOK 2

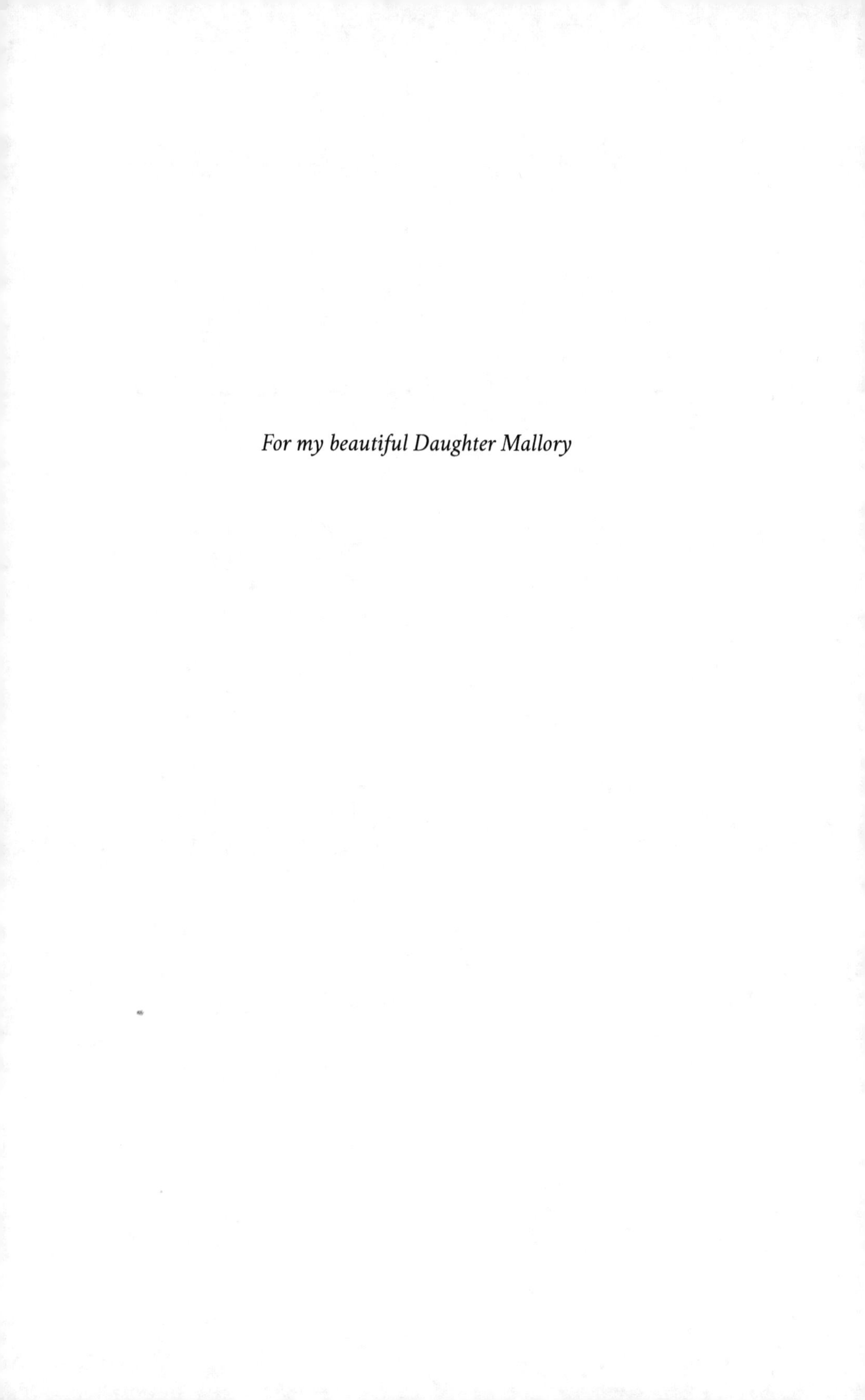

For my beautiful Daughter Mallory

PROLOGUE

Who killed Franny McNeer?

Extract from Thomas Drews' podcast dated March 15, 2022: *Who Killed Franny McNeer?*

...ASSUMING LUTHOR MCNEER DIDN'T KILL HIS WIFE AS HE HAS ALWAYS claimed, we must substitute "It" for "He" or "She" when referencing the killer. And I must warn you, I take a little literary license in my narrative.

At almost midnight on the evening of Friday, July 8, 2016, the killer crept into the McNeer bedroom. Franny McNeer was asleep, alone, in the marital bed, snoring softly, perhaps even dreaming.

The killer stood for a moment in the light of the full moon, staring down at her, knife in hand, then stepped around the bed, took a deep breath, raised the knife and plunged it through the covers into the sleeping woman's breast, and then withdrew it and plunged it again and again and again into Franny's body, each blow more savage than the one before until the killer, exhausted by its efforts, stepped away, blood dripping from the knife blade. Franny McNeer died quickly.

Nineteen of the forty-three stab wounds would have been fatal; this according to Dr. Sheddon, the Hamilton County Chief Medical Examiner. An act of rage, he called it, and rage it must have been for her assailant to stab her so many times.

We know from the bloody footprints that, eventually, the killer took a step back, and the knife, slippery with blood, slid from its fingers and fell to the floor. The killer then turned away and walked quickly and silently from the room, leaving a trail of bloody footprints on the carpet. Franny McNeer, her eyes wide, stared sightlessly up at the ceiling.

Two days later, Luthor McNeer, Franny's husband, was arrested and charged with her murder. It was Luthor who discovered his wife's body. He claimed to have been asleep downstairs on the couch in the living room when something disturbed him and he went upstairs and found her in their blood-soaked bed. He immediately went to her and held her in his arms, but it was too late.

Luthor, now with blood on his clothes and his shoes, called the emergency services and was found standing beside the bed. Of course, he claimed he had nothing to do with her death, but his was the only DNA found at the scene, and there were no signs of an intruder, even though Luthor swore all the doors and windows were locked. The knife handle, slick with the victim's blood, was devoid of fingerprints.

Was Luthor McNeer asleep on the couch as he claims? Was it an intruder that brutally murdered Franny McNeer? In either case, the police didn't think so, and Luthor had no explanation as to why he'd slept through the horrific murder. He denied he was drunk, and blood analysis proved it to be true. Nor were there drugs in his system. So how could he have slept through it all? Luthor himself has no explanation.

Luthor was tried for his wife's murder and was found guilty and sentenced to twenty-five years to life imprisonment. He always claimed he was innocent. But if it wasn't him… who did kill Franny McNeer, and why?

1

Monday, November 18, 2024

8AM

"ANNIE, will you please get yourself in here?" Mallory shouted.

The dog stopped its sniffing, turned and gave her a look of disdain. Rarely did Mallory raise her voice to the Border Collie, but it was eight-thirty on a Monday morning in November. It was cold and drizzling with rain outside, and Mallory was not looking forward to the week ahead. Work of late had been, well, boring. A long-running financial investigation—one of Tucker's many fortes—three nasty divorce cases and a missing person case, only the person wasn't missing at all. She'd simply taken an unannounced leave of absence and had checked herself into a Benedictine convent for a month to "Find my inner self." Even so, it had taken all of Tucker's many skills to track her down, whereupon she'd told him in no uncertain terms to F off and leave her alone with the nuns.

Mallory, a one-time-bartender with a penchant for organization and true crime podcasts, had joined Tucker Randall's one-man organization almost a year earlier after he solved the disappearance of her beloved niece, Julie, with unwavering help from Mallory. Unfortunately, though, the investigation ended in tragedy when it was discovered that Julie had been murdered by Dr. John Williams, a local family GP.

Jennifer Romero, Mallory's older sister and Julie's mother, had hired Tucker, an ex-FBI special agent and something of a loner, to find her missing daughter. Mallory had, much to Tucker's chagrin, insisted on sticking her nose in. At first, he wanted nothing to do with Mallory or her in-depth research. But, as the case wore on, and Tucker, unused to the great outdoors, began to flounder and soon realized that Mallory was much more than the ditsy bartender he'd thought her to be. Thus was born an unusual alliance between the two, and, when the case was brought to its tragic conclusion, he offered her a job as a kind of junior partner. Little did he know what he was letting himself in for.

"Annie," Mallory snapped at the dog, her eyes narrowed, "if you don't come inside right now..." She let the threat dangle unfinished. Annie, smarter even than the average Border Collie, got the message and slunk past her into the office and over to her bed, where she sat down and stared defiantly at her mistress.

"I swear you get worse by the day," she muttered, then went to the door that opened into Randall's home, opened it and yelled, "TUCKER, are you coming, or what?" Then she turned away and went to her desk and sat down.

"Geez, what is wrong with you?" Tucker said as he walked through the door, his jacket over his arm. "You have a rough weekend or something?"

"No," she replied, "but we need to talk. We're hemorrhaging money, and these stupid divorce cases aren't helping. We need something more... meaty. Something we can get our teeth into. Something with a decent paycheck."

"Something *I* can get my teeth into, you mean," he replied with a grin.

"Oh, dear Lord," she said, rolling her eyes. "I'm doing all the work as it is and…" She paused, gave him a grossly exaggerated frown, and then continued. "Speaking of that. Isn't it time you gave me a raise?"

He made a face, shook his head and said, "And what would I pay you with? You just said we're… How did you put it? Oh, yes, hemorrhaging money." He grinned at her triumphantly.

She smiled sweetly at him and said, "How about from that rainy-day account you failed to tell me about?"

"But it's not raining—"

"Oh, yes, it is," she said. "Go outside and look."

"That's not what I meant, and you know it," he said, then sat down in the guest chair in front of his desk. "But you're right. We do need something to pump a little life into things, even if it means we have to travel. There's this thing we've been dodging in Shreveport; well, you've been dodging it."

"Tucker, there has to be plenty to do around here without us having to go gallivanting off into the bayous. Don't you think?"

"I'd hardly call Shreveport bayou country," he retorted. "And, if there's plenty to do around here, as you say, why aren't we getting any of it?"

"Because you're old-fashioned and won't let me do some marketing."

"Marketing? What do you know about marketing?"

"I know if people don't know you're here, they can't hire you," she said.

"So what do you suggest?" he asked, crossing his legs and folding his arms.

"I suggest we hire a marketing company to get our name out there. I've been doing some research… and don't look at me like that. Stop grinning at me, too. You look like… You look silly. Anyway, I found two companies I think might do a good job. What do you think?"

"I think…" he said and paused, smiling at her, "that if I don't let you do as you please, you'll make my life hell. So go ahead and look into it. But do *not* spend any money without checking with me first. Understood?"

"Understood," she replied. "Now, how about that raise?"

"Forget it," he said, uncrossing his legs and rising to his feet when the phone rang.

"Randall and Carver," Mallory said. "How can I help you?"

"Mallory, is that you?"

Mallory frowned. "Vinnie?"

2

"It's Vinnie McNeer," she mouthed with her hand over the phone.

"Hey, Mal. How you doin'?"

"Vinnie..." Mallory hesitated, then said, "I'm doing fine. To what do I owe this honor?"

"You're doin' okay, then, you and that Randall fella?"

"I am, but... Vinnie, I haven't heard from you in almost a year, and we didn't part on the best of terms—"

"Forget about all that," Vinnie interrupted her. "I need to talk to you. Can you come on over?"

"What d'you want, Vinnie?"

"Not on the phone, Mal. I just need... Just come on over, will you? I'll buy you a beer, or whatever." And with that, he hung up, leaving Mallory staring at the phone.

She put the phone back onto its cradle. "He wants to talk," she said, still frowning.

"What about? Did he say?"

Mallory shook her head. "No. He just said he needed to talk and that he'd buy me a beer, and then he hung up. What d'you think? Do you think he's finally gotten around to suing me for the damage I did to his liquor stock?"

She was referring to the day she quit her job at The Saloon and cleared the high-end liquor shelf as she walked out, smashing hundreds of dollars' worth of expensive bottles of scotch, brandy, bourbon, gin and tequila. Vinnie had promised to make her pay for it all but had never followed up… *Until now?* she wondered.

Mallory had worked for Vinnie as his principal bartender for more than ten years until that day when he crossed the line and accused her of having sex with Tucker, at which point she'd lost it.

Tucker shook his head and said, "Nah! If he said he wants to talk to you, that's probably what he wants. He wouldn't offer free beer if he was planning a lawsuit. I think you should go. You want me to go with you?"

"I dunno, Tucker. What if he… Perhaps he…" She shrugged. "I dunno. It's been almost a year. D'you think…? Oh, hell. Let's do it. What have I got to lose except a bunch of money? Yeah, come with me."

She grinned at him, then said, "You should have seen it, Tucker. He almost blew a gasket. The place was in an uproar. I gotta tell you. It was hilarious."

"But possibly costly," Tucker replied, clearly not amused.

"Killjoy," she said as she gathered up her phone and bag.

The Saloon hadn't changed. It was like stepping back in time to a less-than-pleasant era.

Vinnie McNeer was behind the bar wiping a glass, not something Mallory had seen him do more than a couple of times in the ten years she'd worked for him. And he looked nervous, which, to Mallory, seemed out of character. Vinnie, she knew, was the kind of guy who didn't give a damn about anyone or anything except money. And she wondered if she'd been right about an impending lawsuit after all.

"Hey, Mal, Tucker," Vinnie said, putting the glass down. "Good to see you both. Thanks for comin'. What can I get ya? It's on me, okay?" He squinted at them through his steel-framed glasses.

"Nothing for me," Mallory replied. "What is it you want, Vinnie?"

"I'm good," Tucker said before Vinnie could answer.

Vinnie McNeer was a big man. Not tall—about five-ten—but heavy. Some would describe him as stocky. He was broad-shouldered, barrel-chested with an enormous beer belly. He was also bald as a coot. Mallory had never been able to figure out how old he was. She'd asked him once, but he'd just smiled at her and ignored the question.

"Let's sit down," he said as he threw his cloth onto the counter at the back of the bar, then lifted the trap and came out into the room. "Over there," he said. "Where it's quiet.

Over there was a booth in the far corner of the room.

"Geez, Vinnie," Mallory said as they sat down. She and Tucker on one side of the table, and Vinnie facing them on the other. "If you're planning on suing me over the liquor thing, I'm sorry. I lost it and, if you'll give me a bill, I'll pay—"

"Nah!" he said, interrupting her. "That was over and done with a long time ago, and I don't blame you, anyway. I was outta line, what I said, and I should be the one to apologize. I'm sorry, Mal, and I hope you can forgive me."

"Of… course," she replied, frowning. "So, if it's not the liquor, why are we here?"

He squinted down at his fingernails, then looked up at her and said, "Mal, you worked for me for a long time. You know just about everything there is to know about me and my business, but I don't think I ever told you I have a younger brother."

He was right. Mallory had just turned twenty-one when she went to work at The Saloon. Back then, she was a skinny, five-eight natural blonde: a perky, extroverted, smart, witty, observant, talkative individual. Since then, she matured into something quite different; still five-eight. Still blonde. Still perky, extroverted, and talkative, but now, eleven years on, she was also obsessively organized, analytical, thoughtful, and empathetic. And she'd made herself almost indispensable to Tucker's business, something she knew he'd never admit.

Tucker, thirty-five, six-one with black hair and blue eyes, was a good-looking man, well-built, athletic, who worked out for thirty minutes or so almost every day, though he wasn't overly buff. He was a lone wolf kind of PI with a master's degree in criminology and a reputation for solving crime, preferring to work on his own and be left alone in the process. Mallory liked to think she was the bridge between him and the rest of the world.

He was a skeptic with a dry sense of humor. He told Mallory he'd been single most of his life, with just a couple of memorable girlfriends, but that was his fault. She saw that his dedication to his work left little time for a social life, even though he was handsome enough to date any pretty much any woman he wanted.

When she first met Tucker, she got the sense that he couldn't stand her. He found her overtly voluble and annoying. But Mallory had a way of growing on him and, by the time the puzzle of her missing niece had been solved, they'd become something of a team, though Tucker would never admit it at the time.

"He lived out in Polk County, in Greasy Creek," Vinnie continued. "His wife was a sweet girl. We all loved her…" He trailed off, obviously lost in thought.

Mallory paled at the sound of the name Greasy Creek. It held so many memories for her, all of them bad, but she said nothing, and Vinnie continued, "He never came in here…" Vinnie paused for a second, then continued. "Well, he did, but that was before your time. Me and him, we never really got along though and—"

"Vinnie," she said, interrupting him, a concerned expression on her face. "No, you never told me about him. What's happened? Is he dead?"

Vinnie held up his hand and smiled. It was a weary smile, and she could tell something was seriously wrong.

"There you go," he said. "That's the Mal Carver I knew, always jumping to conclusions before she's even heard me out. Let me tell you and then you'll know, okay? But first, I need to show you something."

He reached into his jacket pocket, pulled out a folded newspaper clipping, unfolded it, laid it out on the table and smoothed out the folds, then turned it around so they could see it.

Polk County Man Arrested for Brutal Slaying.

Luthor McNeer was arrested today for the murder of his wife, Franny McNeer. He claims he is innocent despite the mountain of evidence... and the article went on to describe the events of the night of July 8, 2016, in graphic detail.

Mallory read every word, and then she read it again. Then she looked up at him and said, "Vinnie, that's terrible. I don't know what to say."

"He didn't do it, Mal," he replied.

Of course he didn't, she thought cynically. *They never do!*

"That's what they all say," Tucker said. "Whoa, hold on." He held up his hand when he saw Vinnie was about to explode, then said, "Why don't you tell us why we're here, Vinnie?"

"I want you to find who really killed Franny," he said. "Look, Luthor is many things, but he ain't no killer, and he loved her. I know my brother, and I know he didn't do it. That no-good sheriff and his idiot son hung it on him and then quit lookin'. That's Polk County justice for ya. Look, I've been savin' me money for almost eight years. I can pay ya."

He reached into the inner pocket of the worn black leather jacket, pulled out a fat brown envelope, and dropped it on the table in front of Tucker. Mallory reached out, grabbed it, and opened it. It was stuffed full of hundred-dollar bills.

"There's ten thousand there," Vinnie said, "and I have more if you need it."

"Give it back, Mallory," Tucker said, staring at Vinnie, his eyes narrowed.

"Er... No!" Mallory replied.

"I said, give it back to him," Tucker snapped and reached for the envelope. But Mallory leaned away, holding the envelope above her head.

"Not until you hear him out," she said. "This could be just what we're looking for. I know the Cundiffs. You don't. And I believe him when he said they quit looking. That's just like them. Kal Cundiff is a lazy, good-for-nothing dumbass. The word 'work' is an anathema to him."

"It's a whata?" Vinnie said, screwing up his face as if in pain.

"It means he doesn't like work," Mallory explained.

"Oh that. Yeah, you're right about that," Vinnie said, grinning at her. "He's kinda sweet on you, though. Ain't he, Mal?"

"He's a pain in the ass," she replied.

"Look," Vinnie said. "You worked for me for almost ten years. And I always treated you good, didn't I? I mean... He didn't do it. You know?"

Mallory looked at Tucker. His face was a blank slate. She could tell he wasn't buying it.

"Why don't you tell us about it, Vinnie?" she said gently.

Vinnie nodded and said, "So... You see, someone broke into their house, and, well, it was late. I mean, like real late. Midnight. Franny was asleep in bed. Luthor had fell asleep on the couch downstairs... in the living room. And someone got in and stabbed Franny forty-three times. Luthor never heard a thing. He slept right through it. Sometime after midnight, he goes up to bed and he finds her. He tries to resusck... Re..."

"Resuscitate," Mallory said.

"Yeah, that," he said, nodding, "but she's dead, see? So, he calls 911, and that's it. He has blood on his clothes and his shoes and... And Luthor, well, he always was a heavy sleeper. Sleep through a bomb blast, he would." He shook his head at the memory, then continued. "They arrested him two days later. They didn't believe his story, and they didn't look no further. Damn Cundiffs."

Mallory, seeing how upset he was, reached out across the table, took his hand in hers and squeezed it.

Tucker stared at Vinnie for a moment, then said, "I don't believe it either. How could someone sleep through something like that?"

"According to the medical examiner, it was probably the first stab what killed her, so she didn't scream," Vinnie said.

"Why now, Vinnie?" Mallory asked.

"You think I have the kind o' money lyin' around it takes to hire a good investigator, girl? Hell no. I had to save it. That there…" He nodded at the envelope still in Mallory's hand. "…represents the better part of my life savings. You'll do it for me, won't you, Mal? I mean, he swears he didn't do it."

"What about appeals?" Tucker asked.

"Nah!" Vinnie replied with a grimace. "He basically shut down when he went inside. Never did appeal. I think he's accepted the fact he ain't never gonna get out. He misses Franny terrible like. He never sez much about it, but I can tell."

"So, if he didn't kill his wife, who does he think did?" Tucker asked.

"He won't talk about it," Vinnie replied. "All he'll say is he doesn't know and that it wasn't him. I don't know either. Franny was a nice kid, you know? Sweet, lovin', pretty… Damn!"

"I'm going to have to think about it, Vinnie," Tucker said. "Ouch! That hurt, Mallory. What the hell?"

"There's nothing to think about," she snapped. "Vinnie needs our help. It's what we do. And we need something to get our teeth into. Something that isn't so damn boring."

"*I said...* we'd think about it," he said. "And that's what we'll do. Look, we can't just go off half-cocked. We know nothing about the case. We need to do some research. Figure some things out. And, if we decide to take it on, we'll come up with a strategy. Now, give the man his money back."

Reluctantly, she did as he asked and handed the envelope back to Vinnie.

Tucker leaned forward, placed his hands together on the table, looked Vinnie in the eye and said, "We'll be in touch." He looked at Mallory, then back at Vinnie and continued, "And if we do decide to take it on, you can pay us then. For now… Well, we'll see. Let's go, Mallory."

"Vinnie—" Mallory began, but he cut her off.

"It's okay, Mal. I get it. Me an' Luthor, we're just a couple of low-lives, always have been, and—"

"No, you're not," she snapped. "Like Tucker said. We'll be in touch. *I'll* be in touch. So you just hang in there, okay?"

Vinnie nodded despondently, then shook his head, stuffed the envelope in his jacket pocket, stood up, turned away, and walked slowly back to the bar.

"Tucker," she snapped. "Sometimes I could… I just don't get you."

"I know," he said, smiling.

3

THEY WERE BOTH QUIET ON THE RIDE BACK TO THE OFFICE, THOUGH Tucker kept glancing at Mallory, who remained stoically quiet, which was, to say the least, a little unusual and more than a little unnerving.

She spent most of the ride on her phone researching the Luthor McNeer case, and though Vinnie had made it clear the crime had been committed in Polk County, she was a little disturbed to see it had happened in Greasy Creek, a place that held so many sad memories.

"Okay," Tucker said, finally. "What have I done?"

"You refused to take Vinnie's money," she said without looking up from her phone.

"No, I didn't. I said we'd look into it and get back to him."

"But you don't want to take the case, do you?" she asked, still scrolling through the pages.

"No. I can't say I do," he replied.

"Why not?"

"For one, I don't like cold cases. They're time-consuming and expensive, and they rarely end satisfactorily. Two, we'll be dealing with the Cundiffs again. Geez, Mallory, I don't want us to get embroiled in a repetition of your sister's case. That wouldn't be good for you. And three, I hate that frickin' forest.

She looked up at him and smiled. "I'll make an outdoorsman of you yet. But look, it wouldn't require any travel, and I hate travel." She paused for a moment, then said, "You know, it was a big case in its day. Eight years ago, I was working for Vinnie. How come I've heard nothing about it? Why did he never mention it? I don't get it."

"Vinnie's a strange cat," Tucker replied. "He's a loner. No friends that I've ever seen. Have you?"

She shook her head.

Tucker thought for a minute, then said, "There's a lot more crime that happens under the radar than on it, especially when it's a domestic violence case. I don't like it, Mallory. I don't think we should take it. Look, I had a text from a family in Tulsa. Their daughter—"

"You can forget that," she snapped, interrupting him. "I'm not going to spend Christmas in Oklahoma away from my home and family where I don't know a soul or the area. Not when we have a perfectly good case with good money right here at home, and cash, too. So you can forget it. Either that, or you can go on your own, and I'll work Vinnie's case by myself."

"You?" He laughed. "You'll work it? D'you really think you could?"

"Look, Tucker. I may not be a smarty-pants FBI agent, but I know the fundamentals of how to conduct an investigation. I've been studying ever since you hired me. So yes, I think I could."

"You really are something, Mallory," he replied, shaking his head as he pulled into the driveway. "But you know what? I wouldn't be surprised if you could."

"So, no Oklahoma, then?"

"No. No Oklahoma," he replied, rolling his eyes.

"And we'll take Vinnie's case?"

"I didn't say that. I said we'll look into it, and that's what we'll do," he said as he slid the key into the lock and turned it.

"And how d'you propose we go about that?" she asked as he stood aside for her to enter.

When he didn't reply after a second, she continued, "And I don't know what you're so hopped up about," she said as she went to start the coffee. "It's a cold case, yes, but it's a murder case, and we both like those."

"We *like* murder cases?" he asked. "Do you have any idea how that sounds?"

"Oh, come on, Tucker. You know what I mean. So, I'll ask you again. Where do we begin?"

"I think—" he began.

"You know what I think?" she said, cutting him off. "I think we should go talk to Luthor McNeer and see what he has to say. After all, there's nothing to say that Vinnie isn't simply in denial. And if Luthor isn't trying to get out of prison, maybe it's because he's actually guilty… And, if he is, he might even admit it. Especially if we tell him how much money Vinnie is willing to spend. What do *you* think?"

"I think I'll just shut my mouth and let you do all the thinking," he replied dryly. "I was just about to suggest we go talk to him when you so rudely interrupted me."

"Oh, you were? Sorry. You want me to make an appointment, then?"

"Might as well," he replied. "It seems I have little to say about how we run things around here anymore."

She grinned at him. "You really are a big old softy at heart, aren't you, Tucker?"

"You think?" he said. "Just you wait."

She spent the next fifteen minutes on her phone, working her way through the prison bureaucracy and making an appointment for them both to visit Luthor at ten-thirty on Wednesday morning local time.

"Ten-thirty on Wednesday," she said. "That work for you?"

"I guess it will have to if you've already made the appointment. See what I mean when I say I have little to do with how we run things around here?"

"Now that's just not true, Tucker. I trust and I… respect you. So, we're good then?"

"Yes, we're good," he replied with a sigh.

"Good. Now, I've found something interesting. You want to hear it?"

"Do I have to?" he asked wearily.

"You don't, but you should," she replied. "It's one of Thomas Drews' podcasts dated March 15, 2022, and titled *Who Killed Franny McNeer?*"

"Really?" he replied, suddenly interested. "Well, okay then. Let's hear it."

The podcast lasted forty-four minutes, and when it was finished, Tucker leaned back in his chair, linked his hands together behind his neck and stared at the painting of Confederate General Nathan Bedford Forrest on the wall behind her.

She waited as long as she could, about thirty seconds, then said, "Well, what do you think?"

"I think..." he said, then paused, still staring at the painting.

"Oh my God, Tucker. You are so annoying. Are you going to tell me what you think, or not?"

He unclasped his hands from behind his neck, leaned forward, and said, "I think the podcast was interesting. Maybe we should talk to this Drews guy. He seems to know what he's doing. He's local, isn't he?"

"Yes. He's quite famous. He has more than a million followers and some pretty powerful friends in law enforcement. He's from here, local—"

"Okay. I get it," Tucker said, cutting her off. See if you can set something up. In the meantime, we need a copy of the police file. You can handle that too, seeing as you're friendly with that A-hole of a sheriff." He grinned at her. She stuck out her tongue at him. Then made the call.

"Sheriff Cundiff," she began. "This is Mallory Carver. We're investigating the McNeer case— No— Not at all— What? No, of course not — I'm— Of course. Why not? So, you're refusing to cooperate! I wonder what the press will make of that. Huh? Oh, but I would. No, I don't care. Thank you. When can I come and pick it up? Sounds good. I'll see you in an hour, then." She hung up and looked at Tucker.

"That went well," he said.

"He didn't want to give it to me," she replied, rising to her feet.

"So I gathered," he said, dryly.

"Can I leave Annie here with you?"

"You left her here on her own this morning, so I don't see why not. Don't be long. I'm hungry. And stay clear of that Cundiff kid. He's bad news."

"Hah, jealous, are we?"

He looked up at her grinning and said, "As if!"

MALLORY TOLD Annie to be a good girl and then went out to her car. She pushed the starter button, checked the gas, saw she had three-fourths of a tank, then she backed out of the driveway and headed west toward I-75. From there, she headed north to Exit 20 and from there to Highway 64 and Benton, Tennessee.

The Polk County Justice Center was just off Highway 314 on Industrial Access Circle, about a forty-five-minute drive from Tucker's home office. She made it in forty minutes and arrived in the parking lot at eleven-fifteen to find Deputy Kal Cundiff lounging out front, smoking a cigarette.

"Mal," he said, stepping forward as she slid out of her CRV, "Dad… I mean, the sheriff said you were coming. What's this I hear about you guys investigating the McNeer case? I can't see why you would. It was a slam dunk, and he got life. Case closed."

"How've you been, Kal?" she asked.

"Me? I'm good. You?"

"Yes, I'm fine. You want to take me to the sheriff?"

"Yeah, 'course, but you didn't answer my question. Why are you working that old chestnut? Waste of time, if you ask me?"

"I'm not asking you, Kal. Now, will you take me to your dad, or shall I go find him by myself?"

"Okay," he said, frowning. "But I—"

"*Kal?*" she snapped, interrupting him.

"Okay, okay. Keep your hair on. It's this way. Follow me."

Sheriff Kevin Cundiff, an older man in his early sixties, tall with white hair, a heavy gut and a military bearing, was seated at his desk. Just behind him and to his right, his chief deputy, Ryan Wilks, was standing at parade rest: shoulders back, chest out, hands clasped behind his back.

Cundiff rose and extended his hand across his desk to Mallory.

"It's good to see you again, Miss Carver… It is still miss, I take it?"

"If you're asking if I'm married, Sheriff, the answer is no, but it's nice to see you too."

"Please, sit down," Cundiff said, then looked at Kal and said, "That's all, Deputy. You may leave now."

Kal backed out of the door, looking decidedly disappointed.

"You know Chief Deputy Wilks?" Cundiff asked.

"No. I'm sorry, I don't. It's nice to meet you, Chief."

Wilks nodded but remained silent.

"So, talk to me, Mal," Cundiff said. "What's going on? Why are you investigating the McNeer case?"

She stared at him for a moment, wondering what to say and how to say it without upsetting him. She decided the best approach was to tell him the truth.

"We're not actually investigating it… yet. Vinnie, Luthor McNeer's brother and… Well, I worked for Vinnie for nearly ten years. Anyway, he asked us to look into it, so we're in the process of deciding whether or not to take the case. Tucker Randall, my boss… You remember him, right? He doesn't want to take the case, but I think we should. Maybe Luthor's innocent. Maybe he isn't. Either way, Vinnie would like to know. He'd like either closure for himself or his brother set free. Me, I think maybe the original investi… Well, you get the idea, I'm sure. So, do you have the file for me? If so, I'd like to be on my way… What?"

"Geez, girl," Cundiff said, shaking his head. "You haven't changed a bit, have you? You can still talk the hind leg off a donkey." He was smiling when he said it, and Mallory felt a little embarrassed that he'd said it in front of his chief deputy, but she just tilted her head a little to the right, opened her eyes wide, smiled, and stared at him.

"Why don't you finish what you were going to say?" Cundiff asked, leaning back in his chair.

"Oh, I don't think that's necessary," Mallory replied. "Now, can I have the file or not?"

"You were going to say you thought the original investigation was botched, weren't you?" he said quietly, *and a little menacingly*, she thought.

She simply shrugged and continued to stare at him.

"Why would you think that?" he asked.

"Was it botched?" she asked, unsure of how to handle the increasingly difficult conversation.

"Of course not," he replied. "We exercised proper due diligence, analyzed the evidence and the facts, and came to the only logical conclusion that Luthor McNeer stabbed his wife to death. There were no other suspects, and yes, we looked. Now, take the file…" He leaned forward, picked up a thick manila file folder, and tossed it across the desk. "But listen to me carefully, Mal. Think hard before you decide to take this on, because if you do, and if you cause me any more trouble, like you did last year, I'll sue you and your boss. I'll bankrupt you both. I'll own your homes. Now get out of here before I change my mind."

Mallory took a deep breath, nodded, then stood up, picked up the file and, without saying a word, turned and walked quickly out of his office and out into the parking lot.

Well, that went well, she thought as she started the car. *I wonder what his problem is? Can't be little old me. Maybe he's worried we might find something.*

4

"So," Mallory said, "Do we talk to Thomas Drews or not?"

"Eh, I'm not a fan of podcasters and wannabe amateur detectives."

"Wow, did you ever get that wrong?" she replied. "Drews is... well, he was, until he retired a few years ago, a highly decorated and respected detective lieutenant with the Miami PD. I think he probably knows what he's talking about, don't you, Mr. FBI? So he's a podcaster now. So what? It's always good to get another perspective. You said that to me before, and I think—"

"Okay," Tucker said, interrupting her and throwing up his hands. "Talk to him, if you can. But how're you going to do that? These people don't give out their phone numbers to just anyone."

"I'm not just anyone," she replied with a disarming smile. "I already have his number."

"Oh yeah? How come?"

"He's a friend of Kate's."

"Kate? Who's Kate?"

"Kate Gazzara," Mallory replied. "She's a captain with the Chattanooga PD. She's a friend, kinda. I met her at the range. She's quite nice, for a cop. Anyway, she gave it to me."

"Oh, and why would she do that?"

"I asked her for it."

"Oh, come on, Mallory. Don't make me drag it out of you."

"Okay... Okay," she said. "As you know, I'm a big fan of true crime in all its forms, especially podcasts. I have several favorites. Devin Rudd is one, and Thomas Drews is another. I talk to Devin on his Facebook group, and I happened to find out through various channels... well, Kate, actually. She told me that Drews lives in Dalton and that she knows him. Me? I think she more than knows him; I think she's seeing him. It was ages ago; last March, I think. So I called her and told her that you and I were partners and that I needed to talk to him and... Well, I told her I was interested in his Weston case podcast, which I was, and that I had a question, so she gave me his number and... I called him." Mallory shrugged, tilted her head and smiled at him. Then she made a face.

"And how did that go?" Tucker asked skeptically.

Again, she shrugged, then said, "Not as well as I'd hoped. He was courteous, asked me how I had gotten his number—which I didn't tell him, of course—then he thanked me but said he didn't discuss his cases and he... hung up."

"And you think he'll talk to you after that faux pas?" Tucker asked, leaning back in his chair. "I sure as hell wouldn't."

"Probably not," Mallory replied, "but..." She lowered her chin and looked at him seductively through her eyelashes, pouted and said, "I was hoping you might call him, and I could listen in."

"Don't you do that—" he began, but she cut him off.

"Do what? Come on, Tucker. The guy's already done most of the footwork. What have we got to lose?"

"No!"

She actually stamped her foot, then folded her arms across her stomach and glowered at him.

"Why the hell not?" she snapped.

"Because..." and it was then he realized he didn't have a good answer.

"I get it," she said, the snark thick in her voice. "It's because you didn't think of it. Well, that's kind of petty, don't you think?"

"That's not what... Oh, what the hell. Have it your way. What's the number?"

She smiled while wiggling in her seat and gave him the number.

He glared at her for a moment, then picked up his phone and dialed the number. Drews answered on the second ring.

"This is Thomas."

"Good afternoon, Mr. Drews. This is Tucker Randall. I'm the managing partner at Randall and Carver Private Investigations in Chattanooga. I was wondering if you had time for a quick word?"

Drews was silent for a moment, then said, "Of course. What about?"

"We've been asked to look into the McNeer murder, and during our research, we came across your podcast..." He paused and glared at Mallory, who was signaling animatedly and mouthing "speaker."

"Hold on a minute, Mr. Drews, while I put you on speaker so my *secretary* can listen in. There, now, as I was saying—"

"What more can I tell you, Mr. Randall? I remember that podcast. It was an in-depth and thorough narrative of my investigation. Listen to it. You'll find it's all there."

"I have, and you're right, Mr. Drews," Tucker replied. "You covered all the bases, but you didn't offer any opinions. Those are what I'm looking for. Your personal insights. Did he do it? Did Luthor McNeer murder his wife?"

Drews was again silent for a moment, then said, "Honestly, I'm not sure. There was no sign of a break-in. He claims he was asleep on the couch when it happened. They found him covered in blood. And there was blood on his shoes. There was only one set of bloody shoe prints, and they proved to be his. That's all circumstantial, of course. But here's the thing. As far as anyone can tell, McNeer didn't have a motive. The argument was that no one could have slept through that kind of carnage. There were, of course, no fingerprints on the knife, but it was slick with blood, and, as I said, the only shoe prints were his."

He paused for a moment, then continued, "My thought is that the killer would have removed his shoes, and if the first stab wound killed the wife, then McNeer could indeed have slept through it all. I examined the doors and windows, and it's true, there were no signs of a break-in, but the house was old and so were the windows. They have simple catches, so all it would have taken is a thin blade or strip of steel, such as a Slim Jim, to unlatch any of the ground-floor windows. So, in my opinion, yes, he could be innocent, but I also think it's unlikely. Now, if you don't mind, I have an appointment. Goodbye, and good luck, Mr. Tucker. If it goes your way, please call me. I'd like to update my podcast." And he hung up.

They looked at each other. Tucker shrugged and put his phone down. Mallory went back to her desk, sat down and then stared at him, but he said nothing.

"So?" she asked, finally.

"He told us nothing we didn't already know, except for the windows. I, myself, thought the killer could have taken off his shoes; I would have. Guilty or not, I think a good lawyer might have gotten him off."

"Okay," Mallory replied. "So, our next step is to talk to Luthor, then?"

He thought for a moment, then nodded and said, "Yes. You made the appointment for Wednesday. That's good. I need time to think and to study the file. Oh, and by the way, you do realize that Luthor is under no obligation to talk to us. So don't go getting all uppity if he refuses."

"As if I would," she said, frowning.

"Oh yes, you would. I know you only too well."

She ignored him for a moment, then said, "I made the appointment for ten-thirty."

"That's eleven-thirty our time," Tucker said. "It's a two-and-a-half-hour drive, depending on the traffic, so we need to start out at..." He looked at his watch. *Why did he do that?* Mallory wondered. *It's almost three in the afternoon today.* "...seven o'clock, to be sure of getting through the rush hour traffic on I-24. You'll need to be here at six-thirty."

She was about to tell him to pick her up but then realized he'd have to make the trip both ways through the traffic, so she nodded her agreement.

"You want to look this over with me?" he asked as he picked up the file and rose to his feet. He stepped around the desk and walked over to the table set against the wall next to a large whiteboard.

"Sure," she said and joined him at the table.

The file was, in fact, a copy of the murder book containing the crime scene photographs, the investigating officer's notes, witness statements, autopsy report, tox reports, forensics reports, and a somewhat lengthy but lacking in substantive detail, summation by Sheriff Kevin Cundiff.

Mallory picked up one of the photographs, looked at it, cringed, then set it down again. "Wow," she whispered, almost to herself. "She must have really pissed someone off." Then she picked up the photo of Luthor covered in blood. His eyes looked as if they were about to pop out of his head.

"He looks terrified," she whispered. "Or crazy."

"I'd go for crazy," Tucker said, glancing sideways at the photo. "I know what an FBI profiler would make of that, and it's not good."

"He's not crazy," Mallory said. "He's just frightened, poor man, and so would you be, too, if you'd just found your wife murdered like that. I've seen that look before. It's the same one Vinnie had when he was threatened by some bikers over a double charge on their tab. You have no feelings, Tucker."

"Very funny," Tucker replied, then thought for a moment before continuing. "Yeah, well, I've met a lot just like him, and that photo doesn't fill me with confidence," Tucker said thoughtfully as he read the ME's report. "It says here the wounds were all concentrated in the chest area, and that any one of nineteen would have been fatal, and that there were no defensive wounds on her hands or arms." He glanced at Mallory and said, "So, she must have been asleep." He was stating the obvious, but it was more that he was thinking out loud than making conversation. "Which, if Luthor is to be believed," he continued, "is why the attack didn't wake him… It's possible, I suppose."

Together, they continued to go through the file almost in silence until, at last, Mallory said, "I don't know what you think, but there's a lot of filler here and no real substance. Sure, they conducted interviews, but it seems to me they were just going through the motions, covering their asses. They made up their minds from the moment they walked on site that Luthor was the killer. That's what I think. What do you think, Tucker?"

He took a deep breath, blew it out through his nose, then nodded slowly. "I'm inclined to agree with you, but I'm not sure I wouldn't have come to the same conclusion."

"But, from what I can tell," Mallory said, "they never even did a search to see if there were any other similar deaths. Surely, that would be standard procedure, wouldn't it? I mean, it's what I would have done and will do when we get back from Nashville."

Again, Tucker nodded slowly, but this time he didn't reply. Instead, he picked up Luthor McNeer's mugshot and stared at it for a moment, then closed his eyes, tilted his head back and stared sightlessly up at the ceiling. Mallory said nothing. She'd seen him do it before. It meant he was deep in thought.

He opened his eyes, looked at her and said, "We're not going to do anything, not even think about it, until we've talked to McNeer."

5

Wednesday, November 2024

THEY MADE THE DRIVE TO NASHVILLE ALMOST IN SILENCE, WHICH, FOR Mallory, was something of a strain. She wanted to talk about the case, but Tucker was having none of it, preferring instead to keep an open mind.

It was almost ten-fifteen when they arrived at the prison, a dour, imposing collection of tan-colored buildings with arrow slits for windows. They worked their way through the security systems, handed over their weapons, phones and keys until, finally, they were escorted into a large, public room wherein there were some thirty steel tables with seats attached. Some of them were occupied by inmates and their visitors; most were unoccupied.

A guard escorted them to a table where they were told to sit down and that "the inmate" would arrive shortly.

"So," Mallory said, looking around. "This is nice." It was meant to be humorous but somehow fell flat. There was nothing nice about it.

Tucker looked at her, smiled and said, "There's no need to be nervous. I've interviewed cons in rooms like this many times, many of them much worse than Luthor McNeer. You get used to it… eventually."

"I'm not nervous," she said quickly, a bit too quickly, he thought.

"Oh yes, you are," he replied. "I can tell. Just take a deep breath and relax."

She glared at him, then softened and said, "Can you imagine being locked away like this for the rest of your life? I can't. It must be an awful way to live."

"No, I can't," he replied and looked around at the guards. "And you haven't even seen the cells," he continued, "the way they actually live. Not only are they locked up, but they also have to be on their guard every second. One wrong word to the wrong person and it's a beating, or even worse, a shiv in the belly. An inmate's is a dangerous life."

Mallory looked at him, not knowing what to say. It was a subject she'd never thought about, and what he said had shocked her.

It was some fifteen minutes later when the man Mallory recognized from the mugshot was escorted to the table and ordered to sit.

His escort—guard, Mallory supposed—stood by until he was seated, then looked at Tucker and said, "You have one hour. No touching. I'll be over there." Then he turned away and went to the seat under the window and sat down.

Luthor didn't look happy. In fact, Mallory thought he seemed annoyed, irritated, even. *He looks like a younger version of Vinnie.* Mallory thought, *only better looking.*

"I know who you are," he said, looking at Tucker, then at Mallory, "and you. You used to work for Vinnie. I don't like visitors. What are you doing here?"

"If you know who we are, Luthor," Tucker said, "then you know we're private investigators and that we're here at the behest of your brother, Vinnie. He says you're innocent, that you didn't kill your wife, and that he wants us to find out who did."

At that, Luthor slowly shook his head and looked… sad. "Waste of time," he said. "Ain't no one gonna find out what happened that night. I don't even know myself. Tell Vinnie not to waste his money. What's he payin' you, anyway?"

"We haven't decided if we're going to take the case yet," Tucker said, avoiding the question. "That will depend on you."

"Yeah, well. Like I told ya, it'd be a waste of time and Vinnie's money, so why don't you just go away and leave me be?"

"Oh, come on, Luthor," Mallory said. "You can't mean that. Help us to help you. What have you got to lose?"

He looked at her, looked her up and down, and obviously liked what he saw. "I didn't do it," he said after a long moment. "That son of a bitch Kal Cundiff took one look at my wife, then at me, and made up his mind. The rest of the investigation was pure bullcrap. They questioned me, took my statement, then charged me. Took 'em all of two days. That sound like a proper investigation to you? Look, I know it sounds crazy, but I gotta tell ya. When I went upstairs and found her like that, it all seemed like a frickin' dream. Bizarre, huh?"

Mallory stared at him, not knowing what to think of him. *He doesn't seem like a killer to me,* she thought, *but what do I know? I've only ever met one, and he was nothing like this.*

"What do you mean, it felt like a dream?" Mallory asked.

He took a deep breath, shook his head, and said, "I dunno. It was like… I remember sort of wakin' up. You know? Like you do, then goin' back to sleep. I was dreamin' I was at the mall, but it was deserted, no one there, not even in the shops, even though the lights were on. It was weird. Then I woke up again. The TV was on. Jimmy Kimmel. That's all I remember. I must have gone back to sleep again because when I woke up again, Nightline was on. So I got up and went to the bathroom, then up to bed. And that's when I saw it, her, my wife Franny, I mean. I thought I was still dreamin'. I swear I didn't do it. I never heard a thing… not a damn thing."

"Were you drunk, Luthor, when you went to sleep?" Mallory asked.

"No, ma'am, I was not."

"Drugs?" she asked, locking eyes with him.

He looked away, then at her again, shook his head and sighed, "A little weed, is all. And a Trazadone. The doc prescribed it for me. I have trouble going to sleep. That stuff knocks me out in minutes, but I usually wake up around two or three and go to the bathroom. It's not addictive, and it's not a controlled substance. It just helps you to go to sleep. I was takin' one every night back then. Don't get nothin' like that in here. Sleep's a damn nightmare all by itself here."

Hmm, that would account for him not hearing anything, Mallory thought.

"I tried to resuscitate her," he continued, "but she was already gone. That's how I got blood on me, and I must have stepped in it, too. I ran downstairs, grabbed my phone, and called 911. Shit, they took one look at me and cuffed me. I remember Kal sayin' somethin' to me. What it was, I can't remember, but I do remember the shit-eatin' grin he had on his face. They didn't believe a word I said, none of 'em. And that's it. That's all I remember. So now d'you get it?" he asked angrily. "It's over. Done with. Too frickin' late. The horse done run away. Tell Vinnie I 'preciate it, but he's to save his money. Now, are we done?"

Mallory stared at him, and the more she thought about it, the more she was sure he was telling the truth.

"Not quite," Tucker said. "I'd like to ask a few questions, if you don't mind?"

Luthor shrugged but didn't answer.

"I take it that's a yes," Tucker said, so let's begin with this: "if you didn't do it, who do you think did?"

Luthor's eyes lightened up at that, and he leaned forward, looked Tucker in the eye and said, "I've been thinking about that, a lot. And the only thing I can come up with is it must have been like... a serial killer or something."

Mallory looked at Tucker. He was clearly trying not to laugh.

"See, I think Franny was bein' stalked," Luthor said, obviously unaware of what Tucker must have been thinking. "She never said nothin'," he continued, "but she'd been on edge, uneasy, like, you know? For a couple o' weeks or so. I thought nonthin' of it at the time, but now, well, yeah."

"And there's no one you can think of that might have had a grudge against her?" Tucker asked.

Luthor made a face, the corners of his mouth turned down, and said, "Not that I know of. She was a sweet, gentle woman. She didn't deserve to die like that, you know?"

Mallory could see his eyes were watering, and she was moved.

"Could she have been having an affair?" Tucker asked.

"Frickin' hell, no!" Luthor shouted and immediately looked over at the guard, who was already rising to his feet.

Tucker looked at him and nodded, and he sat down again.

"No!" Luthor insisted. "She wasn't like that. She never flirted with no one. Shit, we'd been together since we was kids, since tenth grade. She was… I loved her, and she loved me."

Tucker stared at him. Mallory could tell he wasn't buying the serial killer idea, but she had no idea of what else he might be thinking.

"Luthor," she said. "If you didn't kill your wife, somebody did, and it was up close and personal, and that means it was someone who knew her and, by the violent nature of the attack, that someone was very angry, in a terrible rage. Who could she have upset so much that they would kill her like that?"

"I told ya. I don't know. If she'd pissed someone off, she would've told me, and I would have sorted it out for her. That's how we was. We trusted each other."

"Well," Tucker said. "Thank you for your time, Luthor. We'll think about it and decide what to do—"

"Don't bother," Luthor said, interrupting him. "I told ya. I don't want Vinnie wastin' his money on a lost cause. You tell him thank you for me, and tell him a visit would be nice."

"Luthor," Mallory said. "Vinnie loves you. He believes you, and he's very worried about you."

"Yeah, well," Luthor said, "there's not much I can do about that now, is there?"

To her surprise, Tucker bit his lower lip, tsked, and then said, "Look, Luthor, if there's anything else we should know…" He trailed off when he saw the smirk on Luthor's lips.

"I'll tell you what you should know," he said, leaning forward, his eyes narrowed to mere slits. "You didn't believe me when I said it might have been a serial killer, did you? Well, maybe you should look up the Tiffany Delgado case, is what you should do." Then he leaned back, grinning, turned to the guard and said, "We're done here. You can take me back now."

He stood up, still grinning, cocked his head to one side and opened his eyes wide and smiled, as if to say, *that's got ya thinking, ain't it?* Then he said the name again, "Tiffany Delgado."

They stayed seated and watched as the guard escorted Luthor across the room to the door, where he stopped, turned again to look at them, smiled at them, nodded, and then disappeared through the door.

"Wow," Mallory said. "That came right out of the blue. D'you think he knows something, Tucker?"

"I think," he said, "he's one wily SOB, but…"

"But what?" she asked.

He slowly shook his head and said, "I have absolutely no idea."

6

"Come on, Tucker. Tell me what you think." Mallory said as she closed the car door.

"I think..." he said, smiling, "I'm hungry. How about you?"

"I think you're a selfish, annoying pig," she responded. "No, seriously, what d'you think about the case?"

"Let's find somewhere to eat and then we can talk about it," he replied. "That sound good?"

It was then that Mallory realized she hadn't had breakfast. "Okay," she replied. "Sounds good to me."

Mallory searched nearby restaurants on her phone, but by then they were already heading south on I-24, and the nearest one she could find was the Hickory Falls Restaurant, a few miles south of La Vergne near Smyrna.

It was just after noon local time when they arrived, and the parking lot was packed.

"Oh dear," Mallory complained. "We'll be here for hours."

But they weren't. The service was fast, and the food was excellent. They both ordered burgers and fries, and while they waited, they discussed the case in general and Luthor McNeer in particular. At least, Mallory did. And all the while, Tucker sat quietly, listening to her and smiling stoically. Though when she finally stopped for a breath, he had to admit she'd made a good case.

"By the way, what did you do with Annie?" he asked. "It's not like you to leave her alone for this long."

"Oh, Annie, yes," she said, frowning. "Mrs. Salter, my neighbor, promised to look in on her. She'll be fine. She sleeps most of the day, anyway. Tucker, did you even hear a word I said?"

"I did," he replied.

"And?" she asked.

"And I think you make an excellent case…"

She smiled at him.

"But…" he said.

She frowned at him. "But what?"

"Look," he said, "I agree with almost everything you've said. Luthor may not have killed his wife… Whoa!" He held up his hand as he saw she was about to speak. "I said he *may* not have killed his wife, but I tend to believe him, or I did until he tossed out that serial killer theory. But what I was going to say was that we need to think it through before we commit to spending any more of Vinnie's money. Today alone is going to cost him, and ten thousand isn't going to go very far."

"What about Tiffany Delgado?" she asked.

"Ah, yes, Tiffany Delgado," he replied. "Now, methinks our erstwhile convict has done some research and found something. What it is and how it might be relevant we won't know until *you* have done *your* research, so we must set that aside until you have. Now, if you don't mind, let's eat our food and be on our way, agreed?"

"You really are a pain in the butt sometimes, Tucker Randall, but," she looked down at her as yet untouched food, hoping he wouldn't hear her stomach growling, and said, "Yes. Agreed."

It was after five when they finally arrived back in Chattanooga. The traffic through the Split was still heavy, and by the time they arrived back at Tucker's home, they were both tired and irritable.

"Go home, Mallory," Tucker said as he exited the car. "I'll see you in the morning, bright and early."

Mallory was about to argue but thought better of it, admitting to herself that it was probably a good idea and said, "Right. Have a good night, Tucker."

As she drove home that evening, she couldn't keep her mind from wandering back to what Luthor had said about the Tiffany Delgado case.

"It's… I dunno," she muttered. "We don't even know where it happened." *But I can soon fix that,* she thought as she swung the CRV onto her driveway and cut the engine.

She unlocked the front door and stepped inside to be met by a near-hysterical Annie. The dog's tail was wagging her entire rear end.

She knelt down and hugged her and, in return, received a slathering face-licking that sent her reeling back onto her backside.

"Okay, okay. Stop it. Hahaha. Stop it. I get it. I'm pleased to see you, too." She pushed the dog away and scrambled to her feet. "I bet you're hungry," she said. "Let's go see if I can find you something to eat, but first, you have to go potty."

At that, Annie turned and ran to the back door. Mallory let her out and watched her run down the backyard to the perimeter fence. She stood for a moment and stared at the dark silhouette of the distant mountains in Polk County that held so many memories, most of them bad, most of them generated only a year ago when she lost her niece, Julie, to a murderous doctor.

She heaved a sigh and closed the door, finally ready to admit she was tired. She went to the kitchen, washed Annie's bowl, took some homemade dog food from the refrigerator, added a goodly portion to the bowl and nuked it for a minute in the microwave. Then she went to let Annie in and finally, she set the bowl down and watched the dog inhale it. *Wow,* she thought. *She really loves that stuff, and it's so good for her. Much better than the kibble.*

She sat down at the kitchen table, wondering what she was going to eat. Truth be told, she wasn't really hungry. The burgers and fries in Smyrna had been more than filling, so she decided on an icy-cold hard-boiled egg from the fridge and a glass of Pinot Noir, and then she took both to the living room and set them down, along with her phone, on the coffee table beside her laptop.

She glanced at the TV, then shook her head, heaved a sigh and sat down, ready to admit she was tired out, but she was also restless, fidgety. She took a bite of the egg, set it back down on the paper plate, took a sip of wine, and looked down at the laptop.

"Oh, geez, Annie. Now look what you made me do," she snapped as the dog jumped up on the couch beside her, jiggled her arm and made her spill her wine. *Damn it. I should have changed my clothes. Now look at my pants. That's going to stain and it will never come out!*

She jumped up, went to the kitchen, struggled out of the pants, muttering "vinegar, vinegar, vinegar," and then ran to the cupboard, grabbed a bottle of white vinegar and dowsed the stained section of cloth with it, then put it under the cold water tap and gently massaged it. Next, she sprayed it with OxyClean and gently massaged it some more, then washed it all out with warm water. *Best I can do,* she thought. *I'll leave them to soak overnight. Hopefully, that will do the trick. Now, jammies, then Tiffany Delgado.*

Five minutes later, she was back downstairs and back on the couch. She squinted, bared her teeth, sucked in a deep breath, let it out and grabbed the laptop and googled Tiffany Delgado.

Tiffany Delgado lived in Ringgold, Georgia, a dozen miles south of Chattanooga. She was found by her brother Alfonse on Saturday afternoon, August 20, 2019, three years after Franny McNeer's death.

She was thirty-three, single, blonde, five-nine, described as "pretty," and worked as a sales clerk at Rickerton's, a clothing store at the Hamilton Place Mall. She was in her bed. She'd been stabbed thirty-two times. The Catoosa County Coroner's office established the time of death as between eleven o'clock on Friday evening, the 19th, and two in the morning on the 20th. The crime was listed as unsolved.

Mallory sucked on her bottom lip. *It's the same,* she thought. *No wonder Luthor told us to look into it. She was blonde and five-nine. Franny was blonde and five-eight. Same days, same timeline, same method, same rage. Wow! So Luthor's serial killer theory might not be as crazy as we thought. Hmm... How come I never heard of it?*

She googled the *Chattanooga Times* for coverage and found only two small mentions: one on Sunday, August 20th, and the other two weeks later, stating that the investigation into Tiffany Delgado's death was ongoing. The TV coverage was even less, just a passing comment on Channel 7 the following Sunday morning. *Hah, why is that?* she wondered. *And it's been five years. Why is it still unsolved? And why the lack of media coverage? I mean, it's a pretty horrific murder. I would have thought the police would have been all over it.*

She looked at the dog and said, "What d'you think, Annie?"

Annie cocked her head and gazed sleepily up at her. "Yeah," she said dryly. "Me, too." She took a sip of her wine and went back to her computer.

Maybe they were concerned about scaring the community, she thought. *Who knows?* She sucked on her bottom lip, squinted, scratched her head, pursed her lips and slowly shook her head. *This happened five years ago, and it's still unsolved. Wow!*

She picked up her phone and called Tucker.

"Mallory," he said when he picked up. "It's almost eight o'clock. I was just about to take a shower. What is it?"

"I know, I know, and I'm sorry, but I just had to talk to you. I've been researching the Tiffany Delgado case, and I just know they're related. They have to be. They are the same. I mean, exactly the same and—"

"Hey, hey, slow down," he said, interrupting her. "I told you I didn't want to talk about it tonight, that we'd talk about it in the morning. Now, please, stop it. Watch some TV and then go to bed and get a good night's sleep. We'll talk it over in the morning."

"Yes, but—"

"No buts. Get some rest, okay?"

"But, Tucker…" she began again, but it was no use. Tucker had hung up.

"Geez," she snapped and threw the phone down on the couch. "I can't believe him. He's such a—" She cut herself off, folded her arms, pursed her lips and glowered down at the laptop.

Finally, she made an angry face, unfolded her arms, grabbed her glass and downed the rest of the wine. Then she smacked her lips, stretched her arms above her head, and set the laptop back on the coffee table and leaned back and closed her eyes.

She stayed like that for several minutes, or so she thought. In fact, she woke an hour later with a painful cramp in her right leg, which was curled up underneath her.

"Ouch, ouch, ouch," she muttered as she stood up and flexed her leg.

She looked at her watch. It was two minutes after nine.

"Come on, Annie," she said. "I'll let you out, then I'll get a shower. We'll have an early night. What d'you say?"

Annie said nothing. She just sat there on the couch with her head tilted, looking up at her.

"Yeah, that's what I thought you'd say. Come on. Let's go."

7

Thursday, November 21

MALLORY WOKE AT SIX-THIRTY THE FOLLOWING MORNING TO A COLD bedroom and a light fog over the backyard.

She put on her robe, tiptoed downstairs, hugging herself, turned the heat up to seventy-three, let Annie out, and then ran back upstairs. She'd showered before going to bed, so she didn't bother to take another. Instead, she washed her face, brushed her teeth vigorously, brushed out her dark blonde hair and tied it back in a ponytail, then dressed in a pair of jeans, a tee shirt and a white lambswool sweater. That done, she glanced at herself in the mirror, made a face, then went downstairs and let Annie back in and fed her. She made herself some scrambled eggs on toast, some coffee, and then sat down to eat it, her laptop open in front of her.

So, she thought as she forked some of the egg into her mouth. *I'll go to work, talk to Tucker and see what we can figure out about Tiffany—and then maybe go talk to Vinnie. Did he know about the Tiffany case, I wonder, and is that why he's pushing so hard—?*

The thought was interrupted by her phone ringing. She picked it up and looked at the screen. It was Tucker. She frowned, then answered it. "Hey, what's up?"

"I'm thinking I'll see if I can talk to Crystal Lawrence, Luthor's daughter. She comes off shift at eight. Do you want to come with me?"

She paused for a second before answering, then said, "No, I don't think so, Tucker. I think I'm going to take Annie to the dogsitter, then head on over to the Ringgold police station and see if I can talk to the detective who worked the Delgado case. That okay with you?"

Where the hell did that come from? she thought as she waited for him to answer.

"Sure," he said, "but please behave yourself. I don't want to have to come and bail you out. What's the address, by the way?"

"Very funny," she said and laughed. "I always behave myself."

"The hell you do," he replied, also laughing. "So where is it? I need to know in case you do get yourself locked up."

"It's in Ringgold," she replied. "I don't have the address yet, but I'll send it to you when I do. Just in case, huh? Tucker, why is it you always think I'm going to cause a stir? You know I never do that!"

"Ah, but you do tend to rub folks the wrong way, especially when they don't cooperate the way you want them to. Please take it easy on those poor cops in Ringgold, okay?"

"Geez, Tucker, you're something else. Okay, I'll be sweet. We'll keep in touch, okay?"

"Yup. Talk to you soon. Good luck."

"Thanks," she replied and hung up.

Geez, she thought, *I had no intention of going without him. Still, it should be fun.* "Right, Annie?"

She finished her breakfast, touched up her makeup, checked the H&K P938 in her shoulder bag, slipped on a tan suit jacket, checked herself one last time in the mirror, and then shrugged. Not wanting to leave Annie home alone all day again, especially knowing she was going to be in and out of the office all day, Mallory took Annie out to the car, loaded her up, and took her to the new doggy daycare that her sister Jen took Tobin to sometimes.

And what's this about Luthor's daughter? she wondered as she drove north on I-24 and bore right onto I-75. Where did that come from? *Luthor never mentioned her. Or did he and I missed it? I don't think so. I wouldn't have missed something like that. Would I? I wonder if Tucker has spoken to Vinnie. Huh. I guess he'll tell me when he wants to. Even so, he could've mentioned it last night when I called him.* And so she continued, one thought after another, coursing rapid fire through her brain until, finally, she pulled into the Ringgold Police Department parking lot.

Oh, Lord, she thought as it dawned on her that she'd never done anything like this before. *What am I going to say?* And, for once in her life, Mallory had no answer. She sat there for a moment, gathering herself and her thoughts together, then made sure she had several of her business cards handy, gritted her teeth, stepped out of the car, and walked confidently into the building.

"Good morning, ma'am. How can I help you?" the receptionist asked.

"Um, yes, good morning. My name's Mallory Carver. I'm a private investigator, and I was hoping I could have a few minutes with the detective who's leading the Tiffany Delgado murder investigation." And then she held her breath as the receptionist looked skeptically at her for a moment, then picked up the phone and punched in a number.

Mallory was terrified. She'd just tried to pass herself off as a PI. *Well, I am, practically...* she thought. *Well, not really. But close enough. I'm working on getting my credentials.*

"Hey, Finn," the receptionist said into the phone. "I have a PI out here wants to talk to you about the Delgado case. Says her name is…?" She looked at Mallory.

"Carver. Mallory Carver," she mouthed.

"Carver. What d'you want me to do with her…? Yeah." She glanced at Mallory, then shrugged and said, "Looks legit to me, but what do I know…? Okay, will do." And she hung up and said, "If you'll take a seat over there, Detective Harper will be with you shortly."

Mallory, her heart fluttering, sat down to wait, her hands clasped together in her lap, and looked around the lobby, noting a woman aged about thirty arguing with a young officer. Actually, it was she who was doing the arguing. She was ranting on and on about how she was being stalked, and they were doing nothing about it.

"This is the fourth time I've been in here, and you're not listening to me." Her voice was loud enough for Mallory to hear what she was saying. "When are you going to do something about it? Are you going to wait until he frickin' rapes me or murders me? What's the matter with you people? What do I have to do before you do something, die?"

"And I keep telling you, Miss Wilson," the detective she was talking to said, "there's not much we can do until—"

"Miss Carver?"

"Yes!" Mallory was startled by the sudden interruption, but she jumped to her feet, clutching her shoulder bag.

"I'm Detective Finn Harper," the young woman said, smiling, trying not to laugh. "If you'd like to come on back, I'll be glad to talk to you."

She followed the detective into a large room with several desks and an overabundance of filing cabinets.

"This is me," Harper said, waving a hand at an overly cluttered desk just to the left of the door. "Please, sit down."

"Thank you for agreeing to see me," Mallory said.

"Not a problem. Marcy, that's the receptionist, said you're a PI. Can I see your credentials, please?"

Oh shit! "I'm afraid this is all I have," and she handed her one of her cards. "I'm still working on them, my credentials. I'm working with Tucker Randall. He's an ex-FBI special agent—"

"I know who he is, and you," she said. "I checked you out while you were waiting for me. Good luck with your exams, Miss Carver. Now, you want to talk to me about the Delgado case? You do know it's five-years cold, right?"

Mallory heaved a sigh of relief, then said, "Yes, I know. But we've been asked to look into what we think could be a related case. It's even colder, but the MO is similar and so is the victim. We haven't yet decided to take it, and I was wondering about… the… Delgado case."

"Go on," Harper said, nodding.

"Okay..." She thought for a moment and then continued, "Franny McNeer was stabbed to death in her bed—"

"Wait, whoa," Harper said, interrupting her. "I know that one. Her husband killed her. Well, he was convicted and sent to prison for it. I spoke to... someone at the sheriff's department. Can't remember who it was, but I can look it up. He said it was open and shut, a slam dunk, that they had him dead to rights."

"That sounds like Kal Cundiff," Mallory said dryly.

"Yeah, that's the one. But you think different?"

"His brother does. He's the one who wants to hire us. We went to Riverbend yesterday and talked to the husband. He claims he's innocent."

"Don't they all?" Harper asked with a smile.

Mallory nodded. "Yes, they do, but I have a feeling this guy might just be telling the truth."

"That's hard to believe, knowing what I know about the case. Didn't he say he slept through it all?"

"He says he did," Mallory replied.

"So, you want to know what I know?" Harper said, locking eyes with her.

She was younger than Mallory, *in her late twenties,* she thought, *but she has an... older way about her*. Mallory nodded and said, "Please."

"Tiffany was murdered in the middle of the night in her bed. She was stabbed thirty-two times. There was no sign of forced entry, and the crime scene was clean... Too clean, considering the method of killing. We had a couple of suspects, but neither of them panned out.

"One, she had a stalker, an ex-boyfriend by the name of Ollie Palmer. I don't think Ollie was responsible... But we've not ruled him out, either.

"Two, we had a second suspect, Raul Copper. He was arrested for wounding a woman, a jogger, in the Prentice Cooper Forest with a hunting knife in 2016 and was sent to prison for three years. He was let out of prison on June 5th, 2019, just two months prior to Tiffany's death. Coincidence? I don't know." She paused and thought for a moment. "Anyway, I've been keeping an eye on him. He's back in prison, in Tennessee, in Hamilton County jail for aggravated burglary. Look," she continued, "it's still officially an open investigation, but it's growing colder by the day, even with Raul Copper as a suspect. Whoever killed Tiffany must have had a motive, but, as yet, we don't know what it was. She wasn't sexually assaulted, and we've been unable to find anyone who might have had a problem with her. We just don't know. And it couldn't have been McNeer because he was inside."

"No, it couldn't," Mallory agreed, "but Tiffany's killer could have killed Franny McNeer. That's a possibility, right?"

"Of course," Harper agreed.

"And, if that's the case," Mallory said, "and I'm not saying it is, there could be more."

Harper nodded skeptically and said, "So what you're saying is we might have a serial killer on our hands?"

"It would make sense, don't you think?" Mallory asked.

Again, Harper nodded, more slowly this time, then said, "I don't know, and I'm not sure I want to go there, not yet anyway. To go that route would cause a public uproar and my chief wouldn't go for it, anyway. So, let's do this. If you and your partner want to investigate the Delgado case, that's fine with me. I'll help if I can. Give me a moment and I'll have the file copied for you."

Mallory thanked her, and Harper left, leaving her with mixed emotions. She was gone for almost ten minutes before she returned with the copies. But while Mallory was waiting, she had time to think. *Damn, I screwed up. I should have checked to see if there are more similar unsolved murders. That's my next project. I need to call Tucker and tell him what I've found out.*

She fished her phone out of her bag and tapped the speed dial. The phone rang twice and then went to voicemail.

Damn!

"Oh, thank you," she said as she stood up and took the file from Harper. "Look, I'm going to do some research. If I find anything, I'll let you know. In the meantime…" She fumbled around inside her bag, inadvertently giving Harper a glimpse of the P938.

"Nice weapon," she said with a smile.

"What? Oh. Oh yes. It was a gift from Tucker. Um, here's Tucker's card. If you need to get in touch with either of us…"

"Yep, I'll call you," Harper replied.

8

It was a few minutes to eight when Tucker walked into the hospital lobby that morning, hoping to catch Crystal Lawrence as she came off-shift. He checked in at the information desk and asked if she'd left yet and was told she hadn't, so he sat down to wait.

The lobby was quiet; just a few people he figured must be patients and several nurses scurrying back and forth, as nurses usually do. So engrossed in people watching was he that he almost missed the young woman, who barely looked old enough to be a nurse, though he knew her to be in her thirties, step out of the elevator with a large bag over her shoulder and walk quickly to the front entrance.

Tucker rose to his feet, hurried after her, and caught her at the elevators to the parking garage.

"Mrs. Lawrence?"

She stopped, turned around, frowned, and backed away.

"Who are you? What d'you want?"

He stopped some ten feet away from her and held up his hand. "My name's Tucker Randall—"

"Go away. Leave me alone. I don't do interviews." And she turned away.

"No, no!" he said quickly. "That's not why I'm here. I'm a private investigator. I've been hired by your uncle, Vinnie, to look into the death of your mother. Can you spare me just a few minutes, please?"

"Vinnie?" she asked, frowning. "Why would he do that?"

"He thinks your father is innocent. Can we talk?"

She stared at him for a moment, still frowning, then said, "I suppose... but not here. I have to go home and let the dog out. If you want to follow me, we can talk there. My car's in the parking ramp. Where are you?"

"I'll be waiting for you at the exit," Tucker said.

She nodded, turned, and stepped into the elevator. Tucker watched as the doors closed and then went to his car.

Crystal Lawrence was a petite young brunette with brown eyes and a winning smile, though Tucker saw it only once during their conversation. She lived in a small, Cape Cod-style home on Cannondale Loop off Holly Oak Lane off Igou Gap Road.

"Nice place you have here," he said as he looked around the living room.

"Thank you. Please sit down. I'll get us some coffee."

He was about to refuse when he realized it was still only eight-forty-five and decided to go with the flow.

"Me and Jim, we've lived here since just before my mom died," she said as she returned with the coffee. "She used to come visit us. It's been eight years, but I still miss her."

Tucker nodded, then said, "That was quick," as she handed him the cup.

"Coffee pods," she said tiredly. "What did we ever do without them?"

"I wonder that myself sometimes," he lied. "So, Jim is your husband?"

She looked at him as if to say, 'Of course he is. What the hell d'you think I am?"

"Ah, yes, of course he is," Tucker said. "I'm sorry. I didn't mean to infer that—"

"It's all right," she said, cutting him off. "I understand. You're just trying to make conversation. There's no need, and there's no need to apologize. Yes, Jim is my husband and, if you're wondering where he is, he's already gone to work. Now, if you have something to say, please say it."

He nodded, took a sip of his coffee, and said, "Vinnie thinks your father is innocent. I talked to your father yesterday. He insists he's innocent. What do you think?"

"I think he's innocent, too. My father is… was, many things, Mr. Randall, but he's not a murderer, and he loved my mother dearly."

"I find it kind of strange that he never mentioned you," Tucker said.

"That's because we haven't spoken in years," she replied, "even before my mother's death."

"Oh, really? And why is that?"

She took a deep breath, sighed, and looked down at the coffee table that separated them. "My father," she began, "was always… a little crooked… if there is such a thing as a little crooked." She paused, leaned forward, rested her elbows on her knees, and clasped her hands. "He was an accountant, an independent. He was, I think, well, less than honest would be putting it mildly. He worked for some shady people. I know that because I met some of them."

"How did you know they were shady?" Tucker asked.

"Because they were drug dealers," she replied. "And so was he, though not in a big way, I think, though he certainly was reckless about it. He would go on benders. And he stayed out all night nearly every Friday night… I think he was even seeing prostitutes."

Tucker frowned. This was something new. *Why didn't Vinnie tell me about it?* he wondered.

"Did your mother know about his drug use and…?" he asked.

Crystal shrugged. "I think she probably did. It wasn't a secret. I think my mother condoned it because she had the life she wanted and money to spend."

"On what?" Tucker asked, then thought, *That was a damn silly question.*

Crystal smiled. "Whatever she wanted, of course." But then the smile faded, which Tucker thought was a shame because the smile had lit up her face.

"They were always arguing," she said. "Mostly about money, but isn't that what most married couples do? But I know he loved her. And to stab her forty-three times? No, he was never a violent man; he doesn't have that in him. Now, if you don't mind. I need to shower and then go to the store."

Tucker nodded and rose to his feet. "Just one more question, Mrs. Lawrence. Is there anyone you know of that might have done this?"

She took a deep breath, locked eyes with him and said, "I told you they argued a lot and that it was usually about money, and it was, but that wasn't all they argued about. She was very friendly with one of his clients. Gavin Gray."

Tucker's eyebrows rose. She had his interest.

"Like in an affair friendly?" he asked.

Again, she shrugged. "I don't know. I do know my father didn't like him, though he did his books and sometimes Gavin paid him with product."

"By product, you mean drugs?"

"Make of it what you will," she replied. "I was only twenty-three at the time and in college, UTC nursing school. I left home when I was nineteen to live on campus. Silly really, when you think about it. But I couldn't stand the constant arguing or my father's activities. If I could have afforded to go farther away, I would have. As it was, I had to wait tables to get through school. My father never helped, though my mother did chip in from time to time. I haven't spoken to my father since."

"That's sad," Tucker said.

"It is what it is," she replied.

"So, where can I find this Gavin Gray?" Tucker asked.

"I'm not sure. Last I heard, he was running the Scarlet Pimpernel—emphasis on the pimp—on Dodd's Avenue. You could try there."

Tucker thanked her, handed her his card, and left her on the front porch, her arms folded across her body, watching him go.

9

TUCKER WAS IN THE CAR AND ABOUT TO START THE ENGINE WHEN HIS phone rang. He checked the screen. *Mallory!* He thought as he declined the call. He had every intention of telling Mallory everything he'd learned and to listen to what she'd learned, if anything, but the idea of taking her to a place like the Scarlet Pimpernel... Well, he just didn't feel comfortable about it, even knowing that she'd worked in a bar that might be just as seedy, though sans the strippers, for ten years and thus was hardened to such places. Even so, if he could avoid it, he would, and he did.

It was almost ten o'clock that morning when he strode confidently into the small, low-ceilinged, dimly lit cave-like bar area where a rather lovely, though topless, woman aged about thirty was tending the bar.

Contrary to what you might think, that the place would be deserted at ten o'clock on a weekday morning, there were seven men seated at the small round tables, most of them smoking, all of them watching the all but naked young woman slowly gyrating around a chrome-plated pole. She was, of course, blonde, though from the dark roots it had come from a bottle, and was wearing only a G-string, the tiny scarlet patch of cloth barely covering her... Well, you get the idea.

He stepped up to the bar and asked the topless woman if Gavin Gray was available.

"What you want with him, hun?" she asked, leaning on the bar, her bust flattening on the onyx top.

Tucker smiled at the ploy, nodded in acknowledgment of the obvious show of "talent?" and said, "I just want to talk to him, is all."

"Sure, sweety. If you'll follow me…" And she lifted the hatch, stepped through, and walked toward an even darker opening at the far end of the bar, her hips swaying seductively. Again, Tucker smiled. It was quite a show. She had a knockout figure, that was for sure, and she was wearing only four-inch heels and a micro skirt that left little to the imagination.

She stopped in front of a door at the far end of the dimly lit corridor, turned to face him—she really was stunningly beautiful—and said, "My name is Carly." She lowered her chin, looked at him through her eyelashes, and continued, "If you like what you see, stop by the bar on your way out. I get off at six. It won't cost you a dime."

Then she opened the door and said, "Someone to see you, Gav." Then she walked back toward him, turned sideways and brushed past him, her breasts brushing against his arm. "You'd better go in. He doesn't like to be kept waiting." Then she winked and said, "Not a dime."

He stood for a moment and watched her go. It was quite a performance, and one she'd obviously spent a lot of time practicing.

"Come on in, if you're coming," a voice shouted. "I ain't got all day."

Gavin Gray was much younger than he'd expected, maybe mid-thirties; maybe a little older, but not much. He was seated at his desk, a stocky man with a shaved head and cold, steely blue eyes that even Tucker found a little unnerving. He could see the right-hand desk drawer was open and Gray's hand on the desktop above it.

"You're not going to need that," Tucker said. "I just want to talk."

The steely blue eyes never left his own, but the hand lifted and pushed the drawer closed, and he said, "Who are you, and what d'you want to talk about? And be quick about it. I'm a busy man."

"My name is Tucker Randall, and I'm a private investigator. I want to talk to you about Franny McNeer. Remember her?"

Gray grinned at him. It was more of a snarl than a grin, and there was not a doubt in Tucker's mind that this man was a real badass and wouldn't hesitate to use violence, even deadly force if he thought it was necessary.

"Franny..." Gray said thoughtfully. "Now there's a name I haven't heard in a while. What about her?"

"Did you kill her?" Tucker asked, smiling at him. *Two can play your game,* he thought.

Gray laughed. "Geez," he said. "Why don't you just tell it like it is? What was that about? You trying shock and awe? It won't work, my friend. There's nothing in this world that can shock me. I've seen it all. Two deployments to Afghanistan and this shithole will do that to you. Now, why don't you play nice, and we'll talk?"

"So, what you're saying is that you didn't kill her?" Tucker said quietly.

"No, I didn't kill her, you smart-ass son of a bitch."

"What was your relationship with her?" Tucker asked.

"My relationship was with her husband, Luthor, though..." he blew out a breath, then continued, "She was a great lay. I'll say that for her."

"So, you were having an affair with her?"

"Affair? Hmmm, no! Was I screwing her? Yes! And was I paying well for it? That, too."

"You were paying her?" Tucker frowned. "She was a hooker?"

"Not hardly. I was paying indirectly. I was paying her husband. He was doing my books, and very creatively, I might add. He knew what was going on. The guy loved her, but they weren't doing so good in the bedroom, if you get what I mean." He shrugged. "I think he was kinda grateful I was looking after her, you know? No, it wasn't an affair, but I was very fond of her, in my own way."

Tucker was stunned by the revelation.

"But here's the thing, Mr. PI—is that really a thing, PI, by the way?

Ah, never mind. What I was going to say is, they nailed Luthor for it. Big mistake. That man ain't got it in him. I never seen him angry in all the time I knew him. So, if you're looking for the son of a bitch that killed her, good luck to you. I hope you get him."

"What about you and Luthor?" Tucker asked. "He did your books. Was that on the up and up, or did he cause you some grief?"

Ray smiled at that. "Grief? He was a crooked son of a bitch, that's for sure. But, as I said, he was creative. Let's leave it at that. Look, Luthor was a shady character, and he owed me money, a lot of money, but not enough for me to seek retribution. He was always late with his payments, which cost him more than me in vig, but he always paid, eventually. I've known Luthor for a long time, as far back as when his dad was running the business. No, I wouldn't kill him over a few thousand dollars. That's not me. Ten grand, however. That would be a different story." He grinned, showing two rows of perfect, shiny white teeth. It was a scary sight.

"He didn't do it. He didn't kill his wife, Mr. Randall. He wasn't the violent type, and you can take that to the bank; I know that type very well."

"So, if he didn't do it, who d'you think did?"

He made a face, turned down the corners of his mouth, then shook his head and said, "I don't know," he replied. "If I did, I'd tell you. No, I'd kill the bastard myself. I thought a lot of Franny. She didn't deserve to die, not like that. Bless her heart."

Tucker locked eyes with him, nodded slowly, then said, "Thank you for your time, Mr. Gray. I appreciate it. If you think of anything, anything at all."

"Yeah, yeah. I'll call you, but don't hold your breath… Oh, and steer clear of Carly on the way out. She's bad news. Just sayin'." He grinned knowingly at Tucker.

Tucker nodded, smiled at him, rose to his feet, and closed the door behind him. And so, thoughtfully, Tucker returned to his car and called Mallory.

"Hey," he said when she answered. "Sorry I couldn't take your call.

I was on my way to… Never mind. I'll fill you in when I see you. Where are you? You want to get some lunch?"

"Perfect. I talked to Detective Harper at Ringgold earlier this morning. She gave me a name, Ollie Palmer, and she gave me a copy of the Delgado file and, get this, I came back to the office and did some research. I have two more names and two more cases… Hey, we are taking Vinnie's case, aren't we—?"

"Mallory, please shut up for just a minute. I know you're excited, and so am I, but I have a headache. Can we just talk about it quietly over lunch? I'll pick you up in fifteen minutes. I'm on Shallowford Road. I need to get gas and something for this headache."

"Well, yes, sure. See you… in a little while, then."

Tucker sighed and shook his head as he hung up. *She's a pistol and I love her to death, but she sure can talk. Yeah, boy, but she's also damn good at what she does. Then why don't you tell her that? Shut the hell up, Tucker. Hah, this is just a few blocks from where Crystal lives. How about that?* He sighed as he turned right onto Gunbarrel and then made a left into the Pitt Stop service station. It was a big, busy enterprise with eight sets of pumps, two service bays and a convenience store.

He pulled up to the pump, sat for a moment, then slid out of the car and filled her up. Then he went into the store to pay and get some aspirin and an energy drink. *And if that isn't a paradox, I don't know what is,* he thought.

He found the energy drinks, picked one out, took it to the counter, and asked for a bottle of aspirin from behind the counter.

The guy behind the counter—wearing a name tag that pronounced him Pete—handed them to him, rang him up, and said, "You know those two don't mix well, right? That energy stuff will tear your guts up."

"Yeah, so they say, but you only live once, and I have a terrible headache."

"Well, I'm telling you, that stuff ain't good for you."

"Yeah, well, my job will likely kill me before it does, but thanks, anyway."

Pete nodded and said, "Take care, and have a good rest of the day."

Tucker nodded and went back to his car. And there he sat for a moment, looking at the energy drink, then he shook his head, opened the car door and tossed it into the trash. *I guess the aspirin will have to wait until I get home,* he thought as he pulled out of the gas station and headed toward East Brainerd Road.

10

It was almost noon when Tucker arrived back at the office to find Mallory printing off information about the other unsolved cases she'd found. She'd already marked the locations on a map on the office wall.

"Hey," she said as he entered the office. "How did it go with Crystal?"

"I'm hungry," he replied, grinning. Oh, how he loved to tease Mallory by making her wait for the information he'd gathered. He considered it part of her professional training to learn patience. "You ready?"

She looked at him and sighed, then said, "Sure. Where would you like to go?"

"How about the Acropolis? It's always good, and it's only ten minutes or so away."

"Okay, but can we talk while we eat?" she asked. "I have a lot to tell you."

"Of course. That was the plan," he replied.

The Acropolis at lunchtime is always busy, but Tucker, who seemed to be well known there, was received with a smile and a nod, and they were shown to a table after only a few minutes' wait.

"Okay," he said after they'd ordered. "I can see you're itching to tell me, so go ahead."

"I'm not itching… Oh, yes. I see. Well, okay." She began by telling him about her visit to the Ringgold police department and her talk with Finn Harper.

"…and she gave me a copy of the Delgado file. But here's the thing, as I was on my way back to my car. I began to wonder how many more women had suffered a fate similar to Franny and Tiffany, and guess what?"

She paused, looking at him expectantly.

"Okay," he said. "I'll bite. What did you find?"

"I found two more, and though they're not quite the same MO, the crimes are similar enough that they might well be connected, and so all four could be the work of a single perpetrator. The two new victims—well, they're not really new. They both died before Franny, but… Their names are Bernice Carr, who was murdered late in the evening on April 15, 2016, and Elaine May, who died in the late evening of July 10, 2015. Both women died late on a Friday evening of multiple stab wounds. Both cases are unsolved. That's four, Tucker. What d'you think?"

"I think you did very well, Mallory," he replied. "However—"

"Oh, come *on,* Tucker. There's always a however with you. These two murders, three murders, are all connected to Franny's. I just know it."

"All I was going to say," he said, "was that we need to do our due diligence before we go that route."

"I've already done some," Mallory replied. "You want to hear?"

"Of course I do," he said. "But can we eat first?" he asked as the waiter put their food down in front of them.

Mallory sighed, nodded, shook her head and said, "You're such a killjoy sometimes, Tucker."

Tucker simply smiled at her and picked up his fork.

Mallory took a small bite of her salmon, chewed thoughtfully, swallowed, and said, "I've done some preliminary research into both Ollie Palmer and Raul Copper. Palmer was Tiffany's ex-boyfriend, and he'd been stalking her. Copper had been in prison since August 17, 2016, a little more than a month after Franny was murdered, on an unrelated assault charge… with a knife. He was out again on June 7, 2019, two months before Tiffany was murdered. So, there was a three-year gap between when he went to prison and when he got out when there were no murders. As soon as he does, Tiffany is murdered. I think that's pretty compelling. Don't you?"

"I do," he said. "Now eat your lunch before it gets cold."

"Grrrrr," she said.

He grinned at her, then forked another cut of steak into his mouth and chewed slowly.

Finally, over coffee, he told her about his interviews with Crystal Lawrence and Gavin Gray.

"Look," he said when he'd finished, "I agree that Franny and Tiffany *could* have been killed by the same person. The other two? We have a lot of work to do before we can include them. Agreed?"

"Agreed," she said. "So, does this mean we're taking Vinnie's case?"

He nodded. "It does."

"Good," she said, "then let's drop by The Saloon and pick up the cash."

11

VINNIE WAS, TO SAY THE LEAST, EXCITED AND HANDED THE ENVELOPE containing the cash to Mallory with a smile and a hug.

"Thanks, Mal," he whispered in her ear before releasing her. "I just knew you'd come through for me. How about a drink? Gin and tonic?"

"I know you were, Vinnie," she replied. "We think he's innocent, too, but proving it is going to be hard, and this," she said, waving the envelope in the air, "might not be enough."

He turned the corners of his mouth down and nodded. "Not a problem, Mal. I've been saving everything I've earned from the bar ever since they arrested him. I've got money. That ten grand is just a retainer. I know that. You guys do what you gotta do. I'll pay whatever you ask, and if I run out, I'll take out a loan. Now, how about that drink?"

Mallory looked at Tucker. He nodded. "I'll have a Modello," he said. "Thanks, Vinnie."

Vinnie nodded, went back behind the bar and made the drinks and beer for himself.

It was a given that Vinnie wanted to talk about the case. They filled him in on their progress as best they could without giving too much away, and by the time they'd answered all his questions, it was well after four o'clock.

"I have to go pick up Annie," Mallory said, looking at her watch. She stood up, went around the table, bent down and kissed Vinnie on the forehead. "We'll be in touch, Vinnie. Come on, Tucker."

NINETY MINUTES LATER, after Annie had been fed, and a pizza had been delivered and half-eaten, Mallory had showered and was in her pajamas, but she wasn't done for the day; she still had work to do, be it self-imposed.

She came downstairs, went to the kitchen, made herself a large mug of hot chocolate, then went to the living room, ordered Annie up onto the couch and opened her laptop. Then she sat there for a moment, looking at the lock screen and wondering where to begin.

Finally, after another moment of indecision, she googled Elaine May and was rewarded with several painfully brief articles.

The first was published in the *Chattanooga Times* on Sunday, July 12, 2015. It was the early coverage, if you could call it that, of the murder and a statement by the Cleveland, Tennessee, Police Chief, Otis Woody. The article was short and sparse on detail, saying not much more than Elaine May, aged thirty-two, had been found dead in her home on Spring Place Road. The cause of death? Multiple stab wounds. The police chief had little more to say other than the investigation was ongoing and that he would not answer questions.

The *Cleveland Daily Banner* article dated the same day was equally scant on detail. They were the same articles Mallory had found when she'd done her research earlier that day. The TV hadn't covered it at all. And Mallory wondered why.

And it was the same with Bernice Carr, aged thirty-six of Meigs County, Tennessee. She died in her home off Highway 30 in Decatur on Friday evening, April 15, 2016, also of multiple stab wounds.

Again, there was little media coverage and, again, Mallory wondered why not.

What she did notice was that each victim had lived in a different county, but none in Hamilton County or the city of Chattanooga. *Which,* she thought, *probably accounts for the lack of coverage here. Hmm, we've talked to Ringgold, and Detective Harper was helpful, which was unexpected. And to Kevin Cundiff, who was reluctantly helpful. Now we need to talk to Cleveland and Decatur... hmm... I wonder?* She looked at her watch. It was just after six-forty-five. "Hah, can't hurt to try, can it?" she muttered and picked up her phone and asked Siri to connect her to the Cleveland Police Department.

"Cleveland Police," a female voice said.

"Oh, hi, er, hello," Mallory stuttered. "My name is Mallory Carver. I'm a private investigator and I was hoping to speak with the lead detective on the Elaine May case."

"The who case?" Mallory could almost see the frown.

"Elaine May. She was murdered in Cleveland on July 10, 2015."

There was a moment of silence, then, "Hold on, I'm transferring you to Serious Crimes."

There was another brief silence and then, "Detective Foley!"

"Oh, yes, thank you," Mallory began. "I'm Mallory Carver, and I was wondering if I could speak with the detective who's investigating the Elaine May murder?"

"That would be… no one," Foley said after a brief pause. "That case went cold four years ago. Why are you interested now?"

"We, that is my managing partner, Randall Tucker." She closed her eyes and shook her head. "We're investigating what we think might be a related case, and I thought, after having done some research, that the Elaine May case might also be connected… somehow. So if I could talk to…. Oh, hell. Look, I just want some details. The media coverage was all but nonexistent. I know she was killed late on a Friday evening and that she died of multiple stab wounds. Those two details gel with our case, but I need more. So, can I talk to him, or her, please?"

"You're new to the job, aren't you?" Foley said.

Oh geez, here we go, she thought. "No, not really."

"Come on. Tell me," Foley said, sounding as if he was laughing. "How long have you been a PI? I can tell you were never a cop. You sure you're not just some idiot reporter trying to pull a fast one? If you are, you can forget it."

"I'm the junior partner in Randall & Carver Private Investigations," she replied haughtily. "We're investigating the 2016 murder of Franny McNeer of Greasy Creek, Polk County. Now, if you want to call my partner, Tucker Randall, I can give you his number."

"You still didn't tell me how long you've been a PI," he said.

Now she was sure he was laughing at her.

She took a deep breath and said, "I'm not. I'm still working to get my credentials."

"Hah, I thought so," he said. "I'm Edward Foley. The May case was mine. I closed it out unsolved four years ago. So, where are you?"

"East Chattanooga, why?"

"I was just wondering. Go ahead. Ask your questions. I'll tell you what I can on the understanding that it's off the record and not for publication."

"Well, I know she was stabbed to death, but what else can you tell me?"

"Okay. Let's see. The time of death was, according to the ME, sometime between ten on Friday night and two in the morning. She was stabbed thirty-seven times in the upper torso with a large knife, probably a hunting knife, but we don't know for sure. It wasn't found at the scene. The perp broke in through the back door. That help?"

"Yes. Thanks. And she was in bed?" Mallory asked.

"No, she was on the couch in the living room."

"Oh," Mallory said, sounding disappointed.

"That a problem?" Foley asked.

"Well, yes, and no. My victim was in bed. She was stabbed forty-three times. And we have another potential victim in Ringgold. She was also in bed, and she was stabbed thirty-two times. The fact that your victim was on the couch is a break in the pattern."

"Oh, I wouldn't say that," Foley said. "You're nitpicking the details. Look, you already have two similar killings, and now you have mine, also similar, but for one minor detail. Do we have a serial killer? I would tend to doubt it. But three similar killings, all within fifty miles of one another… A coincidence? Maybe, maybe not."

Mallory was encouraged. "How old was Elaine?"

"Thirty-two."

"And she was blonde, I suppose?"

"Yup, and she was a hooker."

"Oh, wow," Mallory said. "How about the crime scene?" she asked. "Did you find anything, hair, fiber, DNA?"

"A lot of blood, some bloody shoe prints. Otherwise, the place was clean, maybe too clean."

"How about suspects?" she asked.

"Just the one," he replied. "One of her regular clients, Morris Watson. Part-time drug dealer, some-time user, and full-time nasty piece of work. We had him in here twice. One time overnight, but nothing came of it."

"Is he worth talking to?" she asked.

"Possibly," he replied. "Couldn't hurt; a fresh face, and all that. Look, tell you what. I'll have the file copied and FedEx it to you tomorrow, unless you'd like to come and pick it up."

"FedEx will be fine. We'll pick up the cost. Thank you, Detective. You've been most kind."

"No problem. I'd like to see the thing closed. Elaine was… she wasn't a bad person. She was just trying to make it, you know?"

"I do," Mallory replied. "Have a good night, Detective."

"You, too, *detective,*" he replied, then laughed and hung up.

Mallory blew out a deep breath, lay back against the couch, and closed her eyes. *That's three,* she thought. *Three, and possibly four. I think I'll go to Decatur tomorrow morning.*

But Tucker had other plans.

12

Friday, November 22

TUCKER ROSE EARLY THE FOLLOWING MORNING. NOT BY DESIGN, BUT because he couldn't sleep. He'd been lying awake since four, his mind in a whirl. His was essentially a one-case-at-a-time business. His resignation from the FBI had thrown him into an emotional vortex of lethargy and indifference. He was only thirty when he resigned when eighteen-year-old Marsha Cline had been murdered by the perp because of a bad call by his AIC, David Lewis. Now, four years on, there wasn't a night he didn't replay that last scene. But that wasn't what was keeping him awake. It was the fragility of his business.

Over the past year, he'd come to rely on Mallory for her insight, intuition and her ability to analyze a given situation almost instantly, not to mention her organizational skills. And the fact that she was a beautiful woman didn't hurt either. But what bothered him was what he perceived as the fragility of his business. He wasn't short of money. His father, a respected entrepreneur in the field of electronics, had been killed in a car accident and had left Tucker, his brother and his mother more than comfortably off.

No, the continued success of his business was predicated on his continued ability to find new, well-paying clients, and those, locally, were almost as rare as the proverbial hen's teeth. That, and his responsibility to Mallory and her livelihood, was what kept him awake at night. As a loner with just a part-time secretary, he'd been able to pick and choose his cases practically anywhere in the world, but things were different now, and it bothered him.

So, he finally rose that morning at six feeling as if he hadn't slept at all, showered, felt somewhat better, dressed in jeans and a white dress shirt, then went downstairs and made a pot of coffee, all the time thinking about Mallory. Not anything in particular, just a flurry of random thoughts, some of which gave him a weird feeling in the pit of his stomach, almost as if he was crossing some sort of imaginary line.

But, by seven, he'd put such thoughts out of his head and was in his office, cup in hand, staring at the whiteboard and the images thereon.

At seven thirty, his phone rang. He frowned and picked it up. It was Mallory.

"Hey," he said. "Is something wrong?"

"Huh? What? No, of course not. I was just calling to say I wouldn't be in this morning. I'm going to Decatur to—"

"No, no, no," Tucker interrupted her. "I want you to come with me to interview Raul Copper."

"But, Tucker, I called the Cleveland police last night and talked to the detective about Elaine May. It's the same. That's three, all connected. We have a serial killer, and if I can connect—"

"Whoa, slow down," Tucker said. "We need to talk about this. You can't go off half-cocked on your own. You come in here. We'll go and talk to Copper, and while we're at it, you can fill me in on what you've found."

He heard her sigh, then she said, "Oh, very well, but I think we can cover more ground if we split up."

"What's the hurry, Mallory?" he asked. "A thorough investigation is a marathon, not a sprint. Now, I'm hungry. D'you want to stop by Hardee's and get us something, or would you like me to make some waffles?"

"Grrrr, I'll stop by Hardee's. What would you like?"

"A sausage and egg biscuit would be nice. I have coffee made. How long will you be?"

"Oh, I'm ready. I just have to drop Annie off. Say… thirty minutes?"

She arrived thirty-five minutes later at eight-fifteen, and they sat together at Tucker's kitchen table and ate their food almost in silence, something Mallory wasn't noted for.

She's sulking, he thought and smiled at her.

"What?" she asked, her biscuit halfway to her mouth.

"You're quiet this morning," he replied. "That's not like you."

She shrugged, then put her biscuit down and said, "On the way here, I thought about what you said, about it being a marathon and not a sprint. You're right. I'm sorry. I've always been a little…"

"Impetuous?" he finished for her.

"Yeah, that, I suppose, or enthusiastic. I just like to get things done, you know?"

"I do, but we need order, purpose, and to clarify our priorities. We need to identify what must be done and then prioritize. Things are piling up, Mallory. If we don't get a grip on them, they'll overwhelm us. You have two more, possibly connected, cases and we now have a half-dozen possible suspects. You want to go off on your own, but while I respect your enthusiasm, you can't do it like that. We're a team. We need to get our priorities down and tackle them in order. If not… all we'll achieve is chaos."

"Wow," she said. "That's not quite what I expected. I don't know what to say."

"What we're going to do is go to the whiteboard," he said, "and try to put things in some sort of order. I've made a start, but we need to add what you've found out about the May victim."

It was a little after ten-thirty when they took a step away from the whiteboard and stared at it. Two-thirds of it was covered with photographs, names, dates, and notes, including the pertinent details of the Elaine May case and the name Morris Watson, May's client suspect. The remaining third had a list of things they needed to do. Mallory had taken what Tucker had said to heart and had organized the list in order of priority. At the top of the list was: Interview Raul Copper.

"You're sure?" Tucker asked. "You didn't put it at the top of the list just because I said so?"

"No," she replied. "Copper's in Silverdale, the county jail. It's only ten minutes from here, so we don't have to go hunting for him. It makes sense. I'll make the call and see if we can get in to see him."

"There you go," Tucker said, grinning at her.

"Yeah, yeah," she grumbled and then asked Siri to connect her with Silverdale. It took only a few minutes to make an appointment for two-thirty that afternoon.

"Good," Tucker said. "Now. Next on the list is Ollie Palmer, Delgado's ex-boyfriend and stalker. Fire up that computer of yours and see what you can find out about him. Geez, I wish I had access... too... Hmm, I wonder."

"You wonder what?"

"Never mind," he said, thinking better of it. "There should be an address in the file that detective gave you. Her name was Harper, wasn't it?"

"Yeah, I think there is. And there's also Morris Watson," she said. "Detective Foley said he was one of Elaine May's regular clients, and that he's a drug dealer and a user. He also said he was a nasty piece of work, so we need to talk to him, too, right?"

Tucker nodded thoughtfully, his hand to his chin as he stared at the board.

"But before Morris..." she continued, pointing at the list. "And, I know you're not going to like this, but we also need to go to Decatur, to the sheriff's department, ASAP, and talk to the police there about the Bernice Carr murder. I think it's connected."

"Okay," Tucker said after some thought. "We'll run up there tomorrow. There, does that make you happy?"

She grinned at him. "It does."

She stepped over to the map and inserted pins depicting the two new cases, one in Cleveland and one in Decatur, then stood back and said, "There's something weird about this, and I'm not seeing it. Oh well, it will come to me, I guess." She turned to look at Tucker and said, "It's almost twelve. We've got some time. I'll see what I can find on Palmer."

TUCKER, though he said nothing about it to Mallory, had serious doubts about their interview with Raul Copper. From the little he knew about him, he'd come to the conclusion that he was a hard case, and hard cases were always difficult to deal with. This man had attacked someone, a jogger, in the forest and severely wounded her with a knife. The knife, the young woman; they were tenuous links to the Franny McNeer and Tiffany Delgado crimes, and Tucker was skeptical. *Yes, the timeline's right, but if Copper's a serial killer, why did he leave her alive? But it's also true there was no sexual assault. And as Mallory pointed out, it's also true in the Franny McNeer and Tiffany Delgado cases. But what does that mean, if anything?* Tucker wondered as he turned left off Standifer Gap Road and left again into the parking lot of the Silverdale Detention Facility.

"Are you going to talk to me or not?" Mallory asked as he opened his door.

"What?" he asked, frowning.

"Tucker, where is your head?" she asked. "You've barely said a word to me since we got in the car."

"Well," he said, smiling. "You, my dear, have said enough for both of us."

"What's that supposed to mean?" she asked indignantly as she closed her door and stepped around the front of the car to meet him.

"It means nothing," he replied. "Well, not exactly nothing. I mean, you do talk a lot, and, well… you talk a lot."

"I do not… Do I?" she asked, frowning, as they approached the main entrance.

Tucker didn't answer. He just smiled at her and raised his eyebrows.

"I do not," she muttered as they waited.

"Do, too," he whispered, grinning.

She was about to respond again when a corrections officer in a blue uniform stepped into the room and, without a word, beckoned for them to follow him. And they did, to a small interview room with a steel table and four chairs where dour-looking Raul Copper was already waiting for them.

"Who the hell are you?" he snarled, looking up at them, his elbows on the table.

He was, Tucker knew, forty-two and had spent most of those years in one prison or another. His hair was mousy brown. His face was heavily lined with a scar above his left eye that lifted the outer corner of the eye and gave him a look that was more than a little unnerving.

Tucker looked at the officer, nodded, and said, "You can remove the cuffs."

"You sure? This man is—"

"I'm sure," Tucker said. "Take them off, please."

"Okay, but… Ah, what the hell." And took off the cuffs, backed out of the room, and closed the door.

"I said, who the hell are you?" Copper repeated, rubbing his wrists.

"My name's Tucker Randall. I'm a private investigator, and this is my associate, Mallory Carver."

Copper looked at Mallory, did a double-take, and then slowly rose to his feet. "Pleased to meet you, ma'am," he said, offering her his hand.

She looked at it for a long moment, then reached out and took it.

His grip appeared gentle at first. Then, when she tried to take her hand back, Tucker saw that he tightened it and held on, grinning at her.

"Please," she said, as calmly as she could, "let go."

Tucker made a sound in his throat and leaned toward the man.

Copper stuck out his chin and narrowed his eyes. The quirky look turned sinister, but then he smiled, nodded, let go, and sat down.

"So," he said, looking at Tucker, "you're PI's. What d'you want with me?"

"What can you tell me about Franny McNeer?" Tucker asked.

"Who?" he said, frowning.

"Franny McNeer," Tucker repeated. "She was murdered in her bedroom. She was stabbed forty-three times."

He grinned at him and said, "And you think I had something to do with it?"

Tucker shrugged, already realizing he was on shaky ground. "It would make sense," he said. "The timing's right. You're in here for a similar crime."

Copper stuck out his chin, rubbed it with the fingers of his left hand, and then said, "You're kidding me, right? Look, I know why you're here. It's about that silly bitch I cut in Prentice Cooper. Well, you've got me wrong, pal. I didn't hurt her but a scratch, and she asked for it, anyway. Me and Jimmy Bond was out hunting, see? We was on the trail and she comes running up, spots us, and pulls out a frickin' knife, and then she gets all mouthy, calling us names, like. So me, I just steps up and takes it away from her, before she can hurt someone, see? Well, that ain't good enough for her. She tries to take it back, and that's when she got... hurt."

"She got hurt?" Tucker said. "She had a six-inch gash to her upper arm, and where was this Bond guy while all this was going down? How come he didn't testify for you?"

"I told you, it was an accident. Jimmy was off takin' a leak. By the time he come back, she was gone. He didn't see nothing."

"They found the knife on you," Tucker said.

"Well, I wasn't going to throw it away, now was I? It was a nice knife, a Kershaw switchblade."

"She testified that she'd never seen it before," Tucker persisted.

"Well, she would, wouldn't she?" Copper replied, leaning back in his chair and folding his arms, and said, "And as to this... Franny woman, I don't know nothin' about her. I done a lot of bad things, but I ain't never killed no one."

Inwardly, Tucker shook his head, then said, "How about Tiffany Delgado?"

Copper stared at him for a long moment, then said, "Never heard of her."

Tucker then mentioned Bernice Carr and Elaine May, already knowing what the answer would be, so he wasn't surprised when Copper said he'd never heard of either of them.

And, for some strange reason he couldn't explain, Tucker believed him.

Tucker looked at Mallory. She nodded and was about to rise to her feet when Copper said, "You're not leavin', are you? I ain't got to talk to the pretty lady yet. She ain't said not one word to me."

Mallory got up, smiled at him and said, "Goodbye, Mr. Copper."

"Well, now, that just ain't neighborly, now is it?"

She ignored him. Tucker knocked on the door. It opened and they left him sitting there, trying unsuccessfully to look outraged.

"He didn't do any of it," she said as they walked back to the car.

"I agree," Tucker said. "It was a total waste of time."

"Well, you knew it would be," she said. "So why do it?"

"Because…" he said. "We have to cover all the bases. So, now that's out of the way, what we have left is Tiffany's stalker, Ollie Palmer, and the Meigs County Sheriff's Department. It shouldn't be too much trouble to find Palmer. You can do that, right?"

She nodded. "I can, and I have the file Detective Foley FedExed to us, so I can work on that, too. If that's okay with you."

"Yes, that's fine," he replied. Then, after a moment's thought, he said, "Look, I have something I need to do, and it's going to take a while, so I suggest you go home, take the files with you, if you want, find out where Palmer lives, or works, and we'll go talk to him first thing Monday morning."

"But, Tucker, what about Decatur—?"

"Yes, I know, and we'll get there, I promise, but for now, I have other things on my mind."

"But what could be more—?"

Again, he cut her off, saying, "Okay, look. If you must know, I have a doctor's appointment at four-thirty this afternoon. And there's someone I need to see tomorrow. My brother's stopping off on his way back to Tulsa. I don't get to see him very often, so…"

“You have a doctor’s appointment?” she asked. “What? Why? Is something wrong with you?”

I have… I have… I have an ulcer, okay? And I need to go now, or I’ll be late.”

“Oh… Well… Okay, I guess,” she said. “I’ll see you Monday morning then. You’re sure there’s nothing else I can do?”

“No. I’ve got it. I just need to… I’ll see you on Monday morning, and we’ll go see Palmer. Then, depending on how that goes, we’ll figure out what to do next. That sound good?”

“I guess. If you say so,” she replied grumpily.

13

Monday, November 25

THE WEEKEND PASSED SLOWLY AND UNEVENTFULLY FOR MALLORY. SHE spent most of her time going through the files and her notes. She also took Annie for long walks through the fields and woods at the rear of her property and, by Sunday afternoon, she was thoroughly bored. Bored enough to drag herself out and go visit her sister Jennifer.

But, as always, Jen was busy, even on Sunday, and her niece, Jackie, was out with her boyfriend. So, the visit was brief. It lasted no more than an hour, and Mallory left feeling just a little hurt, unwanted, and very much out of place.

And so she went back to her little house, let Annie out for a moment, made herself a grilled cheese sandwich, opened a bottle of Pinot Grigio and, together, she and Annie went to the living room. She turned on the TV, sat down on her couch, and took a very man-sized swallow of the wine.

For twenty minutes she flipped through the cable channels, trying to find something that might stop her mind from collapsing completely, until she happened upon the movie *Outlaws and Angels*. It turned out to be an exceedingly graphic, and at times bloody, western. Even so, before it was halfway through, she managed to fall asleep with Annie cuddled on her lap.

This Ollie Palmer is one creepy guy, was all Mallory could think when they met him that Monday morning. He was working as a mechanic at an auto repair shop on Rossville Boulevard.

Over the weekend, Tucker had an FBI buddy look him up only to find that, other than a stalking complaint, he had a clean record; and the complaint? It was lodged by Tiffany Delgado.

Tiny's Auto Repair and Service was one of a dozen of its kind on the long strip that was Rossville Boulevard, and it was typical of the genre: a onetime tire shop with three service bays and a small office.

Having left Annie in Tucker's office, Mallory had decided she needed to be in control and so had opted to drive her CRV, much to Tucker's displeasure. Be that as it may, Mallory drove and Tucker sat beside her, biting his tongue until she pulled into Tiny's lot and parked in front of the office.

Tiny Garcia—real name Manwell—was indeed a small man. Only five-six, stocky with black hair, a swarthy face and heavy black eyebrows, he was seated behind his battered steel desk whereon were several heavy tomes, some open, some closed, that Mallory assumed to be service manuals. Tiny was a busy man, as was evidenced by the service bays. All three were full.

"Hey," he said when they entered. "What can I do for you?"

"We'd like to talk to Mr. Palmer," Tucker said. "He's one of your mechanics."

Tiny's eyes narrowed; his brow furrowed. He leaned back in his chair, stared at them, then said, "You want to talk to Ollie? What for? You cops, or what?"

"No, we're not police. It's… a private matter," Tucker replied.

"He's busy," Tiny snapped, leaning forward again. "He gets lunch at eleven-thirty. You come back then."

Tucker nodded slowly and was about to leave when Mallory said, "When was your last OSHA inspection, Mr. Garcia?"

Tiny frowned. "Why you ask that?"

"Well, for one, that large oil spill on your forecourt, and I'm sure that's not the only EPA violation they would find, should an inspection become necessary. Oh, and how many illegals d'you have working here? I'm sure ICE would be pleased to know?"

The frown deepened. "You would do that?" he asked.

She shrugged and smiled sweetly at him. "Fifteen minutes with Mr. Palmer, please?" she asked. "In private."

He thought for a moment, the corners of his mouth turned down, his head bobbing from side to side.

"Okay," he said finally, rising to his feet. "I'll go get him. Fifteen minutes. No more. He has work to do."

"Thank you, Mr. Garcia," Mallory said, smiling at him.

Ollie Palmer was everything Mallory hated in a man, and from the moment he set foot in the office, she took a virulent dislike to him. He was tall, a little over six feet, well built, muscular, wearing oil-stained jeans, a plaid shirt with the sleeves cut off at the shoulders, open all the way showing a barrel-like chest covered in a thick matt of hair. His waist was tiny by comparison, and his upper arms were huge, and, from the way he eyed Mallory, he fancied himself as a lady's man.

Tiny ushered him in, then left, closing the door behind him.

"What's this about, then?" he asked, still leering at Mallory. His gaze was penetrating, and Mallory had the distinct feeling he was mentally stripping her of her clothes, one by one.

"My name's Randall. I'm a private investigator. That's my associate, Ms. Carver. It's about Tiffany Delgado," Tucker said, sitting down behind Tiny's desk, leaving Mallory with no option but to take the seat beside Palmer, and she glared angrily at Tucker across the desk.

"You're PI's? I thought you were cops. I don't have to talk to you." He grinned, rising to his feet.

"Sit down, Ollie," Tucker said tiredly. "No, you don't have to talk to us, but if you don't, that will look bad, and you will have to talk to Detective Harper. Remember her?"

He sank slowly back down onto his seat, stared at Tucker, then said, "What about Tiffany?" he asked.

"Well, you and she were an item," Mallory said before Tucker could speak.

He twisted in his chair and looked at her, his eyes narrowed, a half-smile on his lips. "So?" he said softly and licked his lips.

Inwardly, Mallory shuddered. "So, she dumped you and you decided to stalk her," Mallory said. "Did you kill her, Mr. Palmer?"

She saw Tucker roll his eyes. Palmer didn't. He was focused on Mallory.

"What the... Are you serious...? Shit, this ain't happening, lady. I have an alibi. Harper checked it out, and she cleared me."

"That's not what she told me," Mallory retorted. "She told me you're still a person of interest."

"Did she, now?" He was beginning to look worried. "Look, you can't hang that on me. I was at the Billiard Club on Cherry Street till almost one in the morning. You can check it out. I won big that night. No, I didn't kill Tiffany. I loved her. And I wasn't stalking her. I just wanted to talk to her, is all. I would never have hurt her."

There was no other argument Mallory could think of. *If his alibi checks out...* she thought, then said, "What about Franny McNeer?"

"Who?" He looked genuinely puzzled.

"Franny McNeer," she repeated. "Lived in Greasy Creek in Polk County."

"Never heard of her, or it. Greasy Creek? Is that really a place?"

She ignored the question and said, "How about Bernice Carr and Elaine May?"

He slowly shook his head and then said, "Nope. Never heard of either of them."

"Is there anyone, anyone at all, you can think of that might have killed Tiffany or would have wanted to hurt her?" Mallory asked, feeling more than a little frustrated.

"No, missy," he replied. "If there was, I would have told Detective Harper. Tiff was a great gal, sweet as can be. Everybody loved her. I loved her. I don't know nobody as would've wanted to hurt her. If I had, they would've had to deal with me. Maybe it was my fault she got killed. I screwed up, and she finished with me. If we'd still been together, maybe she'd still be alive. Now, we done here? I need to get back to work."

"Yes, we're done," Tucker said, rising to his feet. Thanks for your time, Mr. Palmer."

Palmer also rose to his feet, as did Mallory. He turned to her and offered her his hand.

She took it. His grip was surprisingly gentle.

"Thank you, Mr. Palmer," she said as he released her hand.

"You're welcome, missy. Sorry I couldn't be more help. There's nothing more in the world I'd like to see than the son of a bitch who did it fry." He looked into her eyes, then said, "I don't suppose you'd… Nah, course you wouldn't." And with that, he spun away and walked out the door.

"WELL," she said when they were back in the car. "I think we can write that one off. What d'you think, Tucker?"

Tucker shrugged. "He seemed pretty up front to me."

"D'you think it's worth checking his alibi?" she asked as she started the engine.

"I think your friend Detective Harper already did that, so there's not much point."

"Are you all right, Tucker? You seem a little off."

"Eh, I'm fine. It's just that… Well, we seem to be at a dead end."

"But we still have Decatur—"

"I have a feeling that's going to be a wash, too," he replied. "We're missing something here, Mal. I think you're right, though, that all four cases may well be connected, but whoever this killer is, he's smart. The three crime scenes we have so far—we don't yet know about Decatur—were clean. He didn't leave a trace. He covered his tracks, and now, so it seems, he's gone to ground."

"So, what do we do?" she asked as she pulled out of Tiny's lot onto Rossville Boulevard.

"I don't know," he replied. "We've agreed it's not Raul Copper, Gavin Gray or Palmer."

"I think we should go to Decatur and talk to the detective who investigated the case."

"Let's go get some lunch," he said. "I'm hungry. We can talk about it some more, but I… I dunno, Mal."

As it turned out, when they got back to the office, Tucker received a phone call from a client about an open case, and they spent the rest of the day dealing with that.

It was almost six that evening when Mallory and Annie left to go home.

Tucker, not feeling particularly hopeful about the McNeer case, spent the next two hours going over the three case files. And while he had to admit to himself that all four cases, including the one in Decatur, had to be connected, he still felt there was something he was missing. What it was continued to elude him until, finally, sometime between nine and ten, he fell asleep on the couch.

14

Saturday Morning, December 7

AND THEN THE CASE WENT COLD. FOR ALMOST TWO WEEKS, THERE WAS little they could do but cover old ground. They interviewed Lieutenant Warner at the Meigs County Sheriff's Department, the lead detective on the Bernice Carr case, but he was less than cooperative and seemed to resent the intrusion into what he considered his personal fiefdom. He refused to provide any new information or turn over the files. None of this surprised Tucker. Meigs was, after all, a sparsely populated rural county with a small sheriff's department comprising a half-dozen deputies and two detectives. Mallory, however, couldn't believe Warner's attitude, and she told him so, at which point Warner ended the interview and sent them on their way with a warning to stay out of his investigation.

It wasn't until almost two weeks later, on Saturday, December 7, that things took a turn for the worse, or better, depending upon your point of view, when Tucker, who was eating breakfast, was startled by a thunderous knocking at the front door.

What the hell? he thought as he rose from the kitchen table and went to the door. Barely had he unlocked it when it burst open to reveal Mallory in a state of… excitement.

"Look. Here." Her voice was squeaky, excited. She shoved an iPad in front of his face. "It's the local news at eight o'clock this morning. I recorded it. D'you have coffee? You do. Good. I need some." She handed him the iPad and left him standing there in a state of bewilderment.

"I know her," she said as she poured herself some coffee. "You want me to top that up?" She didn't wait for an answer. She grabbed his cup and filled it almost to overflowing, all the while chattering nonstop. "When I say I know her, I should have said I knew her, but not really. She was at the Ringgold Police Department when I was there to interview Detective Harper. She was telling some detective she was being stalked and complaining about how they were doing nothing about it. I didn't get to hear it all because they came and got me, but I did hear the detective say there was nothing they could do about it. I was going to tell you about it, but it went clear out of my mind. And, anyway, now she's dead, murdered, stabbed multiple times. It has to be connected, Tucker. It just has to be."

She sat down at the table opposite him, took her cup in both hands, placed her elbows on the table, took a sip of her coffee, and then stared at him over the rim of the cup.

He looked at her, slowly shaking his head in wonder at his partner's obvious enthusiasm. Her blonde hair was hanging loosely around her face. She was wearing little makeup, just some lipstick and a little blush, but her blue eyes were sparkling, and he thought, not for the first time, how lovely she was, especially when she was excited.

He took a sip from the over-filled cup, replaced it on the table and reran the news piece. There wasn't much to it. The police rarely released details this early in an investigation. All it said was that Holly Wilson, a resident of Ringgold, had been found dead early that morning in her home and that they were treating it as a suspicious death. In a hesitated response to a reporter's question, Detective Finn Harper admitted that Wilson had been stabbed multiple times, and that was all she could say at that time.

"Could it be Ollie Palmer?" Mallory asked, still nursing her cup in front of her face. "He kind of admitted he was stalking Tiffany."

"And he had an alibi for Tiffany's murder," Tucker countered. "So, no."

"Well, Tiffany could have had two stalkers," Mallory insisted. "I know it sounds kind of crazy, but it's not. It happens. I think we should talk to Detective Harper. Look, Tucker. I saw what happened when she tried to get help. They practically blew her off. She was obviously being stalked. Does Harper even know that? Probably not. She needs to know. We need to tell her."

"Take it easy, Mal," Tucker replied. "I'm sure it's just some sort of coincidence. Are you sure the woman you saw was Holly Wilson?"

"The detective called her Miss Wilson, but—"

"But," Tucker said, cutting her off. "Wilson is a common name. We don't even know if it's the same woman. Where's Annie, by the way?"

"She's at day care. I dropped her off. So, are we going to talk to Detective Harper or not?"

Tucker looked at her for a long moment, then, having realized he was fighting a losing battle, sighed, nodded, and said, "Can I finish my breakfast first?"

15

Saturday Morning, December 7

11am Holly Wilson

Geez, what are we getting ourselves into? Tucker thought as he turned onto I-75, heading south toward Ringgold. *Mallory, bless her, still doesn't get it. We're just a couple of PIs—one, really—and we just don't have the resources for this kind of major investigation. Two states and four counties... geez. And Mallory seems to have it in her head that we're going to be of great service to everyone, but we've already found in Decatur that we're regarded as nothing more than a nuisance. It's exactly how I would have felt —did feel—when I was an agent. Hell, we don't have even the basic resources, like forensics, IT, much less personnel. Sheesh, this is ridiculous.*

He turned his head to look at her and could see she was deep in thought.

"Hey," he said. "What's going on in that pretty little head?"

She looked at him, shocked. It was the first time he'd ever said anything like that to her, and she didn't quite know what to make of it. Was he making fun of her or was it something else?

"What did you say?" she asked, frowning.

"Yep, sorry. I didn't mean anything by it. I was just trying to make conversation… I'm not taking it back, though," he finished with a grin.

Mallory felt herself blushing. She looked quickly away and pursed her lips to stop herself from smiling.

"I was just thinking," she said, finally.

"About what?"

She shrugged. "Nothing, really. Just… you know… stuff."

"What kind of stuff?"

"Oh, I don't know. Stop it, Tucker. You're being weird."

"Me? Weird?" He turned his head to look at her, smiling. "Isn't that a little like the pot calling the kettle black?"

"Tsk," she said. "I never did understand that silly saying. I've never seen a black pot or kettle."

"Of course you haven't," Tucker said. "You're far too young. It goes back to the time when pots and kettles were heated over an open fire and were covered in soot."

"Well, just listen to Mr. Wikipedia," she retorted, smiling.

He grinned at her but didn't reply.

"So, Tucker," she said. "What do *you* think about… all this… mess?"

He nodded, then said, "So you think it's a mess, too."

"Well, not a mess, exactly, but… well… you know?"

"I do know," he replied, "and it *is* a mess, a real mess. Our case is Luthor McNeer, but here we are in the midst of what's beginning to look like an interstate investigation we have no business being involved in, and I'm still not entirely convinced Franny McNeer's death is connected to the other four. And, as yet, we know almost nothing about either the Bernice Carr case or the Holly Wilson case."

"We should be able to get a copy of what they have on Holly Wilson," she replied. "Detective Harper is nice, and she was more than cooperative."

"That was because Tiffany Delgado is a cold case. Holly Willson is not. In fact, it's not even a day old yet. I reckon they'll throw us out. I know I would."

"You're so negative sometimes, Tucker," she said, smiling at him. "You're a real glass is half empty kind of guy. Try to be positive, see the bright side of things."

"I'll happily look at the bright side," he said as he turned off the interstate. "Why don't you give me something?"

She thought for a minute but then shrugged.

"Hah, gotcha," he said. "You can't think of anything, can you? And no, missy, I can't think of anything either. We're in over our heads, and I don't like it. And how about this: suppose Franny's death isn't connected, and Luthor *did* kill his wife? Have you thought about that? What are you going to say to Vinnie?"

Mallory heaved a sigh and pursed her lips, not wanting to admit it was a scenario she'd thought of herself several times, always pushing the thought out of her mind.

"I... I... think... Oh dear, Tucker. I don't know. I just..." She trailed off, speechless.

"Hey," he said. "It's okay. There will always be times like this. Times when we don't even know which way is up. But we'll get through them, as we'll get through this one." *Don't lie to her, Tucker,* he thought, as something deep at the back of his mind dragged him back to the Marsha Cline case. *I really screwed that one up.*

"Okay," he said, "here we are. There seems to be a lot of activity. Let's get to it."

They went inside where, much to Mallory's relief, they found Marcy at the reception desk.

"Miss Carver. Nice to see you again. You'll be wanting to see Finn, I presume?"

"Please," Mallory said, nodding.

"Well, let me see what I can do. She's kinda busy, but she can always say no, can't she?"

She picked up the phone, made the call, asked the question, listened to the answer, then said, "Yes, ma'am." And she put down the phone, stepped out from around her desk, and said, "You're in luck. Follow me, please. They're waiting for you in the conference room."

The minute they walked into the room, everything changed. The FBI had arrived and taken charge of both the Holly Wilson case and the Tiffany Delgado case, but that wasn't all.

Tucker was just about to turn around and walk right out again when, "Hello, Tucker. I was hoping to see you."

16

TUCKER INWARDLY SIGHED AND SHOOK HIS HEAD, THEN SAID, "HELLO, David."

He said it calmly enough, but inwardly he was panicking. He'd been taken completely by surprise.

"What are you doing here?" he asked.

"Interstate crime is federal jurisdiction, you know that, Tucker," David Lewis said, smiling. "Why don't you introduce me to your… charming partner?"

Tucker looked at Mallory. She appeared to be impressed. He looked again at his onetime partner and said, "David Lewis, Mallory Carver."

"Pleased to meet you," they said together and then laughed.

"And this," Lewis said, nodding to the dour-looking middle-aged man sitting at the far end of the table, is Agent Diago Garcia of the Chattanooga Field Office. He'll be working with me and, by extension, you as well, I hope." He smiled at Tucker.

"So, I'll ask you again," Tucker said. "Why are *you* here?"

"Why don't you both sit down and I'll tell you?" Lewis said. They did. They sat down at the table, and he paused for a moment, then said, "You asked what I'm doing here. Well, it's for two reasons. The first is, when I saw this come up on the Chattanooga Field Office roster, I thought it might be a good way for us both to mend some fences and perhaps rekindle what was to me a rather precious friendship. No!" He held up a hand. "Please let me finish, Tucker. I know we've had our differences and that you blame me for… Well, this is not the time nor the place to reopen old wounds. Can we set those aside for now and deal with the here and now?"

Tucker nodded slowly, obviously unhappy with the situation. But he had little choice other than to agree or get up and walk out. He chose the former and nodded.

"Good," Lewis said. "In that case, I'll bring in Detective Harper and bring you all up to speed." And he left the room.

David Lewis, six-two, slim with black hair and a long, narrow face, was in his late forties, or maybe even in his early fifties. Tucker had never known just how old his ex-boss and partner was. Most of what he could remember was contained in those final few weeks when David had put him in charge of protecting Marsha Cline, a key witness in a double homicide. Marsha had been only nineteen when she was shot dead, and Tucker had never forgiven himself, or David. He'd quit the FBI a few weeks later and had never looked back, although Marsha still haunted his dreams.

"Don't," Tucker said as Mallory opened her mouth to speak. "I don't want to hear it, and I will *not* work with him. We'll hear what he has to say, and then we'll get out of here."

Lewis returned a moment later with Detective Finn Harper. Mallory introduced her to Tucker, and then Lewis took over the meeting.

"The second reason I'm here," he began. "As I mentioned, I saw the Tiffany Delgado case on the CFO roster. I also saw that someone, as yet unknown, had linked the case to those of Elaine May and Bernice Carr in Tennessee, thus making it FBI jurisdiction. Rather than assign it as I normally would have, and after a little research during which your name came up, I took it upon myself. I arrived here in Ringgold late yesterday. I came here early this morning and was informed there had been a fourth murder, that of Holly Wilson—"

"What about Franny McNeer?" Mallory asked, interrupting him.

"Who?" he asked, frowning.

"Franny McNeer," Mallory repeated. "Greasy Creek, Tennessee. She was murdered in her bed eight years ago. She was stabbed forty-three times. Her husband is doing life in Riverbend. That makes five cases. His brother hired us to find the real killer."

Lewis slowly shook his head while Tucker stared stoically at him.

Lewis shook his head. "No, I didn't know about that one, probably because it was solved. Anyway, as I was—"

"Wait," Mallory said. "You're blowing it off because it was solved? No way. There's an innocent man in prison, and we're going to get him out. Look, Franny was stabbed forty-three times in her bed, no signs of a break-in. Elaine May thirty-seven times. Tiffany Delgado thirty-three times. And you're telling us the McNeer case is not connected?"

"Typical," Tucker muttered just loud enough to be heard by everyone in the room.

Lewis looked sharply at Tucker, then said, "I'm not saying that. What I'm saying is, it's not an open case so—"

"Well, reopen the damn thing, then," Tucker snapped. "The McNeer case is why we're here. If it's not to be part of the investigation, then we don't need to be here." And he began to rise from his chair.

Mallory put a hand on his arm and said, "Let's hear him out, Tucker."

Tucker paused, glanced at her, nodded, and then settled back down in his chair and stared at Lewis.

"I know how you feel, Tucker. I really do, but we can work together on this. It'll be like old times."

Tucker sat absolutely still, his body rigid, then, "Are you frickin' serious, David? Like old times? Do you think I don't remember *the old times?* I remember them every night when I go to sleep, and in my dreams, and when I wake every morning. You let those two bastards walk free to kill Marsha. I was there. I watched them shoot her in the head. I have this to remember those old times." He held out his hand, palm up, to show the scar. "And where were you? Boozing it up in Cleary's Tavern. You can keep your old times, David. I want no more of it. You want us to work together? Fine. You officially reopen the McNeer case. We'll work together, but we'll keep it purely professional."

Lewis stared at him for a long moment, then picked up the phone, punched in a number, waited for the answer, then said, "I want everything you can find on…" He looked at Mallory.

"Frances McNeer, July 8, 2016."

"A 2016 case. Victim Frances McNeer. Location, Chattanooga, Tennessee."

"Greasy Creek," Mallory corrected him. "Polk County."

"Make that Polk County, Tennessee, and I want it soonest. Got It?" He waited for a moment, then nodded and said, "Then go get it. Have it copied and send a copy to me here? No, wait."

He looked at Mallory and said, "I take it you have a copy?"

"We do, but how complete it is, we're not sure. The source—the sheriff's department—is less than reliable."

He looked at Harper, his eyebrows raised in question. She shook her head.

"Make that three copies," he said into the phone, "and I want everything they have. Go now, and make the copies yourself. If you have problems, call me." And he put the phone down.

"That good enough, Tucker?" he asked.

Tucker nodded, his jaw set, his eyes narrowed almost to slits. He was visibly upset. Mallory had never seen him like it before and she was deeply concerned.

"Very well, then," Lewis said. "Let's get on with what we have. Setting the McNeer case aside until I have the file, what we have is this: Two killings in Tennessee and now two here in Ringgold and maybe a fifth in Tennessee." He smiled at Mallory, ignoring Tucker's icy glare. "I have files for you from the Decatur, Tennessee Sheriff's Office and the Cleveland, Tennessee Police Department, and from Detective Harper here." He glanced at her, then continued. "For the

Delgado case. It's too soon for the Holly Wilson case, but I'll tell you what I know."

He paused for a moment while Finn Harper handed out the files, and to gather his thoughts, then said, "Holly Wilson, age thirty-one, was found dead in her bed at six this morning by her twelve-year-old son, Michael. Preliminary reports indicate she was stabbed to death. How many times we won't know until the autopsy. The coroner estimated the time of death to be between eleven last night and one in the morning. That's basically all I have for the moment. You'll note the similarities between the victims and the killer's MO. Any thoughts. Anyone?"

"We already have Finn's Delgado file and the one from Cleveland," Mallory said as she leaned forward and put the copies on her desk. "The one we didn't have is the one from Decatur, Bernice Carr. Thank you. Now, you asked for thoughts. Well, I have one. I was here, Finn," Mallory said. "I saw Holly pleading for help with one of your officers. I heard him tell her there was nothing he could do. She claimed she was being stalked. I heard her say she'd complained to your department several times, but no one would listen to her. Did you know about that?"

"No. I didn't," Harper said. "Did you, by any chance, get the name of the officer?"

Mallory shook her head.

"I'll look into it," Harper said.

"Tucker," David said quietly. "I know you and Mallory have done a lot of work on these cases. Do you have anything to share?"

Tucker looked at Mallory and nodded. She reached for her shoulder bag, opened it, retrieved a file containing more than eighty single-spaced printed pages, and handed it to Lewis. "You find it's all collated and in chronological order, beginning with Elaine May and ending with Franny McNeer," she said. "It also includes my notes on my interviews and Tucker's, too. I hope you find it all helpful."

Lewis flipped slowly through the pages, then looked at her and said, "This is amazing. It's so… well done. I'll have it copied and returned to you. I need time to go through it, but—"

"Thank you for the kind words, Agent Lewis, but there's no need to return it," Mallory said. "I have it all on my laptop, and I record all my interviews on my phone, even some of those when Tucker and I are discussing… strategy."

"You what?" Tucker said, frowning. "You never told me…"

"It wasn't relevant," she replied. "Everything I recorded was/is work-related, even here." She smiled and held up her phone. "It's always nice to have a complete recording of all business proceedings. That way, there's no argument as to what might, or might not, have been said. Don't you agree, Agent Lewis?"

Lewis looked flabbergasted. Finn Harper, who was seated to Lewis's left, was smiling. She winked at Mallory and nodded, unseen by Lewis, who continued to stare at her.

"What?" she asked innocently.

"Oh… nothing really," he said. "I was just thinking what an enterprising young woman you are. You're very lucky to have her on your team, Tucker."

"She is my team," Tucker snapped. "Can we get on with this, please? We have places to be."

We do? Mallory thought. *That's news to me.*

"I see from this that you've already interviewed several persons of interest," Lewis said, still flipping through the file. "I'll study these, of course, but for now, there's nothing we can do about the Wilson case. Forensics has the crime scene locked down, and it's unlikely we'll have access for at least a couple of days, hopefully sometime on Monday. Nor will we have the autopsy report anytime soon. These rural coroners do like to take their time. No insult intended, Detective Harper."

"None taken," she replied.

"In the meantime, I have a couple of interesting prospects we need to interview: Morris Watson and Levi Rogers. Rogers is Carr's ex-husband, so he's definitely a person of interest. Watson is something else entirely. He was, apparently, friendly with Carr, *and* he was also one of Elaine May's regular clients. Quite a coincidence, don't you think?"

Neither Mallory nor Tucker answered. They just looked at each other.

"No comment, huh?" he said with a smile. "Okay, so here's what I think we should do. These two are a priority, so how about this: I'll track down Levi Rodgers, and you and Mallory take on Morris Watson?"

"I don't—" Tucker began, but before he could finish, Mallory interrupted him.

"We're in," she said, ignoring Tucker's angry look.

"Good," David said. "You have Watson's rap sheet. It's included in the Carr file, as is Levi Rogers. So, that leaves Holly Wilson. There won't be much happening there for a couple of days, so I assume you'll oversee that for now, Detective Harper?"

Harper nodded.

"About the Franny McNeer case," Mallory said.

"Yes?" Lewis replied.

"Are you going to include it as part of the overall investigation?"

"Well, I haven't seen the file yet—"

"But you have to admit the stalker MO fits, right?" Tucker asked.

"Well… yes, but…" He caught the look on Tucker's face, then nodded and said, "Yes, it does, and when I've had time to go through the file, I'll give you my decision. In the meantime, we've all got work to do. I suggest we get on with it."

They all rose slowly to their feet and began to file out of the conference room.

"Tucker, if you'll give me a minute," Lewis said.

Tucker paused at the door, turned, faced him and said, "I know what you're about to say, David, and I don't want to hear it. I told you if you'd reopen the McNeer case, we'd work together, but on a purely professional basis. One, you haven't yet said you'll reopen it. You simply said you haven't yet read the file. And that's typical of you, David. You say one thing and mean another. Second, you're not my friend, and on thinking about it, you never were. You were always out for yourself and your career. So, professional?"

Lewis nodded slowly, maintaining eye contact with Tucker. Then he said, "Professional." And held out his hand.

Tucker ignored it, gave him a grim look, then brushed past him and joined Mallory, who was waiting for him a few yards on down the corridor.

"I heard all that, Tucker. Don't you think you were a little hard on him?"

"No!" Tucker snapped.

"You have to give him a chance—"

"Me? Give *him* a chance?" he snapped, interrupting her. "No. He promised she'd be safe. I told him repeatedly that she was in danger, but would he listen? No. He was too full of himself and his career to listen. Yes, I blame him for it, but I also blame myself, too. If she'd never met me, she'd probably be alive today."

"You can't go on like this, Tucker," Mallory said as they reached the end of the corridor. "This Marsha Cline thing is eating you alive. There was just one of you. There was nothing you could have done."

"And there it is," he snarled. "Just one... Just one agent. Me, to guard a poor kid I'd persuaded against her will to testify. Yes, that was me. If I hadn't... He promised she'd be safe. If he had just... I don't want to talk about it, okay?" He paused, then put a hand on her shoulder, brought her to a standstill, stepped around in front of her, faced her and said, "And don't you ever do that again, tell someone we're in without consulting me first. Understand?"

Mallory was stunned by his intensity. "I'm sorry, Tucker. I didn't mean—"

"I know you didn't," he snapped, "and that's the problem. You don't think. You never do. Look, I appreciate your enthusiasm. It's one of the many things I like about you, but this is my company, small as it is, and every decision we make, even the small ones, has a direct bearing upon whether or not we're successful. We're a team. We make decisions together. We must. If not, it will all come crashing down around our ears. Now, against my better judgment, we'll work with Lewis, but I'm going to watch him like a frickin' hawk, and at the first sign of duplicity, we're out; no arguments. Do you understand, Mallory?"

"Yes, I understand," she whispered.

17

It was already early afternoon when they walked out of the Ringgold Police Department into bright sunshine.

"Look," Tucker said, shading his eyes with a hand. "I've had enough for today. That..." He turned and nodded at the glass doors behind them and then continued, "Was a shock I wasn't prepared for. I thought I'd seen the last of David Lewis, and to walk in there and be confronted like that... Well, I need to do some thinking. So, I suggest you go home and take the rest of the weekend off. I'll take you back to your car."

Mallory nodded. She could tell he was in no mood to talk, so they made the trip in almost total silence.

It was almost one-thirty when they arrived back at the office, and the first thing Mallory did was grab the Carr file and make a copy. Then she went into the house, where she found Tucker seated at the kitchen table.

She stood for a moment at the open door, then said, "I just wanted to tell you I'm sorry. Please forgive me."

Tucker looked up at her, stared at her for a moment, then stood, walked up to her, put his hands on her shoulders and kissed her gently on her lips; then he said, "There's nothing to be sorry for, and nothing to forgive. Now go get Annie and go home. I'll see you here first thing on Monday morning. Stop by Hardee's and get us something to eat."

"But—" she began, totally stunned by what had just happened.

"No buts," he said, smiling at her. "Go home."

She stood for a moment staring at him, not knowing what to say. She bit her bottom lip, then nodded and turned slowly away.

She didn't remember the drive to the doggy day care, nor the ride from there home. She was in a state of disbelief mixed with euphoria. Half of her couldn't believe he'd kissed her, the other with a stunned sense of what it might mean.

It was on the lips, she thought. *Not the cheek... or the forehead. On the lips. Oh, my gosh. What just happened? Monday morning? I can't wait till then, can I? Oh gosh. Oh, my. Frickin' hell. What's the matter with me? It was just a peck. It meant nothing... didn't it?*

Back at the office, at just after five, and with a stomach full of pizza and beer, Tucker settled himself down on the couch in his living room and opened the Carr file. Then he leaned back, clasped his hands together behind his neck, closed his eyes and smiled, remembering the stunned look on Mallory's face when he kissed her. He also remembered how soft her lips had felt on his and how sweet they'd tasted. But then he wondered, *What the hell did I do that for? I shouldn't have done it. It wasn't fair to her. She works for me, for Pete's sake. What the hell was I thinking? Hmm, she didn't seem to mind though, did she?* He made a face. *She didn't say she liked it, either. You didn't give her a chance to, you stupid ass. Maybe I'd better call her... apologize. Hmm. Not tonight. Tomorrow, maybe. Geez, I wish...*

He opened his eyes, heaved a sigh, leaned forward, and took Morris Watson's rap sheet from the file.

Geez, that's one hell of a rap sheet, he thought.

Watson was forty-four years old. Of those forty-four years, he spent twelve of them in prison: five separate sentences ranging from six months to four years, all but one of them for burglary. The exception was the one for beating up a working girl. He'd gotten six months for that, and he'd been arrested but never charged three more times for similar events.

And this guy has a thing for prostitutes. May was a hooker. Carr wasn't. Why was he questioned in the Carr case, then? I guess I'll find out...

He yawned widely, closed his eyes again, and his semi-conscious mind was soon filled with images of Mallory Carver.

He woke three hours later at eight-thirty-five, startled. By what, he didn't know. He looked around the silent room. The curtains were open, and it was dark outside. He picked up his phone. He'd put it in silent mode. He checked for messages. There were none. He checked for missed calls. There were none. He set the phone down, disappointed.

Huh! he thought. *I guess I must have been overthinking it.* He stared at the phone for a moment, then shook his head and went upstairs, took a shower, poured himself a drink, then turned on the TV and tried to relax. He watched a movie: *Mission Impossible Ghost Protocol. Really?* he thought, unimpressed by the unrealities of it all in general and Tom Cruise in particular. *They say he does all his own stunts,* he thought. *Hard to believe, but if he does, way to go, Tom.*

He turned off the TV at a little after eleven-thirty that evening and went to bed, but sleep didn't come easily. He tossed and turned for most of the night with visions of masked men stabbing, stabbing… stabbing…

AT ALMOST THE same time as Tucker opened his file, Mallory, a little more than seven miles away, on the couch in her living room, after a meal of leftover spaghetti and the remains of the bottle of Pino Grigio, opened her copy and extracted the Watson rap sheet, and after she'd scanned through it, she had a similar reaction to Tucker. *Why did they question him about Bernice Carr?*

She put the rap sheet down and began to read through the file. More than two hours later, she was almost three-quarters of the way through it when she came across the reason. Watson, so it seemed, was a long-time friend of Bernice Carr. *Ah, they were in high school together,* she thought. Then, as she read on, she frowned. There was a credit card receipt for an oil change at the service station where he worked. It was dated just two weeks before her death. It was a tenuous connection, but a connection, nevertheless.

That's weird, she thought. *Coincidence? We don't like those, do we, Tucker... Tucker... He kissed me. I wonder...* She looked at her phone, then at her watch. It was eight-thirty. She shook her head and went back to reading and thinking.

So, it looks like Watson knew May and Carr. Hmm, I wonder if he knew Franny, or Tiffany... or Holly. Oh gosh, maybe that's the link, the service station.

She flipped through the other three files but could find nothing to indicate that might be the case. Then she heaved a sigh and relaxed, sucked on her bottom lip, shook her head.*Franny lived less than an hour away from the mall, but that's irrelevant since the mall is the only really decent shopping center anywhere near. Tiffany lived just down the road from the mall, and so did Holly. Elaine lived in Cleveland, fifteen minutes from the mall. And Bernice was also less than an hour away, but it's a straight arrow down Highway 58. Hmm... all roads lead to Hamilton Place Mall, so it seems. I wonder if that's the connection. Could the killer be working there, I wonder? Whew, if he is, and it has to be a he, right? If he is, it's going to take a lot of interviewing to find him.*

Finally, she went to bed, too, but, unlike Tucker, she went to sleep almost immediately, a slight smile on her lips.

18

Monday Morning, December 9

SUNDAY PASSED QUIETLY. TUCKER DIDN'T CALL, MUCH TO MALLORY'S disappointment. She was tempted, not for the first time, to call him but couldn't think of a good reason why she should, so she didn't. She took Annie for a long walk in the morning, called Jen, her sister, and talked to her for almost an hour, went to the store and stocked up on frozen dinners then, after eating a spaghetti dinner, sat down on the couch and stared at the mess of open files and scattered papers.

It took her almost thirty minutes to tidy them up. By the time she had, she was thoroughly fed up and wanted little more than to simply relax with a good book, a glass of nice wine, and the box of Lindor Truffles upon which she'd splurged while at the store.

By six that evening, the truffles were gone and so was two-thirds of the bottle of Pino Grigio.

Mallory woke early the following morning, Monday, excited at the thought they were going to be talking to Morris Watson.

She showered, blow-dried her hair, dressed in jeans and a white roll-neck sweater, fed Annie, ate some cornflakes with two-percent milk, still feeling a little guilty at the way she'd demolished the chocolates the day before, then loaded Annie into the car and dropped her off at her sister's.

Jen was in a funny mood and wanted to talk, but Mallory, wanting to get to the office, cut her off, promising to spend some time with her that afternoon. And then she drove to Tucker's office, excited at the prospect of seeing him and hoping he'd be in a better mood than when she left him.

It was eight-thirty when she arrived at the office, a bag of Hardee's sausage and egg biscuits in hand. She unlocked the door and let herself in to find the office empty: no Tucker.

She frowned. It wasn't like him not to be there. He was always there early. She looked at his desk—it was neat and tidy—then at hers: it was just as she'd left it. She looked at the adjoining door. It was closed. Also unusual.

Hmm, I wonder if he's okay? she thought as she walked to the door, opened it and stepped through into the house.

Geez! she thought as she stared around the living room. *What the hell?*

The place was a shambles and, at first, she wondered if there'd been a break-in, but soon realized there hadn't. There were files and photographs scattered across the coffee table, more on the floor, along with assorted papers and reports. And, in the midst of it all, lying on the couch, wearing only a T-shirt and boxers, was Tucker, fast asleep, breathing deeply.

Wow! she thought as she looked at her watch. *I need to get him moving.*

She went to the kitchen, set the coffee maker brewing, waited until it finished, then poured a huge mug of coffee and took it into the living room to find Tucker sitting up rubbing his eyes.

"Wow," he said. "Sorry. I fell asleep last night."

"That's obvious," she replied. "Here, drink this." She handed him the coffee.

"Thanks." He took it from her, sipped, closed his eyes, sipped again, then set the cup down among the detritus on the coffee table and said, "Give me a few minutes to go take a shower and get dressed.

Sorry. I must look… Oh, never mind." He tilted his head toward the door. She got the message and left him to it.

It took him more than a minute, but by nine-fifteen he'd joined Mallory in the office, dressed in jeans, a white fisherman's sweater, and carrying a heavy leather, sheepskin-lined bomber jacket in one hand and a mug of coffee in the other.

"Okay," he said brightly after setting the coffee on his desk and hanging the jacket on a hook on the office door. "What's the plan? I'm thinking we go find Morris Watson. He has some explaining to do. And I think there might be some kind of connection to the mall. But first… Breakfast. And, speaking of the mall, there's a nice place in the food court. What d'you think?"

"But I brought Hardee's," she protested.

"You did, and I put it in the fridge. I want something more… substantial and… I want to take a quick look around, with different eyes than just a shopper."

"Okay, you're the boss," she said and rolled her eyes. "Lead on, Macduff."

He nodded, drained what was left of his coffee, set the mug back down on his desk, took his holster and Glock 17 from the desk drawer, and clipped the rig to his belt.

"You think you're going to need that?" Mallory asked.

"You never know," he replied, smiling. "How about you?"

She smiled at him and patted her shoulder bag.

"Before we go," he said. "About Saturday—"

"Yes, about Saturday," she said, interrupting him. "My turn." And she stepped forward, kissed him lightly on the lips, and said, "Ready?"

He looked at her for a second, then smiled, reached out and pulled her to him, and kissed her properly.

"Now I am," he said as he turned her loose.

"Oh, my God," she said as she stared at him. "Are you serious?"

"As a heart attack," he replied, grinning. "I've been wanting to do that for a very long time. Shall we go?"

"Yeah… Yeah… You did take your damn time. But wow. Tucker?"

"Yes, I know. Me, too. We need to talk, but not now. We have work to do."

Mallory, still stunned by what had happened, watched as he donned the bomber jacket, then followed him out to his car, her mind whirling. This was a game changer, in more ways than one. He was right; they needed to talk, and soon.

"I meant to come over to see you yesterday," he said as she pulled her door shut and clicked the seatbelt. "But… well… You know."

"I almost called you," she said quietly. "Several times."

He looked sideways at her, smiled, then reached out, took her hand and squeezed it.

Mallory was… Her heart was thumping. Her mouth was dry, and she was, for once, speechless.

Tucker found a parking spot near the front entrance. "I'm thinking The Big Yellow Egg," he said as they walked together into the mall. "That good for you?"

"Umm, err, yes, of course," she replied.

They found a table and sat down to wait, Mallory nervously fiddling with the hem of her sweater.

"Look," he said. "Just relax. Everything will be fine. We'll sort it out later, okay? Now, just take a deep breath and relax. Get your head together. We have work to do."

She nodded and did as he suggested, took a breath and watched the waitress approaching.

"Tell me about David," she said, desperate to change the subject. "I think it's great that we're working together. You know, with the FBI."

"No," Tucker replied sharply. "No, it's not good, and I don't want to talk about Lewis. Besides, there's nothing to tell, other than he was my boss."

"That's not true, is it? You blame him for what happened to that teenager, don't you? What was her name, Marsha… something?"

"Cline. Marsha Cline. She was eighteen, and no; the blame was mine."

"How could you be to blame for what happened? I don't believe it."

"Well, you would be wrong. She was a witness to two murders. She didn't want to testify, but I persuaded her. I also promised her we'd keep her safe. We didn't, and she died. Case closed. Now can we talk about something else, the case in hand, perhaps?"

She looked at him. His face was pale, and he was obviously upset. She reached out and put her hand on his. He withdrew it, as if her hand was red hot. She leaned back in her chair, bewildered.

"Sorry, I didn't mean…" he began, realizing he'd hurt her feelings, then trailed off.

It was at that moment the waitress arrived at their table and introduced herself.

"Good morning. My name's Jessie. What can I get you to drink?"

"Coffee for me, please," Mallory said and looked at Tucker. He merely nodded.

"I'll be back in a minute with your coffee and to take your order," she said with a smile and turned away.

Tucker watched her go, frowning slightly.

"Hey," Mallory said. "Eyes off. I'm over here."

He looked at her for a moment, then said, "There's something about that girl… I can't put my finger on it, but she… reminds me of someone."

He shook it off, then said, "Look, Mallory. About what happened back there. I don't think it's a good—"

"Stop," she said, cutting him off. "I know where you're going. We can't do this here. Let's have a nice breakfast and then maybe this afternoon, after we've both had time to think about it, we can talk about it, over dinner, perhaps."

He nodded reluctantly but said nothing.

The waitress brought their coffee, and they ordered. Tucker noticed her name tag proclaimed her to be Jessie Mills, and he made a mental note of it.

19

THEY ARRIVED AT THE PITT STOP SERVICE STATION ON GUNBARREL Road at a few minutes before ten thirty to find it busy with both bays filled and four more customers in the waiting room.

Tucker looked around for the guy named Pete, but there was no sign of him, so he supposed he must be in the shop. Instead, he approached the counter where a young lady was watching them.

"How can I help you?" she asked. "D'you need a full service or just an oil change?"

"Neither," Tucker said. "I'm looking for Morris Watson. Is he here?"

She didn't answer. Instead, she made a face, picked up the phone and broadcast, "Morris Watson to the service desk. Morris Watson to the service desk." Then she put down the phone and said, "He'll be just a minute if you'd like to take a seat."

Morris Watson was, in Tucker's opinion, the epitome of the word creep. He was about five-ten, well-built, tanned, with dark brown hair and two days of stubble. He was wearing jeans and a black T-shirt that was at least one size too small for him. The thin material sharply defined his biceps and pecs, and when he spotted Mallory as he strode confidently into the waiting room, his lips curled into what Tucker described later as a shit-eating grin.

Tucker and Mallory both stood. He approached them and stopped in front of them, just a little too close for Mallory's comfort.

"You looking for me?" he asked, never taking his eyes off Mallory.

"I take it you're Morris Watson?" Tucker asked.

"You got it," he said, still staring at Mallory. "Who are you, and what d'you want?"

"I'm Tucker Randall. I'm a private investigator. This is my associate, Mallory Carver. We'd like to talk to you about Bernice Carr."

"Oh yeah? What about her? Last I heard, she was dead." And still he hadn't taken his eyes off Mallory.

"Hey," Tucker said. "Stop that. You're making her uncomfortable."

He turned his head to look at Tucker. The smile had turned into a sneer. "Is that so?" he asked. "Delicate, is she?" He turned again to Mallory, his eyes narrowed, and said, "I'm not making you feel uncomfortable, am I?"

She shook her head and said, "Look, we just need to talk to—"

"And why should I want to talk to you if I make you feel uncomfortable? How about we meet up later and I buy you a drink, or two, and then maybe—"

"That's enough, Watson," Tucker snapped. "Show the lady a little respect. Now, are you going to talk to us, or would you rather talk to the FBI?" He took out his phone and locked eyes with him.

There was a long pause while the two men glared at each other. Watson was the first to crack.

"Okay, okay," he said, raising his hands in mock submission. "You win. We'll go to the breakroom where it's quiet."

He was right. The breakroom was empty, and they took seats at a small round table. Mallory pulled her seat back and sat down, the table between her and Watson.

"You said the FBI," Watson said. "How come? Why now?"

"They've reopened the investigation," Tucker said. "That's all I can tell you. What was your relationship with Bernice Carr?"

"What the f..." He trailed off, then said, "She was my cousin... Well, second cousin, really. You didn't know that?"

Tucker frowned. So did Mallory.

"No, we didn't know that," Tucker replied. "Were you having an affair with her?"

"Are you for frickin' real?" he snapped. "I might be what you'd call a frickin' redneck, but I don't screw family."

"And Elaine May?" Tucker said, continuing without even a blink. "What about her?"

"What about her?" Watson countered.

"So you knew her, too, then?" Mallory said before Tucker could speak.

Watson looked at her and shrugged. "What of it?"

"She was a prostitute," Mallory said.

"What of it?" Watson replied.

"She's dead," Mallory replied. "Stabbed to death. Thirty-seven times. But you knew that, didn't you, Mr. Watson?"

He grimaced, shrugged his shoulders, and said, "What of it?"

"Well," Mallory said. "First your cousin is stabbed to death, then Elaine May, whom you also knew. You were one of her clients, I believe. That's quite a coincidence, don't you think?"

"You know, lady," he drawled. "I think you're trying to tag me for something I didn't do. But you've gotten your ducks all about face. One, Bernie and me were friends; nothing more, and Lanie, well... Yep, but I was more than a client. Sure, I paid her, but me and her... We... it was special, is what it was. I think she was in love with me. I was totally pissed off when I found out she was dead. I might even have married her. So, yeah. I was a client, but I didn't kill her. Nor did I kill Bernie. And you can't prove I did."

"But you do like to hurt prostitutes, don't you, Morris?" Tucker asked.

"Hahaha," Watson laughed. "Are you serious? That's what they get paid for, some of them."

"So why were you charged with assault—what? How many times? Three, four?"

"Three, and the charges were dropped. They just get… vindictive, I guess. No big deal."

"When did you last see her?" Tucker asked.

"See who?"

"Elaine May."

There was a pause. He hesitated, his eyebrows furrowed, then said, "Shit, it was nine years ago, man. That… Friday evening. She came here. It was my turn to work late. We had coffee together, and I was supposed to meet her when I got off at nine, but by the time we'd cleared up and when I finally got out of here, it was getting on for ten. She never turned up."

Tucker nodded. So did Mallory. She was recording the interview on her phone.

"How about Bernice?" Tucker asked. "When did you last see her?"

Watson blanched. He stared at Tucker, then said, "Look, I know what you're trying to do, and it ain't going to work. I didn't kill them women."

"You didn't answer the question," Tucker persisted, locking eyes with him. He paused, then said. "I get it, Morris. I don't think you did kill them. But here's the thing: the FBI is all over this thing. We're working with them, officially, which is why we're here. Now, what we'd like to do is eliminate you as a suspect. But if you don't cooperate, you'll find yourself talking to Agent David Lewis, and he's a real asshole. I know. I used to work for him. So, what's it to be? Us or him?"

Watson bit his lip. Gone was the bravado, replaced with a look of genuine concern.

"Okay," he said. "I saw her that Friday afternoon. She brought her car in for an oil change."

For a moment Tucker was speechless, then he said, "Here? You saw Bernice Carr here the day she died?"

Watson nodded. "Look, I know how that looks, but it's not what you think. I didn't kill either of them."

"What time did you get off that night?" Tucker asked.

Again, there was a long pause before he said, "I worked late that night, too, so nine, as usual."

"And then where did you go?" Tucker asked.

"Applebee's On Brainerd. I had a couple of beers to wash the shit of this place out of my mouth, and then I went home."

"What time did you leave Applebee's?"

"I dunno. Ten, maybe ten-thirty. I dunno. I told that deputy from Meigs County. I never heard no more from him, so I figured he was done with me."

"How about the night Elaine died?" Tucker asked. "What did you do after work?"

"I told you. I was supposed to meet Elaine, but she wasn't there?"

"She wasn't where?"

"Starbucks, up on Hamilton Place Boulevard. She wasn't there. I don't think she ever was. I asked a couple of people. They said they hadn't seen her."

"What did you do then?"

"I called her, but she didn't answer. I thought that was kinda strange, so I went on up to her place in Cleveland. I used to go there a lot, you know? But she wasn't there, and her place was locked up tight and the lights were all off."

"And that would be what time?" Tucker asked.

"I dunno. Eleven-thirty… Eleven-forty-five. I never checked my watch. I was tired, man, so I went on home. That's it. That's all I know."

"Can you think of anyone that she might have upset, that might have wanted to hurt her?" Mallory asked.

He grinned at her, then said, "She was a hooker. So yeah, but who or how many? I don't know."

She nodded. "How about friends here?" she asked. "Did Elaine have any in particular?"

He frowned, then said, "Here? You mean here?"

"Yes, I mean here, at the Pitt Stop," she replied.

"None that I know of. She talked to just about everybody, especially the guys, you know? I mean, she was just over-friendly with them all. She was a hooker, right? Why wouldn't she? It's nothing to be ashamed of."

"Anyone in particular?" Mallory persisted.

"I dunno, Pete in the shop, Charlie, who worked the pumps. Me, mostly. I told you. We were close."

"How about Bernice?" Mallory asked.

He pursed his lips and shook his head. "Not that I know of. Just me. Oh, wait, I told that deputy I thought she was cheatin' on that ex-husband of hers. Nasty son of a bitch, he is. Rogers. That's his name. Maybe you should look at him. As I said, I told that deputy, but if he done anything about it, I never heard nothing. Can I go back to work now?"

"In just a minute," Tucker said. "What about Tiffany Delgado?"

"Who?"

"Tiffany Delgado. She was from Ringgold."

He shook his head. "Never heard of her."

"How about Franny McNeer?" Tucker said.

He didn't hesitate. "Never heard of her, either."

"Where were you last Friday night between ten and one in the morning?" Tucker asked.

At that, he grinned and said, "That's an easy one. I was at the Billiard Club on Cherry Street till almost three. You can ask anyone. Why? What's happened?"

Mallory ignored the question and said, "So you must know Ollie Palmer, then?"

"Sure do. He was there, too. You can ask him if I was there. He'll tell you I was."

Tucker nodded, thought for a moment, and then said, "Okay, Morris, you can go, but I wouldn't leave town if I were you."

"Do I need a lawyer?" he asked.

"Do you think you need one?" Tucker responded.

Watson stared at him, shook his head and stood up, then turned away.

"Morris," Mallory called after him.

He stopped, turned and looked at her.

She held up her card and said, "Here, take this. If you think of anything that might help. It has my cell number."

He came back, took the card from her, looked at it, looked at her, smiled slightly, nodded, then turned and walked away without a backward look.

"You think that was wise?" Tucker asked. "Seeing as how he looked at you. He has your number now."

"Maybe, maybe not." She thought for a moment and then looked at him and said, "Well, that was something, wasn't it?" Mallory said. "What do you think?"

"If you're asking if I think he killed those two women," Tucker replied, "I have an open mind. If you're asking me what I think about him, I think he's one slick son of a bitch. He also thinks he's hot stuff. And even though he denies it, I think he has a penchant for beating up on prostitutes. Did you notice how he laughed when I mentioned it, like it was some kind of joke? What do you think?"

Mallory blew out a huge breath, then said, "Well, he has no alibi for Bernice and Elaine, and they were both here the day they died. That can't be a coincidence. Can it?"

"Maybe, maybe not."

"But he does have an alibi for Holly Wilson, and so does Ollie Palmer, by the sound of it. So, if all five murders are connected, that would eliminate both of them, wouldn't it?"

"It would," Tucker replied, "but the Holly Wilson alibi could be bogus, for both of them. And he has no alibi for the May and Carr murders," Tucker said. "And he admits he was there at Elaine's house around the time she died. In fact, I'd bet she was probably lying on the couch while he was outside, if he was outside, not inside. As to Holly Wilson and the others. If we consider there might be more than one killer… That opens up a whole new line of inquiry, and we can eliminate neither Palmer nor Watson. And if they are colluding, and they're providing each other with an alibi…" He trailed off.

Mallory shook her head. "I don't think that's the case. If it was, we'd have known by now, and Watson would have had an alibi for Elaine's time of death, too."

"Look at you," Tucker said, grinning at her. "Aren't you the detective now? Good thinking, Mallory. I'm proud of you—"

His phone rang, interrupting him. He looked at the screen. "It's David. I wonder what he wants."

20

What David wanted was to meet. They settled on Tucker's office.

David and Agent Garcia were already there when they arrived, and David was obviously in a good mood.

"Hey, you two," he said as he and Garcia exited their black Chevy Tahoe. "We should have gone somewhere for lunch. It's not too late. What do you say, Tucker?"

"I say we stick to the plan," he replied. "I have things I need to do, so here is fine."

David shook his head. "Party pooper," he said. "You never were the life and soul, were you, Tuck? Always the first one in and the last one out of the office. Never the one to go for a beer with the troops." He sighed. "Your call, buddy."

"I thought you wanted to talk," Tucker replied caustically. "A restaurant is not the place. We'll talk here… if we must."

He unlocked the office door and stood aside for Mallory to enter, and then David and Garcia. He stood outside for a moment, gathering his thoughts and breathing the crisp December air.

Asshole! he thought, then took a deep breath and followed them inside to find David already seated behind his desk.

He looked at Mallory. She was seated at her desk, leaving only a single guest chair in front of Tucker's desk. She shrugged and looked away, seemingly unable to meet his eye.

He looked at David.

David grinned at him. "No formalities, huh, buddy? Sit where you like," looking pointedly at the guest chair.

Tucker gave him a wry look and closed the door.

Garcia was standing with his back to the wall next to the door, looking more than a little embarrassed.

"So, how did it go with Watson?" David asked as Tucker stood with his back to the door, leaning against it.

Tucker, thinking he might fetch a chair from the house for Garcia, didn't answer. Instead, he looked at Mallory and nodded.

"Well," she said and cleared her throat. "It went well enough, though we didn't learn much. It turns out that Bernice Carr is Watson's second cousin, and it seems they were friends—"

"Was he having an affair with her?" David asked.

"No. Not from what he said. At least I don't think so. His actual words were, 'I don't screw family.' And I believe him. So does that answer your question?"

David smiled at her. "It does. Please continue, Ms. Carver."

Mallory stared at him, unable to make up her mind if he was taking the Mickey out of her or not. She decided not and continued. "So, anyway, we also asked him about Elaine May, and he seemed quite proud that his relationship with her was more than just that of working girl and client. He said they'd been friends." She made quotes with her fingers. "And that he loved her and that he'd even thought of asking her to marry him. Which was, to me at least, a bit of a surprise. He also said he was supposed to meet her the night she died, but she didn't turn up and that he went to her home, but she wasn't there. Tucker thinks she was probably already dead by then. Either that or he killed her." She paused for breath, then continued.

"He's also friendly with Ollie Palmer, claiming they can provide alibis for each other for last Friday night. We haven't checked with Palmer… I mean, what would be the point? If they're buddy buddies, they're going to back each other up, right? Watson was a little short on alibis for the Carr and May murders, though.."

Mallory continued to provide David a narrative of their interview with Watson. In the meantime, Tucker fetched a chair for Garcia and then sat down on the chair in front of his desk, folded his arms, and stared at Lewis.

"So," David said when she'd finished, "that's a lot of information, Mallory..." He made a face, bared his teeth and sucked in a long hissing breath. "We can't rule him out. The alibi for Wilson is iffy at best, and he's a convicted felon. And they could be working together. What d'you think, Mallory? Did he do it? What does your woman's intuition say?"

"If his alibi for Holly Wilson holds up, and if all five cases are connected... No. He couldn't have."

He turned in his chair and looked at Tucker. "Tucker?" he asked, his eyebrows raised in question.

"What Mallory said," Tucker replied. "If the alibi is good, there's no way he could."

"Oh, way to go, Tucker," David said, laughing. Welcome Johnnie Cochran.

Then he was silent for a moment, until, "I still think he's good for it. So he says he has an alibi for last night. But what if he and Palmer are lying for each other? What if they're double-teaming? Maybe they're even working together. Maybe we have two killers."

"Not likely," Tucker said, leaning forward on his chair, his elbows on his knees, his hands clasped together in front of him. "We also talked to Palmer back in November. He has an alibi for both the Delgado and McNeer murders. They might take a bit of checking out, but I think you'll find them to be good, and if so, that would rule him out, too."

"So, we're back to square one," Tucker said caustically. "We have nothing and no suspects."

David nodded. "Basically... yes. I would tend to agree," he replied. "I spoke to Finn Harper while I was on the way over here. The Holly Wilson crime scene was clean, immaculate. She was stabbed either thirty-eight or thirty-nine times. The coroner was unable to specify exactly how many times. And… her throat was cut—that's a first, I think—from left to right. The angle of cut would indicate her assailant was right-handed. There was no DNA present. Not even a stray hair. It would seem, then, that our perp has perfected his craft. I'll have my team research stabbing deaths in the tri-state area over the last twenty-five years and see if we can come up with anything new."

"What about this Charlie guy Watson mentioned?" Mallory asked.

David nodded. "I'll get a warrant for their personnel files. Wouldn't hurt to take a look at all the employees. It's the perfect place to pick up lonely women. Wouldn't you say, Tucker?"

Tucker was about to answer, but Mallory beat him to it. "And how about security footage? There might be some for last night, and I could call them and ask to see the files, too. That might save a little time."

"Hah, good luck with that," David said. "That never works. We'll get nothing from them without a warrant, but by all means, give it a try."

She nodded, picked up her phone and asked Siri to connect her with the Pitt Stop on Gunbarrel. There followed a short conversation, which obviously didn't go the way she hoped, and she hung up.

"We need a warrant," she said ruefully. She was going to say more but was interrupted by a knock on the door.

21

TUCKER MOVED AWAY FROM THE DOOR, TURNED AND OPENED IT AND was almost knocked sideways as Vinnie McNeer rushed in.

"What the hell is going on, Mallory?" Then he noticed the two FBI agents. "Oh, sorry," he said. "I didn't know…"

"It's okay, Vinnie," Mallory said. "This is Special Agent David Lewis, FBI, and that's Agent Garcia. They're here to help."

And at that, Lewis almost choked, but he said nothing. Instead, he rose to his feet and offered Vinnie his hand.

"Vinnie McNeer," I presume. "Pleased to meet you, sir."

"Why are you here, Vinnie?" Mallory asked.

"I want to know what's going on, is what," he blurted. "It's been three weeks, and I've heard nothing from you. You're keeping me out of the loop. It's almost Christmas and… damn it, Mallory, when are you guys going to get Luthor out of prison? I see this Holly Wilson thing all over the news, so he couldn't have killed her, could he? And you know he didn't kill Franny, so what's the holdup?"

Tucker frowned, looked at his watch. It was twelve-thirty-five. He stepped over to the TV and turned it to Channel 7 and, sure enough, "—it appears Ms. Wilson was being stalked and had asked the Ringgold police for help several times," the anchor was saying. "Wilson was found in her home stabbed more than thirty-eight times. The time of death was established to be between—"

"Where the hell did they get all that?" David snapped.

"—appears to be the fourth death in a series of what the authorities are now calling serial killings. The previous deaths include Elaine May of Cleveland, who was found stabbed to death in her home in July 2015, Bernice Carr of Decatur, also stabbed to death, in April 2016, and Tiffany Delgado of Ringgold in August 2019. She, too, was stabbed to death. In each case, the local police admit they have no suspects, and this reporter learned this morning that the FBI has sent a team led by Special Agent David—"

"Are you frickin' serious?" David yelled. "Tucker, Mallory, is this your doing?"

Tucker shook his head, a grim smile on his lips. "I'd say you have a leak, Davis—"

"Never mind that," Vinnie yelled. "They left Franny out. What the hell?"

"Whoa! Stop!" Mallory shouted, rising to her feet. "Calm down, everyone. This yelling at each other is getting us nowhere. I assure you, Agent Lewis, that neither Tucker nor myself have spoken to the media. It has to be… I don't know. It could have come from Cleveland, Ringgold, Decatur, or even your people. But it doesn't matter. The damage is done, and we have to work through it."

"What d'you mean, it doesn't matter?" Lewis snapped. "D'you have any idea what effect this will have on the public? You want to put a scare into them, just announce there's a serial killer on the loose. If I get my hands on whoever it was, I'll… I'll…" He was obviously livid. "And," he continued, "now the killer knows that not only local police are involved in the investigation, not to mention Randall and Carver, but also the FBI, something we needed to keep under wraps. If he goes to ground—"

"What about my brother?" Vinnie persisted.

Mallory glared at him and shook her head, but David turned to him and said, "Yes, Mr. McNeer. We're doing everything we can, but we have yet to establish that your brother's wife's murder is conn—"

"Oh yes, we have," Tucker interrupted him. "This... This... agent has yet to be persuaded. But Mallory and I are working on it, and I can assure you that we're doing all we can to get your brother out as soon as possible. Now, what I need you to do is go back to work and leave it to us. I promise we'll keep you in the loop, won't we, *David?*"

David glared at him, then nodded his head.

"Right... Well then... see that you do," Vinnie growled. "Don't make me come after you again, okay?" He looked around the room, hesitated, nodded, then turned and walked out the door.

"Whew," Mallory said. "I don't know about the rest of you, but I could do with a cup of coffee. Anyone else?"

They all did, so she went to make it and returned ten minutes later with four cups on a tray.

They spent the rest of the afternoon trying to put the pieces together and put the obvious leak to the press behind them, though Mallory could tell David was inwardly churning with anger.

Finally, unable to contain himself any longer, he said, "Tucker, Mallory, I need to get this media thing off my chest. You say you're not responsible for the leak, but I have to get to the bottom of it. You know first-hand how dangerous this kind of thing can be. Do you have any idea who it might have been?"

Tucker shook his head and pursed his lips.

Mallory stared at him for a moment, then said, "I think it's pretty obvious. If it wasn't one of your people, it had to have been someone from Finn Harper's office. No one else knew about the Holly Wilson killing, and that's what they're leading with, and they also know the details, and that could only have come from one of her people."

David stared at her. "That makes sense, but why? Why would she—"

"I'm not saying it was Harper," Mallory insisted, "but one of her people, perhaps."

"Yeah, well, I'm going to get to the bottom of it and when I do—"

"What? What are you going to do, David?" Tucker asked. "Charge them with obstruction? I don't think so. Your big city BS won't work with these people. You might think you're dealing with a bunch of hicks, but they are, for the most part, pretty damn savvy."

Lewis stared at him, breathed out audibly, then nodded, seemed to relax, and said, "Maybe you're right. I'll talk to Harper later and tell her to keep a lid on things. In the meantime…"

It was a little after four when they finally called it a day after beating the dying horse for what seemed to Mallory a lifetime. For some reason she couldn't fathom, she was unable to concentrate and, by the time they finished, the dull buzz of the conversation had all but put her to sleep.

"Okay, that's enough for me," David said, finally, and stood up. "This is getting us nowhere. Come on, Diago. Let's go back to Ringgold and see where Harper and her crew have gotten with it. I'll talk to you tomorrow, Tucker, Mallory. In the meantime, I'll get a warrant for the Pitt Stop."

Tucker nodded while Mallory escorted them to the door.

"Thank goodness they're gone," she said and collapsed into her chair. "I don't know about you, Tucker, but I could do with a drink."

Tucker smiled at her and said, "Me, too. You sit still. I'll go get 'em."

He was gone but a few minutes before returning with a bottle of 2018 Purlieu Cabernet Sauvignon Georges III, Napa, and two glasses.

"I've been saving this for a rainy day," he said, pouring her a generous measure. "Looks like I've picked the right day to open it," he continued as he glanced out the window at the darkening sky and then sat down on the guest chair in front of her.

"Cheers," he said as he raised his glass.

"This looks really expensive," she said, glancing at the bottle and then holding the glass up to the light.

"Eh, it's only money," he said dismissively.

"Oh, come on, Tucker…" and then took a sip. "Mmm." She wrinkled her brow. "This is… lovely."

He smiled. "I bought it for you. Look, I'm sorry about David. He hasn't changed. He's a total ass. Always was, always will be."

"You bought it for me?" she asked, frowning.

"Yeah, a couple of… No, more than that. I bought it two weeks after you came to work with me. I had a feeling it would work out, and I thought it would be nice to... I dunno, celebrate, I suppose."

He paused for a second, staring down into his glass, then looked up at her and said, "Look, Mallory. This thing between us—"

"Tucker, stop," she said, interrupting him. "It is what it is, though what it is, I don't know yet. Instead of trying to figure it out, why don't we just go with the flow and see where it goes?"

He put his elbows on his knees, held his glass in both hands, looked up at her and said, "But what if—"

Again, she interrupted him. "But what if what? We're not exactly kids anymore, are we, Tucker?"

And she got up from behind her desk, grabbed the other guest chair, set it down in front of him, sat down, and then, glass in hand, leaned forward, put the tips of her fingers to his cheek and whispered, "My turn," and then she kissed him.

22

TUCKER RELUCTANTLY PUT A HAND ON HER ARM, GENTLY EXTRACTED himself, leaned back in his chair and stared at her.

She smiled at him, sat upright, and said, "Well, aren't you going to say anything?"

And, for once in his life, Tucker was speechless. His mind was in a turmoil. The situation was rapidly escalating out of his control, and he was feeling helpless. *This isn't going to work,* he thought. *Work relationships never do, and I don't want to lose her.*

"Mallory—" he began, then cut himself off, bit his bottom lip, then slowly shook his head. "It won't work. We have to stop this now, before it gets out of hand."

"But—"

"No! No buts. We're partners. We're working together. That kind of thing never works. We'll end up hating each other. Trapped."

"That's ridiculous," she said, reaching for his hand, but he pulled it away.

"Really?" she asked. "Really? Okay. If that's the way you feel, I'll just quit, because if what you say is true, it won't work either way. You say we'll end up hating each other. I say we'll hate each other if we don't at least try. I can go back to work for Vinnie. That way there will be no working relationship or… Maybe I could go to work for that Starke guy."

He sighed, shook his head, and stared at her for a long moment during which she simply sat still, glass in one hand, the other in her lap, and smiled at him.

"Cat got your tongue?" she asked finally.

"Are you sure you want to…" he began, then stopped, shook his head, and continued, "Of course you are. When were you ever not?"

"What about you?" she asked. "What do you want?"

"I… I… I—"

The office phone rang. He jumped up, went to his desk and picked up the receiver. "Randall and Carver." *Geez, saved by the bell, literally!*

"My name is Jessie Mills. Is this Mr. Randall?"

"It is. How can I help you?"

"I work at The Big Yellow Egg. I served you this morning. And I saw you on TV at lunchtime today." She sounded anxious. Or was it something else?

Tucker frowned. "I wasn't on TV—"

"No, I didn't mean I saw you," she said, cutting him off. "I saw the reporter. She mentioned your name and that you are involved in the serial killer investigation."

Are you frickin' serious? How the hell did they know? He looked at Mallory, who was watching him quizzically.

"Hold on a minute, Ms. Mills, while I put you on speaker… Okay, are you still there?"

"Yes," she replied.

"So, how can I help you?"

"I need to talk to you."

Tucker furrowed his brow and shrugged at Mallory.

"Well…" he began. "We're listening."

"No, I mean in person. I think I'm being stalked. Can I come to your office?"

"She sounds upset," he said with his hand over the receiver.

Mallory nodded. "Tell her to come to the office."

He removed his hand and said, "Sure, come on over. We'll be here till five-thirty."

"Thank you, Mr. Randall. I'll be there in fifteen minutes. I have the address." And she hung up.

He looked at Mallory. She had a sly smile on her lips, and it made him feel uncomfortable.

"So, what d'you think that was about?" he asked for wanting something to say.

"I would have thought that obvious, Mr. Detective," Mallory replied. "She said she was being stalked."

"Yeah, that," he said as he sat down behind his desk.

"So, you still haven't answered my question," she said. "So, I'll ask you again. What do you want?"

He stared at her for a long moment, then said quietly, "I want what's best for you, Mallory."

"Good answer, Sherlock," she replied dryly. "So, how do you want to proceed?"

"Slowly," he said.

"Have you *ever* been in love, Tucker?"

"No, not that I can recall... Well, that's not exactly true. There was this girl in second grade, Lucy Walker, her name was. I used to follow her around like a lost puppy. Pretty little thing, she was—Hey!" he yelled as he dodged the whiteboard eraser she threw at him. "Okay, we have to stop this. We have work to do. Mills will be here in a minute. There's something about her... I noticed it this morning. Something familiar. I can't quite put my finger on it."

"I thought so, too," Mallory said, "and I think I know what it is." She stood up and stepped over to the whiteboard. "Look at these," she said, pointing at four photographs. "Elaine, Bernice, Franny, and Tiffany. They all look alike. And, if I remember her correctly, this Mills woman fits the pattern, too. Same hair, same build, roughly the same age."

Tucker was nodding slowly when there was a knock on the door. It opened, and she stepped inside.

"I'm not too late, I hope," she said.

"No, not at all," Mallory said. "Please, come on in and sit down."

Jessie Mills closed the door and took the seat in front of Tucker's desk.

Mallory, still at the whiteboard, looked at Tucker over Mills' shoulder, pointed again at the four photographs, and nodded. She flipped the board over so Mills couldn't see it, then she came and sat down in the seat Tucker had not so long ago vacated.

"So, Miss Mills," he said. "You're being stalked. Have you reported it to the police?"

"Well… no," she replied. "I didn't really think about it until I saw the news this morning, and then I thought…" She shivered visibly, then licked her lips and continued. "It's just a feeling, really. I've never seen him. It kind of began… one day last week. Tuesday, it was. I was at Hamilton Place Mall, you know? And I had this feeling that someone was watching me. It only lasted a minute. Then, the next day, when I got off shift, a car… well, I think it was a car… the headlights followed me home. And then, yesterday, I was in the front yard, cutting back the hydrangeas, when I had this weird feeling someone was watching me. I looked around and there was this black SUV, a RAV4, I think it was, with tinted windows, parked across the street. It drove away when I turned to look at it."

"Did you get the number?" Mallory asked.

She shook her head. "No, I didn't think. I was so taken aback, you know?"

They both nodded. Tucker glanced at Mallory. She was staring at Mills.

"And that's it?" Tucker asked. "You didn't see the driver, and you didn't see anyone following you at the mall?"

"No," she looked down at her hands. "It's just a feeling, really, but seeing as there's this serial killer out there, I thought… I thought I'd better say something, and then, well, when I saw the news, and they mentioned you guys, I remembered I'd waited on you this morning and I thought…" She obviously didn't know what else to say.

"Okay, Miss Mills," Tucker said. "Here's what I want you to do. I want you to go straight from here to the police department on Amnicola Highway and file a report that you think you're being stalked. They will be skeptical, but that's okay. File it anyway and try to be as specific as possible. Then… Look, I don't want to frighten you, but I do want you to take some basic precautions. I want you to keep all of your doors securely locked at all times. Can you lock your bedroom door?"

"No, there's no lock."

"Upstairs or downstairs?"

"Upstairs."

"Okay, when you go to bed, put a chair under the doorknob. Better yet, go to Lowe's and ask for a portable door security bar or have them cut you a piece of two-by-six exactly thirty-six inches long—that will be a lot cheaper and just as good—and jamb it under your bedroom doorknob. And keep your phone charged and by your bed. Look, I don't really think you're being stalked. I think what's happening here is possibly autosuggestion. You heard the news, and you got to thinking and one thing led to another, and here we are. Having said that, there's no sense in not taking precautions. Now, have you got all that?"

"I think so," she replied nervously.

"Good," Tucker said. "Now tell me what you're going to do."

"I'm going to report it to the police, and I'm going to Lowe's and ask for a portable door security bar or have them cut me a piece of two-by-six thirty-six inches long."

"And you're going to keep your wits about you. You're not going to talk to strangers. And you must not go anywhere on your own."

"I've got it," she said. "But…"

"Yes, you can call me or Ms. Carver anytime. Here are our cards. Put the numbers in your phone, and if anything untoward happens, call us. Immediately. You hear?"

"Yes. I heard you. Thank you both," she said and stood up. "I feel a lot better now." She smiled and went to the door, opened it, then turned and smiled one last time before closing it behind her.

"So, what do you think?" Tucker asked.

"I think she's scared," Mallory replied, staring at the door, "and rightly so."

"I know she's scared," Tucker replied, "but do you believe her? Do you believe she's being stalked?"

Mallory shrugged, then said, "I think *she* believes she is, but do I believe she is? I don't know. If I knew her better... But she seems like a strong woman. Not one for hysteria. What about you?"

"I don't know either," he said, then sighed and continued. "I think maybe she heard all that BS on the news and convinced herself she's next. Who the hell could have leaked it?" It was a rhetorical question that neither of them could answer.

"Hey," he said, looking at her guardedly, "would you like to go somewhere nice for dinner?"

"Why, Tucker Randall, are you asking me out on a date?"

"You want to go or not?" he blurted.

"Yes, that would be nice, but it's almost five-thirty and I have to pick up Annie. Then I have to go home and change. You want to pick me up, say about seven-thirty?"

23

MALLORY ARRIVED AT THE DOGGY DAYCARE AT A LITTLE AFTER FIVE-thirty to find Annie had had a bath and her toenails clipped. She was also in one of her playful moods, bouncing around on the end of her leash while Mallory paid her bill and chatted with the lady owner, who was enthusiastically yakking on about what a wonderful dog she was.

"I bet you say that about all the dogs," Mallory said, smiling as she handed over her credit card.

"No, no. Not at all. She really is. She is very obedient, smart, and she gets along with the other dogs really well."

But Mallory already knew all that. "It's because she's a Border Collie," she said as she signed the receipt. "We're good for the rest of the week, then?" she asked as she handed her the signed copy.

"Yes, of course. See you tomorrow, then, around eight-thirty?"

Mallory nodded, thanked her, and Annie led her to the car, straining at the leash.

It was almost six o'clock and dark when she pulled into her driveway and parked. She opened the car door, unclipped Annie and leaned back as the dog scrambled over her, out and down onto the concrete, ran a couple of yards toward the front porch, and stopped dead, the fur on the back of her neck and rump raised. She went into point mode, staring at the porch, growling softly.

"Annie, what's wrong?" Mallory, still in the car, reached for her purse, took out the P938 and slid cautiously out onto the driveway.

"Go find it, girl," she whispered, then flipped off the safety as she stepped slowly forward, the gun held at arm's length in both hands, as Tucker had taught her.

Annie trotted to the porch, her nose to the ground, up the three steps onto the porch and there she stopped, hackles raised, growling, pointing at a paper fast food sack from McDonald's.

"Annie, come, heel," she snapped.

The dog turned and leaped down the steps in two bounds and sat at her heel.

"We need to take a look around the back," she said, and, together, they made a circuit of the house, ending back in front of the steps.

Mallory looked at the paper sack, took a deep breath, climbed the three steps, peered cautiously inside using the barrel of the gun to open it, and found a Big Mac and fries.

She bit her bottom lip, frowned, stood up and looked around, back toward the road in time to see a pair of headlights come on and a black SUV drive slowly by and disappear into the night.

She set the safety on the P938, went back to the car, got her purse, slipped the gun inside and went to the house and unlocked the front door. And there she had a second thought. She took the gun from her purse, flipped off the safety and went inside. A quick but breathless tour of her home revealed nothing more. She sat down at the kitchen table, put the gun down on the tabletop, ran her fingers through her hair, then put her elbows on the table and her head in her hands, and there she sat for several moments, thoroughly unnerved, trying to compose herself. Finally, she got up, went to the front door, grabbed the paper sack and then went back to the kitchen and threw it in the trash.

"That was quite a fright, Annie," she said.

The dog sat still, looking up at her, panting softly, her tongue hanging out the side of her mouth.

"I bet you need to go out, right?"

Annie jumped to her feet and ran to the back door.

Fifteen minutes later, with Annie safely back inside eating a full bowl of her special homemade food and all the doors and windows securely locked, Mallory was in the shower, the hot water washing away the rigors of the day, especially those of the last half-hour.

She toweled herself off, blow-dried her hair and then went to her bedroom, wondering what she was going to wear. Not that she had a lot of choice. Ten dithering minutes later, after trying to decide on red or black, she slipped into the little black dress and stood in front of the mirror, barely recognizing herself. The dress was sleeveless, cut two inches above the knee and contrasted nicely with her blonde hair. She nodded to herself, slipped on her taupe sandals with three-inch heels, boosting her height to a little over six-one, then went again to the mirror and stood there for several moments, wondering if it was a little too much. Finally, she sighed, gave it up and decided it would have to do; it was seven-twenty. *Almost time,* she thought as she added a little light makeup to her eyes, cheeks and lips.

Tucker arrived punctually at seven-thirty and rang the doorbell.

"Hey," she said as she opened the door and stood aside for him to enter. "Right on time."

Then she led him through to the living room, turned and was about to speak, but before she could, Tucker said, "Wow! Who the hell are you?"

She blushed, speechless.

"You look…" He wanted to say beautiful, but the word hung there on the tip of his tongue. So he settled for, "Amazing. I've never seen you look like this before. You don't look… real."

"Oh, stop it, Tucker," she said, feeling more than a little pleased with herself. "Would you like a drink before we go? I have some nice scotch."

He shook his head. "Better not. I'm driving, so two drinks only. You ready to go?"

"I am." She turned to Annie, who was on the couch watching their every move, and said, "I won't be long, Annie. You guard the house while I'm gone, okay?" The dog tilted her head and looked quizzically at her, then lay down, put her head between her paws and stared up at her.

"Good girl," Mallory said, then turned to Tucker and said, "Shall we?"

And they did, and Mallory, having decided she didn't want to spoil the evening, said nothing about the paper sack or the car that had been parked just down the street. Was the driver watching her house? Did they put the paper sack on the porch and, if so, why? *I mean, who does that kind of thing?* she wondered as Tucker drove to Ruth's Chris.

"By the way," he said, "David figured out who the Pitt Stop employee is. It's Charlie Gibson. I think we'll go see him tomorrow morning. What d'you think?"

She nodded, then said absently, "Yes, all right." It wasn't until they were seated at their table that he noticed how pale she looked.

"Hey," he said, frowning. "Is everything okay? You look kind of pale."

She smiled at him, reached across the table, took his hand, squeezed it and said, "It is now." *But not really,* she thought, took a deep breath and smiled at him.

They enjoyed a delightful meal together, talked about everything except work and, by the time they were through, she knew more about Tucker than she had in all the time she'd known him. He really opened up to her, about his brother, their family, his upbringing, even his past girlfriends, but simmering at the back of it all, even though he mentioned it only once in passing, was the death of Marsha Cline. And so, two steak dinners and a rather expensive bottle of red wine later, he drove her home.

He parked beside her CRV and walked her to the door. As she was about to unlock the door, he took her arm, turned her to him, then took her in his arms and kissed her.

"Oh...my," she whispered. "Tucker—"

He put two fingers to her lips and said, "I'll see you tomorrow. Sleep well, Mallory."

"Don't you want to come in?" she asked, a little bewildered.

He pursed his lips, shook his head and said, "Yes, of course I do. But not tonight. Lock all your windows and—"

"Yes, I know," she said, cutting him off. "But are you sure you won't come in?"

He nodded, put his hands on her shoulders, and kissed her again. "I'll see you tomorrow," he said, then turned, walked down the steps and back to his car, where he stood and watched until she turned, waved, and then went into the house and closed the door.

24

Tuesday morning December 10

TUCKER SLEPT LITTLE THAT NIGHT. HE COULDN'T GET MALLORY OUT OF his head, and it perturbed him. He'd experienced nothing like it before, and what he couldn't understand was why now? He'd known her for more than a year. They'd worked closely together all that time, and never once had he felt for her what he was feeling now, but he really wasn't sure *what* he was feeling, and it was that that was keeping him awake.

And so, last time he looked at his bedside clock, it was after two when he finally fell asleep to be awakened by the jangle of his iPhone alarm at six-thirty.

He literally fell out of bed, grabbed the phone, cut the alarm, and then sat with his back against the bedframe, trying to pull himself together.

He made it to the bathroom, took a hot shower, and then turned it cold, almost giving himself a heart attack. He dressed quickly and went downstairs, turned on the local news and ate some breakfast, checking his watch every five or ten minutes.

She finally arrived at a little after eight-thirty to find him sitting behind his desk, nursing a cup of coffee.

"Hey, you," he said as she closed the door. "There's coffee in the pot. Did you have a good night?"

"I did. You?" she replied as she poured herself a cup of coffee.

"Yep," he lied. "There's nothing on the local news about Holly Wilson," he said, more for something to say than anything else.

"No," she replied. "I saw that."

There followed a moment of strained silence before Tucker said, "Have you eaten yet? I haven't, and I thought maybe we could stop by and check on Jessie Mills on our way to the Pitt Stop."

"No, I haven't. Is there anything we need to do here before we go?"

"Can't think of a thing," he replied, his second lie of the morning. There was always plenty to do at the office, but Tucker was always one to put things off until the last minute. "Let's go."

The Big Yellow Egg was busy, as it always was at that time in the morning. Jessie Mills was, as Tucker had hoped, waiting tables and seemed to be in a good mood.

"Good morning," she said, smiling. "My name's Jessie and I'll be your server today," she quipped. "What would you like to drink?"

"I see your sense of humor has returned," Tucker said, looking up at her. "How are you feeling?"

She shrugged. "I'm okay," she replied. "I took your advice. I had Rachel pick me up this morning, and I got one of those door bar thingies. So yeah, I'm okay, I guess."

"Well, that's good," Tucker said. "You know where we are and how to get a hold of us if you need us." Then he looked at Mallory and said, "So, Mallory, what will you have?"

She ordered two eggs scrambled, sausage, grits, toast and coffee, black.

"I'll have the same," Tucker said.

"What's the matter, Mallory?" he asked as Jessie walked away. "You still look... pale."

"Nothing," she replied sharply. For some reason she couldn't define, she was still unwilling to tell him about the paper sack on her porch. "Really. It's nothing. What are we doing for Christmas?" she asked, changing the subject.

That hit him like a bolt out of the blue. Close as it was, he hadn't even thought about Christmas.

"What? Hah, I haven't thought about it," he said.

"Well," she said, "it's just a couple of weeks away, so maybe you should." And that did the trick. Tucker, now sidetracked to something he didn't want to think about, also changed the subject.

He took a sip of his coffee and said, "I wonder if David has a list of Pitt Stop employees. Hold on to your thoughts while I text him." He tapped on his phone for several seconds, then hit send and set his phone down almost at the same moment as their food arrived.

No sooner had they finished eating than his phone chirped, indicating he had an email. He opened the email, read it, then said, "Do you have your iPad with you?"

"Yes. Why?"

"Take it out. It's an email from David with an attachment. The attachment is too big to read on my phone, so I'm going to forward it to you. I need you to open it so I can read it. It has a list of the Pitt Stop employees, and some of them have records."

"Okay," she replied, taking the iPad from her shoulder bag. "Send it."

She opened the iPad, signed in and, while Tucker tapped on his phone, she went to her email account. Tucker hit send, then looked at her, his eyebrows raised. The email arrived. She opened it, then opened the attachment and handed the tablet to Tucker. All that without saying a word.

Tucker scrolled through the attachment, then looked at Mallory and said, "You want to take notes?"

"How about you talk, and I record it?" she replied.

"Good enough," he said and waited while she set her phone to record.

She nodded, and he began, "There are seven men and eight women on the Pitt Stop staff. We can eliminate the women and concentrate on the men."

Tucker took a sip of coffee and then continued, "First, there's Morris Watson. We talked to him yesterday and decided we can't eliminate him.

"So the rest is as follows. Watson mentioned Charlie Gibson. He's thirty-six. He looks after the pumps and fills in as a sales clerk as needed. He works mostly dayshift. He has a record. He did ten months in County in 2008 when he was twenty for assault. Apparently, he got drunk and tried to rape a female friend. He's been clean ever since.

"Next is Pete Abbott, age thirty-two. Watson also mentioned him. He's a sales clerk, works dayshift seven till seven. No record. I think I met him when I was paying for gas a few days ago.

"Mike Harrell is forty-three. He's a mechanic. Works dayshift seven till seven. No record.

"Larry Talbot, age forty-eight, Mechanic. Dayshift. No record.

"Jarred Marks, age thirty-three. Mechanic. Day shift. Now he has a record. He was arrested in 2015 for bar fighting. The judge let him off with a warning. He was arrested again in 2017 for breaking a man's jaw. He was fined a thousand dollars and given fifty hours of community service for that one. In 2018, he was arrested again. This time for stealing a car. That one got him a hundred hours of community service. He's been clean since. Hmm.

"Finally, we have Jinks Jones, age twenty-five. Mechanic. No record. You get all that?"

She gave him a withering look and said, "Of course I did."

"So," he said, grinning. "What d'you think?"

"I don't know. I've not met any of them yet."

He nodded, caught Jessie's eye, and asked for the check.

He paid the bill, reminded Jessie they were just a phone call away, then looked at Mallory and said, "Let's go meet the cast."

Tucker pulled onto the Pitt Stop lot a few minutes later and parked in front of the convenience store window, taking note of the vehicles in the service bays and the two men working there; one of them was Morris Watson.

Together, they walked through the glass doors into the convenience store and looked around. The register was being tended by an older, frustrated-looking woman.

"Pete around?" Tucker asked.

"Aisle four," she replied without looking at him.

They stepped over to the coolers that lined the far wall and there, at the far end of the store, Tucker spotted the guy he recognized as Pete stocking the shelves.

Pete stood up as they approached, put his hands on his hips and stretched his back.

"Hi," he said. "Looking for more energy drinks? They're back there, to your right."

"Pete Abbott?" Tucker asked.

Abbott frowned, then said, "Yeah. How d'you know my name?"

"I was wondering if we might have a word," Tucker said, smiling at him.

The frown deepened. "What about?"

"My name's Tucker Randall. I'm a private investigator. This is my associate, Ms. Carver. We're looking into the death of Franny McNeer."

"Never heard of her," he replied. "Is this about that serial killer everyone's talking about? I saw something about it on TV this morning. Why would you want to talk to me?"

"Your name came up and—"

"Son of a bitch. It was Watson, wasn't it? I saw you talking to him yesterday. I'll frickin' murder him... Whoa, don't take that the wrong way. I only meant—"

"I know what you meant," Tucker interrupted, smiling at him. "We're talking to everyone who might have known her. You didn't know her, right?"

He shook his head. "Yeah, no. I didn't know her. I never heard of her."

"How about Elaine May?"

Again, he shook his head. "Nope... No, wait. Wasn't she Morris' girlfriend? But that was years ago. She a hooker, wasn't she? I reckon I might have seen her in here, but I don't remember her if I did."

"Tiffany Delgado?"

He shook his head.

"How about Holly Wilson? Did you know her?"

"The blonde on TV? The one that got killed last week? No, of course I didn't," he said, frowning. "Look, what is this? Am I in some kind of trouble?"

"No, of course not," Tucker said. "Where were you last Friday night between ten and one in the morning?"

"Oh, come on, man," he began. "This is ridiculous… I was home. And I was alone." He looked upset, and Tucker didn't blame him.

Tucker nodded, then said, "Thanks for your time, Mr. Abbott. Is Mr. Gibson around?"

"He's out there somewhere, working on pump nine, I think. Hell, I don't know. You're done with me, then?"

Tucker nodded. "Yes, we're done. Thank you again."

"So, what d'you think?" Mallory asked as they walked outside onto the forecourt.

"Oh, he's okay. I told you he's a nice guy."

"You didn't ask him about Bernice," she said as they stood and looked around.

"I didn't think there was any point," he replied. "He didn't remember Elaine, so what were the chances of him remembering Bernice?"

Mallory didn't answer. She looked around and saw Abbott staring at them through the window.

"That must be him," Tucker said, setting off toward a man working on one of the pumps. "You want to take this one?"

"Sure," she said.

Gibson had the front off the pump, exposing its inner workings, and he was on his knees with both his hands inside.

"Mr. Gibson?"

"Yeah," he replied without taking his hands out of the machine.

"Can we have a word?"

"Yeah, but you'll have to give me a minute."

The minute turned into five, but eventually, he pulled out, sat back on his haunches, pulled an oily rag from his pocket and wiped his hands, all the while staring at the inner workings of the pump.

"That should do it," he muttered to himself, then turned his head and looked up at them. When he saw Mallory, he quickly scrambled to his feet, blushing. He offered her his hand, then quickly withdrew it. "Sorry," he said. "Dirty. You want to talk to me? What about?"

"I'm Mallory Carver, and this is Tucker Randall. We're private investigators"—*Well, I will be soon,* she thought—"and we're—"

"I know what you want," he snapped, stuffing the dirty rag into his pocket. "Mo told me all about it after you left yesterday. I don't know nothin' about anything."

"Mo?" she asked, frowning. "Oh, you mean Morris Watson. What did he tell you?"

"He said that you was lookin' into that serial killer thing we saw on TV. Look, lady. I just told you. I don't know nothin' about any of that. So… why don't you just go and leave me alone?"

"It seems some of the victims were known to frequent the Pitt Stop, so we're talking to everyone who worked here over the last ten years, and that includes you, Mr. Gibson. Now, would you rather talk to us or to the FBI?"

He ran his hand through his fair hair, then realized what he'd done, looked at his hand and muttered, "Aw shit!"

He heaved a sigh, shook his head once, then said, "Okay, go ahead. Ask your questions."

"Did you know Holly Wilson?"

"The woman they're talking about on TV? No! Absolutely not."

"Where were you last Friday night between ten and one in the morning?"

"Shit. Here we go," he muttered. "Friday night? I was at the bar in Applebee's on East Brainerd till they closed at eleven and then I went home. I was home by half-after-eleven. That's it."

"Can anyone corroborate that?" she asked.

"Yeah, Mickey. He was working the bar, among other things. Now, are we done?"

"Not quite," she replied. "You say you were home by eleven-thirty. Were you alone?"

"Unfortunately, yes!"

"So you were alone between eleven and one a.m.?" she persisted.

"That's what I said, damn it."

"Do you know Jessie Mills?" she asked.

He frowned. "No. Who is she?"

Mallory shook her head, then said, "Elaine May?"

At that, he grinned and said, "Mo's old girlfriend, the hooker? Sure, I did. Everybody did. I even had me a little of it one time. My, but she was hot, but way too expensive for my blood. What she saw in Mo, I don't know. She could have had her pick. He knew I laid her that one time, and it pissed him off big time. And I know he was pissed at her. Gave her a black eye. What did he say about me? Frickin' rat."

"You say he was angry that you… that you… laid her. How angry?"

Gibson grinned at her. "Angry enough to give her a smack in the eye. He knew better than to mess with me, though. You're asking me if he could have killed her?" He shrugged, still grinning widely, then continued, "Maybe. I dunno. I guess we've all got a little of that in us, given the right circumstances."

"How about you, Mr. Gibson? Did you have it in you to kill Elaine?" Mallory asked.

He was smiling widely now. "I was wondering when you'd get around to that," he said. "No, lady. I didn't kill her. I thought she was pretty damn cool, and I'll remember that night I had with her till I die. Five hundred bucks that cost me, and it was worth every damn dime. She put her heart and soul into her work, that one did, and she was a looker, too."

He paused, stared at Mallory for a second or two, then said, "Look, I know you talked to Morris. He told me you did. He didn't tell me he'd pointed you in my direction, though. I'll have a word with him about that. But let me give you a little advice. Stay on him. He's a nasty little weasel. I think he may even be psychotic enough to have killed those women. I watched him shoot a cat once, for nothing, for just being in the service bay. Beat its head in with a wrench, so he did. Wicked little f..." He trailed off, obviously still thinking about the cat.

"So where were you the night Elaine died?" she asked.

"Hah! God only knows. How long ago was it? Seven years? Eight? How the hell should I know?"

"Nine," she said, exasperated.

"So now go ahead and ask about the other dead women," he snarled. "But before you do, I don't know where I was for any of them. Geez, lady. Where were you on... let's say July 10 this year?"

She looked at him, obviously taken aback, then said, "That's not quite the same—"

"See?" he said. "You don't know, do you, and that's only six months ago. So how d'you expect me to remember where I was six years ago? Damn stupid question, if you ask me."

"Well, here's another stupid question for you," she snapped. "You have a record for assault. You were arrested for sexual assault in 2008, and you served ten months. You tried to rape a young woman. What d'you have to say about that, Mr. Gibson?"

He narrowed his eyes and stared at her. "I say that was blown up out of all proportion," he replied. "I was a kid, and I was drunk. Sure, I pushed her a bit too hard. I never intended to rape her. I don't drink anymore, and I've not been in any trouble since."

"But you're on the Tennessee Sex Offenders Register, are you not?"

He took a long, deep breath, then said, "I am. So what?"

"Think about it, Mr. Gibson. Did you know, Bernice Carr?" she asked. "She was a friend of Elaine May."

He shook his head. "No, ma'am. I did not!"

"Tiffany Delgado?"

He grinned at her and shook his head.

"How about Franny McNeer?"

"Nope." He grinned at her, eyed her up and down, obviously liking what he saw.

It was at that point that Mallory's lack of experience became apparent to Tucker.

She hesitated, and Tucker stepped in and said, "All right, Mr.

Gibson. Thank you for your time. We may need to talk to you again." He nodded to him and turned away.

"You're welcome," he said, "especially you, lady."

"Pig," Mallory muttered as they went back to the convenience store. "Hold on, Tucker," she said, grabbing his arm. "What was that about back there?"

"Yes, sorry about that. I just got the feeling we were wasting our time," he said, trying to be diplomatic. "He's one tough SOB, but I tend to believe him. He maintained eye contact, and he wasn't bothered by the questions."

"True," she said as they walked toward the service bays. "But he has no alibi for any of them, not even Holly Wilson. And he has all the attributes of a serial killer."

"Hah," he half-laughed. "Yes, I suppose he does. Let's see who else we can find."

"Well, I think he's a good fit," she said petulantly.

Morris Watson met them at the service bay doors, wiping his hands, and said, "What did Charlie have to say for himself, then? I saw you talking to him. Piece of work, he is. Ain't he?" He looked at Mallory and said, "You need to watch him."

"Hello, Morris," Tucker said. "You've had time to think about our chat yesterday. Anything to add?"

Watson grimaced, shook his head, and said, "Can't think of a thing, Detective."

"Who's your friend?" Tucker asked.

Watson turned to look at the young man who'd joined them. He was fair-haired, tall, wiry and obviously worked out.

Watson turned to look at him, then said, "Jinks, say hello to Mr. Randall and… Sorry, ma'am. I forgot your name."

"Carver," she said.

"Mallory Carver," Watson said. "They're what they used to call in the movies, private *dicks*." He emphasized the word dicks.

Jinks nodded but said nothing.

"Jinks Jones?" Tucker asked.

"Yeah, so what?"

"Can we have a word, please? In private?" Tucker asked.

"You can say whatever you want to say in front of him," he said belligerently.

"Beat it, Morris," Tucker said to Watson in a tone that made it clear he would brook no argument.

Watson grinned, nodded, then said, "Careful what you say to them, Jinks. Things have a way of getting twisted, if you get what I mean." Then he turned away and walked to the back of the service bay. There, he sat down on an oil barrel and stared at them.

This kid is too young to have had anything to do with Franny, Carr and May... Tucker thought. *Still, it's worth a shot.*

"Just a few quick questions, Jinks. Can you tell me where you were between ten and one on Friday night?" *Might as well begin there.*

"Yeah, Mo told me about you guys," he said. "I don't have to say nothin' to you."

"That's true," Tucker said, "but if you have nothing to hide, why wouldn't you want to answer our questions?"

Jones shrugged, locked eyes with Tucker, then said, "I was with Jenny, my girlfriend."

"Jenny who?"

"Lawrence. Jenny Lawrence. I was with her at her place all night. You can call her. The number is..."

He gave them the number. Tucker nodded at Mallory. She turned, walked away, and made the call. She was gone only a couple of minutes before returning.

She nodded at Tucker, and he turned and said, "Thank you, Jinks. That's all we need. See? Easy, wasn't it?"

Their next stop was back in the convenience store where they checked on the other employees on the list and found that Harrell was on sick leave, having had hernia surgery on December 3, three days before Holly Wilson's murder. Marks was off until the weekend. And Talbot had the day off.

"If Harrel has just had surgery for a hernia, I doubt he could have been fit enough to have killed Holly Wilson. Hmm, time to get some lunch," Tucker said. "What d'you fancy?"

By then, they were back in the car and she leaned back in her seat and closed her eyes.

"The Acropolis would be nice," she said, her eyes still closed. Then, "Why did you let him off the hook, Tucker?"

"I thought you'd ask that," he replied as he started the engine. "A couple of reasons. One, his alibi checked out, right?"

"It did," she said.

"So he couldn't have killed Holly Wilson and, by extension, neither could he have killed Delgado. As for the others, he would have been in his teens, so I didn't think so. All we needed was a confirmed alibi for Wilson, and we got it. No sense in prolonging an interview when we didn't need to."

"Makes sense, I suppose," she said and yawned.

25

BEING A TUESDAY LUNCHTIME, MALLORY EXPECTED THE ACROPOLIS TO be busy, and it was, though the wait time was only a few minutes.

They were seated by the window at the far side of the dining room opposite one another, something Mallory was—though she couldn't explain why—somehow grateful for.

"Mallory, you've been quiet all morning. Something's wrong," Tucker said, leaning across the table and taking her hand. "What is it?"

She shook her head and squeezed his fingers. "Nothing. Really. I promise."

"Is it... You know?"

"Us, you mean?" she asked, smiling. "No."

"Well, I know you well enough by now to know when something's off. Come on. Tell me."

She locked eyes with him and sighed. "Tucker, it's nothing. I'm probably making a big deal out of it, but—" She cut herself off, shook her head again, then continued, "When I got home last night, I let Annie out of the car, and as soon as she hit the ground she started growling. She knew something was wrong. I followed her to the porch and... and someone had left a bag of McDonald's at the front door. No note. Nothing. Just the bag of food. We checked around the house." She shrugged. "Look, it's probably nothing. Someone being nice. But..." She bit her bottom lip. "Considering what we're dealing with, it's a little unnerving."

He squeezed her hand and was about to speak when the server arrived to take their order. He let go of her hand and leaned back.

The server left, and Mallory said, "Well, any comment?"

"You're probably right," he said. "Much ado about nothing. But... Where's your Sig?"

She reached for her purse, opened it and showed him the weapon nestled in the interior, safety on, hammer cocked.

He nodded. "Keep it with you locked and loaded at all times. Keep your doors and windows securely locked and bar your bedroom door. You need some security cameras. I have some and a spare laptop. I'll come over this evening and install them... If that's okay with you."

"Of course it is. How about I cook spaghetti?"

"That would be nice," he replied, smiling at her as his phone buzzed.

"Hello, David," he said when he answered the phone. "Okay... Uh-huh... Yep... Say..." he looked at his watch, then said, "Two o'clock... Yes... Of course." Then he hung up and shook his head. "He wants an update. Our office at two." Then, under his breath, "Son of a bitch!"

"I heard that," Mallory said. "You have to get over it, Tucker. Put your grievances behind you. Being adversarial is non-productive."

"Easy for you to say," he muttered, then took a deep breath, smiled and said, "I'll try to do better, but only for you."

THEY ARRIVED BACK at the office to find David and agent Garcia already there, waiting for them.

"Nice lunch?" David asked as they got out of the car.

"Nice until—"

"Yes, it was very nice, thank you, David," Mallory cut in, giving Tucker the look. He just smiled at her and unlocked the office door, then stood aside for them to enter.

"Coffee, anyone?" she asked brightly.

It was a yes for everyone.

"So," David said. "What have you been up to this morning?"

"Why don't you go first, David?" Tucker said. "How did it go with Levi Rogers yesterday?"

David nodded. "He has a record for violence, as you know, mostly domestic. He's remarried to a girl almost half his age; Alicia Aguirre. She opened the door. Nasty black eye. Said she tripped and fell. I don't believe it. Kid can't be more than twenty-five. I think he's knocking her about."

He thought for a moment, then continued, "His alibi for Friday night is Alicia, which isn't worth a damn. She's scared of him. We asked him about Bernice Carr, his first wife. He said he was out of town on a fishing trip and came home as soon as he heard what happened. Your buddy and his, Morris Watson, called him and gave him the news. So I'm pretty confident it's *not* Levi. As for Delgado; he has a solid alibi for that one. It was easy to confirm. All it took was a phone call. He was at work, at the Amazon distribution facility on Discovery Drive. Garcia talked to his foreman, and he confirmed it. As to the rest…" He shrugged. "He wasn't working at Amazon before December 2018 when he signed on for the Christmas rush and they kept him on. It's no more than what's in Detective Warner's report. You have a copy, right?"

"We do now," Mallory said. "Thank you."

She handed him and Garcia a mug of coffee, and another to Tucker. Then sat down at her desk with a cup for herself.

"So," David said after taking a sip of coffee. "How did you do?"

"No better than you," Tucker said. "We interviewed the main suspect, Morris Watson. He and Palmer have complementary alibis for the Wilson murder, but they're buddies and would probably back each other up no matter what. And, of course, there's the possibility that they could be working together."

"Maybe we should talk to Palmer again," Mallory said. "About Wilson."

"Yes, I think we should," Tucker said, then to David he said, "We also interviewed a Pete Abbott. He has no alibi for the Wilson murder and was pretty pissed off that Watson had pointed the finger at him.

"We also talked to Charlie Gibson. He did ten months for sexual assault back in 2008, but he's been clean since. He has a partial alibi for the Wilson murder. He admitted he knew Elaine May and that he'd had sex with her, for a fee, but insists he didn't kill her. He can't remember where he was the night she died, but he did point the finger at Watson. He said, and I quote…" He looked at his notes and read, "'He's a nasty little weasel. I think he may even be psychotic enough to have killed those women.'"

"And we talked to Jinks Jones. If his alibi for the Wilson murder checks out, we can eliminate him for that one. And he's too young to have killed May, Carr or McNeer."

"So," David said, "we have some work to do, though it feels like we're at a bit of a dead end. I wonder—"

He was interrupted by the door opening and Jessie Mills bursting into the room, pale as a sheet.

"You've got to help me." She was in a panic, her voice trembling. "Someone's been following me. A car followed me home last night. A black SUV, and I saw it parked across the street from the Egg, just a few minutes ago. It drove away when I went outside and stood looking at it. I tried to get the number, but it was too quick for me. You've got to help me. *Please!*" And she burst into tears.

Mallory got up from her desk, went to her, put an arm around her shoulder, and steered her to her chair.

"Calm down, Jessie," she said gently. "Of course we'll help you. Just… calm down, okay?"

Jessie stopped crying, heaved a shuddering breath, wiped her eyes, sniffled, and nodded.

"We need to see the Egg's security footage," Tucker said. "Mallory and I can do that. Anything more you need from us, David?"

"No, but stay in touch. If there's anything on that footage, let me know ASAP, okay?"

Tucker nodded, and the two FBI agents rose to their feet and left.

"Jessie?" Mallory asked, handing her a tissue. "Would you like some coffee?"

Jessie shook her head and looked ready to burst into tears again.

"Come on, now," Mallory said. "That's enough. You're safe now. Tucker and I will go talk to your boss and hopefully look at the security footage. What I want you to do is go home. You have a door bar, right?"

"I have three," she muttered. "One each for the downstairs doors, back and front, and one for my bedroom."

"That should do it," Mallory said, taking her arm. "Now then, off you go. We're on it... D'you have a gun?"

Jessie shook her head.

"Hmm, maybe you should."

She looked at Tucker. He shook his head, frowning. "No!" he mouthed, so Jessie couldn't hear him.

"Now look," she said as Jessie rose to her feet. "You have my number, and you have Tucker's. You can call us anytime, okay?"

She watched her go to her car and then closed the door, turned to Tucker and said, "We could have given her a gun. You have plenty."

"Err, no, we couldn't," he replied. "We don't know if she can handle a gun. Hell, Mallory, no one should own a gun, or even handle one unless properly trained. They could be a danger to themselves, much less anyone else."

"Sorry. I didn't think," she replied.

"Let's go take a look at that footage..." he said, then thought for a moment before continuing, "Look, Mallory. I know you feel for her, as do I, but we don't even know for sure that she's being stalked. It could all be in her imagination. And even if she is, we've done all we can, short of moving in with her. She's taken all the precautions, so she should be safe enough, at least for now, until we know who it is."

Mallory shook her head. "I guess you're right," she said. "It's just that I... I wish... Oh, I don't know what I wish. Let's just go."

The owner of the Big Yellow Egg, Brad Lincoln, was only too pleased to show them the footage for that day and the previous evening and even made them a copy.

"She was right," Tucker said. "That's a RAV4. A late model."

They watched the footage as Jessie appeared and stood with her hands on her hips, staring at the SUV. Its windows were heavily tinted, so it was impossible to see the driver. Then, not more than a minute after Jessie had stepped outside, the SUV took off at a high rate of speed. And she'd also been right about that. It was impossible to catch a glimpse of the license plate.

"Well," Mallory said. "So much for that. What are we going to do now?"

"We're going to go back to the office, pick up the cameras, go get Annie, and then you're going to cook us some spaghetti while I install them," he said with a big grin. "And it will, I think, be nice to have a little downtime and relax. No phones, no texts, no work. Just you, me and Annie. Sound good?"

She smiled at him and nodded. "But if she is being stalked, don't you think we should get Jessie some sort of protection, just in case?"

"We don't know for sure that she is," Tucker replied. "But I'll talk to David about it tomorrow."

She nodded dubiously, then shrugged and said, "Well… okay, I suppose."

26

Wednesday, December 11

Tucker arrived home after a pleasant evening with Mallory at just after eleven, tired but feeling better than he had in quite a while, but with a lot of questions bubbling in the back of his mind, not the least of which was his burgeoning relationship with Mallory. They hadn't spoken about it, but it had been there, hovering between them like a beautiful butterfly, and when he kissed her goodnight on the porch steps, it had been just a little more than a casual peck on the lips, and he couldn't help but smile at the memory.

As usual, he woke early the following morning after a night of tossing and turning, feeling far from refreshed or revitalized and wondering what insurmountable challenges Hump Day held for them.

He lay for several moments on his back, hands behind his head, staring up at the ceiling, thinking that it was a strange situation for a private investigator to find himself in. He was potentially dealing with four police jurisdictions as well as the FBI, and his status with all of them was unclear at best and nonexistent at worst, and it worried him; David Lewis worried him. He was smart, devious, and could be a sneaky son of a bitch whenever the mood took him. And, for once in his life, Tucker felt, professionally, out of his depth.

He sighed, rolled out of bed, went to the bathroom, turned on the shower, and slipped inside.

The hot water hammered his back like a thousand red-hot needles. He tilted his head back, closed his eyes and let the near scalding water wash over his face. For a good two minutes, he tortured himself before turning down the heat and washing his hair. Five minutes later, he stepped out of the shower, his skin still tingling, and toweled himself off.

He dressed in a pair of blue jeans and a white dress shirt, open at the neck, and then went downstairs to make coffee, only to find the jar was empty.

Damn! he thought, then sat down at the table, put his elbows on the tabletop and his hands to his temples. *That's all I need: no coffee and a headache.*

He picked up his phone and texted Mallory, *Hey you. Good morning. I hope you had a good night. Look, I'm out of coffee. Would you mind stopping by Starbucks on your way here, please?*

The reply came almost immediately. *Sure, and yes, I did have a nice night. Thank you. See you soon.*

He stared at the message for more than a minute, trying to read something into it that may or may not have been there. Finally, he set the phone down, sighed, looked at the kitchen clock, got up and went into the office and stood before the now hopelessly cluttered whiteboard, trying to make sense of it.

MALLORY WATCHED from the porch as Tucker walked to the car after kissing her goodnight. And then, with the butterflies still circling around in her stomach, she waved, turned around and walked back into the house, smiling like the cat who'd just drank a bowl full of cream. And, to say she slept well that night would have been very much the understatement.

She, too, woke early the following morning, her thoughts immediately turning to the events of the previous evening, but only for a moment.

She slipped out of bed, ran downstairs, Annie at her heels, let her out into the backyard, then made a pot of coffee and went back upstairs to shower and get dressed.

By eight, she was back downstairs. Annie had been fed, and she was ready to go to work. She decided to take Annie to work with her and was just attaching the leash when her phone beeped, indicating she had a message.

It was from Tucker. She smiled as she read it, typed a quick reply, and said, "Come on, Annie. The boss needs his morning fix."

TUCKER STARED at the images on the whiteboard, thinking there were still three Pitt Stop employees yet to be interviewed. *Or maybe only two,* he thought vaguely as he looked at the timeline. *Harrell had hernia surgery three days before Holly Wilson's murder. Could he have managed it after such a serious surgery? Huh! Maybe he could. I was thinking we could eliminate him, but maybe not; not yet, anyway. So the priority is Marks, who's off work until the weekend. And Talbot, who should be back at work today.* He stared at the photo of Holly Wilson. *There's a five-year gap between the deaths of Tiffany Delgado and Holly Wilson. Hmm, five years. What was the killer doing during those five years? Was he locked up? If he was, he isn't one of our persons of interest. Has he moved away? If so, we can again eliminate all of them. If not, what the hell was he up to? Why the break?*

His thoughts were interrupted by a knock on the door. He'd forgotten to unlock it. He opened it to find Mallory there with Annie at her heel, two Grande containers of coffee and two bags of House Blend in hand.

"Oh, thank God," he muttered, taking one of the containers from her. Then he leaned in close and kissed her gently on the lips. "Thank you. I don't think I could have lasted much longer."

"For the coffee or the kiss?" she asked as she followed him into the kitchen.

"Both," he said as he added a little milk and two packets of sweetener to the coffee. "Take a seat and let's talk."

They sat down at the table and Tucker said, "I've been thinking. Serial killers don't stop. They escalate over time. So what was our killer doing during the five years between Delgado and Wilson? Where the hell was he?"

"In prison?" she asked.

"That would be the obvious answer," Tucker replied. "And if that's it, then we've been wasting our time. It couldn't have been any of the people we've been talking to. Same goes if our killer moved out of state for five years. I think we've gotten it all wrong right from the start. What if he was still killing and we just haven't found them yet? I think we should widen our search." He sighed. "Geez, David's not going to like that."

"So what you're telling me is that none of the people we've been interviewing is the killer?"

"No, I'm not," he replied. "What I'm saying is that there's more, a lot more. How wide was your search area?"

"Southeast Tennessee and Northwest Georgia."

"Not Alabama or… Hmm. What if…? Look, we've been assuming we're looking for someone local. What if… I think we should expand the area to include Middle Tennessee, Knoxville and Northwest Alabama. What d'you think?"

"I think you're wrong," she said.

He sat back in his chair and looked at her in surprise. "You do? Why?"

"Because, if Jessie is being stalked, then it makes sense that the stalker's local."

"That doesn't make me wrong," he countered. "Our killer could be local but likes to travel. And we don't yet know for sure that Jessie's being stalked," he said, frowning.

"Well, I think she is. And I remember listening to the conversation between Holly Wilson and that Ringgold detective. She was certain she was being stalked, and she was right. And if we're not careful, Jessie is going to end up just like Holly, and I'm not going to stand by and let that happen."

Tucker stared at her, stunned. "You're serious," he said.

"Damn right I am," she replied. "We already have five victims. We have to get this guy before he kills again, and I have a deep-seated feeling that we've already talked to him, and that I'm a target. The food..." She trailed off, her eyes watering. "Tucker...?"

"Yeah, I know," he said. "I've been thinking about the food that was left on your doorstep..." He bit his top lip, wondering how he was going to handle it without upsetting her further. "And I get it, but I think maybe you're reading things..." He paused and shook his head. "Okay, look. Maybe you're right. Maybe you should stay here until we get this thing solved. I have two spare bedrooms. You can take your pick."

She shook her head. "Thank you, Tucker, but no. I have Annie, and I have my Sig, so I'll be just fine. You're right. I've been letting my imagination run away with me. People drive by and dump trash all the time."

"Not on your porch, they don't," he argued. "That was a blatant message if ever I saw one."

"Yes, well, I love my home, my fortress, and Annie and me will defend it to the death." She grinned at him, but he didn't find it funny.

"Mallory, this guy has killed five times that we know of. He's going to kill again. I don't want it to be you. Please, stay here with me where I can protect you. Just till it's over. Then you can go home."

She shook her head. "No. I'm not going to let the son of a bitch drive me out of my home. It's not going to happen. And besides, we have the cameras now."

"Whatever," he said, sounding totally frustrated. "I'm hungry. Let's go eat, then interview Larry Talbot. He should be back at work today."

"Fine," Mallory replied, "But let's go to the Big Yellow Egg. I'd like to see how Jessie's getting along, if she's even there, and I wouldn't blame her if she wasn't."

She looked at Annie, who was snoring softly in her bed.

"Annie?" The dog lifted her head and looked at her. "You be a good girl, okay?" Then to Tucker. "Maybe we should drop her off at the doggy sitter. It's not far, and I don't feel comfortable leaving her on her own."

Tucker nodded absently. Something was obviously on his mind. She grabbed the leash, hooked Annie up, and said, "Ready then?"

"What?" he asked, frowning. "Oh, yeah. Okay."

IT WAS Jessie who served them. She seemed upbeat, but Mallory could see she wasn't doing as well as she would have them believe.

"Are you okay, Jessie?" she asked. "You're looking a little peaky."

"I'm fine," she said and was about to turn away when Mallory said, "Did you have a good night? Any… problems?"

"No. Not really," she replied. "I didn't sleep well, but I don't think I was followed. When I got home, I ran into the house and locked all the doors. I went to bed early, but…" She shook her head. "I'll go get your order."

She brought their food a few minutes later, set it down in front of them and then turned quickly away without saying a word.

"She's going to make herself sick, if she's not careful," Mallory said. "We need to catch this guy, and soon."

Tucker nodded, forked some scrambled eggs into his mouth, looked at her as he chewed, then said, "I don't know, Mallory. We have three, maybe four, persons of interest so far. And now we have victim number five, Holly Wilson. We have to rule out Raul Copper; he's in prison, which means we're left with Palmer, Watson and Gibson."

"What about Harrell, Talbot, and Marks?" she asked, consulting her notes.

"I think we can rule out Harrell for the Wilson murder. I doubt he could have killed her if he's recovering from hernia surgery, and if he didn't do that one, we can also rule him out for the other four. We still have to talk to Talbot and Marks, but I'm not liking it, Mallory. Palmer, Watson and Gibson have dodgy alibis at best. Maybe we'll have better luck with Talbot or Marks." He heaved a sigh, shook his head and ate another bite of his eggs.

After a refill of their coffee, Tucker paid the bill, and they headed for the Pitt Stop, where they found Larry Talbot replacing a stolen catalytic convertor on a late-model Ford Explorer.

"Mr. Talbot?" Tucker said, peering under the lift.

"Yep, and you must be the two private eyes Mo told me about. What can I do for you? As if I didn't know."

"Do you have a minute?" Tucker asked.

"Sure," he said, coming out from under the lift, wiping his hands on a dirty piece of rag. "Anything for a break."

He was forty-eight, tall, slim, dark-haired, with a crooked nose and a nasty-looking scar on his chin. He was also smiling broadly.

Tucker didn't waste any time. He introduced himself and Mallory, and then said, "Would you mind telling us where you were between ten and one in the morning last Friday evening?"

"Wow," he said, frowning. "You're a bit of a hard ass, aren't you?"

Tucker didn't answer, nor did he smile. He simply stared him down.

Talbot broke eye contact, turned his head to look at Mallory, and stared at her. Then he literally looked her up and down. "I was working at home. I write romance novels." His eyes glittered, and the smile slipped a little as he continued to stare at her, then he continued, "With a little murder thrown in to make it interesting. My main character would look a lot like you, Miss Carver, if she were real."

"You were alone?" Tucker asked.

He turned again to Tucker. "I was. Sorry. See? I've been single since early 2015. My wife divorced me. Ran off with a piece of shit from Nashville, would you believe? I'm almost always alone these days." And he turned again to look at Mallory. "How about you, Miss Carver? You dating anyone?"

"That, Mr. Talbot, is none of your business." She looked at Tucker, who took the hint.

"Two-thousand-fifteen, you say?" he said. "When?"

"April, why?"

"No reason," Tucker lied. "How did you feel about that?"

"How d'you think I felt?" He snapped. "Nineteen frickin' years we were married. Two kids. Then she starts this girl's night out crap and I find out from a buddy she's been screwin' around on me with this guy from Nashville for two years, and I didn't know a thing about it. How the hell would you feel?"

Tucker stared at him for a moment, then said, "I'd feel pretty pissed off, and I'd want to get back at her. Is that how you felt, Mr. Talbot?"

"Yes... I... did, but as soon as I found out about it, she hightailed it to him in Nashville. Took the kids with her. They've been together ever since. I ain't seen my kids in more'n two years."

"So you were pretty angry then?"

"Yeah, I was angry. I'm still frickin' angry. Wouldn't you be?"

Tucker ignored the question and said, "Angry enough to kill?"

"Are you frickin' kidding me?" he asked, seemingly outraged by the question.

Tucker shook his head. "No, Mr. Talbot. I'm not kidding. Did you by any chance know a Miss Elaine May? She was a prostitute. She lived in Cleveland in 2015."

He frowned, looked away, and shook his head. "You don't have to shade it, Mr. Randall. I know who she was. She was Mo's girlfriend. He told me all about her and what happened to her. I met her a couple of times. She was murdered. But I never had anything to do with her, if you get my meanin'. See, I don't pay for it. I don't have to. I have friends, lady friends." He turned his head to look at Mallory and... it was more a sneer than a smile and inwardly Mallory shuddered.

"Hey," Tucker said, noticing the look he was giving her. "How about Bernice Carr?"

He turned again to Tucker and said, "Yeah, Mo told me about her, too, but I never met her. Look, I know you've been poking around here talking to all the other employees. I didn't kill nobody. I just work here every day, and I've never been in no trouble, not for nothin'... Ever!"

How about Franny McNeer from Polk County?" Tucker persisted, watching him closely. "Did you know her?"

He made a face and shook his head.

"Tiffany Delgado, Ringgold?"

Again, he shook his head.

"All right, Mr. Talbot," he said. "I think we're done here. We'll be in touch." He looked at Mallory and said, "Let's go."

And they did. They went into the convenience store where the guy Pete was behind the counter doing something on his phone.

"Oh, hey. Hi," he said after looking up at them. He straightened up. "What can I do for you today? More questions?"

"No," Tucker replied. "We were just wondering if you know where we can find Jarred Marks. I know he's off until the weekend, but…?" He left the question open.

"He's gone fishing. Lake Eufaula, Alabama, I think. He should be back on Friday, late. I shouldn't wonder."

"Good to know. Thanks," Tucker said and turned to go.

"Have a nice day."

Tucker turned, but Pete was already hunched over his phone again. Tucker shook his head and smiled, and together they walked back to the car.

"I did not like that guy Talbot," Mallory said as she opened the car door. "I think he's a real possibility." She slid into the passenger seat and pulled the door closed. "He obviously hates women."

Any other time, Tucker would have played devil's advocate, but this time he had little to say other than to agree. "You could be right," he replied, "but that doesn't make him a killer."

"He's the most likely prospect we've talked to yet," she persisted.

"I think we need to know more about him," he replied.

"But he knew Elaine and Bernice, and his wife left him in April, and Elaine was murdered in July, just three months later. Is that a coincidence? I don't think so."

"You really don't like him, do you?" Tucker asked, glancing sideways at her.

"No, I don't. And did you see the way he was looking at me? It made my skin crawl... What are you going to tell David?"

"Nothing yet. In fact, I wish to hell he'd gather his crap and go on back to where he came from."

"Oh, come on, Tucker. Get over it. I think he's nice."

"Not too nice, I hope. What have you got planned for tonight? I was thinking Mexican."

She blew out through her lips, thought about it for a moment, and then said, "Not tonight, if you don't mind. I was thinking maybe I should have an early night. You could probably use one, too. Or... Maybe... you... could... come over," she finished shyly.

He thought for a moment, then said, "You know, I'd love to. I really would, but you're right; we both need an early night. How about if I come over tomorrow night instead?"

"That sounds lovely," she said. "Thank you, Tucker."

As it turned out, though, at a little after five-thirty that afternoon, David Lewis called Tucker and invited himself over for a beer and a chat—just a chat. Not to talk about the case.

Tucker reluctantly agreed, and David arrived an hour later with a twelve-pack of Modello.

27

It was a little after six-thirty when Mallory arrived home with Annie that Wednesday evening, and it was almost totally dark. After she unlocked the front door, they stepped inside, and Mallory turned and set both the lock and the deadbolt Tucker had installed. That done, she followed Annie to the back door, unlocked it, opened it and let Annie out. She was about to close the door and let Annie do her thing when she saw the dog running back and forth on the deck, her nose to the boards; then she went to the steps, went into a low crouch and began to growl.

Mallory, who'd already been thinking about the sack of food someone had left on the front porch, froze, the hair on the back of her neck prickling.

"Stay, Annie," she whispered, backing into the house.

She grabbed her purse from the kitchen table, opened it and took out the compact nine-millimeter pistol, checked the safety and the load, grabbed a flashlight from the kitchen counter, and then stepped cautiously out onto the back deck.

If it's him and he's still out there, I'll get him, she thought. *He's into knives, not guns.*

"Annie, go seek," she whispered, and the dog took off down the steps into the backyard, heading toward the trees that bounded her property.

Mallory took a deep breath, bit her bottom lip, and then followed Annie into the darkness, waving the flashlight back and forth as she went. It wasn't until she'd almost reached the boundary that she spotted Annie almost hidden by the long grass, sniffing and pawing at something on the ground.

"Annie, bring it to me!" she shouted. It was a command with which Annie was entirely familiar, having learned it as a puppy playing with her toys.

She pawed whatever it was some more, grabbed it between her jaws, then turned and trotted back to Mallory.

Mallory frowned when she saw what it was. "Bring it to me, Annie," she repeated, holding out her hand.

The dog obediently placed it gently in her hand.

"Good girl," she said as she shone the flashlight onto what appeared to be a pocket-size notebook. She turned it over and looked at the back, thinking it couldn't have been there long. The air was damp from the low-lying mist over the fields beyond her property, but the notebook was perfectly dry.

"Come on, Annie," she said, looking around, playing the beam of the flashlight back and forth over the trees and the fields but seeing nothing out of the ordinary. Together, they walked the path back to the house, mounted the three steps up onto the deck and there she stopped, staring at the partially open door, unable to remember if she'd closed it or not.

After a moment's thought, she decided she'd left it open. She looked down at Annie. She seemed perfectly at ease now, looking up at her, panting gently.

She went back inside, locked the door, absentmindedly staring at one of the pages in the notebook as she filled Annie's bowl with food, and then sat down at the kitchen table and began to flip through the pages. It was small but thick, measuring roughly four-by-six-by-one, with perhaps a hundred pages, and all but a dozen of them filled with small, but neat, cursive handwriting, and she was stunned by what she read. Page after page was filled with the private information of dozens of women, including age, description, address, phone number, social security number, even credit card numbers complete with the three-digit security codes. Each entry was dated, going back to January 2019. One by one, she flipped through the pages until she came to the one headed Tiffany Delgado, which she read in detail. What horrified her most was that Tiffany's name had been crossed out in red and the date, August 9, 2019, written in the margin.

Mallory bit her bottom lip, knowing exactly what that meant and what she was looking at. She flipped through the rest of the pages, almost to the end, until she read Holly Wilson. It, too, was crossed out in red ink and the date December 6, 2024, written in the margin. But it was when she turned to the final few pages that her blood turned to ice water. The penultimate entry was for Jessie Mills. It hadn't been crossed out, but the date December 11, 2024, had been written in the margin. *Oh, my God.* She thought. *That's today*. She was about to jump to her feet when she realized there was one more entry. She turned the page and, sure enough, there it was, Mallory Carver.

There was no date in the margin, but the information was all there, all but her credit card information, and she wondered why it wasn't.

She sat for a moment, staring at her name. Then she looked up at the clock. It was a little after seven-thirty. *Oh geez! What was I thinking?* She jumped up from the table, grabbed her keys, phone and gun, told Annie to stay and be a good girl, then ran to the door, opened it, set the lock and flung it closed behind her. She ran down the porch steps to her car, started the engine, backed out onto the street, and peeled away, heading for Jessie Mills' home.

And then she called Tucker. It was seven-forty-five.

28

It was almost seven o'clock when David arrived at Tucker's door with a twelve-pack of Modello and a paper sack containing two Subway sandwiches.

"I thought you might like something to eat," he said as he set both down on the kitchen table. "How was your day?"

"So, so," Tucker replied. "How was yours?"

"Unproductive," he replied as they sat down at the table and began to unwrap the sandwiches. "I thought you might like turkey and Swiss on rye. And Modello is always a good choice, right?"

"What d'you want, David?" Tucker said dryly. "I know you well enough to know you never do anything without a motive."

"That's the Tucker I remember. Ever the optimist," he replied sarcastically. "I don't want anything other than a quiet, catch-up evening with my old friend and partner. No talk about the case. Just a chat and a pleasant evening."

Tucker shook his head, opened two bottles of beer, pushed one across the table to the FBI agent, stared at him for a moment, then said, "Let's get things straight, David. You were never my friend, and I was never your partner. I was your go-to when you needed dirty work done. So cut the crap and tell me why you're really here."

"Now that's just not true," David said before taking a sip of beer. "I always thought of our relationship as mentor and mentee." He shrugged. "And, by the look of things, I did a pretty good job…" he said, looking around. "And, talking about pretty, where's that lovely partner of yours? I was hoping she'd be here, too. Lovely girl, that. Where d'you find her? Or did she find you?"

"She's at home. Where d'you think she'd be?" Tucker asked, his hackles raising. "And how I found her, as you put it, is no damn business of yours."

"Calm down, Tucker. I meant no harm, but having seen how you two respond to each other, I would have thought you'd have moved her in with you." He grinned at him.

"As usual, you've gotten it all wrong, David," Tucker snapped. "Mallory and I are business partners. No more than that."

"Bullshit," David said, leaning back in his chair. "The woman's in love with you. Anyone can see that by the way she looks at you, and you at her, for that matter."

Tucker was stunned. *Geez, is it that obvious?*

Obviously, it was, but he denied it again, anyway. "As I said, you've gotten it all wrong, just as you always do, just as you did with Marsha Cline," he said, deftly changing the subject.

"Marsha Cline!" David said. "There you go again, Tucker. For God's sake, please get over it…" He stared at him, bottle in hand, and then continued, "And that's why you decided to quit, isn't it? You know, that's one thing I would never have believed of you, Tucker, that you're a quitter."

"Why don't you just take your—"

But it was at that moment that Tucker was cut off before he could finish the sentence when his phone rang. He glanced at the screen. *Mallory? What the...*

He picked up the phone. "Mallory—?"

"Tucker, you've got to come. I found a notebook in the backyard—well Annie found it—but it's full of stuff about the victims. It must belong to the killer. He must have dropped it. He's stalking me, too—"

"Slow down, Mallory," Tucker said. "I can't understand a word you're saying."

"I'm saying you need to meet me at Jessie's house," she yelled. "He's going to kill her. Tonight. Then he's going to kill me. It's all in the notebook. The victims, the dates, everything."

"Not if I have anything to say about it," Tucker growled. "Where the hell are you, Mallory?"

"I'm in the damn car," she yelled. "Where d'you think I am? I'm on my way to Jessie's house. You've got to come. He's going to kill her, Tucker. Tonight. He might already be there."

"Mallory. Stop. I'm at least thirty minutes away from Jessie's home. You've got to wait for me. Do not go to that house by yourself. Do you understand?"

"Yes, but—"

"Stop it, Mallory. Who is it? Who are we dealing with?"

"I don't know who it is. Tucker, the notebook is full of information about the victims, everything. Tiffany, Holly, Jessie, me. But there's nothing in it about the killer. Are you coming?"

"Yes, I'm on my way," he replied as he jumped to his feet. "Mallory, do not go without me. Do you hear me?"

Mallory babbled something he couldn't understand and then the phone went dead.

Damn it, he thought savagely. She hung up. She's doing it. She's going there alone. She doesn't know what the hell she's doing or what she's getting herself into.

By then he was on his feet. "Come on, David. You're coming with me." He grabbed his jacket and his gun and turned to David, who was also on his feet.

"What's going on, Tucker?" he asked. "I heard some of that, but what I'm getting is that Mallory knows who the killer is and is on her way to Jessie Mill's home. Yes?"

"Yeah," Tucker replied. "Come on. We need to hurry and get there before she gets herself into more trouble than she can handle. We'll talk in the car."

They'd been in the car for five minutes with Tucker driving like he was insane and not saying a word before David finally shouted, "Are you going to tell me what the hell's going on?"

"I'm not entirely sure," Tucker answered, his knuckles white on the wheel. "It seems Mallory's dog found a notebook with a lot of names and information in it, including some of the victims, including hers and Jessie Mills. She thinks she's being stalked and that whoever it is the notebook belongs to is going to kill Mills tonight, and she's on her way to stop him. She's going to get herself killed if we don't get there fast."

"Holy shit!" David whispered. "That changes everything. D'you think it's legit?"

"If she said she found it, she found it," Tucker replied as the speedometer crept past seventy. "As to the information… who the hell knows? But I think we're about to find out. Oh, shit!" he growled, looking up at the rearview mirror.

"What? What's wrong?"

"We've got ourselves a tail, a cop."

As he said it, the red and blue lights on the car behind began to flash and the siren wail.

Tucker pulled over, put the car in park, rolled down the window, put both hands on the wheel and waited, tapping the wheel with his fingers in frustration.

"In a bit of a hurry, weren't we, sir?" the cop said, leaning forward, his right hand on the butt of his gun.

Tucker was about to answer, but David beat him to it, leaning across the console, offering his creds to the officer.

"Special Agent David Lewis," he barked at the officer. "We have an emergency. There's possibly a crime in progress. We need backup. Call it in, please. The address is…" He looked at Tucker.

Tucker nodded and gave the officer Jessie's address.

The officer handed David's creds back, nodded, and ran back to his car while Tucker put the car in drive and pulled out onto the street.

"Thanks, David," he muttered. "I wouldn't have gotten away with that."

"You're welcome, Tucker. Now let's do this, yeah?"

Tucker nodded grimly and said, "Yeah!"

29

It was a little after eight when Mallory arrived outside Jessie Mills' house. There was no garage, so she assumed the older model Honda Accord parked in the driveway must belong to Jessie, which was a good sign.

She looked up at the rearview mirror and saw the street behind her was empty, then she looked ahead through the windshield. A dark-colored SUV was parked about half a block away on the same side of the road, and other driveways had cars in them, but that was all. Nobody was creeping around, no cars were moving, and she didn't see any headlights approaching. The area looked safe, so she heaved a sigh of relief, turned off the engine, stepped out of the car and stood for a moment, listening. All was quiet. The air still. Mallory hesitated, wondering what to do, looking back and forth, up and down the street. *Tucker said to wait,* she thought. *But what if...*

She looked up at Jessie's bedroom window. The lights were on, and the drapes were closed, but she could see shadows moving inside, then... She furrowed her brow, listening. *She's not on her own... Ooh, what was that?* she thought. *It sounded like a scream. Oh, my God. He's already here.*

She fumbled for her phone. Dropped it. Picked it up and hit the speed dial for Tucker.

"Where are you?" she screamed. "He's here. He's already inside. He's killing her."

"We're about ten minutes out," Tucker shouted. "The police are on their way. Stay where you are. Do not attempt to go inside."

"But he's killing her, Tucker. I can't just stand here and do nothing."

"You'll do exactly what—" but she'd already hung up.

Mallory ran to the front door, her P938 in her hand. She tried the doorknob. The door was locked. She heard another scream. She backed away from the door, looked up. The bedroom lights were still on, but as far as she could see, nothing was moving. She ran around to the back of the house. A window was ajar. She hesitated only for a second, then crawled into the house. She could hear screaming upstairs.

"Jessie, Jessie, Jessie," she yelled at the top of her voice as she ran to the stairs and then up, taking them two at a time. The bedroom door was busted wide open, and she could hear sounds of a struggle and someone whimpering.

"Jessie," she shouted again as she ran to the bedroom door. Jessie was on the floor, on one elbow between the bed and the window, a figure dressed in black on top of her, its arm raised, knife in hand, about to stab her. Her right arm was raised, her forearm in front of her face as if to ward off the blow.

"Back off, you son of a bitch," Mallory yelled and fired a shot that hit the wall just above the figure's head.

The figure reared up, turned, stared at her, then threw the knife at Mallory. She ducked. It bounced off the wall beside the door and fell to the floor. She froze as the figure hurled itself over the bed, grabbed her arm, and slammed it against the edge of the open door. The gun flew out of her fingers, skittered across the hardwood floor and slid under the bed.

"You frickin' bitch," a male voice screamed in her ear. "I almost had her. Why d'you have to stick your stupid nose in where it don't belong?"

He threw her to the ground, jumped on top of her, and reached across her for the knife. She slammed her fist into the side of his face as hard as she could. He grunted and hammered his fist into her jaw. Pain seared through her head. She almost blacked out. She went for his eyes with both hands and managed to press her right thumb to his left eye. He screeched, twisted his head away, grabbed her hand and wrenched it away from his eye, then hit her again in the face. She rolled sideways. He was in mid-swing at her and lost his balance. She clawed at his face and only managed to grab the balaclava, but she ripped it from his head and found herself staring at a familiar face.

"You frickin' bitch," he yelled. "I'm going to frickin' kill you now. I was going to anyway, but you couldn't wait, could you, you stupid bitch? You just couldn't wait."

"You!" she yelped. "It's you!"

"Of course it's me, you frickin stupid..." He trailed off and punched her in the face again, and then again, and then again, all the while looking wildly around, searching for the knife. He spotted it, reached for it, but before he could grab it, she grabbed him between his legs and squeezed as hard as she could.

He squealed and backhanded her with all his might. Her head snapped back, connected hard with the edge of the door, and everything went black.

He sat back on his heels, rocking back and forth, breathing hard, his left eye closed, his right eye watering, nursing his genitals, staring at her. "Frickin' bitch," he muttered. Then he lost it and screamed, "Bitch, bitch, bitch." He slapped her face as hard as he could. "Bitch!" And he slapped her again. "You hear me, bitch?" he yelled.

She heard nothing, and she felt nothing. She was unconscious. A deep wound to the back of her head.

He slapped her again. Her head rolled from one side to the other. He reached over, almost fell off her, grabbed the knife, turned again to the still unconscious Mallory, raised it over his head with both hands, paused for a second and snarled, "Your turn now, bitch!"

BAM! And before he could blink, something slammed into his left shoulder. He tipped over backward, the knife flying from his fingers. His head slammed into the footboard of the bed and, for several seconds, he seemed to lose consciousness. He blinked several times with his good eye, coughed, rolled over onto his stomach, then tried to sit up.

"You," he said, staring at Tucker who was down on one knee beside Mallory, gun in hand, pointing at him, two fingers of his left hand at her throat, feeling for a pulse.

"You!" Tucker snarled. "If you've—"

"Yeah, fooled y'all, didn't I?" He grinned at Tucker through gritted teeth, his hand on his wounded shoulder. "I wondered when you'd catch on, but you didn't, did you? You never would have. I had y'all fooled. Even that silly bitch didn't know until she pulled my frickin' hood off. Dumbasses, all of you. Geez, it frickin' hurts. I ain't never been shot before. Why didn't you kill me, Randall? You couldn't have missed, close as you were. Is she dead?"

Tucker shook his head. "I didn't kill you because I wanted to make sure you suffer for what you've done. And no, she isn't dead, and you'd better pray she doesn't die, because if she does—"

"You'll do what?" he asked, cutting him off and grinning at him. "You can't do a damn thing, Randall. I'm in the system now, and it will protect me." He paused for a second, looking at Mallory, then continued, "A few seconds more and I would've had her. I hate people like her. Arrogant, stupid bitches, all of 'em." He looked up at David, who was standing in the doorway. "Who's your friend?"

"Your worst nightmare," Tucker snarled.

"Who is he?" David asked, standing in the doorway, also with a gun in his hand.

"Pete Abbott, from the Pitt Stop. Boy, did I ever get that one wrong? Did you call an ambulance?"

"Yeah, they're on their way," he replied. "Where's Jessie Mills?" He was looking at Abbott.

"Over there," Abbott said. "Other side of the bed."

"She dead?"

Abbott shrugged, winced, closed his good eye, then opened it and said, "I sure as hell hope so… Frickin' hell, I think that frickin' bitch has put my eye out."

But Jessie wasn't dead. She was lying on her side with her hands covering her ears. Her face was covered in blood, and she was crying.

"Jessie," David said gently, holding out a hand.

She opened her eyes and looked up at him, blood streaming from a deep knife wound to the left side of her head where Abbott's knife had slid by as she'd jerked her head away.

She didn't answer. Instead, she reached out, took his hand, and he helped her to her knees. Then he put his arm around her and helped her to her feet. Jessie staggered painfully to the door, where she stopped and looked down at Mallory.

"She saved my life," she whispered. "Is she going to be all right?"

Tucker looked up at her, closed his eyes, opened them again, and nodded. "I hope so. I sure as hell hope so."

30

Thursday, December 12

It was almost nine the following morning when Mallory woke up. She opened her eyes and stared up at the brightly lit white ceiling. And she knew almost immediately that she was in the hospital. She lay there for a moment with her eyes closed, feeling comfortable and a little euphoric, wondering what had happened to her.

She opened her eyes again, turned her head a little to the right, closed them again and winced as pain speared through her head. She waited until it dissipated, then opened her eyes again and smiled. Tucker was asleep at her bedside, and he was holding her hand.

She closed her eyes again, still smiling, and was almost asleep when she heard a voice that said, "Tucker?"

She opened her eyes and saw David Lewis standing at the foot of the bed.

"Hey, Mallory," he said. "You're awake—"

"What?" Tucker, suddenly awake, sat up and let go of Mallory's hand, his face flushing.

Mallory scoffed, reached out, and took his hand again.

Tucker looked at her, then at David.

"I guess I dozed off," Tucker said.

"Could I have some water?" Mallory asked, her voice cracked and dry.

"Yes, of course." Tucker rose quickly and rounded the bed and David to get it for her.

"Can you sit me up a bit, please?"

"Yeah… Yes," he said, searching for the control unit.

He raised the head of the bed and handed her a cup with a lid and a straw.

She sipped some ice water, closed her eyes and sipped again, then she looked up at him, smiled and handed him the cup.

Tucker rounded the bed again and sat down.

"What happened?" she asked. "Did you get him? Is Jessie all right? And, Tucker, just so you know, I recorded the whole thing."

"You got yourself into one hell of a scrap," he replied. "Abbott beat you pretty badly. You have a concussion, but the doc says it will pass over the next couple of days. But yes, we got him. And Jessie's all right, too. She's in a room just down the hall."

He looked at David. "What's the word on Abbott?"

"He's here. The wound was through and through. What ammo were you using?"

"FMJ," Tucker replied ruefully. "Full metal jacket."

"A bit chancy, that, don't you think?" David asked.

"An oversight," Tucker replied. "Range rounds. My bad."

David nodded. "You look like hell, Tucker," he said. "You've been here all night?"

Tucker merely nodded.

Mallory turned her head to look at him and said, "Thank you, Tucker. You should go home now. I'll be fine."

Tucker wrinkled his brow, looked at David and said, "So, what about Abbott? Have you interviewed him yet?"

"No. I was waiting to see if he'd be fit enough. The surgeon says the wound is clean, no internal damage, so they patched him up and will turn him loose this afternoon. He's officially in my custody, but he'll be released to the Chattanooga PD. I've arranged to interview him there. I'd like you to attend. You up for it?" David asked.

Tucker looked at Mallory. She smiled at him and nodded.

"Oh, yeah," he said. "You bet."

"Good," David said. "I'll leave you two alone, then." He looked at Tucker and said, "Two o'clock. Amnicola Highway."

"I know where it is, David... Thanks."

David nodded and turned and left the room.

"How are you feeling?" Tucker asked as the door closed behind him.

"Not so hot," she replied. "I must look a mess."

"Eh, not so bad for someone with a bandage around her head, a split lip, two broken ribs and multiple bruises. Why did you do it, Mallory? I told you to wait for me."

"Yes, I know you did, and I was going to, but I could hear Jessie screaming and a window was open and... Tucker, he was just about to stab her when I got there. I had to do something, so I shot at him and missed. I was nervous, I guess. Did you find my Sig? He knocked it out of my hand. It went under the bed and—" She burst into tears.

"Hey, come on," Tucker said. "You did great." He wanted to put his arm around her, but with the IV and the monitor cables he couldn't, so he took her hand in both of his and kissed it.

"No, I didn't," she blubbered. "I almost got myself killed. If you hadn't arrived when you did..."

"Stop it, Mallory," he said, then rose to his feet, leaned over the bed and kissed her.

The door opened. "Ah, feeling better, are we?"

Tucker sat down again. "Doctor," he said.

"So, how are you feeling?" she said to Mallory.

"I'm good," she replied. "When can I go home... Oh, geez, Tucker. Annie!"

"She's fine," he replied. "I called your sister. She went by this morning and let her out and fed her. She'd peed on the kitchen floor, I'm afraid. But Jen cleaned it up. I'll go by when I leave here. So stop worrying. Oh, and by the way…" He looked at his watch. "She'll be here in about ten minutes." He looked at the doctor.

"Hmm," she said, looking at her iPad. You have a mild concussion, two cracked ribs and quite a bit of bruising. Other than that… D'you have anyone at home?"

"She does," Tucker said, jumping in before Mallory could answer. "Me."

Mallory almost choked, trying to suppress her surprise.

The doctor looked at him over her glasses, frowning, then looked at Mallory, who was blushing. The frown deepened. "Well, I suppose… We'll see how the rest of the day goes. If all goes well, she can go home this evening." With that, she nodded, turned on her heel, and left the room.

She hadn't been gone more than two minutes when Jen burst into the room. She took one look at her sister, then said, "Oh, my God, Mallory. What the hell happened? What were you thinking?"

"You've been talking to Tucker," Mallory accused her.

"Damn right, I have. Have you gone mad, taking that monster on by yourself? What were you thinking?" she repeated.

Mallory shrugged, winced, and wished she hadn't. "I couldn't let him kill her, now could I?" she replied.

Jen looked at Tucker. "And you can wipe that silly grin off your face. Mallory, I just spoke with your doctor and you're coming home with me this evening."

"Er… no!" Mallory replied. "Thank you, Jen, but I want to go home."

"But—"

"I said I want to go home," Mallory said gently.

Jen looked at Tucker. "Is this your doing?"

Tucker just shrugged.

"The doctor said she has to have someone… with… her… Oh, I see. That's how it is, is it?"

At that, Tucker stood and said, "I have to go. You two decide who does what and let me know."

He bent over the bed and kissed Mallory, who put her hand to his neck. "Call me later," he whispered. Then he turned to Jen, winked at her and walked quickly out of the room.

Jen stared after him, then at her sister. "Seriously?" she asked. "When did that happen?"

Mallory shrugged again and winced.

"Is it serious?" Jen asked.

"I don't know," Mallory replied. "We haven't really talked about it yet."

"Have you..."

Mallory frowned at her. "*No.* Of course not."

"Just asking," Jen said and sat down in the chair Tucker had just vacated. "So, tell me all about it."

31

David met Tucker in the front parking lot of the Chattanooga Police Service Center on Amnicola Highway and escorted him inside.

"How's Mallory?" he asked as he followed Tucker through the glass doors.

"Last time I spoke to her, she was eager to come home."

"What's your relationship with her?" he asked after he'd signed Tucker in.

"That's none of your business, David."

"I was just asking, is all," the FBI agent said.

"Why? What's it to you?"

"Well, I was hoping I could talk you into coming back to us."

"Not a chance, David," he replied. "I have a good life now, and besides, I hate the damn bureaucracy. I have no one to answer to. I make my own decisions, take only the cases that interest me. As I said, it's a good life."

"Will you think about it?" David asked. "You can pick up where you left off."

Tucker stopped walking. "Are you serious?"

David had taken another couple of steps before stopping and turning to look at him. "Of course," he replied, not catching the tenor of Tucker's question. "Same deal, same pay grade. It will be as if you never left."

Tucker shook his head in amazement. "I can't believe you'd say that. Not after what happened. You may have gotten over Marsha, but I haven't. No, I will *not* think about it. Now let it go and let's do what we're here for."

"Okay," David said. "Your loss, my friend."

Tucker was about to respond to that, but he gritted his teeth and together they walked to the interrogation room, where Peter Abbott was already waiting for them with his attorney.

Abbott was dressed in an orange jumpsuit and wearing a full set of chains, including leg cuffs. His right hand was handcuffed to the table with his attorney, a blonde woman Tucker knew slightly named Helena Charles.

How ironic, Tucker thought. *The woman could have been one of his victims.*

"Here they are," Abbott, his arm in a sling, said brightly, looking up at them. "No energy drink today, Mr. Randall?"

Tucker looked at him and shook his head in disbelief. He and David took their seats on the opposite side of the table to Abbott and his attorney.

Abbott clamped his lips together in a tight smile, looked from one to the other and then said, "So?"

David began the interview by announcing the date, time, and those present. "Interview of Peter Abbott, December 12, 2024, at two-seventeen p.m. Present are Mr. Abbott, his attorney Ms. Helena Charles, FBI Special Agent in Charge David Lewis and Detective Tucker Randall. Also present is corrections officer Michael Grady."

He paused, staring at Abbott. Abbott, his head tilted to one side, stared back at him, the same tight smile on his lips.

What the hell is he thinking? Tucker wondered.

"Peter Abbott," David began, "I'm charging you with the attempted murders of Jessie Ann Mills and Mallory Carver. You have the right to remain silent. Anything you say can and will be used against you in a court of law. You have the right to talk to a lawyer for advice before we ask you any questions. You have the right to have a lawyer with you during questioning. If you cannot afford a lawyer, one will be appointed for you before any questioning if you wish. If you decide to answer questions now without a lawyer present, you have the right to stop answering at any time. Do you understand these rights?"

Still smiling, Abbott looked at Charles. She nodded, and he replied, "Yes, but I wasn't trying to kill her."

"Seriously—" Tucker began, leaning forward, but David put a hand on his arm and cut him off.

"Would you like to explain that statement, Mr. Abbott?" David asked.

"I wasn't trying to kill her," he repeated. "It was the other way round. She was trying to kill me. See, I met her at the store a couple of weeks ago. She came beboppin' in all uppity, like, and we kinda hit it off, you know? I just went to her house to see if I could ask her out. She invited me in and, well, I must have said something to set her off because she just went nuts, grabbed a knife from the drawer and went for me."

Tucker looked at him, not believing what he was hearing.

David merely nodded and said, "So, you were in the kitchen when this happened?"

Abbott thought for a minute, then grinned and said, "No, the bedroom."

"So, Jessie Mills, a woman you barely knew, invited you into the house, then up to the bedroom, where she took a kitchen knife from one of her drawers and attempted to stab you?"

"That's about the size of it," he said.

David nodded and said, "Please continue, Mr. Abbott."

"Well, I had to defend myself, didn't I. We fought, and I was able to get the knife away from her and—"

"Bullshit," Tucker snapped. "I'll tell *you* what happened. You saw her in the store as you said, just as you did all the other women you killed, and you stalked her. You broke into her house through a window. She was in the bedroom where you attacked her. But, unlike the other women, she fought you, didn't she, Pete? Would you like to know how

I know all that?" He didn't wait for an answer. He slammed the notebook, sealed in a plastic evidence bag, down on the table. "Recognize it?" he asked. "You should. It has your fingerprints all over it."

Abbott stared at it. Tucker watched as his face paled.

"Where d'you get that?" he whispered.

Charles put a hand on his arm and shook her head. He shrugged her hand away.

"You dropped it in Mallory Carver's backyard. It was you who put the paper sack of fast food on her doorstep, too, wasn't it?"

He hesitated for a second, then said, "I've never seen that before."

"Really?" Tucker said, taking a pair of latex gloves from his pocket. "Let's see, shall we?"

He snapped on the gloves, broke the seal on the envelope, took out the notebook, opened it and rifled through the pages. "Ah, here we are. Jessie Mills, December 11, and here are all her private and personal details. Why December 11, Pete?"

"That was..." He realized his mistake, closed his mouth and folded his arms.

"You were going to say that was the date you met her, weren't you? But you just said you met her a couple of weeks ago, during which time you were able to gather all this information, so why December 11?" Abbott didn't answer. He just stared stoically at Tucker. "But there's more, isn't there, Pete? Let's try this one. Holly Wilson? Remember her?"

Abbott stirred uncomfortably in his chair but said nothing.

Tucker nodded and pressed on, "Now that one is a little different. It's dated December 6, the day she was murdered, and look at this." He showed the entry to Abbott, Charles, and then David. "Her name has been crossed out in red. What does that mean, Pete? You entered the date you intended to kill her, didn't you? Then, when you had, you crossed out her name."

"Let's take a look at another one." He flipped through the pages, then looked up at him and said, "Tiffany Delgado, August 9, 2016. Same thing. The name's crossed out in red. And how about this one,

Mallory Carver? No date yet, but the intention is clear, isn't it, Pete? And not only are your fingerprints all over it, but a handwriting expert will testify you wrote it all—"

"Okay, okay, okay," Abbott shouted. "That's enough. I did it. I killed—"

"Stop!" his lawyer shouted, grabbing his arm.

"Get off," he shouted, snatching his arm away from her. "I killed 'em, and I would have killed the Mills woman, too, if that silly bitch hadn't charged in when she did. So what? They deserved it. All of them stupid blonde bitches. I frickin hate women. They're sneaky, conniving, sly, shitty bitches, especially the blonde ones. They're the worst. Just like my mother was, frickin' bitch. And where the hell did they dig you up from?" He turned to his attorney and continued his rant. "You're just like the rest of them. Lousy, lying bitches. Do your frickin' worst? I don't give a shit."

It was at that moment Officer Grady stepped forward to restrain him, but David held up a hand.

"So," he said, after Abbott had seen Grady, a huge man, step forward and he'd calmed down, "you admit to the attempted murders of Jessie Mills and Mallory Carver?"

He nodded.

"Say it, please, Mr. Abbott, for the recording."

"Yes, damn you. Yes!" he snarled.

"And you admit to the murders of Tiffany Delgado and Holly Jennifer Wilson?"

Again, he nodded, then, almost as an afterthought. "Yup!" And then he reverted to the tight smile and folded his arms across his chest and leaned back in his chair, staring at them, waiting.

"How about Elaine May?"

"Ah, pretty little Elaine, Mo's lover," he said, staring at the far wall. "She was the first. She was always in and out of the store. Beboppin' around in those tiny little skirts and halter tops. She'd screw anything with a pulse if they had enough money, women included. She was a hooker, you know?"

"You stabbed her thirty-seven times," David said. "Why so brutal? One or two would have done the job."

"Thirty-seven, was it? I didn't count. I guess I must have gotten lost in the moment." He grinned at Tucker. "That *associate* of yours," he said with a sneer, "the Carver woman; you screwin' her, Detective?"

Tucker jumped to his feet, but David grabbed his arm, restraining him. "Easy does it," he said, and Tucker slowly sat down again.

"How did you gain entry to May's home?" Tucker asked.

"Easy enough," he replied. "Old house, old windows. I went in through one at the rear. I just had to slip a Slim-Jim between the two sashes and push the catch to the side. She was asleep on the couch." He smiled at the memory. "You should have seen her face when I woke her. I'll remember that look for the rest of my days."

The two detectives were silent for a moment, then David said, "And Bernice Carr?"

Again, Abbott made with the tight smile and nodded, then said, "Bernie, Mo's cousin. Yep, her too. She was always in and around the store. What more can I say?"

"How about Frances McNeer, Franny? Did you kill her, too?"

At that, he burst out laughing. "Now that one was a trip—"

"A trip?" Tucker asked, horrified. "You stabbed that poor woman forty-seven times, you frickin' monster."

"Forty-seven, was it? I guess I must have been in a bad mood that day. Hmm, I remember the day she came into the store... she only came in once. There was... something about her... I dunno. I never did figure it out. She... just... Eh," he frowned. "I don't know. As I said, there was just something about her that didn't sit well with me."

"So you decided to kill her," Tucker pressed him.

"Yeah, I suppose I did, but here's the kicker. Here's why I said it was a trip. They convicted her dumbass husband for it and sent him away for life. Can you believe that? That was a turn-on, believe me."

"So something about Franny McNeer didn't sit well with you, so you killed her?" Tucker pressed, trying to make sure he got a viable confession from him.

"I know what you're doing, Detective, so let me help you out here."

He uncrossed his arms and leaned forward. "Yes, I killed, murdered, Frances McNeer. There. Feel better now?"

Tucker took a deep breath and leaned back in his chair. He had what he wanted. And, internally, he was elated. Luthor McNeer would go free.

David glanced at Tucker, then looked at Abbott and said, "How many more, Pete?"

"Ah-hah," Abbott replied. "Now there's the question. What makes you think there are more?"

"You say Elaine May was first, then you waited almost a year before you killed Bernice Carr and then Franny McNeer three months later, but there was no one between May and Bernice."

"There wasn't?" Abbott asked. "What makes you say that?"

"So there was?" David asked.

"Was there?" Abbott replied, grinning.

"Okay, we'll come back to that later," David said. He sounded frustrated. "There was a three-year gap between the murder of Franny McNeer and Tiffany Delgado. There were none during that time either," he said.

"Weren't there?" Abbott asked, beaming at him. "Okay, so here's the thing—"

At that point, Helena Charles again put her hand on his arm and tried to stop him from talking, but he was having none of it. He shrugged her hand away and said, "Stop it, you silly bitch. Can't you see it's over? Just sit there quietly and listen or piss off. Now, where was I? Oh yes. So, here's the thing. I'm not stupid, Agent Lewis. I know interstate murder is a federal capital offense, and I could be sentenced to death. So I want a deal. You promise to take the death sentence off the table—and I want it in writing—and I'll tell you about the rest. Who they are and where they are. Deal?" He looked at Helena. She nodded and looked at David, her eyebrows raised in question.

David nodded and said, "I can't promise—"

"Then you don't get the others," Abbott said, cutting him off.

"How many?" David asked.

Abbott leaned forward, his eyes narrowed to mere slits, and said, "Eight!"

Tucker stared at him in disbelief.

David also stared at him for several seconds, then said, "Give me a moment. I need to make a call." And he stood up and left the room.

"Agent Lewis has left the room at three-twenty-three p.m.," Tucker said for the record and then sat back, his arms folded, staring at Abbott.

"What's up, Doc?" Abbott asked.

"You're one sick son of a bitch," Tucker muttered. "You almost killed my partner. Would have if I hadn't stopped you."

"Them's the breaks, I guess," he replied, sounding totally at ease. "The silly bitch shoulda kept her nose out of what doesn't concern her. How is she, by the way?"

"She's fine," Tucker muttered.

"You are, aren't you?" he said. "You're screwin' her. I don't blame you. She's a looker, that's for sure."

It was at that moment that David reentered the room, just in time, as Tucker was about to go across the table at him.

"Whew, that was close. Did you know he was screwin' his partner?" Abbott said, grinning broadly. "So, what did your boss say?" he asked as David sat down. "Do I get a deal or not?"

"You get a deal," David said and nodded at the attorney. "Draw up the papers, and the director will sign them." He turned his attention back to Abbott and said, "So, start talking."

And he did. It turned out there were victims all over the tri-state area. Two in northern Alabama, two more in Georgia, and four in Tennessee, in Rhea, Marion, and Sequatchie counties, and one in Knoxville; thirteen in all. And all of them had stopped by the Pitt Stop, usually during visits to the various medical centers off Gunbarrel Road. That was the connection Tucker had been looking for, The Pitt Stop.

They questioned him at length for almost three hours more, until David finally called it a day and Abbott was taken away.

Tucker and David left the police department together and stood for a moment in the parking lot.

David offered Tucker his hand, and Tucker shook it.

"You sure you won't take me up on my offer?" David asked.

Tucker shook his head, then said, "No, but thanks, David. As I told you, I'm done with all the BS and the bureaucracy."

David nodded. "We have a new president and a new AG. I have a feeling things are going to be different."

"How different can they be, David? The agency is a monolith. Nah, I'm done with it. Look, I have to go and see if Mallory's going home." He offered David his hand again and said, "I can't say it's been a pleasure, or fun, but I appreciate your help proving Mr. McNeer innocent."

David shook his hand and replied, "Stay safe, Tucker, and look after that girl. She's a keeper. Call me if you change your mind." And with that, he turned and walked away to his car.

Tucker watched him go, then went to his car and called Mallory.

Mallory answered on the first ring. "Tucker. How did it go?"

"Well enough. I'll tell you all about it later. You ready to go home?"

"Yep, the doctor says I can. Jen wanted me to go and stay with her, but I told her no. You want to come and get me?"

"Of course. My place or yours?"

There was a moment of silence before she said, "Yours, but we'll have to pick up Annie."

Tucker smiled to himself, then said, "We can do that. I'll be there in thirty minutes."

"I'll be waiting," she said.

EPILOGUE

Peter Abbott was transferred to the FBI field office in Nashville two days later, on Saturday morning. It was over, all but the shouting, as they say. Over the next several weeks, he led them to the eight remaining bodies. At his trial, he pled guilty and was sentenced to life imprisonment on all charges.

Luthor McNeer was released from prison on New Year's Eve. Vinnie was there to meet him and to take him home. They hugged each other for the first time in more than eight years. It was a poignant moment.

Mallory spent the next seven days at Tucker's home recovering from her injuries. The head wound healed quickly, but the two broken ribs were painful and slow to heal. She'd been given Hydrocodone for the pain but refused to take it, preferring Tylenol instead.

She found the environment strange, at first. Tucker was the perfect gentleman, but their relationship had changed, and she could feel it stirring beneath the surface. So, it was three days later, on Sunday, when she decided to bring it to the surface.

"Tucker," she said as he poured them a second cup of coffee. "We've been dodging it for almost two weeks, but no more. We need to talk."

He looked at her, coffeepot in hand, not knowing what to say. “Oh yeah?”

She nodded. “Come and sit down.”

He sat down and said, “Hey, we have a new case… and you'll never believe who it involves.”

“Stop it,” she whispered and reached out across the table and took his hand.

She looked into his eyes, her own eyes glistening, and said, “I'm in love with you, Tucker.”

THANK you so much for reading, ***Happily Never After***, the second book in the Randall & Carver Mysteries series. I hope you enjoyed it! Keep reading with ***Evil Never Sleeps***.

EVIL NEVER SLEEPS

A RANDALL & CARVER MYSTERY BOOK 3

DEDICATION

To my beautiful daughter Mallory for whom the main character in this story is named.

PROLOGUE

THERE WAS NO MOON THAT NIGHT, JUST A WASH OF STARS SCATTERED across the Tennessee sky like salt spilled on a black velvet blanket. A soft breeze rustled through the trees, nature's fingers playing across the leaves in the gentle rhythm of approaching autumn. In this remote corner of rural Tennessee, the darkness belonged to the crickets, to the occasional hoot of an owl, and to the secrets that only darkness could keep.

Terry Fisher moved quietly along the gravel road, his boots crunching softly with each step. The twenty-eight-year-old had the lean build of someone who worked with his hands, shoulders squared under a denim jacket despite the warm September evening. His dark hair fell into his eyes as he walked, head down, hands shoved deep in his pockets. The thin line of his mouth betrayed tension, the crease between his eyebrows showing he was lost in thought.

As the fence line for the Parsons farm appeared in the distance, Terry slowed his pace. He'd agreed to this meeting against his better judgment. It wasn't like him to be out this late, especially on a weeknight, and he didn't like it one bit, but the reply to his message had been insistent. *I understand. It needs to be tonight. You know where. Do not tell anyone.* And so here he was, walking the Tennessee back roads at eleven-thirty, the small flashlight in his pocket barely used, his eyes having adjusted to the darkness.

"I am… I'm getting out," he whispered to himself, rehearsing the words he'd say soon. "This is the last time, for sure. Tiffany and I are moving forward. Getting married. Starting clean. No arguments."

The old oak tree loomed ahead; its massive trunk silhouetted against the star-filled sky. It marked the corner of the Parsons' property, a natural landmark where the fence turned ninety degrees to follow the property line. It was also where the meeting was to take place, far from any roads, far from any homes, far from curious eyes and ears.

Terry checked his watch. It was 11:42 PM. He was early, but that was intentional. He wanted to arrive first, to have the psychological advantage of waiting rather than being waited for. It was a small thing, but tonight… Well, he knew he needed every advantage he could get.

He leaned against the oak tree and took a cigarette from his pocket. He rarely smoked anymore—Tiffany had asked him to quit—but he kept a few for moments of stress. This certainly qualified. The flame from his lighter briefly illuminated his face, the sharp planes of his cheekbones, the hint of stubble along his jaw, the tightness around his blue eyes.

"Last time," he muttered again, exhaling smoke into the night air. "Last time and I'm done."

The events of the past year flashed through his mind. It had started so innocently. A favor for a friend, he'd thought. Just look the other way, just hold something for a few hours, just make an introduction. But favors had a way of multiplying, of growing teeth, of becoming demands. And now he was in too deep, knowing too much about things he'd never wanted to be part of.

Gun running wasn't what he'd imagined for his life. He'd grown up in this small town, had gone to the church youth group, had played football at the high school, had helped his mother with the groceries. He'd been the boy who walked old Mrs. Henderson's dog when her arthritis got bad. And now he was the man who helped move illegal firearms, who kept his mouth shut about shipments and buyers, who looked the other way when money changed hands.

All for what? The extra cash hadn't been worth it. The excitement had worn off quickly. The realization that he was breaking the law—serious federal laws—had settled in his stomach like a stone. And lately, the fear. The growing, gnawing fear that he was into something he couldn't escape.

But tonight, he would. Tonight, he would end it. He'd rehearsed what he would say, how he would say it firmly but without accusation, without threat. He wasn't going to the police. He wasn't going to talk. He just wanted out. He wanted to marry Tiffany, maybe start a family, be the man his father had raised him to be.

Terry checked his watch again. 11:58 PM. Almost time.

The sound came from behind him—a twig snapping almost imperceptibly over the nighttime chorus of insects. Terry turned, dropped his cigarette and ground it underfoot.

"You're early too," he said, squinting into the darkness, trying to make out the approaching figure. The silhouette was familiar in its movements, the way it approached with purpose but without hurry.

"Have you been waiting long?" The voice was measured, calm.

"Just a few minutes," Terry replied, straightening up from the tree. "Thanks for meeting me."

"No problem." The figure stopped several feet away, still partially obscured by the shadows. "Something about you wanting out?"

Terry swallowed, his rehearsed speech suddenly forgotten. He nodded. "Yeah. I… I can't do this anymore. The guns, the money… I'm getting married in a few months. I need to be done with all this."

Silence stretched between them, punctuated only by the rhythmic chirping of crickets and the distant call of a night bird.

"Just like that?" The voice remained even, emotionless. "You think you can just walk away?"

"I'm not going to cause any trouble," Terry said quickly, holding up his hands. "I won't say anything to anyone. I just want to be done. Clean slate."

"After everything you've seen? Everything you know?" A small, humorless laugh. "That's not how it works, Terry."

A chill ran down Terry's spine that had nothing to do with the night air. "Look, I've been loyal," he said. "I've kept my mouth shut. I'm not asking for anything except to be left alone."

"And if I say no?"

Terry took a deep breath. "Then I'll leave town. Me and Tiffany. We'll start fresh somewhere else. No one needs to worry about me."

The figure took a step closer, the moonlight now catching the outline more clearly. "You know, I actually believe you, Terry. I believe you'd keep quiet."

Relief flooded through Terry. "Then we're good? I'm out?"

"The problem isn't what you'd do," the voice continued, as if he hadn't spoken. "It's what you represent. If you walk away, others might think they can too. And then what? My whole operation falls apart because Terry Fisher wanted to play house with his girlfriend?"

"That's not—"

"You made commitments," the voice hardened. "You took money. You knew what you were getting into."

Terry shook his head, desperation creeping into his voice. "I didn't, though. Not really. It got bigger than I expected. More dangerous."

"And that's supposed to be my problem?"

"Please," Terry took a step forward. "I'm begging you. I'll do one last job if that helps. Whatever you need. But after that, I'm done."

The silence that followed was heavier than before, laden with unspoken threats and calculations.

"One last job," the figure finally said. The voice sounded thoughtful.

Hope bloomed in Terry's chest. "Yes. Anything."

"And then we never see each other again."

"Exactly," Terry nodded eagerly. "Clean break."

"Turn around."

Terry blinked, confused. "What?"

"Turn around. Look at the view. I want to discuss what this last job would entail, and I think better when I'm looking at the stars."

It was an odd request, but Terry was too relieved to question it. He turned, facing away from the figure, looking out over the Parsons' property. The field stretched before him, a sea of tall grass silvered by starlight, rolling gently toward the tree line in the distance.

"Beautiful, isn't it?" the voice said, now just behind him.

"Yeah," Terry agreed, shoulders relaxing slightly. "Peaceful."

"Do you know what I've learned in this business, Terry?" The voice was calm, almost philosophical. "I've learned that peace is an illusion. There's always trouble brewing under the surface. Always someone wanting more than they deserve."

Terry started to turn. "I don't—"

"Don't move," the voice commanded sharply. "Just listen."

Terry froze, a new fear creeping up his spine.

"I trusted you," the voice continued, now with an edge of disappointment. "I brought you in. Made you part of something bigger than this backwater town could ever offer you. And this is how you repay me? By trying to walk away?"

"I told you, I won't—"

"Quiet." The word was delivered without heat, but with absolute authority. "I know what you think. That you're different. Special. That the rules don't apply to you."

Terry felt the presence move closer, just inches behind him now. "Please," he whispered. "I just want—"

"What you want doesn't matter anymore, Terry. What matters is the message."

The first shot came without further warning, a muffled crack that seemed impossibly loud in the quiet night. The bullet entered the back of Terry's skull with surgical precision, stealing his words, his thoughts, his future with Tiffany. Before his body could crumple, a second shot followed the first, a redundancy born of professionalism rather than passion.

Terry Fisher fell forward, face first into the tall grass of the Parsons' farm. No last words, no dramatic clutching at life, just a sudden, brutal transition from existence to absence.

The figure stood over the body for a long moment, breathing

steadily, no hint of panic or regret. The gun, still warm, disappeared into a pocket. Hands reached down, checking for a pulse more out of habit than necessity. Finding none, the figure straightened and surveyed the scene with clinical detachment.

Terry Fisher lay dead in the gentle slope of the field, his blood soaking into the earth, his body already beginning to cool under the indifferent stars. The crickets, momentarily silenced by the gunshots, gradually resumed their chorus.

The killer turned and walked away unhurriedly, footsteps deliberate and careful, leaving no trail, no evidence, nothing but a cooling body in a farmer's field. The night swallowed the retreating figure, darkness embracing darkness, secrets kept in the shadows where they belonged.

By morning, dew would settle on Terry's still form. By midday, a teenage boy cutting across the field would discover him and make the panicked call to the sheriff's office. By evening, the rumors would begin—drugs, gambling debts, love triangles—the small town trying to make sense of the senselessness.

But for now, in the deep of night, there was only silence, only stars, only the soft footsteps of someone walking away from murder, already calculating the next move in a game where the taking of human lives was merely collateral damage.

1

Mallory Carver suppressed a yawn as she flipped through yet another bridal magazine, her finger tracing over glossy images of wedding dresses that, after three hours, all seemed to blend together. She sighed, shook her head, and watched the dust motes dancing in the late afternoon sunlight streaming in through Jen's bay windows, highlighting the scattered wedding paraphernalia that had gradually consumed her sister's living room. Across from her, Jen sat at the table, meticulously organizing swatches of fabric and photos of floral arrangements into a binder that had grown to the size of a small dictionary.

The coffee table between them had disappeared beneath layers of wedding magazines, cake design options, and invitation samples. Mallory's eyes burned slightly from the endless parade of white, cream, and ivory, each shade supposedly distinct but looking maddeningly similar after hours of scrutiny.

"What about this one?" Jen asked, rotating a magazine toward Mallory. "The lace detail on the sleeves would complement your figure beautifully." She tapped a manicured nail against the page, her wedding ring catching the light. Jen, at forty-four, had been married to Jared for nearly twenty-four years, and sometimes Mallory wondered if her sister was more excited about this wedding than she was.

Mallory tilted her head, studying the dress. It was elegant—maybe a bit too elegant for the outdoor ceremony she and Tucker had agreed on. The intricate beadwork and cathedral-length train seemed better suited to a grand church with stained glass windows than the botanical garden venue they'd secured.

"It's pretty, but isn't it a little formal for a garden wedding?" she asked, trying to picture herself navigating grass and gravel in something that elaborate. "I'd probably trip over that train and face-plant into the wedding cake."

Jen rolled her eyes. "You can never be too formal on your wedding day, Mal. Besides, I thought you wanted the dress to be the one extravagant element." She closed one magazine, immediately opened another, and flipped to a dog-eared page. "And there are ways to bustle the train for the reception. Jackie could help with that—she's got nimble fingers."

Mallory smiled at the mention of her sixteen-year-old niece. "Jackie would probably add hidden pockets for my lock picks and pepper spray."

"Don't even joke about that," Jen said, but her lips twitched. "That girl has been obsessed with your cases ever since..." she trailed off, the unspoken reference to Julie's murder hanging in the air between them.

Mallory reached across the table to squeeze her sister's hand. It had been nearly three years since they'd solved her older niece's murder, but the pain was still raw for all of them. Julie would have been almost twenty-four now, probably finishing graduate school, perhaps even planning her own wedding.

Jen blinked rapidly and refocused on the magazine. "Anyway, back to your dress. I do like the sweetheart neckline on this one, but maybe with a simpler skirt? What d'you think?"

"Yes... but—" Mallory's phone vibrated on the coffee table, the screen lighting up with a notification, and she reached for it instinctively. Work had been hectic lately, with three active surveillance cases keeping her and Tucker occupied from dawn until well past dusk most days.

"Don't you dare," Jen warned, slapping her hand away with a fabric swatch. "We agreed. Two hours of uninterrupted wedding planning." Her tone was light, but Mallory could hear the underlying frustration. This wasn't the first time they'd tried to nail down wedding details, only for Mallory to get distracted by work.

"It's been three hours," Mallory countered, checking her watch. "And I'm pretty sure my brain will leak out of my ears if I look at one more variation of white fabric."

She rubbed her temples; a dull headache had been building for the past hour. While she loved her sister dearly, Jen's approach to wedding planning was exhaustingly thorough. No detail was too small to dissect, no option too remote to consider.

Jen sighed dramatically, tucking a strand of hair behind her ear. At forty-four, Jen Romero was still strikingly beautiful, with only the faintest lines around her eyes betraying the twelve-year age gap between the sisters. Her dark hair was expertly highlighted, her clothes tastefully expensive, her home immaculately decorated—everything about Jen screamed polished perfection.

Beside her, Mallory often felt like the perpetual kid sister—the "accident" their parents had had in their forties, the family wild card who'd never quite fit the mold. Where Jen was elegant and traditional, Mallory was practical and unconventional. Where Jen had married young and built a picture-perfect family life, Mallory had bounced between relationships and careers before finding her calling as a private investigator.

"Therefore, you have to make decisions now, Mal," Jen insisted, her voice taking on the patient tone she typically reserved for her teenage daughter. "The wedding is only six months away. Vendors need deposits. Dresses need alterations. Invitations need to be ordered. Do you have any idea how quickly time will fly?"

"Six months is an eternity," Mallory argued, stretching her arms above her head until her shoulders popped satisfyingly. She'd spent too many hours sitting still. "Tucker and I could solve a dozen cases in that time. Remember the Wilkins inheritance fraud? We cracked that one in three days."

"Speaking of Tucker," Jen said, flipping to another section of her wedding binder, "has he made any decisions on his tux yet? The groomsmen need to coordinate, and Jared will need time for alterations." She pulled out a color-coded spreadsheet of timeline milestones that made Mallory's eyes cross.

"We haven't even confirmed who the groomsmen are yet," Mallory reminded her. "Besides, Tucker thinks the entire wedding planning process is an elaborate form of torture specifically designed to break hardened criminals. He keeps saying we should just elope."

"He wouldn't," Jen gasped, clutching her wedding binder to her chest as if it were a shield against such blasphemy. Her expression of genuine horror made Mallory laugh.

"Relax," she said, reaching for her water glass. "He's not serious. Well, mostly not serious." She paused, considering. "Okay, he's about sixty percent serious, but I've vetoed the idea. He'll come around."

Mallory had known from the beginning that Tucker wasn't the type to dream about big weddings. At thirty-four, he'd been a dedicated bachelor before they'd met, focused entirely on his career. He approached wedding planning the same way he approached surveillance—as a necessary but tedious task to be endured rather than enjoyed.

"What's his issue, anyway?" Jen asked, making a note in her binder. "I thought men just had to show up in a tux and say 'I do.' It's not like he's the one trying on fifty dresses."

"He's not thrilled about the outdoor venue," Mallory admitted, remembering Tucker's face when they'd toured the botanical gardens. He'd looked like a man marching to his doom.

"What's wrong with the garden? It's gorgeous in spring. Those cherry blossoms will be perfect for photos."

"He says it's too weather dependent," Mallory replied. "What if it rains? What if there's a freak heat wave? What if a swarm of locusts descends upon our nuptials?" Mallory deepened her voice in a surprisingly accurate impression of Tucker's baritone, complete with his characteristic eyebrow raise. "Mallory, statistical analysis of Chattanooga springs shows a thirty-two percent chance of precipitation during our designated time window."

Jen laughed despite herself, setting down her pen. "Tucker Randall, afraid of a little rain," she chuckled, shaking her head. "The man who chased down that armed robber is worried about getting his hair wet? I don't believe it."

The memory of that case flashed through Mallory's mind—Tucker sprinting through a crowded farmer's market, vaulting over a produce stand to tackle a suspect who'd pulled a gun. He'd ended up with a black eye and a sprained wrist, but the embezzler had been arrested, and their client's stolen retirement funds recovered. It had been over two years ago, their third case together, before their professional partnership had evolved into something more personal.

"It's not the rain he's worried about. It's the unpredictability," Mallory explained, her voice softening with affection. "You know how he is. He likes to control variables, to plan for every contingency. A man who keeps three backup weapons and memorizes the floor plan of every building he enters doesn't like leaving things to chance."

Tucker's methodical nature was what made him such an excellent investigator—and sometimes such a challenging partner. Where Mallory followed hunches and intuition, Tucker relied on evidence and logic. Their different approaches had led to more than a few heated arguments, but they'd also helped them solve cases that had baffled others.

"Most PI's do," Jen nodded sagely, as if she hadn't learned everything she knew about private investigators from true crime podcasts and her sister's stories. She had eagerly devoured every detail of Mallory's cases since she'd joined Tucker's agency, asking questions that ranged from insightful to amusingly naïve.

"Is it always like on TV?" she'd asked once. "Do you wear disguises and have car chases?" The reality—hours of monotonous surveillance, mind-numbing paperwork, and witnesses who misremembered crucial details—was far less glamorous than fictional depictions, but occasionally they did get cases that rivaled anything on screen.

Mallory's phone buzzed again on the coffee table, the screen lighting up with another notification. An email had come through to their business account—the one that forwarded to both her and Tucker's phones. Usually, it was just routine inquiries: potential clients asking about rates, current clients requesting updates, occasionally spam that made it through the filters.

"Mallory," Jen warned, her tone that of a kindergarten teacher catching a student reaching for cookies before lunch.

"Just a quick peek," Mallory promised, already reaching for the phone. She'd developed the ability to quickly triage communications during her years working on cases, separating urgent matters from those that could wait. "It could be important. Maybe the Hendersons have new information about their neighbor's suspicious late-night activities."

"The murderers will still be there tomorrow," Jen said, her tone half-joking, half-exasperated. She tapped her watch meaningfully. "Your wedding dress decisions won't wait. The boutique needs six months for custom orders, and even off-the-rack options need alterations."

But Mallory was already skimming the email, her posture straightening instinctively as she read. The subject line had caught her attention immediately: "Unsolved Murder - My Brother Deserves Justice."

She'd seen plenty of cold case inquiries over the years. Most were rambling, fueled by grief that hadn't faded with time, often lacking crucial details. This one was different. The message was from someone named Gary Fisher, detailing the unsolved murder of his brother Terry eleven years earlier. Terry had been found on a farmer's property, shot twice in the back of the head execution-style. No arrests had ever been made, no suspects had ever been named publicly.

What struck Mallory was the methodical organization of the email. It was huge. Gary Fisher had included dates, times, locations, names of the original investigating officers. He'd attached a PDF timeline of events surrounding the murder, along with scanned newspaper clippings and what appeared to be copies of the initial police statements from several witnesses. This wasn't just a grieving relative reaching out in desperation—this was someone who had been conducting his own investigation for years.

"Jen, listen to this," Mallory said, reading aloud from the email. "My parents are elderly and in declining health. My father has only a few months to live. All they want to know before they pass is who killed their son and why. The local police have given up. You guys are my last hope for justice."

The urgency resonated with Mallory. She remembered all too well the agonizing weeks when Julie had first disappeared, the desperate need for answers that had consumed their family.

"That's sad," Jen conceded, her expression softening, "but you get emails like this all the time, don't you? People whose cases have gone cold, looking for whatever help they can find."

"Not like this," Mallory said, continuing to scroll through Gary's message. She skimmed the detailed timeline he'd created, noting how each event was documented. He'd listed every person his brother Terry had contact with during the days before his death, every location he'd visited, even the weather conditions on the day the body was found.

"So what makes this one different?" Jen asked, closing her wedding binder with a resigned sigh, clearly sensing that their planning session was effectively over.

Mallory wasn't entirely sure she could articulate it. Part of it was the thoroughness of Gary's documentation, part of it was the looming deadline of his parents' failing health, but there was something else—a pattern in the details that tickled the back of her mind, though she couldn't quite place it yet.

"I don't know exactly," she admitted, biting her lower lip as she continued to read. "But there's something about this case… It feels… different, important. The execution-style killing, the rural setting, the complete lack of progress after eleven years. And the parents who might die without ever knowing who killed their son."

She scrolled through more of the attached documents, finding a photograph of Terry Fisher—a young man with an easy smile, dark hair falling over bright eyes, his arm slung around a woman Mallory assumed was his fiancée. According to Gary's notes, Terry had been planning to get married just three months after he was killed.

"I need to show this to Tucker," she said, already dialing his number. The wedding magazines lay forgotten on the coffee table as Mallory began pacing across Jen's living room, phone pressed to her ear.

Tucker answered on the third ring, his voice carrying that slightly guarded tone he used when expecting wedding-related questions. "Please tell me this is about dinner plans and not flower arrangements."

"Check your email," Mallory said without preamble, too focused to be amused by his wariness. "The business account. Something just came in from a Gary Fisher about his brother's murder."

"Give me a second," Tucker replied, and she could hear the faint clicking of his keyboard through the phone. Tucker would be sitting at his desk in their small home office, probably reviewing surveillance photos or drafting a client report. He was meticulous about documentation, keeping their case files organized with a precision that sometimes bordered on obsessive.

Jen caught Mallory's eye across the room and mouthed, "Wedding plans?" with an exaggerated pout, gesturing to the abandoned magazines.

Mallory covered the phone with her hand. "Tomorrow, I promise. Dinner and full wedding focus." She knew she was making a promise she might not keep, but in the moment, she meant it.

"You've got that look in your eyes," Jen sighed, gathering up some of the scattered fabric swatches. "The one that means you're about to disappear into a case for weeks and forget that the rest of the world exists."

Mallory couldn't argue with that. The familiar buzz of anticipation was already coursing through her veins, the same feeling she got at the start of every challenging case. She was like a bloodhound catching a scent—once she had it, she couldn't let go until she'd followed it to its source.

"I'm reading it now," Tucker's voice came through the phone, pulling her attention back. "Cold case, rural area, execution-style killing..." She could practically see him frowning as he analyzed the information. "Sounds like a long shot, Mal. These rural jurisdictions don't always preserve evidence properly, witnesses disappear or die, documentation gets spotty."

"Duckwood isn't exactly rural, Tucker, and... His parents are dying," Mallory pressed, pacing more quickly now. "His father only has months left to live. Don't they deserve answers before it's too late?" She walked to the window, looking out at Jen's backyard, thinking of the Fisher family living with an open wound for eleven years.

There was a moment of silence. Tucker wasn't one to make hasty decisions, especially when it came to taking on new cases. She could imagine him mentally reviewing their current workload, calculating billable hours, assessing their resources.

"You know how difficult these cold cases can be," he finally said, his tone cautious. "Small-town police departments with limited resources, evidence that's probably been mishandled or lost by now, witnesses whose memories have faded or who've moved away—"

"So we don't even try?" Mallory countered, cutting him off, her voice rising slightly, passion creeping in. "We've solved cases with less to go on. Remember the Caldwell fraud? All we had were bank statements from six years ago and a hunch."

"That was different," Tucker said, but she could hear the slight waver in his voice. Despite his rational, methodical approach to cases, Tucker was at heart a man driven by justice. It was why he'd left the FBI after a case went wrong—not because he'd stopped caring, but because he cared too much.

"We should drive out there," Mallory said before he could fully formulate his objections. "Meet with Gary Fisher in person, get a feel for the situation on the ground. If it's a dead end, we'll know quickly enough."

"Mal, we've got three active cases here in Chattanooga, plus all this wedding stuff—" Tucker's voice held a note of exasperation now.

"The wedding isn't for six months," she interrupted, ignoring Jen's dramatic gasp from across the room. "And those other cases are just surveillance jobs. They can wait a day or two." She knew she was pushing, perhaps too hard, but there was something about this case that was pulling at her.

The silence on the line told her Tucker was wavering. She knew better than to push harder; after nearly three years together, she'd learned when to let him come to a decision on his own. Tucker didn't respond well to pressure, but he did respond to reason and to his own moral compass, which invariably pointed toward helping those in need.

Finally, she heard him sigh, a sound that signaled surrender. "Fine. I'll reach out and set up a meeting. But we're not committing to anything yet, understood? This is just a preliminary reconnaissance."

"Understood," Mallory agreed, a smile spreading across her face as she turned back to face her sister. "Let me know when you've arranged it."

She ended the call and tucked her phone into her pocket, already mentally packing for their trip. Jen was staring at her with a mixture of annoyance and affection, arms crossed over her chest.

"There goes our wedding planning," Jen said, but there was no real anger in her voice. After decades of Mallory's unpredictable nature, Jen had developed a tolerant resignation to her younger sister's sudden changes of direction.

"Just for… a few days. Maybe only one," Mallory promised, gathering her purse from the side table. The wedding magazines could stay; she'd pick them up next time. "Besides, you've already done most of the work. I just need to pick a dress and show up, right?"

"If only it were that simple," Jen muttered, but she stood to walk Mallory to the door. "Just promise me one thing?"

"What's that?" Mallory asked, slinging her bag over her shoulder.

"Try not to get shot this time? Jackie's still traumatized from your last big case, and I don't want to have to explain to Mom and Dad why their youngest daughter has a new bullet hole."

Mallory thought of her sixteen-year-old niece, who had developed a fascination with true crime after Mallory and Tucker had solved the murder of her older sister Julie the previous year. Jackie had gone from a typical teenager obsessed with social media to someone who listened to true crime podcasts and asked unsettlingly specific questions about investigative techniques. Trauma manifested in strange ways sometimes.

"I'll do my best," Mallory said, giving her sister a quick hug. "No promises, though. You know how these things go."

"That's what worries me," Jen replied, her smile not quite reaching her eyes. "Just… be careful. And maybe check in more than once a week this time?"

"I will," Mallory promised, meaning it. Three years before, during the investigation into Julie's disappearance and murder, she'd gotten so absorbed in the case that she'd barely communicated with her family. Looking back, she regretted not being more present for Jen during that horrific time.

"Oh, and would you mind looking after Annie while I'm gone?" she asked. Maggie was her seven-year-old Border Collie.

"You know I will," Jen replied. "Drop her off whenever you like."

"Thanks, sis. I…" She was going to say I owe you one, but she owed her many more than one, so she simply turned, smiled, and hugged her, then pivoted and walked away, leaving her sister staring after her.

2

As she walked to her car, Mallory could already feel her mind shifting into investigative mode. Already, she was mentally cataloging the details from Gary's email. Two shots to the back of the head. Execution-style. A rural setting. An investigation that had apparently stalled almost immediately. A family still seeking answers after more than a decade.

She couldn't explain exactly why this particular case had caught her attention the way it had. They received literally dozens of cold case inquiries each month, and very rarely did one grab her the way this one had. Perhaps it was the methodical way Gary had presented the information, or the urgency of his parents' failing health. Or perhaps it was simply that Terry Fisher had been engaged to be married when he was killed—a young man on the cusp of starting his life with someone he loved, only to have it all ripped away.

Whatever it was, her instincts rarely led her astray. Tucker often teased her about her "hunches," but even he had learned to trust her intuition. *There's something here,* she thought, *something worth pursuing. I can feel it in my bones.*

Her phone buzzed with a text from Tucker: *Meeting with Gary*

Fisher tomorrow at 11 AM. It's a 90-minute drive. Pack overnight. I'll pick you up at 9 AM.

Mallory smiled to herself as she slid into the driver's seat of her Honda CRV.

Tucker might pretend to be reluctant, she thought, *but he's already planning ahead, already assuming we'll need more than a day to assess the situation.*

And that was the thing about Tucker; once he committed to something, he did it thoroughly. No half measures, no cutting corners.

And that was the thing about their partnership. It was personal and professional. They balanced each other perfectly. Where she was intuitive, he was analytical. Where she rushed in, he proceeded with caution. Where she followed her heart, he followed the evidence. She provided the intuitive leaps, the passionate pursuits; he contributed the methodical planning, the careful consideration. They pushed each other, challenged each other, and ultimately made each other better investigators.

Together, they solved cases that neither could crack by themselves.

This one would be no different. Someone had killed Terry Fisher eleven years ago, and his family deserved to know why. If the local police couldn't or wouldn't provide those answers, then Mallory and Tucker would just have to do it themselves.

As she drove home to pack, Mallory felt that familiar tingling sensation at the base of her skull, the one that told her they were about to uncover something big. Something dangerous. The feeling she'd had three years before when she and Tucker had gone after Julie's killer, and a dozen times since. She shook her head and smiled as she remembered that first meeting, how it almost never happened, and how he insisted he worked alone. Persuading him to let her tag along hadn't been easy. *But look where we are now,* she thought.

Her phone rang again, breaking into her thoughts. She answered through the car's Bluetooth system. It was Tucker.

"I need you to download everything Gary Fisher attached to his email," he said without preamble. "There's a lot to go through before tomorrow, and I want us both up to speed before we meet him."

"You got it," she replied, making a mental note to stop for coffee on the way home. It would be a late night of research. "Anything jump out at you?" she asked.

Tucker was silent for a moment, and she could almost see him organizing his thoughts, choosing his words carefully as he always did. "Maybe, he replied. The victim's girlfriend at the time is now married to his cousin. That's an interesting development. And the local police chief, Nate Winson; his name appears in some online forum posts speculating about corruption. Nothing concrete, but it's worth looking into."

"I saw that too," Mallory said, feeling a surge of excitement. "And there's the murder itself, the execution style—two shots to the back of the head. That's smacks of a professional hit, don't you think?"

"Possibly," Tucker replied. "Or maybe it was made to look that way. Rural Tennessee has plenty of hunters, so familiarity with firearms is common. Don't jump to conclusions about hitmen or organized crime just yet."

Mallory laughed. "You know me too well."

"Indeed, I do," he agreed, his voice warming slightly. "That's why I already called the hotel in Duckwood and booked us a room for at least three nights. Two beds," he added quickly. "For propriety's sake, since we're not married yet."

The formality made her smile. Despite their engagement and the fact that they almost lived together, Tucker maintained certain old-fashioned sensibilities when they were working. "Always the gentleman," she joked.

"Professional," he corrected. "We're representing the agency. I don't want small-town gossip interfering with our investigation."

"Fair enough," she conceded, turning onto her street. "What else did you find in Gary's materials?"

"There's a mention of some local Baptist church that Terry attended regularly. The pastor there might be worth talking to if he's still around after eleven years."

"Good thinking," Mallory said as she pulled into her driveway.

"Churches are information hubs in small towns. People talk to their pastors, share things they wouldn't tell police."

"Exactly. There's also—" Tucker paused, and she heard keyboard clicks in the background. "Hold on, I just got another email from Gary. He's sending more documents. Old newspaper clippings about the case, some photocopied police statements… Mallory, this guy has been working this case for years."

"I told you there was something here," she said, unable to keep the satisfaction from her voice.

"Let's not get ahead of ourselves," Tucker cautioned. "Having a lot of documents doesn't mean they contain a lot of useful information. For all we know, Gary's spent a decade compiling irrelevant details."

"We'll find out tomorrow," Mallory said, gathering her purse as she parked. "I'm home now. I'll go through everything tonight."

"I'll call you in the morning at seven sharp and pick you up at nine

"I'll be ready. And Tucker?"

"Yeah?"

"Thanks for taking this seriously. I know we're busy, but… I just have a feeling about this one."

There was a pause on the line. "Your feelings have panned out before," he admitted grudgingly. "Just… keep an open mind. Don't get tunnel vision on any one theory."

"I promise," she said. "See you at nine. Love you."

"Love you, too," he replied.

Mallory ended the call and sat in her car for a moment, watching the last rays of afternoon sunlight filter through the trees in her front yard. Her thoughts drifted to Terry Fisher, a young man whose life had been violently cut short eleven years ago, whose parents were now dying without answers, whose brother hadn't stopped searching for justice.

Her phone buzzed with a text from Jen: "Since we didn't decide on a dress today, I'm making an appointment at Bridal Elegance for next week. Non-negotiable."

Mallory smiled and texted back: "Deal. And I'll actually show up this time."

Setting her phone on the passenger seat, she reached into the glove compartment and pulled out a small notebook—an old-fashioned habit in a digital age, but one that had served her well. On a fresh page, she wrote "TERRY FISHER CASE" and underlined it twice.

Below that, she jotted her initial questions:

- Why execution style? Professional hit or made to look that way?
- Connection to other victims?
- Nate Winson - corrupt cop or victim of rumors?
- Tiffany (ex-fiancée) - now married to the victim's cousin. Suspicious timing?
- Local church connection - what did Terry confide in his pastor?
- Why has the case gone cold for 11 years despite Gary's efforts?

She tapped her pen against the page, then added one more question:

- Who stands to benefit from Terry Fisher's death? Follow the money/motive.

It wasn't much to go on, but it was a start. Tomorrow they would meet with Gary, see the actual town where the murder took place, begin to get a feel for the cast of characters in this long-dormant mystery. And, if Tucker was right, it would probably lead nowhere—just another cold case destined to remain unsolved, another family left without closure.

But if Mallory's instincts were correct, they were about to uncover something that had been deliberately buried for over a decade. Something dangerous enough that someone had been willing to kill to keep it hidden.

She closed the notebook and stepped out of her car. She had packing to do, research to review, sleep to grab before their morning departure. Tucker would arrive exactly at nine—not eight-fifty-nine, not one minute after nine—and he'd expect her to be ready to go.

That was one more thing about their partnership she had come to appreciate. They kept each other accountable, balanced each other's strengths and weaknesses. His methodical nature tempered her impulsivity; her intuition complemented his logic.

Together, they made a formidable team. And starting tomorrow, they would put that partnership to work on behalf of a family that had waited far too long for answers.

As she turned the key in her front door, Mallory felt that familiar surge of anticipation that came with starting a new case. The late nights, the dead ends, the breakthrough moments, the rush of finally piecing together a puzzle that others had abandoned. And that was what she lived for. Not wedding dresses or flower arrangements, but the pursuit of truth, however uncomfortable or dangerous it might be.

She was met enthusiastically by Annie, her energetic border collie.

"Hello, girlfriend," she said. "Have you been a good girl? I have a surprise for you. You're going to visit your aunt and uncle for a few days. Won't that be nice? Come on, let's go potty and then I'll give you some dinner."

That done, she grabbed a soft drink from the fridge, sat down at the table, took her laptop from her bag, opened it, and got to work.

Forty-five minutes later, she gave it up, pushed the laptop away, folded her arms, frowned, then muttered, "This isn't working. We should be doing this together."

3

Tucker Randall leaned back in his office chair, stretching his neck from side to side as he scrolled through the surveillance photos on his computer screen. Three hours of watching the Henderson property had yielded exactly two usable images of their neighbor's suspicious late-night activities. The rest were just shadows and normal neighborhood comings and goings. Nothing that would definitively prove the illegal subletting that Mrs. Henderson suspected.

The office—an addition to the left side of his home—was quiet this late in the afternoon, just the hum of the air conditioning and the occasional car passing on the street outside. Tucker preferred it that way—no distractions, no interruptions, just him and the evidence. It wasn't fancy, but it was functional, and most importantly, affordable.

The walls were lined with filing cabinets—Tucker's insistence, despite Mallory's argument that everything should be digital now. He'd compromised by maintaining both paper and electronic records. Technology failed; paper endured. It was a lesson he'd learned the hard way during his FBI days when a server crash had temporarily wiped out months of case files.

Tucker clicked through several more photos, making notes in his precise, squared-off handwriting that Mallory often teased him about.

"It's like a robot is writing in hieroglyphics," she'd said once, peering over his shoulder at a case report. He'd retorted that at least his notes were legible, unlike her hasty scrawl that sometimes even she couldn't decipher later.

The memory made him smile slightly. For all their differences in approach, he and Mallory made an effective team. Her intuitive leaps sometimes led them down rabbit holes, but just as often, they cracked cases wide open. His methodical process ensured they didn't miss crucial details along the way.

When his phone rang again, Tucker glanced at the screen and felt a twinge of apprehension when he saw Mallory's name. She'd been wedding planning with her sister Jen, which meant the call likely involved flower arrangements, color schemes, or some other detail he was supposed to have an opinion on but genuinely didn't.

He took a deep breath and answered. "Please tell me this is about dinner plans and not flower arrangements."

"Check your email," Mallory said immediately, her voice carrying that distinct tone of excitement he recognized from the start of promising cases. "The business account. Something just came in from a Gary Fisher about his brother's murder."

Tucker sat up straighter, her enthusiasm momentarily contagious. He clicked over to their email, finding the message already at the top of their inbox. The subject line was direct: "Unsolved Murder - My Brother Deserves Justice."

"Give me a second," he said, opening the email and scanning the contents. They received plenty of cold case inquiries—enough that he'd created a standardized response for the ones they couldn't take on, which was most of them. But even at first glance, this one seemed more substantive than most.

The email was methodically organized, with clearly delineated sections for background, evidence, witness statements, and investigation notes. The writer, Gary Fisher, had included several attachments: a PDF timeline, scanned newspaper articles, and what appeared to be copies of police reports. Tucker's investigator instincts perked up at the thoroughness, even as his practical side noted the challenges inherent in such cases.

The basics were straightforward enough. Terry Fisher, twenty-eight years old, found shot execution-style on a farmer's property eleven years ago. No arrests, no named suspects, no apparent motive. The local police investigation had gone nowhere. Now the victim's parents were elderly and ill, seeking closure before they passed.

Mallory was already pushing for them to take the case, her voice growing more animated as she described the details he was still reading.

"I'm reading it now," Tucker said, tempering his response. "Cold case, rural area, execution-style killing..." He frowned as he scrolled through the attached timeline. "Sounds like a long shot, Mal. These rural jurisdictions don't always preserve evidence properly, witnesses disappear or die, documentation gets spotty."

"His parents are dying," Mallory pressed, the passion in her voice unmistakable. "His father only has months left to live. Don't they deserve answers before it's too late?"

Tucker sighed internally. Mallory's compassion was one of the things he admired most about her, but it sometimes clouded her professional judgment. He shook his head. Eleven years was a long time. Evidence degraded. Memories faded. Witnesses moved away or died. And rural police departments often lacked the resources and expertise to properly maintain case files for that long.

"You know how difficult these rural cold cases can be," he reminded her. "Small-town police departments with limited resources, evidence that's probably been mishandled or lost by now, witnesses whose memories have faded or who've moved away..."

"So we don't even try?" Mallory countered, her voice rising slightly. "We've solved cases with less to go on. Remember the Caldwell fraud? All we had were bank statements from six years ago and a hunch."

"That was different," Tucker said automatically, though he knew she had a point. The Caldwell case had seemed impossible until Mallory had spotted a pattern in the bank records that everyone else had missed. But financial fraud cases left paper trails; murders often didn't.

Tucker ran a hand through his short black hair, mentally reviewing their current caseload. Three active surveillance cases, all relatively straightforward. The Hendersons, worried about their neighbor illegally subletting. The Martins, suspecting their business partner of embezzlement. The Davidson divorce, where the husband was allegedly hiding assets. None were particularly time-sensitive or complex.

"We should drive out there," Mallory suggested, interrupting his thoughts. "Meet with Gary Fisher in person, get a feel for the situation on the ground. If it's a dead end, we'll know quickly enough."

That was actually a reasonable approach, Tucker had to admit. An initial assessment wouldn't commit them to taking the case, but it would give them enough information to make an informed decision.

"Mal, we've got three active cases here in Chattanooga, plus all this wedding stuff—" he began, more as a token protest than a genuine objection.

"The wedding isn't for six months," she interrupted, dismissing his concern. "And those other cases are just surveillance jobs. They can wait a day or two."

Tucker glanced at his calendar. She wasn't wrong. The surveillance cases could be paused briefly without issue. And a part of him was intrigued by the methodical way Gary Fisher had compiled his brother's case information. It suggested a careful, detail-oriented person—the kind of client Tucker preferred to work with.

He was also aware that Mallory's interest in this particular case likely stemmed partly from her own family's experience with her niece Julie's murder. The Fisher parents' desire for closure before they died resonated with her on a personal level.

After a moment's consideration, Tucker made his decision. "Fine. I'll reach out to set up a meeting. But we're not committing to anything yet, understood? This is just a preliminary reconnaissance."

"Understood," Mallory agreed, the smile clear in her voice. "Let me know when you've arranged it."

As soon as they ended the call, Tucker opened a new email to Gary Fisher, introducing himself and Mallory as investigators interested in discussing his brother's case. He suggested meeting the following day at 11 AM, noting they would drive from Chattanooga to—he checked the address—Duckwood, a small town about ninety minutes away in rural Tennessee.

The response came less than five minutes later. Gary was available and eager to meet. He provided his home address and phone number, along with effusive thanks for their interest.

Tucker texted Mallory with the details, and then he did a search for hotels in Duckwood, found one he liked and booked a room for three nights.

With the logistics handled, Tucker returned to the Fisher case materials, methodically working through each document. The execution-style killing—two shots to the back of the head—suggested either a professional hit or someone trying to make it look like one. The lack of robbery or sexual assault ruled out certain common motives. The body had been left where it fell, not hidden or moved, which indicated either confidence or panic on the killer's part.

The victim, Terry Fisher, had no criminal record. He'd worked as a contractor, was engaged to be married, attended church regularly. So, by all accounts, he was an ordinary young man in a small town. Nothing in his background screamed "murder victim." *So what the hell happened?* he wondered, *And why?*

Tucker opened an online forum thread Gary had linked in his email. Local speculation about the case ran rampant: wild theories from organized crime connections to satanic cult activity. Most of it was the usual nonsense that proliferated around unsolved murders, but one name kept appearing: Nate Winson, a local police officer who was now apparently the chief. Several anonymous posters suggested he might have deliberately mishandled evidence or even steered the investigation away from certain suspects.

This was potentially significant. Police corruption could explain why the case had gone unsolved despite the seemingly straightforward evidence. Tucker made a note to look into Winson's background and history with the department.

And then another detail caught his attention: Terry's fiancée, Tiffany Springer, had married his cousin Louis shortly after his death. *Hmm, interesting,* he thought. *That's an unusual development worth exploring.* Grief sometimes pushed people together, but the timing raised questions.

As Tucker continued reviewing the materials, his phone rang again. Seeing Mallory's name, he answered it.

"Hey, I just sent you everything Gary Fisher attached to his email," he said without waiting for her to speak. "There's a lot to go through before tomorrow. I want us both up to speed before we meet him."

A brief conversation followed about the case during which he told her of the arrangements he'd made in Duckwood and his plan to pick her up at nine in the morning.

After they ended the call, Tucker continued working through the case materials, creating a preliminary timeline and suspect list. As the sky outside his office window darkened, he finally stood, stretching his back and shoulders. He'd been hunched over his computer for hours, so absorbed in the Fisher case that he'd lost track of time.

The office was silent now, so Tucker grabbed his laptop and the notes he'd printed out, locked the front door, turned off the lights an made his way into the house. He would, he decided, continue reviewing the materials later.

As he walked through to the kitchen, he reflected on the investigation ahead and what it might entail. Cold cases were always challenging, but they had their own particular satisfaction when solved. Bringing closure to families, justice to victims long forgotten by everyone except those who loved them—it was work worth doing, even when the odds seemed long; too long, in some cases.

His phone buzzed with a text from Mallory: "I picked up dinner. Thai food. I'll be there in a few minutes."

Tucker smiled, typing back a quick affirmative. *Geez, does she never quit?* He shook his head. He knew just exactly what she was doing. She wanted to discuss the case and figured they could do it over dinner.

Tucker's mind continued working the Fisher case, turning over the sparse facts, looking for angles they could explore. He'd spent eight years with the FBI before resigning after the Marsha Cline case went so tragically wrong. Those years had taught him that even the most seemingly straightforward cases often contained hidden complexities. What might appear to be a simple rural murder could have tendrils extending in unexpected directions.

Mallory arrived a few minutes later to find the case materials spread across the surface of the table.

"Oh, that's nice," she said, her hazel eyes bright with the energy she always had at the beginning of a promising case.

"I thought I told you to go home and get some sleep?" he said.

She shrugged. "Sleep? Seriously?" she joked. "It's only six-thirty. And besides, what was the point of me going over everything on my own and then have to discuss it all with you tomorrow? It's better we do it together, over dinner, don't you think?"

It was logical enough, and he could see she was full of enthusiasm, so, rather than argue with her, he nodded, got up and they both went to the kitchen.

He grabbed a couple of plates from the cupboard and they sat down at the table to eat.

"I've been cross-referencing the witness statements with the timeline Gary created," she said through a mouthful of food. She swallowed, then continued, "There are some inconsistencies in what people reported seeing the night Terry disappeared—"

"Can we give it a moment?" Tucker asked, cutting her off. "Let's eat, then we'll talk."

She pursed her lips, narrowed her eyes, stared across the table at him.

He stared stoically back at her, unyielding.

Finally, she gave it up, smiled, nodded, and said, "Oh hell, have it your way. You always do. And on that note, I'm not sure I want to marry you after all."

"Really," he replied. "I—"

"No, not really, you idiot," she snapped. "Now shut up and eat."

Thirty minutes later, coffee in hand, they were back, standing at the dining room table, staring down at the dozens of printed sheets.

"What I was going to say when you so rudely cut me off," she began, "was that there are inconsistencies in what people reported seeing the night Terry disappeared, and…"

She paused, opened her briefcase, took out a sheet of paper, and said,, "And look at this." She pushed a photocopy of a newspaper article toward him. "Three months after Terry's murder, there was another killing with the same MO. Corey Robar, a local contractor, found on the edge of a property about a mile from where they found Terry. Two shots to the back of the head."

"No kidding?" Tucker said, closing his laptop and examining the article with interest. "Connection to organized crime, perhaps? Or a serial killer, maybe?"

"That's what I'm thinking," Mallory said, holding up a map she'd printed. "Gary mentions this briefly in his notes but doesn't develop it. I found more details in some of the forum posts. And there's more." She paused, stared at him, waiting for a response.

"Well," he said. "Go on. What more?"

"Apparently, there have been four similar murders, all with the same MO, over the eleven years since Terry's death, all within a five-mile radius."

Tucker's eyebrows rose. He leaned back in his chair and stared at her. If what she said was true, it changed the entire complexion of the case.

"Five murders with the same MO, all unsolved, all in the same area?" he said, thoughtfully. "That can't be a coincidence."

"Exactly," Mallory nodded, her excitement palpable. "And get this; the local police never publicly connected the cases. Each one was treated as an isolated incident. Either they're incompetent, or…"

"Or someone's deliberately keeping them separate to hide the pattern," Tucker finished, his mind already calculating the implications. Multiple related murders increased the complexity but also provided more evidence, more potential witnesses, more opportunities to find connections.

They ate dinner while continuing to discuss the case, Mallory's enthusiasm a counterpoint to Tucker's methodical analysis. By the time they finished, Tucker had a clearer picture of what they might be dealing with: either a serial killer who had somehow managed to operate undetected in a small community for over a decade, or a series of related murders connected to some local criminal enterprise that powerful people wanted to keep hidden.

Either way, it was potentially dangerous, and certainly more complex than the routine surveillance jobs that made up the bulk of their business lately.

"We should get some sleep," Tucker said finally, checking his watch. "It's after ten, and we need to leave by nine to make the meeting on time. You going to stay over?"

"I thought I might," she replied. "I dropped Annie off with Jen on the way here. I told her it might be a couple of days. That okay?"

Tucker made a face but didn't argue.

"Good," she said. "I'll set three alarms."

"Make it four," Tucker suggested, knowing her tendency to sleep through alarms. "And I'm thinking at least three days, so you might want to update Jen. I know it's only a little over ninety minutes away, but if we decide to take the case it might be prudent to stay in Duckwood for a while."

"Already packed," Mallory grinned, gesturing to a duffel bag by the door that Tucker hadn't noticed when she came in.

As they cleaned up, Tucker found himself reviewing mental checklists: equipment they should bring, questions to ask Gary, background information to verify. Cold cases required a different approach than fresh investigations. Evidence had to be reconstructed, witnesses re-interviewed with an understanding that memories had faded and changed. Time was both an obstacle and occasionally an ally, as people who'd kept secrets for years sometimes became willing to talk as they aged, as relationships changed, as old loyalties died.

Before turning in, Tucker made one more call—to Mike Preston, a former FBI colleague who now worked with the Tennessee Bureau of Investigation. He didn't expect Mike to answer this late, and he didn't, so Tucker left a brief message asking if the TBI had any information on the Fisher case or other unsolved murders in Duckwood over the past decade.

Mallory was already in bed when he joined her, but he could tell from her breathing that she wasn't asleep.

"Nervous about tomorrow?" he asked quietly in the darkness.

"Not nervous," she replied after a moment. "Just… I can't stop thinking about those parents. Waiting eleven years for answers about who killed their son, now running out of time."

Tucker reached for her hand beneath the covers. "We'll do our best," he promised. It was all he could offer; not certainty of success, but the assurance that they would pursue the truth with every tool and skill at their disposal.

"I know," Mallory murmured, squeezing his hand. "That's why I love you. You always do your best, even when the odds are long."

There was a moment of silence, then Mallory said, "Tucker!" Then rolled over, put her arm around him, then slid on top of him, and—

Tucker lay awake long after Mallory's breathing had deepened into sleep, his mind still working through the Fisher case. There was something about it that nagged at him; not just the details they'd uncovered so far, but some pattern or connection he couldn't quite grasp yet. Experience had taught him to trust that feeling, to let his subconscious mind process the information until the insight emerged.

As he finally drifted toward sleep, images from the case files floated through his mind: Terry Fisher's smiling face in a photograph with his fiancée, the stark police photos of his body in a rural field, and the newspaper clippings about subsequent murders. Something connected these deaths beyond the obvious similarities in method. Something that had remained hidden for eleven years.

Tomorrow they would begin unraveling that mystery, for the sake of parents who deserved to know the truth, and for a young man whose life had been cut short just as it was about to begin.

The last thought Tucker had before sleep claimed him was a simple promise, made to himself and to the victim he'd never met but whose cause he was already beginning to take as his own: *We'll find out who did this, Terry. No matter how long it takes.*

4

Mallory Carver bit back a yawn as Tucker's SUV sped along Highway 27 toward Duckwood. The clock on the dash read 9:32 AM.

"Tell me again why we needed to leave at the crack of dawn when our meeting isn't until eleven?" she asked, taking another sip from her travel mug.

Tucker kept his eyes on the road. "I texted Fisher. I changed the time to eleven-thirty. I want to take a look at the town," he replied. "I want time to get the lay of the land before meeting him. Besides, it's not the crack of dawn. I've been up since six."

"Of course you have," Mallory muttered, but there was affection in her tone. Tucker's sometimes mechanical, even fastidious, approach had saved their lives more than once.

As they drove, Mallory flipped through the case notes on her tablet. *Terry Fisher,* she thought, *twenty-eight years old, found shot execution-style on a farmer's property eleven years ago. No arrests, no suspects, a textbook cold case that had likely been mishandled from the start. Small-town police departments rarely had the resources or expertise for complex homicide investigations. Hah! So now what? Where do we begin?*

"So now what?" Mallory asked. "what's our strategy?" She set aside the tablet and turned her head to look at him. "Gary Fisher has been compiling information for years without cracking the case. What can we offer that local law enforcement couldn't?"

"Fresh eyes," Tucker replied simply. "No preconceptions, no local politics influencing our perspective. Plus, you have good instincts for these things."

Mallory smiled at the compliment. Tucker wasn't generous with praise, which made his rare acknowledgments all the more meaningful.

"I've been thinking about the location," she said, grabbing her tablet and bringing up the map. "The body was found on a farm property outside town. Owned by someone named Carl Parsons, according to Gary's notes."

"Farmer's field, middle of nowhere, execution-style killing," Tucker mused. "Suggests the killer's confident, experienced."

"But who hires hits on contractors in small Tennessee towns?" Mallory questioned. "Terry Fisher wasn't wealthy, wasn't involved in drugs, at least not according to the tox screen. He was just a regular guy planning his wedding."

"That's what we're here to find out," Tucker replied.

They lapsed into silence as Duckwood appeared on the horizon. It was a picturesque small town nestled in the rolling hills of eastern Tennessee—red brick buildings lining a traditional Main Street, church steeples rising above the tree line, American flags fluttering from lampposts. It was the kind of place that appeared on postcards captioned "Small Town America."

"Doesn't exactly scream murder capital of Tennessee," Mallory observed as they drove past the Cumberland County Justice Center on the left.

Tucker checked his watch. "Appearances can be deceiving," Tucker replied. "It's only ten after ten. We've made good time. Let's drive around a bit, then get some breakfast."

Tucker navigated the quiet streets methodically, giving Mallory a chance to observe the town waking up. Shopkeepers unlocked doors, elderly men gathered at a diner, mothers dropped children at a daycare center. Everything seemed perfectly normal—which made the eleven-year-old unsolved murder seem even more incongruous.

Mallory made mental notes of each location, creating a mental map of the small community. They continued driving, eventually reaching the outskirts where houses gave way to more rural properties.

"That place looks interesting," Tucker said, nodding to the Crossroads Café. "Looks busy. Might be a good place for breakfast and maybe some local gossip. But before we do, I want to take a quick look at the place where the body was found. It should be just… this way," he said as he turned onto a county road that wound through the farmland.

Using GPS coordinates from the case file, they were able to locate the spot where Terry Fisher's body had been discovered eleven years earlier. Now it was just an unremarkable field, part of a working farm with no sign of the tragedy that had occurred there.

"Middle of nowhere," Mallory observed, staring up at the old oak tree, then turning to scan the open landscape. "But close enough to that access road that whoever did it could get in and out quickly."

Tucker nodded. "Local knowledge. Whoever it was that killed him knew this area well."

After surveying the location, they returned to town and stopped at the Crossroads Cafe, a quaint establishment with gingham curtains and the smell of fresh-baked biscuits wafting through the door. A bell jingled as they entered, and several patrons glanced up to assess the newcomers.

They found an empty booth by the window and sat down opposite one another.

A middle-aged waitress approached with a coffeepot in hand. "Hello. I'm Donna," she said as she filled their cups without asking, then set the coffeepot down on the table and pulled a pad from her apron pocket. "Passing through?" she asked conversationally. "What can I get you?"

"We're here on business for a few days," Tucker replied, his voice taking on a slight Southern drawl that Mallory recognized as his "blending in" technique.

"What kind of business brings folks to Duckwood?" Donna asked, her tone friendly but curious.

Tucker kept his answer deliberately vague. "Research. Looking into some local history."

"Well, our breakfast special will keep you fueled for your research," Donna smiled. "All you can eat biscuits and gravy today."

They placed their orders, and Mallory waited until the waitress moved away before leaning across the table. "You didn't mention we're investigating a murder."

"No point raising red flags yet," Tucker replied quietly. "Small towns have efficient gossip networks. By lunchtime, everyone would know why we're here."

Their food arrived quickly; fluffy biscuits smothered in sausage gravy for Tucker, a vegetable omelet for Mallory. They ate quietly, occasionally glancing around the cafe to observe the other patrons.

"So what's our first move after meeting with Gary?" Mallory asked, keeping her voice low.

"Depends on what new information he provides, if any," Tucker replied. "But I do want to speak with Tiffany Springer, Terry's former fiancée, who married his cousin. That's an unusual development."

"And the police," Mallory added. "We should ask to see and review the full case files if possible."

Tucker nodded. "I'll request a meeting with chief. Winson."

After finishing breakfast, they still had a little time before their appointment with Gary. They decided to drive by the Baptist church again, where, according to Gary Fisher's case materials, Terry had been a regular attendee.

The Whitehaven Baptist Church was a white clapboard building with a modest steeple, set back from the road on a well-maintained lot. A sign out front announced Sunday services and Wednesday prayer meetings.

"Pastor Henry Pearcy," Mallory read from the sign. "Same pastor as eleven years ago and, according to Gary's notes, he conducted Terry's funeral."

"Add him to our interview list," Tucker said. "Religious leaders often know more about their congregants than anyone else."

As eleven-thirty approached, they headed to Gary Fisher's address in a modest subdivision on the edge of town. Two children were playing catch in the front yard when they arrived—a teenage boy and a younger girl. The boy noticed them and called back toward the house. A moment later, a tall, slim man with dark hair and a prominent nose appeared at the front door and raised his hand in greeting.

"That must be him," Mallory said, gathering her notebook and digital recorder as they parked in the driveway.

They approached the house, and Fisher extended his hand. "Mr. Randall? Ms. Carver? Gary Fisher. Thank you for coming."

"Call me Tucker, please," Tucker replied, shaking his hand firmly. "And this is Mallory."

"Gary," he responded and offered Mallory his hand. "Please, come inside. My wife Linda has coffee ready."

The modest home was neat and comfortable with family photos prominently displayed. Several showed Terry Fisher—at high school graduation, fishing with an older man who must have been his father, arm-in-arm with a blonde woman Mallory assumed was his fiancée, Tiffany.

Gary led them into a living room where a woman was arranging coffee mugs on a side table. "This is my wife, Linda," he introduced them. "Linda, these are the private investigators I told you about."

Linda nodded politely, but Mallory detected a certain reservation in her manner. Not exactly unwelcoming, but perhaps not entirely comfortable with their presence.

"Thank you for looking into Terry's case," Linda said as they took seats. "It means a lot to Gary, especially with Bill and Margaret's health declining so rapidly."

"How are your parents doing?" Tucker asked Gary directly.

Gary's expression tightened. "Dad's been given two months, maybe three. Lung cancer. Mom's health isn't much better—heart problems.

They've held on this long hoping for answers about Terry, but I'm afraid time is running out."

Mallory felt a pang of empathy. She understood all too well the desperate need for closure when a loved one was killed. Her sister Jen had been the same way after Julie's murder—unable to move forward without knowing why her daughter had died.

"We've reviewed the materials you sent," Tucker began, "but we'd like to hear from you directly. Tell us about Terry, what happened, anything you think might help us understand this case better."

Gary took a deep breath, as if mentally preparing himself. "Terry was seven years older than me. We weren't especially close growing up. The age gap made that hard. By the time I was in high school, he was already working as a contractor."

He paused, glancing at a photo of his brother. "About three years before he was killed, when Terry was twenty-five, he started showing some strange habits. Staying out late, being secretive about where he'd been, getting phone calls that he'd take in another room. My parents were worried he might be involved with drugs, but whenever he had drug tests for work, they always came back clean."

"What kind of contracting work did he do?" Mallory asked, jotting notes.

"Home renovations mostly. He was good with his hands, could fix just about anything. He had a solid reputation in town." Gary's pride in his brother was evident in the way he looked at the photograph. "He had his own business. It was small but growing. He was saving to build a house for himself and Tiffany after they got married."

"Tell us about Tiffany," Tucker said. "Your notes mentioned she's now married to your cousin?"

A flicker of discomfort crossed Gary's face. "Yes, to Louis. They got together a few months after Terry died. It was... unexpected. Tiffany took Terry's death hard, completely fell apart at first. Louis helped her through it, and I guess one thing led to another." His tone suggested he had more thoughts on the matter than he was expressing.

"Where does Tiffany live now?" Mallory asked.

"Just a street over, actually. She and Louis have two kids now." Gary hesitated. "She doesn't like talking about Terry anymore. Says it's too painful, and she's moved on. I'm not sure how cooperative she'll be if you try to interview her."

Mallory made a note to visit Tiffany, regardless. Sometimes people who claimed to have moved on were actually holding secrets they were afraid would be discovered if they reopened old wounds.

"Let's talk about the night Terry disappeared," Tucker suggested, steering the conversation back to the central events.

Gary nodded, his expression growing more somber. "It was a Tuesday. Terry had been acting strange for days, according to Tiffany. Distracted, checking his phone a lot. That night, he told her he had to meet someone on business. Didn't say who or what it was about. Just that he'd be back in a couple of hours. That was the last time anyone saw him alive."

"When was his body discovered?" Tucker asked, though they knew the answer from the reports.

"The next morning. A high school kid cutting across Parsons' farm found him." Gary's voice tightened. "Shot twice in the back of the head, left there like garbage. Whoever did it made no attempt to hide the body."

"You mentioned in your notes that the local police investigation seemed inadequate," Mallory prompted. "Can you elaborate on that?"

Gary's expression darkened. "Detective Bradley was in charge initially. He seemed earnest enough, but after a few weeks, the case just... faded away. No arrests, no suspects named publicly, no actual progress."

"What's your opinion of Chief Winson?" Tucker asked carefully.

"Nate?" Gary looked surprised. "He's a good man. Been chief for about six years now. He was just an officer when Terry was killed, so he wasn't in charge of the investigation."

Mallory noted the discrepancy between Gary's positive view of Winson and the online forum posts suggesting corruption. Either Gary was unaware of the rumors, or he didn't believe them.

"We noticed in our research that Pastor Henry Pearcy conducted

Terry's funeral," Mallory observed. "Did Terry attend his church regularly?"

Gary nodded. "Every Sunday. Pastor Henry was a huge support to our family after Terry died. Still is. He visits my parents weekly, even though they're too ill to attend services now."

As they continued talking, Mallory sensed there was something Gary wasn't telling them—some detail or suspicion he was holding back. His answers were forthcoming but occasionally seemed rehearsed, as if he had decided in advance what narrative to present.

Tucker evidently noticed it too, because he shifted tactics, asking more unexpected questions about Terry's friends, his business competitors, any arguments or conflicts he might have had in the weeks before his death.

"Terry got along with everyone," Gary insisted. "That's what made his murder so shocking. He didn't have any enemies."

"Everyone has someone who dislikes them," Mallory pointed out gently. "Even minor disagreements could be relevant."

Gary hesitated, then conceded. "Well, there was some tension with a competitor—Walsh Construction. The owner, Bill Walsh, accused Terry of underbidding him on purpose for a big renovation contract at the high school. But that was just business rivalry, not something worth killing over."

"We'd like to follow up with some of the people you've mentioned," Tucker said as they wrapped up the interview. "Tiffany, Pastor Pearcy, maybe some of Terry's former clients or coworkers. Would you feel comfortable providing their contact information?"

"Of course," Gary agreed quickly. "Anything that might help." He went to his home office and returned with a printed list. "I anticipated you might ask. These are the people who knew Terry best, with their addresses and phone numbers where I have them."

As they stood to leave, Gary suddenly looked hesitant. "There's something else you should know," he said, his voice lower. "Something I didn't put in the emails."

Mallory and Tucker exchanged glances.

"What is it?" Tucker asked.

Gary glanced toward the front yard where his children were still playing, then back to them. "There are rumors in town... about why these men were killed. You know there were more, right? four more!"

Tucker nodded.

"Rumors about what they might have been involved in."

"We're listening," Mallory encouraged when he paused.

"Some people say there's a... gun running operation. That they move illegal firearms through this area, using the back roads, small private airstrips on farms, that kind of thing." Gary's voice had dropped to nearly a whisper. "I don't know if it's true, but the rumor is that Terry and the others somehow got caught up in it."

"And you didn't include this in your written materials because...?" Tucker prompted.

"Noooo..." he drew the word out. "Because it's just gossip," he said, looking uncomfortable. "And because if it is true, it might be dangerous to put it in writing. These people—if they exist—have been operating for years without getting caught. They've killed before. They wouldn't hesitate to kill again if they felt threatened... would they?"

"As you say," Tucker replied, "it's probably just rumors. We'll look into it, though. In the meantime, say nothing about why we're here. If what you say is true, we do not want to stir the hornet's nest, not yet."

"I won't," Fisher replied. "I'll not say a word. You go careful now."

The warning hung in the air as they said their goodbyes. As they walked back to the SUV, Mallory processed this new information. If Terry Fisher had indeed been involved in gunrunning, it provided both a motive for his murder and an explanation for why the case had never been properly solved. Rural gun smuggling operations often involved local power players; sometimes even law enforcement.

"What do you think?" she asked Tucker as they pulled away from Gary's house.

Tucker's expression was thoughtful. "I think we need to talk to Tiffany Springer; or Tiffany Fisher, as she is now, I suppose. She was the last person to see Terry alive. And I'm increasingly interested in meeting Pastor Pearcy, given his connection to the family."

Mallory nodded. They had their first real lead, their first glimpse beneath the surface of Duckwood's peaceful exterior.

"Where to first?" she asked, already knowing the answer.

"Tiffany's," Tucker confirmed. "Let's see what Terry's fiancée has to say about the man she supposedly loved and the cousin she married after his death."

As they drove through the quiet streets of Duckwood, Mallory couldn't shake the feeling that they were being watched. In a town this small, with secrets this big, strangers asking questions rarely went unnoticed for long. And if Gary's rumors about gun running were true, they might already have attracted the attention of some very dangerous people.

The thought should have frightened her, but instead, it only intensified her determination to uncover the truth. Someone had evaded justice for eleven years. Five families had been denied closure. Whatever secrets Duckwood was hiding, Mallory was resolved to bring them into the light—no matter the risk.

Her phone buzzed with a text from Jen: "Don't forget. Bridal Elegance appt Friday 2pm!!"

Mallory sighed and slipped the phone back into her pocket without responding. Some things would have to wait. Right now, they had a murder to solve.

5

Tucker pulled up to the curb across the street from Tiffany Fisher's address, a two-story home with beige siding and dark green shutters. Like Gary's house, it was in a modest subdivision—newer homes built for middle-class families, each with similar layouts but with different cosmetic details to provide the illusion of uniqueness. A basketball hoop stood in the driveway next to a silver SUV, and carefully tended flower beds lined the front walkway.

"Doesn't exactly scream widow of murder victim, does it?" Mallory remarked, studying the property.

"Very few things are what they appear to be," Tucker replied, turning off the engine. "Especially in cases like this."

He observed the house for a moment longer, noting the children's bicycle leaning against the porch and the American flag hanging beside the front door; outward signs of a normal, stable household. But his years in law enforcement had taught him that the most disturbing crimes often happened behind the most ordinary facades.

"Let's be careful with our questions," he said as they exited the SUV. "If Terry was involved in something illegal, and if Tiffany knows about it, she might be protective, either out of loyalty to his memory or fear for her own safety."

Mallory nodded. "And if she doesn't know, we don't want to be the ones to shatter her image of him."

They approached the house together, Tucker slightly in the lead. He was aware of Mallory's tendency to dive straight in with the difficult questions, which sometimes yielded surprising confessions but other times shut down interviews before they'd gathered useful information. This situation called for a more measured approach.

Tucker rang the doorbell, and they waited. After about thirty seconds, the door opened to reveal a blonde woman in her early thirties. She was attractive in a carefully maintained way: highlighted hair styled in a neat bob, subtle makeup, a pastel blouse and khaki capris that suggested she'd dressed for the day but wasn't expecting company.

Her eyes widened slightly as she took in the two strangers on her doorstep. "Can I help you?" she asked.

"Mrs. Fisher?" Tucker asked politely. "I'm Tucker Randall and this is my colleague, Mallory Carver. We're private investigators working with Gary Fisher regarding his brother Terry's case. We were hoping to speak with you for a few minutes, if you have time."

Tiffany's expression flickered through several emotions in rapid succession: surprise, wariness, and something that might have been fear before settling into a carefully neutral look.

"Gary didn't mention he was hiring investigators," she said, her voice was controlled but slightly tight.

"It was a recent decision," Mallory explained. "As you probably know, his parents' health is declining, and he's hoping to bring them some closure."

Tiffany hesitated, glancing past them toward the street as if checking whether any neighbors were watching. Finally, she stepped back. "You might as well come in, I suppose," she said, reluctantly. I don't have a lot of time, though. I need to pick up my daughter from soccer practice in an hour."

She led them into a living room decorated in the contemporary farmhouse style that had dominated home design shows for the past several years: lots of neutral tones, shiplap accents, and inspirational phrases stenciled on wooden signs. Family photos adorned the walls and side tables, showing Tiffany with a man Tucker assumed was Louis Fisher and two children—a boy around eleven and a girl about nine.

"Please, sit down," Tiffany waved a hand toward a beige sectional sofa. "Can I get you anything? Water? Coffee?"

"We're fine, thank you," Tucker replied, taking a seat while maintaining eye contact. "We appreciate you taking the time to speak with us."

Tiffany settled into an armchair across from them, her posture straight, hands folded in her lap. "What exactly do you want to know? It's been eleven years, and I've told the police everything I know multiple times."

Tucker nodded understandingly. "We're aware of your previous statements, but sometimes details that seemed insignificant at the time become important with new perspectives. We're hoping you might help us understand Terry better; who he was, what was happening in his life in the weeks before his death."

It was a deliberate strategy to start broadly rather than zeroing in on the night of Terrys disappeared. Tucker wanted to establish rapport, get Tiffany talking comfortably before addressing more sensitive areas.

"Terry was…" Tiffany paused, seeming to search for the right words. "He was charming. Hardworking. Everyone liked him." Her description was positive but generic, the kind of bland eulogy that revealed little of substance.

"How did you two meet?" Mallory asked, her tone conversational.

A genuine smile flickered across Tiffany's face for the first time. "High school. He was a senior when I was a sophomore. We didn't start dating until after he graduated, though. My parents wouldn't have allowed it otherwise."

"And you were engaged to be married when he died?" Tucker prompted.

Tiffany nodded, twisting a ring on her right hand, not her wedding band, but perhaps a memento from her relationship with Terry. "We'd been engaged for almost a year. The wedding was scheduled for that June."

"That must have been devastating," Mallory whispered.

"It was." Tiffany's voice tightened. "I didn't think I'd ever recover. Louis—my husband now—he really helped me through that time. He was Terry's cousin, so he was grieving, too. We understood each other's pain."

Tucker watched her carefully as she spoke. There was genuine emotion there, but also what appeared to be rehearsed elements, as if she'd told this version of events many times and had settled on a narrative that was both true and carefully curated.

"Gary mentioned that in the weeks before Terry died, he'd been acting differently," Tucker said. "Staying out late, being secretive about phone calls. Did you notice these changes as well?"

Tiffany's posture stiffened slightly. "Yes. He said it was work-related—a big project he was bidding on. I didn't question it much. Terry was ambitious, always looking for ways to grow his business."

"But you were concerned enough to mention it to the police after his death," Tucker noted, referencing her initial statement from the case file.

Her eyes narrowed slightly. "Only because they asked if I'd noticed anything unusual. In hindsight, maybe I should have paid more attention, asked more questions. But you can't change the past, can you?"

The defensiveness in her tone was subtle, but unmistakable. Tucker changed tack, moving to a seemingly unrelated topic. "Terry was religious, I understand? A regular at Pastor Pearcy's church?"

The question seemed to catch Tiffany off guard. "Yes. We both were. Pastor Henry was very supportive after… after what happened."

"He conducted the funeral service?" Tucker asked.

"Yes. It was beautiful, actually. He talked about Terry's spirit, his good heart." Tiffany's expression softened momentarily. "Pastor Henry has a way of bringing comfort even in the darkest times."

Tucker nodded sympathetically. "And the night Terry disappeared; you were the last person to see him, correct?"

The shift back to the central event was deliberate, coming after

Tiffany had relaxed slightly while discussing the pastor. Her guard went up again immediately.

"As far as I know, yes. He left our apartment around nine. Said he had to meet someone about work, though it seemed late for a business meeting."

"Did he say who he was meeting?" Mallory asked.

"No. Just that it wouldn't take long and not to wait up." Tiffany looked down at her hands. "I fell asleep watching TV. When I woke up around two in the morning and he wasn't home, I tried calling his cell phone. It went straight to voicemail."

"What did you do then?" Tucker prompted.

"Nothing, at first. It wasn't completely out of character for Terry to work late. I figured he'd gotten caught up in something and would be home soon." Her voice caught slightly. "By morning, when he still wasn't back and wasn't answering calls, I called his parents, then Gary. We were about to file a missing person report when..."

She trailed off, and Tucker finished the thought for her. "When Terry's body was found on the Parsons' property."

Tiffany nodded, blinking rapidly. "It was surreal," she said. "Like a nightmare I couldn't wake up from. One minute we're planning our wedding, the next I'm planning his funeral."

Tucker allowed a moment of respectful silence before continuing. "Tiffany, in the years since, have you heard any theories about why Terry was killed?"

She hesitated, glancing toward a window. "What do you mean?"

"Small town talk," Mallory interjected gently. "Especially about unsolved murders. There must have been rumors, speculations about what Terry might have been involved in."

Tiffany's gaze snapped to Mallory. "Involved in? Terry wasn't 'involved' in anything. He was a good man who was in the wrong place at the wrong time."

The defensiveness was revealing. Tucker pressed further, keeping his tone casual. "Of course. But Gary mentioned there are rumors around town about gunrunning, illegal activities that might have led to these murders. Five men killed the same way over eleven years. That suggests something serious."

Tiffany stood abruptly. "I don't know anything about that. And I don't appreciate you coming into my home and suggesting Terry was mixed up in something criminal. He wasn't that kind of person."

Tucker remained seated, maintaining a calm demeanor despite her agitation. "We're not suggesting anything, Mrs. Fisher. We're just trying to understand all the possibilities. Terry's parents deserve to know what happened to their son before they pass."

"And you think I don't want that?" Tiffany's voice rose slightly. "Terry was the love of my life. His death destroyed me. But dragging his name through the mud won't bring him back or give anyone closure."

Mallory adopted a softer approach. "We understand this is difficult, Tiffany," she said, softly. "But sometimes people get caught up in situations without fully understanding what they're involved in. If Terry was in trouble, or if he witnessed something he shouldn't have, that information could help us find who killed him."

Tiffany seemed to struggle with herself for a moment before her shoulders sagged. "Look, I don't know anything concrete. But..." she lowered her voice, glancing toward the hallway as if ensuring no one else was listening, "about a week before he died, I found a gun in his truck. A handgun. Terry never owned firearms. He didn't even like them. When I asked him about it, he got defensive, said it was for protection, that times were changing."

Tucker leaned forward slightly. "Did he elaborate on what he needed protection from?"

"No. And I didn't push it. We had a big fight about the wedding venue that same day, so the gun conversation got lost in that." She twisted her hands together. "I've always wondered if I should have asked more questions, if I could have somehow prevented what happened."

"You couldn't have known," Mallory assured her. "Did you tell the police about the gun?"

Tiffany nodded. "I told Detective Bradley. He made a note of it, but

I don't think anything ever came of it. The gun wasn't on Terry when they found him."

This was new information, something not mentioned in the police reports Gary had provided. Either it had been deliberately omitted, or the paperwork had been lost over the years.

"When did you start dating Louis?" Tucker asked, the question seemingly coming out of nowhere.

Tiffany blinked at the abrupt change of subject. "What does that have to do with anything?"

"I'm just trying to establish a timeline," Tucker replied calmly.

She exhaled slowly. "I don't... About four months after Terry died. Louis had been checking on me regularly; bringing groceries, helping with household repairs, things like that. It evolved..." She paused, twisting her fingers together. "It evolved naturally," she continued. "We were both grieving. We understood each other."

"And Terry's family; were they supportive of the relationship?" Tucker asked.

A flash of something—guilt, perhaps, or maybe defiance—crossed Tiffany's face. "Not initially. Gary especially thought it was too soon, disrespectful to Terry's memory. His parents were more understanding. They've always liked Louis."

Tucker nodded, mentally filing away the information. "Just one more question, Tiffany. Did Terry ever mention anything about the other victims? Cory Robar, Samuel Jenkins, Malik Williams, or Freddy Paul?"

Tiffany frowned. "I recognize Cory's name—he did some work for the school district—but I don't think Terry ever mentioned him specifically. I don't know the others at all. Why?"

"They were all killed the same way as Terry over the past eleven years," Mallory explained. "Two shots to the back of the head, bodies left in similar rural locations around Duckwood."

Tiffany's face paled. "I knew about a couple of other murders, but not four. That's... that's horrible."

"Yet the police never publicly connected the cases," Tucker observed, watching her reaction carefully.

"Small towns," Tiffany said with a faint, bitter smile. "Things get buried, don't they? Forgotten. Life goes on. That's the way it is here." She glanced at her watch. "I'm sorry, but I really do need to leave soon to pick up my daughter."

Tucker recognized the dismissal and rose to his feet. "Thank you for your time, Mrs. Fisher. If you think of anything else, no matter how insignificant it might seem, please call us." He handed her a business card.

Tiffany accepted it reluctantly. "I've told you everything I know. And I'd appreciate it if you didn't mention to Louis that we spoke. He… he thinks I should leave the past in the past. He worries about me getting upset."

"Of course," Mallory assured her. "We understand."

6

As they walked back to the SUV, Tucker processed the interview, mentally cataloging what had been said and, perhaps more importantly, what had been deliberately avoided. Tiffany had been cooperative on the surface but guarded in substance. The revelation about the gun was significant, but Tucker suspected there was more she wasn't sharing.

Once they were inside the vehicle, Mallory took her recorder from her jacket pocket, turned to him expectantly, wagged it in the air and said, "Well? What do you think?"

"I think she's hiding something," Tucker replied, starting the engine. "The question is whether it's something directly related to Terry's murder, or just uncomfortable details about their relationship that she'd rather keep private."

"The gun is interesting," Mallory noted. "If Terry wasn't typically a gun owner, why suddenly have one for 'protection' a week before his death? He must have felt threatened."

Tucker nodded. "And it wasn't found with his body, which suggests either the killer took it, or Terry hid it somewhere before the meeting that led to his death."

"What about her relationship with Louis? Starting to date your murdered fiancé's cousin within a few months seems... fast."

"People process grief differently," Tucker said, not entirely dismissing the observation. "But it's worth looking into Louis Fisher more thoroughly. If Terry was involved in something illegal, Louis might have known about it. They were cousins, after all."

They drove in silence for a few moments, each considering the implications of Tiffany's statements and body language. Duckwood passed by outside the windows, its quiet streets and modest businesses concealing what was clearly a more complex and dangerous reality than first appearances suggested.

"Where to next?" Mallory asked. "Pastor Pearcy?"

Tucker checked his watch. "It's nearly lunchtime. Let's grab something to eat and review what we've learned so far. I'd also like to stop by the police station to see if we can speak with Chief Winson, and I'd like to track down Detective Bradley, even if he's retired."

"The pastor conducted all five funeral services," Mallory reminded him. "That can't be coincidence."

"Agreed, but in a town this size, there might only be one or two churches. We'll definitely speak with him, but let's be methodical about it."

They found a small deli near the town square and secured a booth in the corner, where they could talk privately while observing the other patrons. Tucker ordered a turkey sandwich, Mallory a salad, and they spread their notes across the table while they waited.

"So far we have a gun that appeared shortly before Terry's death, rumors of gun running in the area, five victims killed in the same manner over eleven years, a fiancée who married the victim's cousin, and a pastor who conducted all the funeral services," Tucker summarized. "Plus a police department that either couldn't or wouldn't connect the cases."

"And Gary's parents dying without answers after more than a decade," Mallory added, her expression softening with empathy. "That's the part that gets me. Imagine living all those years not knowing who killed your child or why."

Tucker nodded, understanding her connection to that aspect of the case. Mallory had seen firsthand how Julie's murder had devastated her sister Jen's family. That personal experience undoubtedly fueled her determination to solve cold cases like Terry Fisher's.

"Let's focus on the gun running angle," Tucker suggested. "If Terry suddenly had a gun for protection, it suggests he might have been involved in something dangerous or had knowledge of something dangerous."

"But if he was part of a gun running operation, why would he need protection from his own associates?" Mallory questioned. "Unless... Unless he was planning to leave or threaten exposure."

"Exactly. If Terry wanted out, or if he was going to talk to authorities, that would give the organization motive to silence him."

As they continued discussing theories, Tucker noticed a man in uniform enter the deli. He was in his mid-forties, with a solid build and the confident bearing of someone used to authority. Several patrons nodded respectfully as he passed, and the server behind the counter immediately began preparing what appeared to be his usual order without him having to ask.

"I'm guessing that's Chief Winson," Tucker murmured to Mallory, who glanced over her shoulder casually.

"Should we approach him?" she asked.

Tucker considered the options. "Not here. Too public. Let's finish up and head to the station formally. Better to establish ourselves as professionals conducting an investigation rather than ambush him during his lunch break."

They paid their bill and left, Mallory resisting the urge to stare at the police chief as they passed. Once outside, they walked back to their SUV, parked a block away.

"I've been thinking about the gun," Mallory said as they walked. "What if it wasn't for protection? What if Terry was actually delivering it as part of the operation? Or maybe he found it and was concerned about it?"

"All possibilities worth considering," Tucker agreed. "But without the weapon itself, it's hard to draw conclusions. I'd like to know if it was ever logged in as evidence, or if that detail somehow disappeared from the official record."

As they approached their vehicle, Tucker spotted something tucked under the windshield wiper. He glanced around, checking to see if anyone was watching them, but the street was busy with normal lunchtime activity. No one was paying them particular attention.

"What's that?" Mallory asked as he carefully removed what appeared to be a folded piece of paper.

Tucker unfolded it, a handwritten note that read: "Stop asking questions about Terry Fisher. Leave Duckwood while you can. This is your only warning."

He handed it to Mallory, who read it quickly, her eyes widening. "Well," she said with a grim smile, "looks like we're on the right track. Someone's nervous."

"Or someone's trying to protect us," Tucker countered, examining the paper for any identifying marks or characteristics. The handwriting was deliberately disguised, printed in all capital letters with no distinctive flourishes.

"You think it's a genuine warning rather than a threat?" Mallory asked.

"Could be either," Tucker admitted, carefully placing the note in an evidence bag from his pocket. "But it confirms what we've suspected; there's something significant connecting these murders, and there are people in Duckwood who know more than they're saying."

As he scanned the surrounding buildings and parked cars, his law enforcement instincts on high alert, Tucker made a decision. "Let's head to the police station now. We'll report this, establish an official record of our presence and purpose in Duckwood."

"And watch how Chief Winson reacts," Mallory added, catching onto his strategy.

"Exactly." Tucker opened the car door for her before walking around to the driver's side. "But we'll keep certain details to ourselves for now; particularly our suspicions about gun running and potential police involvement. You have your weapon with you, I assume."

"Always," she replied.

As they drove the short distance to the Duckwood Police Department, Tucker couldn't shake the feeling that they'd stirred up something dangerous, something that had remained hidden for eleven years and wouldn't easily be exposed. The threatening note was a tangible reminder that their investigation carried real risks.

Whatever secrets Duckwood was hiding, powerful people wanted them to remain buried. But Tucker hadn't resigned from the FBI to let injustice prevail elsewhere. Five men had been murdered, five families had been left without answers. He and Mallory would get to the truth, no matter the cost.

7

Mallory followed Tucker through the glass doors into the Duckwood Police Department, between Highland Avenue and Archer Street, next to Duckwood Fire and Rescue. They entered the reception area and stepped up to the desk behind which sat a middle-aged female officer. A bulletin board on the wall displayed community notices and wanted posters, while a glass case nearby housed trophies from police softball tournaments and community service awards.

Small-town law enforcement at its most stereotypical, she thought, approaching the reception desk beside Tucker.

"Can I help you?" The receptionist glanced up from her computer, her expression professionally neutral but her eyes curious.

Tucker produced his identification. "Tucker Randall and Mallory Carver. We're private investigators from Chattanooga working on behalf of the Fisher family regarding the Terry Fisher case. We'd like to speak with Chief Winson, if he's available."

The woman's eyebrows rose slightly. "The Fisher case? That's going back some years." She picked up her phone. "Let me see if the chief is available."

While she made the call, Mallory studied the room more carefully. A framed photo on the wall showed the current police force—forty sworn officers, including the chief, posed in three lines, one behind the other. Another showed what appeared to be a retirement party, with an older man receiving a plaque while surrounded by colleagues. The name plate read "Detective James Bradley, 35 Years of Service."

"Chief Winson can see you," the receptionist announced, hanging up the phone. "Last door on the right."

Tucker thanked her, and they walked down the hallway. Mallory noted the building's layout, a habit she'd developed over her three years of investigative work. Two interview rooms, a break room, a half dozen offices, a situation room, a door marked "Evidence," an unmarked door at the end of the corridor and, finally, the chief's office on the right.

The door was open when they reached it. Chief Nate Winson was seated behind a desk cluttered with paperwork, a half-eaten sandwich from the deli they'd just left pushed to one side. He was better looking up close than Mallory had observed from across the deli—early forties, athletic build, salt-and-pepper hair cut in a military style, and sharp green eyes that assessed them with professional interest.

"Come in," he said, gesturing to two chairs opposite his desk. "I understand you're looking into the Fisher case. That's ancient history around here."

"Not for Gary Fisher and his parents," Mallory replied before she could stop herself. Tucker gave her a subtle glance, a reminder of their agreement that he would lead this conversation.

Winson's expression didn't change. "Of course not. That poor family never got closure. Please, sit down."

They settled into the chairs, and Tucker smoothly took control of the conversation. "Thank you for seeing us, Chief. We've been retained by Gary Fisher to review his brother's case, considering his parents' declining health."

"Understandable," Winson nodded. "Though I'm not sure what you expect to find after eleven years that our department and the sheriff's office couldn't."

"Fresh eyes sometimes help," Tucker said diplomatically. "And we're hoping you might provide access to the original case files. The copies we have are incomplete."

Winson leaned back in his chair, studying them. "I wasn't chief when Terry Fisher was killed. Wasn't even the lead detective. That was Jim Bradley. He's retired now. I was just a patrol officer."

"But you're familiar with the case?" Mallory asked.

"Everyone in the department is familiar with it," Winson replied. "Unsolved murders aren't common around here, thankfully. And the Fisher family has been… persistent in keeping it on our radar."

There was something in his tone when he said "persistent" that caught Mallory's attention—not quite resentment, but a subtle sign that the family's efforts were viewed as an irritation rather than a rightful pursuit of justice.

"We've also become aware of four similar murders in the area over the past eleven years," Tucker said, watching the chief carefully. "Cory Robar, Samuel Jenkins, Malik Williams, and Freddy Paul. All killed in the same manner as Terry Fisher, all found within a five-mile radius."

Chief Winson's expression tightened almost imperceptibly. "Those cases aren't officially connected."

"But unofficially?" Mallory pressed.

The chief sighed. "Look, I understand what you're doing. You're trying to build a narrative, connect dots to give the family answers. But sometimes coincidences are just coincidences."

"Five execution-style murders in a small rural community within eleven years doesn't strike me as coincidental," Tucker observed calmly.

"When you've been in law enforcement as long as I have, you learn that pattern recognition can be misleading," Winson countered. "Yes, the MO is similar. But these men had different backgrounds, different social circles. We've never found a concrete connection between them."

Mallory bit back a skeptical response, letting Tucker continue the conversation. She focused instead on observing the chief, his body language, his eye contact, the subtle tells that might show he was being less than forthcoming.

"We'd still appreciate access to the files," Tucker said. "For all five cases, if possible. It would help us be thorough in our report to the Fisher family."

Winson hesitated, then nodded. "I can arrange that. But I'll need to have someone from the department present while you review them. Chain of custody, you understand?"

"Of course," Tucker agreed. "There's another matter we'd like to discuss as well." He reached into his pocket and produced the threatening note they'd found on their SUV. "This was left on our vehicle while we were having lunch."

Winson took the evidence bag, examining the note with a frown. "How long have you been in town?"

"Since this morning," Mallory answered. "We interviewed Gary Fisher and Tiffany Fisher, drove by the locations where the bodies were discovered, and had lunch at the deli."

"And someone's already warning you off," Winson mused, setting the note on his desk. "Interesting."

"We thought you should be aware," Tucker said. "In case there are other incidents."

The chief nodded. "I appreciate that. I'll have one of my officers take your statement and file a report." He seemed to consider something before continuing. "I should warn you—Duckwood is a close-knit community. People here don't appreciate outsiders stirring up old troubles."

"We're not here to cause trouble," Mallory assured him. "We just want the truth."

"The truth," Winson repeated, with a slight smile that didn't reach his eyes. "In my experience, that's rarely as straightforward as people hope." He stood up, signaling the end of the meeting. "I'll have Officer Daniels supervise your review of the case files tomorrow morning, if that works for you. And I'll assign someone to take your statement about this note."

"We'd also like to speak with Detective Bradley," Tucker added, remaining seated. "I understand he's retired now, but as the original investigator, he might have insights that aren't in the official reports."

Something flickered across Winson's face; reluctance, perhaps, or concern. "Jim's in the Golden Years Retirement Home on the edge of town. His health isn't great, and his memory comes and goes. I can't guarantee he'll be helpful."

"We'd still like to try," Mallory said.

"Your prerogative," Winson shrugged. "Just don't get your hopes up. And don't upset him. The staff there is protective."

As if on cue, a knock came at the office door, and a young officer appeared. "Sorry to interrupt, Chief, but the mayor's on line one. Says it's urgent."

Winson nodded. "I need to take this," he said.." Officer Daniels will help you with your statement about the threat." He extended his hand to Tucker, then Mallory. "Good luck with your investigation. I hope you find what you're looking for."

Mallory couldn't help but notice he didn't say he hoped they solved the case.

Officer Daniels, a fresh-faced young man who couldn't have been more than twenty-five, led them to an interview room where he took their statement about the threatening note. He seemed earnest and thorough, asking detailed questions about the exact location of their vehicle, whether they had noticed anyone suspicious, and if they had received any other threats.

"Does this sort of thing happen often in Duckwood?" Mallory asked casually while Daniels was writing.

He looked up, surprised. "No, ma'am. We're a peaceful town, generally speaking. Some drunk and disorderlies on weekends, occasional domestic disputes, teenagers causing mischief, but threatening notes? That's unusual."

"What about the murders we're investigating?" Tucker inquired. "Those aren't exactly 'peaceful town' activities."

Daniels shifted uncomfortably. "That's different. Those were… isolated incidents. And they happened over many years." He cleared his throat. "Have you folks arranged accommodation while you're in town?"

The change of subject wasn't subtle, but Mallory went with it. "We're staying at the Duckwood Inn. Why?"

"Just asking," Daniels said, looking back down at his form. "In case we need to reach you." He completed the report and slid it across the table for them to sign.

After finishing with Officer Daniels, they left the station and returned to their vehicle. Mallory waited until they were inside, with the doors closed before speaking.

"Well, that was enlightening," she said, her voice low despite being alone. "Winson is definitely holding back."

Tucker nodded as he started the engine. "The question is whether it's because he's involved, or because he genuinely doesn't believe the cases are connected."

"Did you notice how quickly he changed the subject when you mentioned Detective Bradley? Almost like he didn't want us talking to him."

"I caught that," Tucker agreed. "Which means Bradley moves to the top of our priority list. Let's head to the Golden Years now and see if he's in any condition to speak with us."

8

The Golden Years Retirement Home was a single-story brick building on the outskirts of town surrounded by several acres of well-maintained gardens. A covered porch with rocking chairs fronted the entrance, though no residents were outside in the afternoon heat.

Inside, the facility was clean and bright, with a faint smell of industrial cleaner barely masking the underlying scent of age and illness. A cheerful woman at the reception desk greeted them with a practiced smile.

"We're here to see James Bradley," Tucker explained.

"Are you relatives?" she asked, frowning.

"No, ma-am," Tucker replied. "We're private investigators working on a case he handled years ago."

The woman's smile faltered slightly. "Well…" She hesitated, then continued, "Mr. Bradley doesn't get many visitors except for his daughter. And his condition…" Again, she hesitated.

"We understand he has memory issues," Mallory said gently. "But we'd like to try. It's for the family of a murder victim."

The appeal to empathy worked. The receptionist nodded. "Let me check to see if he's having a good day. Sometimes mornings are better than afternoons for him."

She made a quick call, then directed them to a sunroom at the back of the facility. "Twenty minutes, please. Don't tire him out."

They found Bradley sitting in a wheelchair by a large window overlooking a garden, a blanket draped over his legs despite the warm day. He was thin, his once-powerful frame now diminished with age, his white hair neatly combed to one side, and his eyes, though clouded with cataracts, still held a sharp intelligence.

"Detective Bradley?" Tucker approached, extending his hand. "I'm Tucker Randall, and this is my colleague, Mallory Carver. We're private investigators looking into the Terry Fisher case."

Bradley's hand was cool and papery as he shook Tucker's, then Mallory's. "Fisher," he repeated, his voice stronger than his appearance suggested. "Terry Fisher. He was found on Pearcy's land."

Mallory glanced at Tucker. This didn't sound like someone with severe memory issues. They sat in chairs opposite Bradley, positioning themselves where he could see them clearly.

"That's right," Mallory confirmed. "You were the detective in charge of the investigation."

Bradley nodded slowly. "Shot twice in the back of the head. Execution-style. No casings found. Professional job."

"Do you remember anything specific about the case that might not have made it into the official reports?" Tucker asked.

The old detective was quiet for a moment, his gaze drifting to the garden outside. "You know about the others?" he finally asked.

"Cory Robar, Samuel Jenkins, Malik Williams, and Freddy Paul," Mallory listed. "All killed the same way over the past decade."

"All within five miles of each other. All just inside the city limits," Bradley added. "I always thought that was significant. We started calling it 'the Graveyard,' you know. Just among ourselves. Not officially, of course. Officially, they were separate cases."

"Why?" Tucker pressed gently. "Why not investigate them as connected homicides?"

Bradley's eyes shifted back to them, suddenly sharper. "Politics. Money. The usual reasons. Duckwood depends on tourism from the lake, the golf, the state park, and so on, and on being seen as a safe, quiet community. Serial killings are bad for business."

"So you were told to keep the cases separate?" Mallory asked, leaning forward.

"Not in so many words," Bradley replied. "But the message was clear. Especially after I started asking questions about certain local businesses, certain shipments coming through the area."

Tucker and Mallory exchanged glances. "What kind of shipments?" Tucker asked.

Bradley's gaze drifted again, and for a moment, Mallory worried they'd lost him. Then he focused on them with renewed clarity. "Guns. Modified automatic weapons. Coming up from the south, passing through here on the way north and east. Using the back roads, the lake access points. Terry Fisher… I always thought he must have been involved, or that maybe he witnessed something he shouldn't. Either way, if he talked to the wrong person…" He trailed off with a slight shrug.

"Do you know who was behind the operation?" Mallory asked, frowning, inwardly excited by this confirmation of their suspicions.

Bradley shook his head slowly. "Never got that far," he replied. "After I started pulling on those threads, I had an accident. Nasty fall down the stairs at home. Three broken ribs, concussion. When I came back to work, the Fisher case was officially cold, and I was assigned to petty theft and vandalism until I retired." His rheumy eyes held a mixture of regret and resignation. "I knew when to take a hint."

"The other victims," Tucker prompted. "Do you think they were connected to the same gun running operation?"

"Had to be," Bradley nodded. "Too many similarities otherwise. But I never got to investigate properly. By the time the second victim turned up, I was already sidelined."

"What about Nate Winson?" Mallory asked. "Was he involved in any way?"

Bradley's expression closed off slightly. "Nate was a good officer. Young, ambitious. Didn't ask too many questions, which is how you advance in a department like ours." He paused. "That's all I'll say about the current chief."

A nurse appeared in the doorway. "Mr. Bradley needs his medication and rest now."

Sensing they wouldn't get much more, Tucker handed Bradley a card. "If you remember anything else, or if you're willing to talk again, please call us."

Bradley took the card, studying it before tucking it into the pocket of his cardigan. "Be careful," he said quietly. "Duckwood looks peaceful, but the currents run deep. People who ask the wrong questions tend to have accidents."

"Like falling down stairs?" Mallory asked.

The old detective's eyes met hers. "Among other things," he confirmed.

The nurse wheeled Bradley away, leaving Tucker and Mallory alone in the sunroom. They remained silent for a moment, both aware that conversations in such facilities often carried.

"You get all that?" Tucker asked, referring to her recorder.

She nodded, patted her pocket, and said, "Of course."

"Then let's go," Tucker said, rising to his feet.

9

TWO MINUTES LATER, WITHOUT SAYING ANOTHER WORD TO EACH OTHER, they stepped out into the sunshine.

"Well, that confirms the gunrunning theory," Mallory said once they were safely inside the vehicle. "And it suggests local law enforcement was pressured into keeping the cases separate and unsolved."

"But it doesn't tell us who's behind it," Tucker pointed out. "Or why these men were killed."

"At least we know we're on the right track, though," Mallory replied. "And Bradley seemed much more coherent than Winson would have us to believe."

"Another reason to be skeptical of the chief," Tucker exclaimed as he started the engine. "Let's regroup at the hotel and review what we've learned today and plan our next steps."

The Duckwood Inn was a modest two-story motel with a new red metal roof on the edge of town, its vintage neon sign and recently repainted exterior suggesting an establishment trying to maintain standards despite limited resources. Their room was on the second floor, simple but clean, with two queen beds, a small table with two chairs, and a bathroom with a coffee maker that had been updated sometime in the early 2000s. It was generic, and just like a million other hotel rooms scattered across the United States from east to west and one end to the other.

Tucker dumped his suitcase on the bed nearest the window, leaving the one closest to the bathroom for Mallory, and his briefcase on the table. The he went to the minibar, took out two soft drinks, spread their notes on his bed while Mallory took a seat at the small table and opened her laptop.

"So we have confirmation of gunrunning through Duckwood, five victims killed the same way, a detective whose investigation was deliberately derailed, and a police chief who seems reluctant to acknowledge any connection between the cases," she summarized, typing as she spoke.

"Plus a threatening note warning us to leave town, a fiancée who married the victim's cousin and seems to be hiding something, and a pastor who conducted all five funeral services," Tucker added. "It's starting to take shape, but we're still missing the key connections."

Mallory nodded, scrolling through the notes they'd compiled. "Let's focus on the gun angle," she said. "If Terry had a gun for protection shortly before his death, it suggests he knew he was in danger."

"Or maybe he wasn't part of it at all," Tucker suggested. "Maybe he simply stumbled onto something, acquired the gun for protection, and was killed before he could go to authorities."

"Either way, the gun is significant," Mallory agreed. "And it's not mentioned in the official reports we have, despite Tiffany saying she told Detective Bradley about it."

"Tomorrow, we'll review the complete case files," Tucker said. "See if there's any mention of it there, or if that detail was deliberately removed."

Mallory shifted her focus. "What about this Pastor Pearcy? Bradley said Terry was found on 'Pearcy's land,' but Gary told us it was the Parsons' farm."

Tucker frowned. "That's a discrepancy worth exploring. Could be Bradley's memory playing tricks, or it could be significant. We should talk to the pastor tomorrow, see what he knows."

"And Louis Fisher," Mallory added. "Tiffany's current husband,

Terry's cousin. He might have insights that Tiffany wasn't willing to share."

They continued planning their investigation until the early evening, ordering pizza delivered to their room rather than risk being overheard in a local restaurant. As they ate, Mallory's phone rang. She looked at the screen. It was Jen calling, as promised.

"I should take this," she said, stepping out onto the walkway for privacy.

"Hey," she answered, watching the sun beginning to set over Duckwood.

"Finally!" Jen's voice came through. "I was starting to worry. How's the mysterious cold case going?"

"Interestingly," Mallory replied, careful not to share any details over the phone, "we're making progress."

"Enough progress that you'll be back for the dress appointment on Friday? The boutique had a cancellation, and it's the only slot they have for weeks."

Mallory hesitated. Two days from now? It was possible they'd wrap up the investigation by then, but unlikely given the layers of complexity they were uncovering.

"I'll try, Jen. But this case is important, and complex. It could take a while."

She heard her sister's sigh. "Your wedding is important too, Mal. Six months will go by faster than you think."

"I know, I know," Mallory assured her. "Look, if I can't make it back by Friday, maybe you could FaceTime me from the appointment? I trust your judgment anyway."

They chatted a few minutes longer before ending the call. When Mallory returned inside Tucker was reviewing a map of the area, marking the locations where each body had been found.

"Everything okay?" he asked, glancing up.

"Just wedding stuff," Mallory replied, sitting beside him on the bed. "Jen's worried I won't make it back for a dress appointment."

Tucker studied her face. "If you need to go back for that, I can handle things here for a day."

The offer was generous, especially given their growing concerns about the case's danger. But Mallory shook her head. "No, we're partners in this. The dress can wait."

Tucker's expression softened slightly. "You're sure?"

"Positive," she affirmed, turning her attention back to the map. "So, what's next for tomorrow?"

"Case files in the morning, then the pastor, if he's available. We should try to track down Louis Fisher as well." Tucker circled the area where the bodies had been found. "And I think we need to physically check out this area again, more thoroughly this time. Bradley called it 'the Graveyard' for a reason. There might be something about the location itself that's significant."

"He mentioned they were all found just inside the city limits," Mallory said, nodding. "Why would he do that? Why would that be significant? she asked, though she thought she already knew the answer.

Tucker glanced at her, then said, "Whoever killed them may have planned it that way. Outside the city limit the sheriff's office would have had jurisdiction. As it is, it's Chief Winson's purview. Kind of convenient, don't you think?"

Mallory nodded. "That's what I thought," she replied thoughtfully. She was excited despite the long day. They were making progress, piecing together a puzzle that had remained unsolved for over a decade. It was exhilarating, and whatever dangers might lie ahead, the promise of justice for Terry Fisher and the other victims was worth the risk.

As night fell over Duckwood, Mallory couldn't shake the feeling that they were being watched. The threatening note, Bradley's warning about "accidents," the chief's carefully measured responses—all suggested they were stirring up trouble for some powerful people who wanted the past to remain buried.

And the note on the windshield? That made it personal.

10

THEY ARRIVED AT THE DUCKWOOD POLICE DEPARTMENT PRECISELY AT eight-thirty the next morning. Tucker had been awake since five, reviewing their notes and planning their approach. Experience had taught him that when examining cold case files, organization and focus were essential. They needed to identify discrepancies, missing information, and connections that previous investigators had either missed or deliberately ignored.

Officer Daniels was waiting for them in the reception area, his demeanor professional but slightly nervous. "Chief Winson asked me to supervise your review of the case files," he explained, leading them down a hallway to a small conference room. "I'll need to remain present while you examine them."

"Understood," Tucker replied, noting the young officer's discomfort. Daniels couldn't be much more than a rookie, probably assigned to this task because the chief wanted someone who wouldn't provide additional insights.

Five cardboard boxes were arranged on the conference table, each labeled with a victim's name. Tucker immediately noticed that Terry Fisher's box was significantly larger than the others.

"The Fisher case received the most thorough investigation,"

Daniels explained, following Tucker's gaze. "It was the first, and Detective Bradley was... very methodical."

Tucker nodded, pulling a pair of latex gloves from his pocket and putting them on before opening the first box. Mallory did the same, settling into a chair across from him. They had agreed to each focus on different aspects—Tucker would examine the forensic evidence and official reports, while Mallory would review witness statements and personal effects.

The first folder contained autopsy photos of Terry Fisher. Despite his years of law enforcement experience, Tucker had never completely desensitized to such images. The young man lay face-down in tall grass, two neat bullet holes visible at the base of his skull. The clinical precision of the wounds confirmed what they already knew: this was no crime of passion. It was a calculated execution.

The medical examiner's report estimated the time of death to be between eleven in the evening and one in the morning on the night Terry disappeared. Cause of death: two gunshot wounds to the occipital region of the skull, fired at close range. The bullets had passed through the brain and exited through the frontal bone. No bullet casings had been found at the scene, suggesting either they were collected by the killer or a revolver was used.

Tucker turned to the ballistics report. One of the bullets had been recovered from a tree trunk at the scene, a 9mm, consistent with numerous handgun models. Without casings or the weapon itself, more specific identification had been impossible.

Next came the crime scene photos and diagrams. Tucker studied them carefully, noting the rural setting, the lack of cover that would have made the shooting visible from a distance, should anyone have been nearby. The body had been found approximately fifty yards from a dirt access road that connected to a county highway.

"Officer Daniels," Tucker said without looking up, "whose property was Terry Fisher's body found on? These reports list it as belonging to Carl Parsons, but Detective Bradley referred to it as Pearcy's land."

The young officer shifted uncomfortably. "I believe it's the

Parsons' farm, sir. But Pastor Pearcy leases part of it from Carl Parsons for his church's annual events. Has done for years."

Tucker noted this information, exchanging a glance with Mallory. They hadn't known about this connection.

As he continued through the file, Tucker found statements from the initial responding officers, Detective Bradley's detailed notes from the first forty-eight hours, and canvass reports from nearby properties. All appeared thorough and professionally executed. But when he reached the evidence log, something caught his attention.

"There's no mention here of a handgun belonging to Terry Fisher," Tucker observed, looking up at Daniels. "His fiancée told us she informed Detective Bradley that Terry had acquired a gun shortly before his death, supposedly for protection."

Daniels frowned. "I don't know anything about that, sir. I wasn't on the force back then."

"Is there a supplemental evidence log? Something that might have been filed separately?" Tucker pressed.

"Not that I'm aware of," the officer replied. "Everything should be in that box."

Tucker continued searching, but found no reference to the gun Tiffany had mentioned. Either she had lied about informing Detective Bradley, or the information had been deliberately removed from the official record. Given Bradley's statements about being sidelined after pushing the investigation too far, Tucker figured the latter seemed more likely.

Meanwhile, Mallory was reviewing witness statements, occasionally making notes in her small notebook. They worked in methodical silence for over an hour, the only sounds being the rustle of papers and Officer Daniels occasionally shifting in his chair.

When Tucker opened the box containing Cory Robar's case file, he immediately noticed the difference in thoroughness. Where Terry Fisher's investigation had filled a dozen folders with hundreds of pages of documentation, Robar's entire case fit in less than half the space. The autopsy photos showed the same execution-style wounds, and the crime scene was similarly rural, but the follow-up investigation appeared cursory at best.

"Who was the lead detective on the Robar case?" Tucker asked Daniels.

"Detective Mercer," the officer answered. "He retired about five years ago. Moved to Florida, I think."

The pattern continued with the remaining cases. Each subsequent murder received less investigative attention than the one before, despite the obvious similarities in method and location. By the time Tucker reached Freddy Paul's file—the most recent victim—killed just two years earlier—the investigation appeared to consist of little more than basic crime scene processing and a few perfunctory interviews.

"Chief Winson handled the Paul case personally," Daniels volunteered, noticing Tucker's frown. "We were short-staffed at the time."

Tucker made a note of this. The chief's direct involvement in the most recent murder added another dimension to consider.

After nearly three hours of review, Tucker nodded to Mallory. They had extracted what they could from the official records.

"We'd like copies of certain documents," Tucker told Daniels, indicating several key pages they'd flagged.

"I'll need to get approval from the chief," Daniels replied, looking uncertain.

"It's standard procedure when working with a private investigator on a cold case," Tucker assured him, maintaining a professional tone despite his frustration. "Just the autopsy reports, crime scene photos, and witness statements. Nothing that would compromise any ongoing investigation."

Daniels hesitated, then nodded. "I'll check with the chief and let you know."

As they prepared to leave, Tucker studied the young officer. "How long have you been with the department, Officer Daniels?"

"Three years, sir."

"And you're familiar with these cases?"

Daniels shifted his weight. "Only what I've heard around the station. They're... not really discussed much."

"Five unsolved murders in a small town, all with the same MO, and they're not discussed?" Mallory asked, her tone making it clear how unlikely she found this.

"It's just… it's sensitive," Daniels replied, looking uncomfortable. "Chief Winson prefers we focus on current cases, things we can actually solve."

Tucker nodded, catching the implication. "Thank you for your assistance today, Officer Daniels. We'll be in touch about those copies."

11

Outside in the parking lot, they paused by the passenger side door of their vehicle, out of sight of the PD, to discuss their findings.

"There was no mention of the gun anywhere in Fisher's file," Tucker said quietly. "And the investigations get progressively less thorough with each victim."

"I noticed that too," Mallory agreed. "And there's something else. In the witness statements for Terry's case, there's nothing from Tanya Broadbent."

Tucker frowned. "Who's that?"

"She's mentioned briefly in Malik Williams' file as his girlfriend," Mallory explained. "But when I cross-referenced the witness lists from all five cases, her name jumped out. She's the only person who appears in connection with two different victims. She was a waitress at a local café who knew both Malik Williams and Terry Fisher."

"And yet she wasn't formally interviewed in the Fisher case," Tucker noted. "That's an oversight… or a deliberate omission."

"Either way, she should be on our list to interview," Mallory said. "After the pastor."

Tucker checked his watch. "It's almost noon. Let's get lunch, then head to the church. I called this morning and left a message that we'd like to speak with Pastor Pearcy this afternoon."

They found a small sandwich shop a few blocks from the police station and sat down at a table near the back of the room, where they could talk privately. The lunch crowd was just starting to filter in—mostly locals, judging by the familiar greetings exchanged.

"So, what's your assessment after seeing the files?" Tucker asked, keeping his voice low.

Mallory sipped her iced tea before answering. "Deliberate suppression of the investigation. Bradley did a thorough job with Terry's case, but after he was sidelined, each subsequent murder received less and less attention. Almost like they were going through the motions without any real intention of solving them."

Tucker nodded. "And the missing reference to Terry's gun is significant. Tiffany specifically told us she informed Bradley about it."

"Do you think Bradley removed it from the file himself?" Mallory questioned. "Maybe to protect Tiffany somehow?"

Tucker considered this. "It's possible," he replied, "but unlikely given his reputation for thoroughness. More likely it was removed later, perhaps after his 'accident' and reassignment. Yeah, and I'd like to know more about that accident. I wonder if we should talk to his wife."

"She's passed," Mallory said. "I checked. But, if you're right, it must have been removed by someone who wanted to eliminate any connection to gunrunning, right?"

They ate quickly, discussing their next steps. Tucker's phone vibrated with a text message. The pastor was available to meet them at one-thirty.

The sun was shining on Whitehaven Baptist Church when they arrived. The sign out front announced not only the Sunday services and Wednesday prayer meetings, but also a quote from Proverbs: "The fear of the Lord is the beginning of wisdom."

Tucker parked in the small lot beside the church, noting the well-maintained grounds and fresh paint. Whatever its other secrets, Duckwood clearly supported its house of worship financially.

"Kind of appropriate, don't you think?" Tucker asked, nodding at the sign as they walked toward the front entrance.

Mallory smiled and nodded.

"Over here," a middle-aged woman called from a side entrance.

She introduced herself as Mrs. Larson, the church secretary. "And you must be Mr. Randall and Miss Carver," she said. "Pastor Henry is expecting you. Please follow me." And she led them down a hallway to an office. "He's just finishing up his sermon notes for Sunday."

The pastor's office was surprisingly austere, given the church's prosperous appearance: a simple desk, bookshelves filled with theological texts, and a small seating area with worn but clean furniture. The only decoration was a large wooden cross on the wall and framed photos of what appeared to be mission trips to developing countries.

Pastor Henry Pearcy rose to greet them as they entered. He was tall and lean, with silver hair and piercing blue eyes that suggested intelligence and intensity. Tucker estimated him to be in his late fifties or early sixties, though he moved with the energy of a younger man.

"Mr. Randall, Ms. Carver. How nice to see you," he said and extended his hand to each of them. "Mrs. Larson said you're investigating Terry Fisher's death. I'm so pleased hear that. Please, sit down. Can I get you something? Water perhaps. Mrs. Larson makes the best iced tea."

"Not for me, thank you," Tucker said as he sat down on one of the two chairs in front of the desk.

"I'm fine, thank you," Mallory said as she sat down next to him.

Tucker assessed the pastor as they settled into their chairs. There was a quiet authority about him, the practiced ease of someone accustomed to being listened to and respected.

"Thank you for agreeing to meet with us, Pastor," Tucker began. "As you may have heard, we're private investigators working on behalf of the Fisher family. We understand you knew Terry well."

"Yes, that's true. I know all the Fisher family," Pearcy replied, his voice deep and resonant, a preacher's voice, designed to carry to the back pews. "Terry attended our church regularly until his tragic death.

His parents also until their health declined. I visit them weekly now, bringing communion and comfort."

"You also conducted Terry's funeral service," Mallory noted.

Pearcy nodded solemnly. "One of the most difficult services I've ever led. A young man cut down in his prime, about to be married, full of promise. The community was shocked."

"We understand you also conducted funeral services for Cory Robar, Samuel Jenkins, Malik Williams, and Freddy Paul," Tucker said, watching the pastor's reaction closely.

If Pearcy was surprised by this direct connection, he hid it well. "Yes, that's correct. All tragic losses to our community."

"All murdered in exactly the same way as Terry Fisher," Mallory added.

"God's ways are indeed mysterious to behold," Pearcy replied, his expression somber. "But evil is real in this world of ours, as any pastor can attest."

Tucker shifted tactics. "We visited the site where Terry's body was found. Detective Bradley referred to it as 'Pearcy's land,' but the official reports list it as the Parsons' farm."

"A common misunderstanding," Pearcy explained smoothly. "The Parsons own the property, but our church has leased a portion of it for over twenty years for our annual revival meetings and summer youth camps. Some locals have taken to calling it 'the church land' or 'Pearcy's field.' It's where Terry was found, yes."

"And what about the other victims?" Tucker pressed. "Were they also found on or near this same property?"

The pastor hesitated briefly. "I believe some were in that general vicinity, yes. Duckwood is small, Mr. Randall. Many locations are in relative proximity to each other."

"Five murdered men, all found within a five-mile radius, all killed execution-style, all with funeral services conducted by you," Mallory summarized. "That seems like more than coincidence."

Pearcy's expression remained composed, but Tucker noted a slight tightening around his eyes. "I'm one of only two Baptist pastors in Duckwood, Ms. Carver. Most local families from this end of town attend our church, or at least turn to us in times of crisis. It's not unusual that I would be called upon to provide funeral services."

"Did you know all five men personally?" Tucker asked.

"To varying degrees," Pearcy replied. "Terry better than the others, of course. Cory attended services occasionally. The others, less so, though I had met each of them through community events or mutual acquaintances."

"Did any of them ever confide in you about being involved in or witnessing illegal activities?" Tucker asked directly. "Gunrunning, for instance?"

The pastor's calm demeanor slipped for just a moment—a flash of something in his eyes that might have been anger or fear—before his professional mask returned.

"I'm afraid I can't discuss what may have been shared in pastoral confidence," he said, his tone cooling slightly. "But I can assure you that if any of these men had come to me with knowledge of serious crimes, I would have encouraged them to go straight to the proper authorities."

"Even if those authorities might have been compromised?" Mallory suggested.

Pearcy's gaze sharpened. "That's a serious allegation, Ms. Carver. Our local police department serves this community with dedication and integrity."

Tucker decided to take a different approach. "We're not making accusations, Pastor. We're simply trying to understand why five men would be murdered in the same manner in a small town like this over the course of eleven years, with seemingly no progress in any of the investigations."

"Sometimes evil goes unpunished in this life," Pearcy replied, his voice taking on a preacher's cadence. "But rest assured, God's justice is inevitable, if not always immediate."

"We're more concerned with earthly justice at the moment," Tucker said evenly. "For the families who have lost loved ones."

The pastor nodded, his expression softening. "As am I, Mr. Randall. The Fisher family has suffered greatly, and I pray daily for their comfort and for a resolution to this tragedy. It's good that you're here. I will pray to God that you're successful."

"One more question," Mallory said. "Do you know Tanya Broadbent? She worked as a waitress at a local café and was dating Malik Williams when he was killed."

Something flickered across Pearcy's face: recognition, certainly, but it might also have been concern.

"Yes, I know Tanya," he acknowledged. "A troubled young woman with a difficult past. She came to our church a few times after Malik's death, seeking comfort. I haven't seen her in some months, though."

"Do you know where we might find her?" Tucker asked.

Pearcy hesitated. "I believe she lives in a small house near the lake. Green siding, on Lakeview Drive. But I'd approach carefully if I were you. Tanya has struggled with… substances… over the years. Her perspective may not be entirely reliable."

Tucker noted the warning; similar to ones they'd received about Detective Bradley. It seemed everyone in Duckwood was eager to discredit potential witnesses before they could even speak.

As they prepared to leave, Pearcy rose and extended his hand again. "I hope you find the answers you're seeking. For the Fishers' sake, and for all the families who have lost loved ones."

"Thank you for your time, Pastor," Tucker replied, shaking his hand firmly. "We may have additional questions as our investigation progresses."

"My door is always open," Pearcy assured them, though his smile didn't quite reach his eyes. "God bless you both, and your efforts."

Back in the car, Tucker and Mallory processed the conversation in silence for a moment before Mallory spoke.

"He definitely knows more than he's saying."

Tucker nodded, starting the engine. "That's a given," he said. "The question is, though, whether he's involved directly or simply protecting information shared in confidence."

"Did you notice how he reacted when I mentioned Tanya Broadbent? That was more than just recognition."

"Yes, I caught that, too," Tucker agreed. "Let's go find this Tanya

Broadbent. If she knew both Terry and Malik, she might be the connection we've been looking for."

As they drove toward Lakeview Drive, Tucker pondered their conversation with the pastor. Pearcy had been polished, controlled, revealing little beyond what was necessary. But there had been moments—brief lapses in his composed facade—that suggested deeper knowledge of the events surrounding the murders.

Whether that knowledge made him a witness, an accessory, or something else entirely remained to be seen. But Tucker's instincts told him that Pastor Henry Pearcy was a key piece in the puzzle they were assembling—a puzzle that someone in Duckwood was willing to kill to keep unsolved.

The lake area was more upscale than the rest of Duckwood, with newer homes and well-maintained properties taking advantage of the water views. Lakeview Drive curved along the shoreline, featuring a mix of year-round residences and summer cabins.

"Green siding," Mallory reminded him, scanning the houses they passed.

Tucker spotted it first—an older, small somewhat neglected house set back from the road, its green paint faded and peeling in places. A ten-year-old blue sedan was parked in the gravel driveway, and a set of wind chimes hung from the small front porch.

"That must be it," he said, pulling over a short distance away. "Let's approach carefully. If she knew two of the victims, she might be wary of strangers asking questions."

They walked up to the house together, Tucker slightly ahead. The porch steps creaked under their weight as they approached the front door. Tucker knocked firmly, listening for movement inside.

Nothing.

He knocked again, louder this time. Still no response.

Mallory peered through a front window, then shook her head. "I don't see anyone moving inside."

Tucker tried the doorknob—it was locked, as expected. They circled the small house, checking windows and calling Tanya's name.

The back door was secured as well, and there was no sign of forced entry or struggle.

"She could be at work," Mallory suggested. "Or running errands."

Tucker nodded, but a sense of unease was growing in his gut. "Let's check with the neighbors, see if anyone knows when she was last seen."

The nearest house was about fifty yards away, a better-maintained property with flower beds and a boat in the driveway. An elderly man was watering plants near the road as they approached.

"Excuse me, sir," Tucker called. "We're looking for Tanya Broadbent. Do you know if she's home?"

The man turned, regarding them suspiciously. "Who's asking?"

Tucker introduced themselves as private investigators, explaining they needed to speak with Tanya about a case they were working on.

The man's expression changed from suspicion to something like concern. "I haven't seen Tanya in a couple days. Not unusual, though. She keeps to herself mostly. She works odd shifts at the café."

"Has she lived here long?" Mallory asked.

"Bout three years," the man replied. "Rents the place from Carl Parsons, the same fella who owns the farm where they found that Fisher boy's body years back." He peered at them more closely. "That what you're investigating? Those murders?"

"We can't discuss the details," Tucker said diplomatically. "But if you see Tanya, could you ask her to call us?" He offered a business card, which the man accepted reluctantly and then stared at it.

"You folks be careful," the neighbor warned, glancing toward Tanya's house. "Strange things happen around here sometimes. People who ask too many questions about those killings tend to regret it."

It was the third such warning they'd received since arriving in Duckwood. Tucker was beginning to think it was less coincidence and more orchestrated intimidation.

"We'll keep that in mind," he assured the man. "Thank you for your help."

As they walked back to their SUV, Mallory leaned close. "Another connection to the Parsons property," she murmured. "And another missing witness."

Tucker nodded grimly. "Let's check the café, see if she's working today. And if not..."

"If not, we might need to be concerned about her safety," Mallory finished his thought.

The pieces were coming together, but the picture they formed was increasingly disturbing. Five murdered men. Missing evidence. Witnesses who couldn't or wouldn't talk. And now, potentially, another victim.

Whatever secrets Duckwood was hiding, they were worth killing for. And Tucker had the growing conviction that he and Mallory had stumbled into something far more dangerous than a simple cold case investigation.

12

MALLORY SCANNED THE BUSY INTERIOR OF MOLLY'S CAFÉ, SEARCHING for Tanya Broadbent among the waitstaff. The afternoon crowd filled most of the tables—a mix of locals having coffee and tourists passing through. A server—middle-aged with tired eyes and a harried look—approached their table.

"Help you folks?" she asked, order pad ready.

"We're looking for Tanya Broadbent," Mallory replied. "Does she work today?"

The waitress's expression shifted subtly, a flicker of something that might have been concern. "Tanya? No, she hasn't been in for her shifts the last two days. And it's not like her to miss without calling. You friends of hers?"

"We needed to speak with her about an investigation," Tucker explained, showing his PI credentials discreetly. "Do you know where we might find her?"

The waitress—Sally, according to her nametag—glanced around before leaning closer. "Look, Tanya's had a rough go of it. After what happened to Malik, she was pretty broken up. Started asking questions nobody around here wants answered."

"Questions about his murder?" Mallory pressed.

Sally nodded. "She said she had theories about who was behind it, why he was killed. Most folks just thought she was messed up from grief and, well, other issues." She tapped her temple meaningfully. "But lately she seemed clearer, said she had proof of something. Then she just stops showing up."

Mallory felt her pulse quicken. "When exactly did you last see her?"

"Monday morning. She worked the breakfast shift, left around two o'clock." Sally paused. "The strange thing is, she seemed excited. She said she finally had what she needed to 'blow it all open,' whatever that means."

Today was Wednesday. Tanya had been missing, or at least unreachable, for almost two days, right around the time they'd arrived in Duckwood.

"Did she mention what kind of proof she had?" Tucker asked.

Sally shook her head. "Tanya talked big sometimes, especially when she'd been drinking. But she seemed different this time. More… I dunno, certain." She hesitated, then added, "You might try Louis Fisher. They were kinda friendly."

"Louis Fisher?" Mallory repeated, surprised. "Terry's cousin? Tiffany's husband?"

"That's him. He'd stop by the café when Tanya was working, sit at the counter, talking with her. Nothing inappropriate. It just seemed like they had some kind of understanding, like, you know?"

Mallory exchanged a glance with Tucker. This was an unexpected connection—Louis Fisher, who had married Terry's fiancée, was also friendly with a woman connected to another victim.

"One more question," Mallory said. "Do you know if Tanya knew Terry Fisher before his death?"

Sally's eyebrows rose. "Terry? Yeah, they knew each other. They grew up together. Dated briefly in high school before he got with Tiffany. Why?"

This was significant, a direct personal connection between Tanya and both victims. "Oh," Mallory said, shaking her head. "No, I'm just… trying to establish connections. Thank you so much for your help."

They ordered coffee to avoid drawing attention, waiting until Sally moved away before discussing what they'd learned.

"So Tanya dated Terry in high school, then later dated Malik, another victim," Mallory summarized quietly. "And she's friendly with Louis Fisher, who married Terry's fiancée after his death."

"And now she's missing after claiming to have proof of something," Tucker added. "We need to find her. And we need to speak with Louis Fisher."

"I'll check social media for any recent activity from Tanya," Mallory suggested, pulling out her phone. "You try Gary; see if he knows where his cousin might be."

While Tucker stepped outside to make the call, Mallory searched for Tanya Broadbent online. She found a Facebook profile that hadn't been updated in months and an Instagram with occasional posts of nature photos and inspirational quotes. Nothing that indicated where she might be or what "proof" she might have discovered.

Tucker returned as she was scrolling through Tanya's sparse social media presence. "Gary says Louis works at the hardware store on Main Street. Should be there until six o'clock today."

"Anything else?"

"Gary seemed surprised we were asking about Louis. Said they're not close since Louis married Tiffany, but as far as he knows, Louis is a straight arrow; works hard, attends church, coaches Little League."

"And apparently has secret conversations with a woman connected to two murder victims," Mallory added.

They paid for their coffee and left, deciding to drive past Tanya's house once more before approaching Louis. The small green house looked exactly as they'd left it: quiet, seemingly unoccupied, with no new signs of activity.

"I'm getting worried," Mallory admitted as they pulled away. "The timing is too coincidental. She discovers some kind of proof as to what happened to Malik, then disappears right when we arrive in town and start asking questions."

"Let's not jump to conclusions," Tucker said, though she could see by his expression he was equally concerned. "But let's find Louis Fisher and see what he knows," he said.

THE GOODMAN HARDWARE Store was a local institution, judging by the worn but well-maintained facade and the "Serving Our Community Since 1952" sign in the window. Inside, the narrow aisles were packed with everything from paint supplies to fishing gear, the smell of sawdust and metal permeating the air.

A young clerk directed them to the back, where a man in his early-forties was cutting keys for a customer. Louis Fisher was broader than his cousin Gary, with a solid build and calloused hands that spoke of physical work. His brown hair was neatly trimmed, his expression pleasant as he handed the keys to the customer with a friendly comment.

Tucker and Mallory waited until the customer left before approaching. "Mr. Fisher? Louis Fisher?" Tucker began. "We'd like to speak with you if you have a moment."

Louis looked up, his expression curious but not alarmed. "That's me. What can I help you with?"

"I'm Tucker Randall, and this is Mallory Carver. We're private investigators working with Gary Fisher regarding his brother's murder."

The change in Louis was subtle but immediate: a stiffening of his shoulders, a slight narrowing of his eyes. "Gary hired private investigators? He didn't mention that."

"It was a recent decision," Mallory explained, observing his reactions. "Given his parents' declining health, he's hoping for a solution before it's too late."

Louis nodded slowly. "Understandable. Though I'm not sure what I can tell you that the police haven't already covered. Terry died long before Tiffany and I got together."

There was a defensiveness in his tone that caught Mallory's attention—as if he expected to be judged for marrying his murdered cousin's fiancée.

"Actually, we're hoping you might help us locate someone," Tucker said. "Tanya Broadbent. We understand you know her."

Louis's expression shifted again to one of surprise, followed by something that might have been concern. "Tanya? Why would you need to find her?"

"She knew both Terry and Malik Williams," Mallory explained. "We believe she might have information relevant to our investigation."

"Have you checked Molly's café?" he asked. "She works there."

"She hasn't shown up for her shifts in two days," Tucker replied. "Her house appears empty, and no one seems to know where she is."

Louis ran a hand through his hair, a gesture that reminded Mallory of Gary. The family resemblance was stronger in movement than appearance. "That's… concerning. Tanya's had her struggles, but she's reliable about work."

"When did you last see her?" Mallory asked.

Louis hesitated, his gaze flicking between them. "Monday evening. She stopped by the house briefly to drop off a book she'd borrowed from Tiffany."

"Did she seem unusual in any way? Excited, worried, afraid?"

"Not that I noticed," Louis replied, but there was a slight delay in his response that made Mallory doubt his sincerity. "Look, why all these questions about Tanya? What does she have to do with Terry's murder?"

"We're exploring all the avenues," Tucker said smoothly. "Tanya dated Terry in high school, then later dated Malik Williams; both were murdered in identical fashion. That makes her perspective potentially valuable. We need to speak with her."

Louis's eyebrows rose. "I knew she'd dated Malik, but Terry? That's news to me." He paused. "Does Tiffany know you're investigating all this again? She's worked hard to move forward with her life."

"We've spoken with Tiffany," Mallory confirmed. "She mentioned

Terry had acquired a gun shortly before his death, supposedly for protection. Did he ever discuss that with you?"

Louis's expression closed off further. "No. Terry and I weren't especially close back then. Different circles, different interests." He glanced at his watch. "Look, I need to get back to work. Is there anything else?"

Tucker handed him a business card. "If you hear from Tanya, please let us know immediately. We're concerned about her safety."

Louis took the card reluctantly. "Sure. Though Tanya sometimes goes off-grid when she's having a rough patch. She might just be taking some personal time."

As they turned to leave, Mallory paused. "One more question, Mr. Fisher. Do you know Pastor Henry Pearcy well?"

"Pastor Henry?" Louis seemed surprised by the shift. "Of course. He's our pastor. He conducted Terry's funeral, counseled Tiffany after his death, and he performed our wedding ceremony. Why?"

"Just establishing connections," Mallory replied with a smile. "Thank you for your time, Mr. Fisher."

Outside, they walked a block before discussing the interview, wary of being overheard.

"He's hiding something," Mallory stated confidently. "That business about Tanya returning a book to Tiffany? I don't buy it. Tiffany never mentioned being friends with her."

Tucker nodded. "And he seemed genuinely surprised that Tanya had dated Terry. If they were as friendly as the waitress suggested, wouldn't that have come up?"

"We need to find Tanya," Mallory said, feeling increasingly uneasy about the woman's absence. "If she had proof of something related to the murders, and now she's missing…"

"Let's check with the police first," Tucker suggested. "File a missing person report, make it official. If something has happened to her, we want a paper trail documenting our concerns."

13

The Duckwood Police Department was quiet when they returned. The receptionist from that morning replaced by a young male officer. He looked up as they entered, recognition flickering in his eyes.

"You're the private investigators, right? How can I help you?"

Tucker explained their concerns about Tanya Broadbent, her missed work shifts, the empty house, her claims of having proof related to the murders they were investigating.

The officer—Peters, according to his nameplate—typed notes into his computer as they spoke, but Mallory noted his lack of urgency. "So she's been missing since Monday afternoon?" he asked. "That's not very long. Adults are entitled to go wherever they want without reporting in."

"Under normal circumstances, yes," Mallory agreed. "But given the context, her connection to two murder victims, her claim to have evidence, and the threatening note we received after asking questions about those same murders, we believe there's cause for concern."

Officer Peters looked uncomfortable. "I'll file the report and pass it along to the chief. But without signs of foul play or a much longer absence, there's not much we can do officially."

"We understand," Tucker said. "We'd just like our concerns documented. And we'd appreciate being notified if she turns up."

After completing the paperwork, they left the station, both frustrated by the lukewarm response but not surprised.

"They're not going to look for her," Mallory said as they walked to their vehicle. "At least not seriously."

"Which means it's up to us," Tucker agreed. "But where do we start? We've checked her home, her workplace. No one seems to know where she might go."

Mallory considered the puzzle pieces they'd collected. "The waitress said Tanya claimed to have proof. What if she didn't just discover something? What if she went somewhere to get that proof?"

"Like where?"

"The Parsons' farm," Mallory suggested. "It's where Terry's body was found, and apparently where the church holds events. Tanya even rents her house from Carl Parsons. Those are connections, but there's something we're missing."

Tucker nodded slowly. "It's worth checking out, I suppose. But we should wait until dark. If someone's watching us—and that note suggests they are—we don't want to telegraph our movements."

They decided to return to their hotel to review their notes and plan their approach to the Parsons property. As they drove, Mallory's phone rang. It was her sister, Jen, again.

"I should take this," she sighed, answering the call. "Hey, Jen."

"Please tell me you're heading back tomorrow," Jen said without preamble. "The dress appointment is at two on Friday, and I've already had to reschedule twice."

"I'm not sure," Mallory admitted, glancing at Tucker. "Things are getting complicated here."

Jen was quiet for a moment. "Mal, I know your work is important. But so is your wedding. And your safety. Maybe you should let the local police handle the investigation."

Mallory suppressed a bitter laugh. "The local police aren't exactly eager to investigate anything. That's part of the problem."

They talked a few minutes longer, with Mallory promising to call the next day with a definite answer about the dress appointment. When she hung up, Tucker gave her a sympathetic glance.

"You should go back for that appointment if you want," he offered. "I told you, I can handle things here for a day."

Mallory shook her head firmly. "Not with Tanya missing and the case heating up. The dress can wait."

Back at the hotel, they spread their notes across Tucker's bed and began creating a timeline of events and connections between the various players in Duckwood.

"So we have five victims over eleven years, all killed the same way," Tucker summarized. "Terry Fisher, who was engaged to Tiffany, who later married his cousin Louis. Terry dated Tanya in high school. Years later, Tanya dated Malik Williams, another victim."

"And apparently Tanya and Louis were friendly recently, despite there being no obvious reason for them to interact," Mallory added. "Pastor Pearcy conducted all five funeral services and leases the land where Terry's body was found from the Parsons family, who also happen to be Tanya's landlord."

"Then there's the gunrunning operation that Detective Bradley was investigating before his accident," Tucker said. "And the gun that Terry acquired shortly before his death, which mysteriously disappeared from the case files."

Mallory stood and paced the small room, trying to see the connections more clearly. "What if the gunrunning operation is the key to everything? Say Terry somehow got involved, or discovered it, then was killed before he could expose it. The other victims followed the same pattern. Say they knew something, threatened exposure, and were eliminated?"

"Possible, and what about Tanya?" Tucker prompted.

"Maybe she finally figured it out. Maybe she found evidence of who's behind it all." Mallory paused by the window, lifting the edge of the curtain to peer outside. "That's why we need to check the Parsons property. If there's some kind of operation centering on that land, there might be physical evidence: a building, equipment, something that would explain why five bodies were found in that same general area."

Tucker checked his watch. "It's almost seven. We should get dinner, then wait until after dark to check out the property."

They chose a different restaurant for dinner, a small Italian place off the main street where Tucker figured they'd be less likely to encounter people they'd already interviewed. Over pasta, they continued refining their theory, keeping their voices low and watching for anyone paying them undue attention.

"Even if we find evidence of gun running," Tucker pointed out, "we'll need to determine who's behind it. Is it the Parsons family? Pastor Pearcy? Chief Winson? Or some combination of all three?"

"Or someone we haven't even considered yet," Mallory added. "Duckwood might be small, but there are still plenty of people we haven't spoken with."

By the time they finished dinner, darkness had fallen. They returned to their hotel room briefly to change into darker clothing and gather flashlights and weapons, then they headed out toward the Parsons property.

14

ONCE THEY LEFT THE MAIN ROAD, TUCKER DROVE WITH THE HEADLIGHTS dimmed, following a winding country lane that led toward the area where Terry's body had been discovered. They passed occasional houses set back from the road, but the properties grew larger and more isolated as they continued onward.

"The main farmhouse should be up ahead," Tucker said quietly, referring to the map they'd studied. "We'll park well back and approach on foot."

Mallory felt the familiar mixture of tension and excitement that accompanied potentially dangerous investigative work. Her hand instinctively checked the pepper spray in her pocket and the Sig P938 she carried by habit. Tucker, she knew, carried a Glock 17 in a holster on his belt and a small Smith and Wesson revolver in an ankle holster, a habit from his FBI days that had proven useful more than once.

They parked in a small turnoff hidden by trees, then began the half-mile walk toward the Parsons property. The night was clear but moonless; the darkness broken only by distant porch lights and the glow of their carefully shielded flashlights.

"Terry's body was found in that field to the east of the main farm buildings," Tucker whispered as they approached. "The area where the church holds its events."

Mallory nodded, scanning the landscape. The silhouette of a large barn was visible ahead with what appeared to be equipment sheds and the main farmhouse some distance away. No lights burned in any of the buildings.

"Let's check the barn first," she suggested. "It's the most logical place to store or transfer illegal goods."

They moved silently across the open ground, staying low and using the sparse tree line for cover when possible. As they neared the barn, Mallory noticed something that made her pause—fresh tire tracks in the dirt driveway, despite there being no vehicles visible.

"Someone's been here recently," she whispered to Tucker, indicating the tracks.

He nodded, eyes alert as they continued toward the barn. The massive door was secured with a padlock, but a smaller side entrance stood slightly ajar. Tucker approached it cautiously, listening for any sound from inside before slowly pushing it open.

The interior was pitch black. Tucker clicked on his flashlight, keeping the beam low and sweeping it across the concrete floor. Farm equipment filled much of the space: tractors, attachments, tools hanging on the walls. Nothing immediately suspicious.

They moved deeper into the barn, checking behind equipment and scanning for anything out of place. Mallory was beginning to think they'd made a mistake when her beam caught something reflective in the far corner—a tarp covering what appeared to be crates.

"Tucker," she whispered, pointing.

They approached carefully, Tucker taking the lead while Mallory watched their backs. He lifted the edge of the tarp, revealing a stack of wooden crates with foreign markings.

"Military-grade weapons shipping containers," he murmured, recognizing the markings from his FBI training. "Russian manufacturer."

Mallory felt a surge of vindication. "So the gunrunning operation is real. These must be in transit to somewhere else."

Tucker was about to respond when a sound from outside froze them both—the crunch of tires on gravel, headlights sweeping across the barn walls through cracks in the siding.

"Someone's coming," Mallory whispered urgently. "We need to hide."

They quickly replaced the tarp and moved behind a large tractor, crouching low as vehicle doors slammed outside. Voices approached—at least two men, maybe more.

The side door creaked open wider, flashlight beams cutting through the darkness. Mallory pressed closer to Tucker, her heart pounding as footsteps entered the barn.

"Let's make this quick," a man's voice said, his tone authoritative and vaguely familiar. "The shipment needs to be on the road by midnight."

"What about the woman?" another voice asked. "Pearcy says she's asking too many questions."

"She's contained for now," a third voice said. "We'll deal with her after the shipment's gone."

Mallory felt her blood run cold. The woman had to be Tanya. And if she was "contained," it meant she was alive—for now.

Tucker's hand found hers in the darkness, squeezing once in silent communication. They were outnumbered, potentially outgunned, and had stumbled into the middle of an active illegal operation. Their only advantage was that they hadn't been discovered... yet.

The men moved toward the crates, unaware of the hidden investigators hiding behind the tractor.

Tucker remained perfectly still behind the tractor, controlling his breathing as the men moved about the barn. Years of FBI training had prepared him for situations like this: discovery meant danger, not just for him and Mallory, but also for Tanya Broadbent, who was apparently being held somewhere.

He counted the footsteps, trying to determine exactly how many men had entered. Three, possibly four. Their flashlight beams swept across the barn's interior, illuminating dusty farm equipment and the covered crates in the corner.

"Start loading them now," the authoritative voice commanded. "Truck's waiting on the north access road."

"What about those investigators asking around town?" another man asked, his tone betraying nervousness. "Pearcy said they filed a report about the Broadbent woman."

Tucker felt Mallory tense beside him at the mention of the report.

The authoritative voice replied with a dismissive snort.

"Winson will handle that. Small-town PI's from Chattanooga; they're nothing to worry about. Focus on getting this shipment out. We've got buyers waiting."

The sound of the tarp being pulled back echoed in the cavernous space, followed by the scraping of crates being moved. Tucker carefully shifted position to peer through a gap in the tractor's machinery. Four men were visible now, working methodically to load the wooden crates onto hand trucks.

One man, whose face remained in shadow, appeared to be supervising rather than assisting with the physical labor. From his stature and the deference the others showed him, Tucker assumed he was the leader, and the source of the authoritative voice.

Tucker reached down slowly to the Glock 17 on his belt, confirming his weapon was accessible if needed. He had no intention of engaging in a firefight while outnumbered, but if they were discovered, having options might make the difference between life and death.

The loading continued for several minutes; the men working efficiently in near silence. Tucker noted their practiced movements. These men weren't amateurs; they were people who had done this many times before. The operation was clearly well-established, explaining why it had continued uninterrupted for over a decade.

"Last one," one of the men announced, loading a final crate.

"Good," the leader replied. "Meet at the rendezvous in thirty minutes. I need to check on our guest first."

Guest. Tucker exchanged a glance with Mallory in the darkness. That had to be Tanya. If they followed the leader, he might lead them right to her.

The men began moving toward the door, taking the loaded hand trucks with them. Tucker calculated rapidly—they needed to avoid detection but not lose their chance to find Tanya. He leaned close to Mallory's ear.

"Stay here until they're gone," he whispered, barely audible. "I'll follow at a distance. Wait five minutes, then return to the car."

She gave a nearly imperceptible nod, though he could sense her reluctance to separate. But it was the safest approach—one person trailing was less likely to be detected than two, and if something went wrong, Mallory would be free to contact authorities.

15

As the men exited the barn, Tucker counted to thirty, then carefully moved from their hiding place toward the door. The night outside seemed to have grown darker, clouds now obscuring what little starlight had illuminated their approach. He could see flashlight beams moving away toward different vehicles—two heading north, presumably with the weapons, and one moving west, toward what appeared to be a smaller outbuilding about a hundred yards from the barn.

Tucker slipped out the side door and pressed himself against the barn's exterior wall, using the shadows for cover. The leader was walking alone toward the outbuilding, his flashlight bobbing with each step. Tucker waited until there was sufficient distance, then began following, moving from shadow to shadow, careful to avoid making a noise on the gravel and dirt.

The outbuilding appeared to be a storage shed, perhaps twenty feet square, with a metal roof. Unlike the barn, it had a sturdy-looking door with what appeared to be a modern electronic lock. The leader approached it, his flashlight illuminating a keypad mounted beside the door. Tucker watched from behind a stack of hay bales as the man punched in a code, the lock disengaging with an audible click.

The door opened, spilling light from inside onto the ground. The leader entered, closing the door behind him. Tucker moved closer, circling to approach from the side where a small window might offer visibility inside. Crouching beneath it, he slowly raised his head just enough to peer inside.

The shed's interior had been converted into a makeshift holding cell. A camp bed stood against one wall, and a woman he assumed was Tanya Broadbent sat on it, her hands bound in front of her but her feet free. She appeared disheveled but uninjured, her expression defiant as she faced the leader, who was now illuminated in the overhead light.

Tucker felt a jolt of recognition. The leader was Carl Parsons, owner of the farm, Tanya's landlord, and a man whose name had repeatedly surfaced during their investigation, a man whose photograph he'd seen several times during his research.

He was speaking to Tanya, his tone was condescending. Tucker put his ear to the glass.

"...just need to cooperate, and this ends well for everyone. Where's the evidence you claimed to have?"

"Go to hell," Tanya spat back. "I know what you did to Malik. To Terry. To all of them."

Parsons sighed, as if dealing with a troublesome child. "We've been through this, Tanya. You have theories, not evidence. If you had actual proof, you would have produced it by now."

"Maybe I already gave it to someone for safekeeping," she countered. "Maybe if anything happens to me, it goes straight to the state police."

Tucker couldn't see Parsons' face from his angle, but the man's posture stiffened. "You're bluffing. There's no one in Duckwood you trust enough for that."

"Who said anything about anyone in Duckwood?" she snapped.

The statement hung in the air between them. Tucker recognized the strategy. Tanya was trying to create doubt, to make her captors hesitate before doing anything permanent. It was a smart play, but she was clearly in serious danger.

Tucker weighed his options. He was armed, but engaging in a direct confrontation with Parsons now could put Tanya at greater risk. He needed to get back to Mallory, formulate a plan, and call in reinforcements—though given Chief Winson's apparent involvement in the conspiracy, the local police weren't an option, and neither could he assume the sheriff wasn't involved.

He carefully backed away from the window, keeping low and using the ambient noise of the rural night to mask any sounds. Once at a safe distance, he circled wide around the buildings, heading back toward where they'd parked. His mind raced with the implications of what he'd witnessed. The gunrunning operation was real, and had been operating for years, and Carl Parsons appeared to be a key figure, perhaps even the leader, though from what had been said in the barn, it was clear that the pastor was also somehow involved..

Halfway back to their parking spot, Tucker heard the soft crunch of footsteps ahead. He froze, hand moving toward his weapon, then relaxed slightly as Mallory's familiar outline emerged from the darkness.

"I told you to wait at the car," he whispered as she approached.

"You know I don't follow instructions well," she replied quietly. "What did you find?"

"Tanya's alive. She's being held in one of the sheds. Carl Parsons is holding her, and he appears to be running the gun operation. We need to get back to the truck and call for help."

They moved quickly through the darkness, staying off the main access road and using the tree line for cover. Once they reached their vehicle, Tucker did a quick check to ensure it hadn't been tampered with before they got inside.

"Who do we call?" Mallory asked as Tucker started the engine, keeping the headlights off as they pulled away. "Not the local police, not if Winson is involved somehow."

"State police," Tucker decided, putting distance between them and the Parsons farm before turning on the headlights. "But we need to be careful about what we say. We don't know how far this conspiracy extends."

"Did you hear what he said about the pastor?" Mallory asked.

"Yes, it seems he must be somehow involved, too," he replied as he drove toward the main highway, planning to get well outside Duckwood before making the call. As they rounded a curve in the country road, headlights suddenly appeared behind them, closing fast.

"We've got company," Mallory warned, looking back.

Tucker accelerated, but the pursuing vehicle—a large pickup truck—gained on them rapidly. "Call now," he instructed Mallory, tossing her his phone. "Tennessee Highway Patrol. Tell them we're being pursued and believe it's connected to illegal weapons trafficking."

Mallory went to her contacts and tapped the number while Tucker focused on driving, pushing their small SUV to its limits on the winding rural road. The pickup behind them was now close enough that its headlights filled their rear window, illuminating the interior as bright as day.

"It's ringing," Mallory reported. "Wait—we're losing signal."

Tucker glanced at the phone and saw the "No Service" indicator. "We must be in a dead zone. Keep trying."

The road ahead straightened as they approached the highway intersection. Tucker accelerated further, hoping to reach the main road where there might be other traffic or better cell reception. The pickup responded in kind, its engine roaring as it closed the gap.

"Hold on," Tucker warned as he took the turn onto the highway, tires squealing in protest. The pursuing truck followed, now just car lengths behind them. In the side mirror, Tucker could see the driver clearly; it was one of the men from the barn.

"They're going to ram us," Mallory said tensely, bracing herself against the dashboard.

The impact came seconds later; the pickup slammed into their rear bumper, causing their vehicle to fishtail briefly before Tucker regained control. He sped up again, but their vehicle was no match for the more powerful pickup.

Another impact, harder this time, sent them skidding toward the shoulder. Tucker fought the wheel, keeping them on the road, but a third hit knocked them into a spin. The SUV rotated one-hundred-eighty degrees before sliding to a stop on the opposite shoulder, facing back the way they had come.

The pickup braked hard and skidding to a stop some twenty yards away. Its headlights illuminated their disabled vehicle as two men emerged, both carrying what appeared to be handguns.

"Get down," Tucker ordered, drawing his weapon. "When I engage them, run for the trees on your side."

"I'm not leaving you," Mallory protested.

"This isn't a debate. One of us needs to get help." His tone left no room for argument. "Now get ready."

The men approached cautiously, weapons raised. Tucker waited until they were thirty feet away before making his move. He pushed his door open, using it as partial cover while aiming at the closest attacker.

"FBI! Drop your weapons!" he shouted, falling back on his old authority out of instinct.

The men hesitated briefly, just long enough for Tucker to fire a warning shot over their heads. They dove for cover, returning fire almost immediately. Bullets pinged against the SV's body and shattered the driver's side window.

"Go!" Tucker yelled to Mallory, firing again to provide covering fire as she slipped out the passenger side and sprinted for the tree line.

One of the men noticed her escape and turned to fire in her direction. Tucker adjusted his aim and shot more deliberately this time, hitting the man in the shoulder. He went down with a cry of pain as Mallory disappeared into the darkness beyond the road.

The second attacker unleashed a barrage of bullets, forcing Tucker to duck behind the engine block for cover. He was pinned down now, with limited ammunition and an injured but still armed opponent, plus the second attacker methodically closing in on his position.

"You're just making this worse for yourself," one of the men called out. "We only want the woman. Tell us where she's going, and maybe you get to walk away from this."

Tucker didn't respond, using the moment to assess his options. His position was deteriorating rapidly. The SUV offered some protection, but they would eventually flank him. His best hope was that Mallory had gotten far enough away to find help or signal passing traffic.

A new sound cut through the night, distant sirens, growing louder. Someone had reported the gunfire, or perhaps a passing motorist had seen the confrontation. Either way, it changed the equation.

"Cops are coming," the uninjured attacker said urgently to his partner. "We need to go. Now."

"What about him?" the wounded man asked, gesturing toward Tucker's position with his good arm.

"Leave him. If he's still alive, Winson can deal with him."

Tucker heard them retreating, car doors slamming, and tires squealing as the pickup reversed course and sped away. He remained in position, gun ready, until the vehicle's taillights disappeared into the distance.

Only then did he allow himself to take stock of his own condition. A sharp pain in his left arm suggested he'd been hit, though adrenaline had masked it during the confrontation. Sure enough, blood was soaking through his sleeve from what appeared to be a graze rather than a direct hit.

The sirens were very close now. Tucker holstered his weapon and raised his hands as the first patrol car came into view, its light bar painting the scene in alternating red and blue. He needed to be careful here. If Winson had been alerted, the responding officers might not be friendly.

To his relief, the cruiser had Tennessee Highway Patrol markings rather than local police. Two officers emerged cautiously, weapons drawn.

"On the ground! Hands where we can see them!" one shouted.

Tucker complied immediately, calling out as he did so. "I'm a licensed private investigator. I was just attacked by armed men. My partner fled into the woods for safety."

The officers approached carefully, one keeping him covered while the other checked the immediate area.

"Anyone else here?" the officer asked, holstering his weapon after confirming Tucker was not an immediate threat.

"No, they fled when they heard your sirens. Two men in a dark pickup, one injured. They're connected to an illegal weapons trafficking operation based at the Parsons farm in Duckwood. And they're holding a woman captive there, Tanya Broadbent."

The officer looked skeptical but radioed the information in while his partner helped Tucker to his feet.

"You're bleeding," the second officer noted, examining Tucker's arm. "We should get you checked out."

"My partner," Tucker insisted. "She ran into those woods. We need to find her first."

"We've got additional units on the way," the officer assured him. "They'll help search for her. Meanwhile, I need your identification and a statement about what happened here."

Tucker provided his PI credentials and gave a concise account of their investigation, the discovery at the Parsons farm, and the subsequent pursuit. He omitted certain details—particularly those that might reveal Mallory's location if she was still hiding—until he could be certain these officers weren't connected to the Duckwood conspiracy.

"This is a serious allegation," the officer said when Tucker had finished. "Weapons trafficking, kidnapping, possible involvement by local law enforcement. We'll need to contact our captain."

"I understand," Tucker replied. "But time is critical. Tanya Broadbent is in immediate danger, and now my partner is missing as well."

The sound of someone emerging from the woods interrupted their conversation. Tucker turned, relief washing over him as he saw Mallory approaching, hands raised to show the officers she wasn't a threat.

"That's my partner," he called out quickly. "Mallory Carver."

The officers verified her identity while Tucker explained what had happened after they separated. Mallory looked shaken but unhurt, her eyes widening at the sight of blood on Tucker's sleeve.

"It's just a graze," he assured her before she could ask. "Did you see which way they went?"

"Back toward Duckwood," she confirmed. "Tucker, I got through to 911 while I was in the woods. State Police dispatch. They're sending units to the Parsons farm."

The highway patrol officer's radio crackled with confirmation. Units were indeed en route to the location, with a warrant being expedited based on the weapons trafficking allegations and suspected kidnapping.

"We need to go there," Tucker insisted. "We can identify Parsons and the shed where Tanya is being held."

The officers exchanged glances. "That's not standard procedure for civilians," the senior officer began.

"We're not civilians," Mallory interjected. "We're licensed investigators who've spent days documenting this case. And I'm an ex-FBI agent. We know the layout of the property and can identify the suspects. And every minute we waste puts Tanya in greater danger."

After some discussion over the radio with their supervisor, the officers reluctantly agreed to escort Tucker and Mallory to the Parsons farm, where other units would be converging. An ambulance would meet them there to treat Tucker's wound.

As they drove toward the farm, Tucker's mind raced with contingency plans. If Parsons and his men realized law enforcement was closing in, Tanya might become a liability they couldn't afford to leave alive. And if Chief Winson was alerted before the state police secured the scene, evidence could disappear.

"We found the gun running operation," Mallory said quietly beside him in the back of the patrol car. "Just like Detective Bradley suspected eleven years ago."

Tucker nodded. "And likely the motive behind five murders. But we still don't have all the players. Parsons is clearly involved, probably Winson too. But what about Pastor Pearcy? The men at the barn mentioned him."

"One connection at a time," Mallory replied, her hand finding his in the darkness. "Right now, let's focus on saving Tanya."

The patrol car's lights illuminated the rural landscape as they sped toward the Parsons farm. Ahead, Tucker could see the flashing lights of other law enforcement vehicles already on the scene. The operation that had remained hidden for over a decade was about to be exposed —but at what cost?

As they approached, gunfire erupted from the direction of the main farmhouse, answering his question with chilling clarity. The confrontation was far from over.

16

Mallory tensed as more gunfire erupted ahead. The Highway Patrol officer driving their cruiser immediately slowed, speaking rapidly into his radio to coordinate with the units already on scene at the Parsons farm.

"Shots fired, multiple officers engaging. All units approach with caution. Civilians present."

Tucker leaned forward. "Any word on the status of the female hostage?"

"Negative," the officer replied, his expression grim. "The team was attempting to clear the outbuildings when they encountered armed resistance."

Mallory's thoughts flew to Tanya, locked in that shed with a firefight raging around her. And she knew if Parsons or his men reached her first, they'd eliminate the witness rather than let her talk.

Their cruiser turned onto the farm's access road, now illuminated by the flashing lights of nearly a dozen police vehicles. Officers in tactical gear had taken positions behind vehicles and outbuildings, their weapons trained on the main farmhouse where muzzle flashes occasionally lit up the windows.

The officer parked well back from the action, turning to his passengers. "You two stay in the vehicle. This is an active shooter situation."

"But the hostage isn't in the main house," Mallory protested. "She's in a storage shed about a hundred yards west of the barn. If you're focusing all your resources on the farmhouse, she's vulnerable."

The officer hesitated, then radioed the information to the command post, which appeared to be set up behind a large SUV with State Police markings. Moments later, a tactical team of four officers detached from the main group and began moving cautiously toward the western outbuildings.

"She's going to be okay," Tucker said quietly, though his expression remained tense. Blood had soaked through the makeshift bandage on his arm, and his face was pale in the flashing lights.

A paramedic approached their vehicle, directed there by one of the officers. "Sir, we need to check that wound."

Tucker reluctantly allowed himself to be guided to a waiting ambulance at the edge of the secured perimeter. Mallory followed, unwilling to let him out of her sight after the close call on the highway.

"It's just a graze," Tucker insisted as the paramedic cut away his sleeve to examine the injury.

"That 'graze' took a chunk of flesh with it," the paramedic countered, cleaning the wound. "You'll need stitches, but it can wait until we get you to a hospital."

"I'm not leaving," Tucker stated firmly. "Not until we find Tanya Broadbent."

The paramedic looked like he wanted to argue, but instead focused on bandaging the wound properly. Mallory stepped a few paces away to speak with the officer in charge, a State Police captain who had approached the ambulance.

"Ms. Carver? I'm Captain Reynolds. I understand you and your partner discovered an illegal weapons operation and a kidnapping victim?"

"Yes," Mallory confirmed, quickly explaining what they'd witnessed in the barn and the shed. "Tucker saw Tanya Broadbent being held by Carl Parsons. She's alive, or was when we left, but in imminent danger."

"We have a team approaching the storage structures now," Reynolds assured her. "Can you describe exactly which building she's in?"

Mallory provided detailed directions to the shed, including the keypad lock she'd glimpsed during their escape. "It's a modern security system; not what you'd expect on a farm storage building."

Reynolds nodded, relaying the information via radio to the tactical team. Meanwhile, the situation at the farmhouse appeared to be escalating. More officers had arrived, including what looked like a SWAT unit from a larger jurisdiction.

"How many hostiles are we dealing with?" Reynolds asked.

"At least four that we saw," Mallory replied. "Parsons and three others. But there could be more."

A burst of radio chatter interrupted them. Reynolds listened intently, then turned back to Mallory, his expression serious.

"The shed's empty. No sign of the hostage."

Mallory felt her stomach drop. "That's impossible. They must have moved her after we left."

"There are signs someone was held there," Reynolds said, "a chair with restraints, some food wrappers. But no hostage."

By then, Tucker had joined them against the paramedic's protests. "They must have relocated her when their men failed to return from pursuing us. Parsons would have realized something went wrong," he said.

Reynolds considered this. "If they moved her, she's likely in the main house now."

"Which complicates your assault," Tucker finished grimly.

The standoff at the farmhouse continued as officers maintained their positions, occasionally exchanging fire with those inside. From their vantage point, Mallory could see tactical officers working their way around the sides of the property, preparing for a coordinated breach.

"We need to get closer," she said to Tucker. "If they bring Tanya out, we're the only ones who can identify her."

"Captain," Tucker addressed Reynolds, "we're both experienced investigators, and I have eight years FBI tactical training. Let us move to your command post where we can assist in identifying the suspects and the hostage."

Reynolds hesitated, then nodded. "Stay behind the vehicles, keep your heads down, and follow my officers' instructions implicitly. Understood?"

They agreed and followed the captain to the SUV serving as the command center. From this new position, they had a clearer view of the farmhouse and the officers surrounding it. A negotiator was attempting to communicate with those inside through a loudspeaker, demanding they release any hostages and surrender.

"Carl Parsons, this is the Tennessee State Police. The building is surrounded. Come out with your hands up and release Tanya Broadbent unharmed."

There was no response except another burst of gunfire from an upstairs window.

"How long has this been going on?" Mallory asked one of the officers manning the radio.

"About twenty minutes," he replied. "They're not responding."

"They know they're cornered," Tucker said. "Men like Parsons don't surrender easily. They've been operating this gun running scheme for over a decade, and they're probably responsible for five murders. They're looking at life sentences."

"Or they're buying time," Mallory suggested, a new thought occurring to her. "Maybe they're waiting for reinforcements."

Tucker looked at her sharply. "You think Winson might show up with local officers?"

"It's possible," she replied. "If he's involved, he can't afford to let Parsons talk."

Captain Reynolds overheard this exchange. "We've notified the County Sheriff's office, not the Duckwood PD. But you're saying the local chief might be corrupt?"

"We have reason to believe Chief Winson is connected to the weapons operation," Tucker confirmed. "And possibly implicated in covering up several murders related to it."

Reynolds' expression hardened. "I'll alert my teams to be cautious about any local law enforcement arriving on scene."

Suddenly, movement at the farmhouse caught Mallory's attention. The front door opened slightly, and someone waved a white cloth.

"They're trying to signal," she said, pointing.

The negotiator immediately responded: "Carl Parsons. Come out slowly with your hands in the air."

Instead of Parsons, a woman was shoved through the doorway, stumbling onto the porch, her hands bound in front of her, squinting in the harsh lights directed at the house. Even from a distance, Mallory was able to recognize Tanya Broadbent.

"That's her," Mallory confirmed to Reynolds. "That's Tanya."

"Hold your fire," Reynolds ordered over the radio. "Female hostage on the porch. Do not engage."

A male voice shouted from inside the house: "We want safe passage! A helicopter to the county airport, or she dies!"

"Standard procedure is not to negotiate transportation," Reynolds muttered, then raised the megaphone. "Release the hostage first, then we can discuss terms!"

Tanya stood frozen on the porch, shaking with fear. Then, something unexpected happened. She suddenly dropped to the ground and rolled off the porch into the shadows below, disappearing from the line of fire.

The move caught everyone by surprise, including her captors. Gunfire erupted from the house, spraying wildly in the direction she had fled.

"Covering fire!" Reynolds ordered. "Team Two, extract the hostage!"

Officers responded immediately, laying down suppressing fire while a tactical team rushed forward to retrieve Tanya. Mallory held her breath as the officers reached the area where Tanya had disappeared, then exhaled in relief as they emerged moments later, half-carrying the woman to safety behind the police line.

Tanya was quickly brought to the command post area, where paramedics rushed forward to attend to her. She was disheveled and had bruises on her face and wrists, but otherwise appeared unharmed. Her eyes widened when she saw Mallory and Tucker.

"You're the investigators," she said, her voice hoarse. "You're the reason they were freaking out in there."

"Are you okay?" Mallory asked, kneeling beside her as the paramedics checked her vitals.

"I'll live," Tanya replied grimly. "Better than they're going to."

"How many people are there in the house?" Reynolds asked, kneeling on her other side.

"Three now. Parsons, his son Mike, and a guy named Dunbar who works for them. They've got a stockpile of weapons in there. And they're expecting help."

"From who?" Tucker asked.

Tanya's expression darkened. "Winson. Parsons called him when the police showed up. Said to 'bring everyone' and 'take care of it like before.'"

Reynolds immediately dispatched officers to block the access roads and watch for approaching vehicles.

"What about Pastor Pearcy?" Mallory asked. "The men at the barn mentioned him."

"Pearcy?" Tanya laughed bitterly. "He's as dirty as they come. He's the connection to the buyers. He uses church mission trips as cover to make the arrangements."

"What happened to Terry Fisher? D'you know?" Mallory asked.

"He was involved somehow," she replied. "Exactly how, I don't know."

"So why did they kill him?" Mallory pressed her.

She just shook her head, but didn't reply.

The pieces were falling into place now. "And the others? Cory, Samuel, Malik, Freddy?" Mallory asked. "What about them?"

"Same thing," she replied. "Wrong place, wrong time. They all discovered something they shouldn't. Cory caught them moving guns through the church basement. Malik overheard Parsons and Pearcy talking about a shipment. They eliminate anyone who might expose them."

A fresh barrage of gunfire from the house interrupted their conversation. Reynolds pulled Mallory aside. "We need to move the hostage to safety, and you two as well. We're preparing to breach."

"Wait," Tanya protested, overhearing this. "There's something you need to know. There's evidence—documentation of their entire operation. That's what I found. That's why they grabbed me."

"Where is it?" Tucker asked urgently.

"Hidden at my house. Under the floorboards in my bedroom closet. Names, dates, photos—everything. I've been collecting it for years, ever since they killed Malik."

Reynolds dispatched officers to secure Tanya's residence and retrieve the evidence. Meanwhile, the tactical teams had completed their preparations for breaching the farmhouse.

"We need to clear the area," Reynolds insisted. "This is about to get very active."

Mallory and Tucker followed the officers escorting Tanya toward the medical staging area. As they walked, headlights appeared on the distant access road—multiple vehicles approaching rapidly.

"Incoming!" an officer shouted. "Multiple vehicles, no emergency lights!"

"That'll be Winson," Tucker said grimly, drawing his weapon despite his injured arm.

Reynolds immediately redirected officers to establish a new perimeter facing the approaching vehicles. Mallory, Tucker, and Tanya were hustled behind an armored tactical vehicle for protection as the newcomers arrived at the edge of the police line.

Five Duckwood police cruisers skidded to a stop, and several officers emerged from the first two, including Chief Winson. He approached with an air of authority, apparently unfazed by the state police presence.

"Captain Reynolds? Nate Winson, Duckwood PD. What's the situation here?" His tone was professional, betraying no awareness that his involvement was suspected.

Reynolds met him at the perimeter line. "We have an armed standoff," he replied. "Carl Parsons and two others are barricaded inside, refusing to surrender."

Winson nodded. "I've known Carl for years. Maybe I can talk him down."

"That won't be necessary, Chief," Reynolds replied evenly. "We have the situation under control. In fact, we've already rescued the hostage they were holding."

For the first time, Winson's composed façade cracked slightly. His eyes darted around, eventually landing on Tanya, who was just visible behind the tactical vehicle. Recognition and alarm flickered across his face before he masked it.

"Glad to hear it," he recovered smoothly. "My officers are at your disposal if you need assistance."

"Actually, Chief," Reynolds said, "I'd like you to come with me to discuss something that's come to light during this investigation."

Winson stiffened, his hand drifting subtly toward his sidearm. "What kind of information?"

"It concerns your involvement in an illegal weapons trafficking operation and the cover-up of multiple homicides."

Mallory watched the confrontation tensely, aware that it could go violently wrong in seconds. The Duckwood officers behind Winson looked confused, uncertain whether to follow their chief's lead or stand down.

For a long moment, Winson seemed to calculate his options, his eyes flicking between Reynolds, the state police officers around him, and his own men. Then, with a movement so quick it was almost a blur, he drew his weapon.

"Gun!" someone shouted.

Reynolds reacted instantly, tackling Winson before he could aim. State police officers swarmed forward, subduing the chief while others kept their weapons trained on the Duckwood officers, ordering them to raise their hands.

Most complied immediately, looking shocked at their chief's actions. One younger officer—Daniels, who had supervised their file review—actually stepped forward to help secure Winson, his expression a mixture of disillusionment and resolve.

"I knew something wasn't right," he said as Reynolds cuffed the struggling chief. "The way those murder cases were handled... it never made any sense."

With Winson secured, attention returned to the farmhouse. The distraction had given the tactical team time to move into final position. Reynolds rejoined them at the command post, leaving Winson in custody of several officers.

"We're ready to breach," the SWAT commander reported. "On your order, Captain."

Reynolds gave a short nod. "Execute."

The next moments unfolded with the controlled chaos of a tactical operation. Flash-bangs detonated at multiple points inside the farmhouse, followed by the crash of doors and windows being breached simultaneously. Officers poured into the building, shouted commands echoing in the night air.

Gunfire erupted again—a brief, but intense exchange—then silence.

Everyone at the command post waited tensely for the radio to crackle with news. When it finally came, the message was concise:

"Building secure. Two suspects in custody, one deceased. No other casualties."

Mallory exhaled a breath she hadn't realized she'd been holding. Beside her, Tucker's rigid posture relaxed slightly.

"It's over," she said quietly.

"This part is," he agreed. "But we still need to connect all the dots. Parsons, Winson, Pearcy, and any others involved."

"Pearcy," Tanya said suddenly from her seat nearby. "Has anyone gone to the church? He'll know something's wrong by now."

Reynolds overheard and immediately dispatched officers to locate and detain Pastor Henry Pearcy. But Mallory suspected the pastor was already long gone. Men like him, who maintained respectable facades while orchestrating violence, were usually the first to flee when the operation collapsed.

As the night progressed, the scene transformed from an active tactical situation to a massive crime scene as state evidence technicians arrived to process the farm and its outbuildings. The weapons crates Tucker had discovered earlier were documented and secured. Officers returning from Tanya's house confirmed they'd recovered a substantial cache of evidence hidden exactly where she said it would be.

Tanya herself was transported to the hospital for evaluation, along with two officers assigned to protect her. Before she left, Mallory approached her one last time.

"Thank you," she said simply. "For never giving up on finding the truth."

Tanya looked up at her with tired but determined eyes. "Malik deserved justice," she said. "So did Terry and the others. I couldn't let them get away with it."

"They won't," Mallory assured her. "Not anymore."

As dawn began to lighten the eastern sky, Mallory and Tucker finally allowed themselves to be transported to the hospital. Tucker's arm needed proper medical attention, and they both required treatment for exhaustion and minor injuries sustained during their escape.

In the back of the ambulance, Mallory leaned against Tucker's good shoulder, the adrenaline finally ebbing from her system.

"We did it," she murmured. "We solved five cold case murders in four days."

Tucker put his good arm around her shoulders. "And we exposed a weapons trafficking operation that had corrupted an entire town. Not bad for a couple of private investigators."

"Gary Fisher will finally have answers for his parents," Mallory said, thinking of the family that had waited eleven long years for justice.

"And maybe peace," Tucker added quietly.

As the ambulance wound its way toward the hospital, Mallory felt the weight of the case begin to lift. There would be statements to give, evidence to review, perhaps testimony at trials. But the central mystery—what had happened to Terry Fisher and why—was solved.

Five men had died because of a criminal operation hiding behind the respectable facades of Duckwood. Their killers had believed they could silence the truth forever. But they hadn't counted on the persistence of those left behind; a brother seeking justice and a woman collecting evidence for years.

17

TUCKER SAT ON THE EDGE OF HIS HOSPITAL BED, IMPATIENT TO LEAVE despite the doctor's advice to rest. The wound on his arm had required twelve stitches, and the doctor had warned him about the risk of infection. But there was still work to be done—loose ends to tie up in Duckwood before he could consider the case closed.

Mallory entered the room, tucking her phone away. "Gary Fisher's on his way to see his parents now. He said they've been watching the news coverage all morning."

"It's been on every channel," Tucker said, carefully pulling on his shirt, mindful of his bandaged arm.

"The raid on a gun running operation, the arrest of a small-town police chief, five murders solved, it's a big story." Mallory sat beside him. "It's over, Tucker."

"I'm not so sure," Tucker replied, buttoning his shirt one-handed. "We still have work to do."

"What d'you mean, you're not so sure?" she asked, frowning. "What work? Parsons is in custody, Winson too. The state police have the evidence from Tanya's house. We've given our statements."

"Pastor Pearcy is still unaccounted for," Tucker reminded her. "And

I want to talk to Louis Fisher again. His connection to Tanya still bothers me."

A knock at the door interrupted them. Captain Reynolds entered, looking tired but satisfied. "I thought I'd find you both here. Figured you'd want an update."

"We were just discussing the loose ends," Tucker said. "What's the latest?"

Reynolds leaned against the wall. "Parsons is talking, trying to get himself a deal. He's confirmed everything Tanya told us. The operation has been running for about fifteen years. They've been moving weapons through from the south to northeastern markets, using Duckwood as a transit hub because of its isolated location and Winson's protection."

"And the murders?" Mallory asked.

"All connected, just as you suspected. Terry Fisher was inducted into the operation by Pastor Pearcy. Apparently, he was a low man on the totem pole; one of the worker bees, if you like. His mistake was he wanted out. He wanted to get married, to start over. Well, they could have that. They couldn't trust him to keep his mouth shut, so they eliminated him."

Tucker nodded. "We figured it must have been something like that. It's a story as old as time. What about the others?"

"Absolutely," Reynolds confirmed. "Cory Robar worked the farm for Parsons occasionally. He stumbled onto something he shouldn't have seen in one of the outbuildings. Malik Williams overheard a conversation between Parsons and Winson. Samuel Jenkins was a county inspector who got suspicious about activity at the farm and began poking around. They caught him nosing around the outbuildings one night. Freddy Paul was actually part of the operation but was skimming profits."

"Has Pearcy been found yet?" Mallory asked.

Reynolds shook his head. "Not yet, but we have officers at the church and his residence, but, as yet, there's no sign of him. We've issued a BOLO and alerted border patrol in case he tries to leave the country."

"And Louis Fisher?" Tucker prompted. "He was friendly with Tanya, according to the waitress at the café. Did Parsons mention him? Was he involved?"

"Not that I know of," Reynolds said, looking curious. "You think he's connected?"

"I don't know," Tucker admitted. "But he married Terry's fiancée shortly after the murder, and he lied to us about his relationship with Tanya. Those aren't necessarily criminal acts, but they're an anomaly and worth looking into."

"I've got officers going through Tanya's evidence now. If Louis Fisher is involved, there might be something there." Reynolds checked his watch. "Speaking of Tanya, she's being released today. She's agreed to enter witness protection until after the trials."

"She'll need it," Mallory observed. "Pearcy is still out there, and an operation this size probably has connections beyond Duckwood."

"That's exactly why I've got a protective detail with her," Reynolds confirmed. "Now, about you two…" he paused for a moment, then continued, "my department owes you a debt of gratitude. This case might never have been solved, or even come to light, without your persistence."

Tucker shrugged, uncomfortable with praise. "We were just doing our job."

"Still, it's impressive work. I've spoken with your former colleagues at the FBI, by the way. They remember you well."

Tucker tensed slightly. "You contacted the Bureau?"

"Standard procedure with weapons trafficking cases this size. They're sending agents to coordinate the broader investigation, follow the supply chain, identify buyers. Agent Lewis sends his regards, by the way."

Tucker bit his lip. David Lewis, his former supervisor, the man whose bad call had resulted in Marsha Cline's death, the incident that had prompted Tucker's resignation from the FBI.

"Tucker?" Mallory asked, noticing his reaction.

"I'm good," he said, his tone clipped. "When are the FBI agents arriving?"

"They're already here," Reynolds replied, studying Tucker with interest. "Is there something I should know?"

"No," Tucker said firmly. "Ancient history. Water under the bridge. Is there anything else we can help with?"

Reynolds seemed to sense the change in mood. "Not at the moment. Your statements have been processed. You're free to leave when the doctor clears you."

"The doctor already has," Tucker lied smoothly. "We were just about to leave."

After Reynolds left, Mallory turned to him. "Lewis," she said. "It's been a while since we last saw him."

"Not long enough," Tucker said.

"I thought you two had made up," she said.

"We did, sort of, but..." he paused, staring at the floor, then looked up and said, "Let's focus on what's in front of us. I want to talk to Louis Fisher before we leave town."

"Are you sure that's a good idea? You're injured, and if Louis is involved—"

"If he's involved, we need to know," Tucker interrupted. "And I doubt he'd try anything with the town swarming with state police and FBI."

Mallory didn't look convinced, but she knew better than to argue when Tucker used that tone. "Fine. But we go together, and we keep Reynolds informed of our movements."

They checked out of the hospital and retrieved their SUV, which had been towed to a local garage and hastily repaired after the highway confrontation. The damage was still visible—a cracked windshield, dented rear bumper, and bullet holes in the driver's side door—but it was drivable.

Duckwood looked different in the harsh light of day, its picturesque small-town facade now seeming like a thin veneer over deeper corruption. Police vehicles were stationed throughout the town, and news vans clustered near the municipal building. Locals gathered in small groups, talking in hushed tones about the shocking revelations.

They drove to the hardware store first, but were told Louis Fisher hadn't shown up for work. That in itself was unusual, according to his boss. Louis had never missed a day without calling in.

"Let's try his house," Tucker suggested. "If he's involved, he might be planning to run."

As they approached the Fisher residence, Tucker noticed something wrong immediately. The front door stood partially open, and there was no sign of the family SUV in the driveway.

"Stay behind me," he instructed Mallory, drawing his weapon despite his injured arm. They approached cautiously, Tucker leading the way to the open door.

"Mr. Fisher?" he called out. "Louis Fisher? It's Tucker Randall and Mallory Carver."

No response.

Tucker pushed the door open wider with his foot, revealing a scene of hasty departure. Drawers hung open, contents half-emptied. A suitcase lay on the living room floor, partially packed with children's clothing.

"They left in a hurry," Mallory observed, checking the kitchen. "Recently, too. The coffee pot is still warm."

Tucker moved deeper into the house, checking rooms systematically. The master bedroom also showed signs of rapid packing—closet doors open, dresser drawers pulled out.

"Tucker," Mallory called from another room. "You need to see this."

He found her in what appeared to be a home office, kneeling beside a small safe that had been left open and emptied. Papers were scattered across the floor, and the desk drawers had been ransacked.

"Someone left in a panic," Tucker observed, scanning the room. "Question is, was it Louis or someone else?"

Mallory held up a document. "It's a deed to property in Mexico. Purchased six months ago in the name of Louis and Tiffany Fisher."

"An escape plan," Tucker said grimly. "Or at least a contingency. But... why would he have left the deed? That makes no sense."

"Maybe it wasn't him," Mallory said. "I mean, it looks to me like someone was looking for something. Maybe Louis disturbed them"

"Anything's possible," I suppose," Tucker said as he moved to the desk, examining the papers strewn across it. Most were ordinary household documents—bills, insurance papers, tax forms. But underneath a scattered pile, he found something more interesting, a photograph of Louis Fisher with Pastor Henry Pearcy, both men in hunting gear, standing over a dead deer. They were smiling broadly, arms around each other's shoulders.

"It appears Louis and Pearcy were friends," he said, holding up the photo for her to see.

She nodded, "They're certainly closer than Louis let on," she replied. "He said Pearcy was just their pastor and performed their wedding. Maybe they're just hunting buddies. she suggested. "That photo doesn't prove criminal involvement."

"No, but it's another connection." Tucker continued searching, finding a bank statement showing regular monthly deposits of $5,000 in cash, far more than a hardware store employee could legitimately earn.

Tucker shook his head. "I think this proves he was involved in something," he said. "I mean, it makes sense that if his cousin Terry was involved, then it's likely he was involved, too."

Mallory didn't answer.

They searched the rest of the house, finding more evidence of a hasty departure, but nothing directly linking Louis to the gunrunning operation. When they returned to the living room, Mallory paused by a family photo on the wall.

"What about Tiffany?" she asked. "Do you think she knew?"

"Hard to say," Tucker replied. "She seemed genuinely distraught about Terry's death, but that doesn't mean she didn't know what Louis was involved in later."

A car pulled into the driveway, and Tucker moved quickly to a window, peering out cautiously. "It's the state police," he said, recognizing Captain Reynolds stepping out of an unmarked vehicle.

Reynolds approached the house, his expression grim. "Thought I might find you here. You should have told me you were visiting a potential suspect."

"We were just following a lead," Tucker explained. "The house was open when we arrived. Looks like the family left in a hurry."

Reynolds surveyed the scene. "We've got a situation developing. Pastor Pearcy has been spotted at a storage facility on the edge of town. Officers attempted to approach him, but he fled inside a unit. He's believed to be armed."

"Is a tactical team on the way?" Tucker asked.

"En route, but it'll take time. The facility is being evacuated now." Reynolds hesitated. "There's more. We found evidence in Tanya's documents that Louis Fisher was not just connected to the gunrunning operation; he was Pearcy's right-hand man. He managed the finances, laundering the money through various off-shore accounts and shell companies."

"Including the hardware store?" Mallory asked.

Reynolds nodded. "And his wife's interior design business. It explains how a hardware store clerk and a part-time designer could afford this house."

"Do you have any idea where they might have gone?" Tucker asked.

Reynolds shook his head. "Nope, but we've put out alerts at airports, bus terminals, and border crossings. But they had at least a few hours' head start." Reynolds glanced around the house again. "Find anything useful here?"

Tucker handed him the property deed and bank statements. "Looks like they may be heading to Mexico. They own property there."

Reynolds nodded. "I'll have our people look into it. Meanwhile, I need to get to that storage facility. According to the officers who spotted him, Pearcy's becoming increasingly unstable. He was talking to himself, behaving erratically."

"We'll come with you," Tucker said immediately.

"With all due respect, you're injured, and this is now a law enforcement operation," Reynolds countered. "You've done more than enough already."

"Captain," Mallory interjected, "we've been investigating these people for days. We might see something your officers would miss. And if Pearcy is unstable, having familiar faces around might help de-escalate the situation."

Reynolds considered this. "You can observe from a safe distance. But I want your word you won't engage unless explicitly authorized."

"Agreed," Tucker said, though he had no intention of standing by if the situation turned dangerous. "Let's go."

18

They followed Reynolds to the storage facility—a modern complex of ten single-story buildings, each divided into thirty individual units with roll-up doors. A perimeter had already been established, with officers positioned behind vehicles and concrete barriers. The facility manager had provided a diagram showing that Pastor Pearcy was holed up in unit 60, a large corner unit with no windows or alternate exits.

"What's his mental state?" Tucker asked as they joined the command post behind a police SUV.

"Deteriorating," an officer replied, handing Reynolds a radio. "He's been shouting biblical references, claiming he's being persecuted. He says he won't be taken alive."

"Has he made any specific threats?" Mallory asked.

"Nothing beyond refusing to surrender. But the manager confirms he rented the unit six years ago and visits regularly. No one knows what's inside."

"Given what we've learned about the operation, it could be weapons," Reynolds speculated. "Maybe documentation they couldn't risk keeping at the church. A negotiator has been trying to establish communication, but Pearcy's not responding consistently. Now and then, he can be heard reciting scripture or making ominous declarations about judgment day, but so far, he's refused to engage in an actual dialogue."

"SWAT team is ten minutes out," an officer reported. "And FBI agents are also en route."

Tucker tensed at the mention of the FBI, wondering if Lewis would be among them. It was true. They'd put the past behind them more than a year ago, but he'd still not gotten over Marsha Cline's untimely death. *But, it is what it is;* he thought.

"Let me try talking to him," he suggested to Reynolds. "I've interviewed him before. He might respond to a familiar voice."

Reynolds looked skeptical. "He knows you're investigating him. That might make him more volatile, not less."

"True, but he also knows me as someone who listened to him, who treated him with respect. Right now, he's surrounded by anonymous officers with guns. A known face might help."

After considering the options, Reynolds reluctantly agreed. "You can use the bullhorn, but stay behind cover. If he becomes more agitated, we pull back immediately."

Tucker positioned himself behind a concrete barrier, where he could see the door to unit 60 but remain protected. Through the bullhorn, he called out: "Pastor Pearcy. It's Tucker Randall. We spoke at your church yesterday, remember? I'd like to talk to you. Can we do that?"

For a long moment, there was silence. Then the door rattled slightly, and Pearcy's voice came through, strained and higher-pitched than Tucker remembered.

"Mr. Randall? Have you come to witness the final reckoning?"

"No, sir! I've come to talk," Tucker replied evenly. "To understand."

"Understanding comes too late," Pearcy responded, his voice taking on a preacher's cadence. "The wages of sin is death, but the gift of God is eternal life through Jesus Christ our Lord. Romans 6:23."

Tucker glanced at Mallory, who had moved to his side despite his gesture to stay back. "He's quoting scripture about consequences and redemption," she whispered. "Maybe appeal to that?"

"Pastor," Tucker called, "whatever has happened in the past, there's still a chance for truth. For redemption."

A harsh laugh echoed from the storage unit. "Truth? The truth is that I did God's work! Those men were sinners, obstacles to a greater purpose. The weapons we moved saved Christian lives in regions where believers are persecuted. The end justified the means!"

Tucker motioned for Mallory to take notes. Pearcy was confessing, and they needed to document it. "Five men died, Pastor. Terry, Cory, Samuel, Malik, Freddy. How was killing them God's work?"

"They were going to destroy everything! Years of mission work, millions in funding for our brothers and sisters abroad." Pearcy's voice grew more agitated. "Terry was the first. He wanted to leave. He would have gone to the authorities. He didn't understand the greater good!"

"And the others?" Tucker prompted, keeping his tone conversational, non-judgmental.

"All the same!" he replied. "They all transgressed. I tried to guide them, to make them understand, but they were blind!"

Reynolds had moved closer, listening intently. "Keep him talking," he whispered. "SWAT's two minutes out."

"Pastor," Tucker continued, "were you alone in this work, or did others help you?"

"There are many servants in the Lord's vineyard," Pearcy replied cryptically. "Winson protected our mission. Parsons provided the means. Louis managed our finances. We were all serving a higher purpose!"

"And Tiffany?" Mallory suddenly called out, ignoring Tucker's warning glance. "Did she know what happened to Terry? That her new husband helped kill her fiancé?"

The question hung in the air for a long, tense moment. Then Pearcy let out a sound that was half laugh, half sob.

"Poor Tiffany. She never knew. Louis made sure of that. She was his prize for faithful service. I blessed their union, though it was built on blood."

Tucker shot Mallory a look—both impressed by her insight and concerned about provoking Pearcy further. But the pastor continued unprompted, his voice growing more unhinged.

"It's all falling apart now. The temple veil is torn asunder. But they won't take me. I've long prepared for this day."

The hairs on the back of Tucker's neck stood up at those words. He turned to Reynolds. "He's going to blow it up. We need to pull back. Now."

But before they could move, a gunshot echoed from inside the storage unit, followed by silence.

"Pastor Pearcy?" Tucker called. No response.

Reynolds motioned for officers to approach cautiously. "Pastor Pearcy, this is the State Police. We're coming in."

Still no response.

The tactical team, which had just arrived, moved into position. On Reynolds' signal, they breached the door of unit 60, rushing inside with weapons raised.

Moments later, an officer emerged and signaled the all-clear. "He's down. Self-inflicted gunshot wound."

Tucker felt a complex mix of emotions: relief that no officers had been harmed, frustration at the loss of a key witness, and a grim satisfaction that Pearcy had at least confessed before taking his own life.

Reynolds approached, his expression somber. "You got him to confess on record. That will help with prosecuting the others."

"What's in the storage unit?" Mallory asked.

"Documents. Lots of them. Financial records, shipping manifests, photographs. And weapons—enough for a small army. This place was essentially their archive and emergency cache."

As crime scene technicians arrived to process the scene, Tucker and Mallory stepped back, watching the activity from a distance.

"It's really over," Mallory said quietly. "Parsons, Winson, and Pearcy are all accounted for. Louis and Tiffany will be found eventually."

Tucker nodded, but his expression remained troubled. "There's still something I want to understand. Why did Tanya date both Terry and Malik? Was it just coincidence, or was she somehow involved?"

"We can ask her," Mallory suggested. "She's still at the hospital."

But before they could leave, a black SUV pulled up, and three people in suits emerged. Tucker recognized one of them immediately; David Lewis, his former FBI supervisor, looking older but still carrying himself with the same officious authority that had grated on Tucker all those years ago.

"Tucker. Mallory," Lewis said, approaching with an extended hand. "It's been a while, but it's good to see you both again. It's not something I expected, and definitely not on a case like this."

Tucker shook his hand briefly, his expression neutral. "Agent Lewis. You're heading the Bureau's involvement?"

"Coordinating with state and local authorities, yes." Lewis glanced at the storage facility. "I understand the pastor took the easy way out."

"After confessing to orchestrating five murders," Tucker replied evenly.

Lewis nodded. "Good work on that. The Bureau's been tracking weapons movements through this corridor for years, but we never connected it to Duckwood. Sometimes it takes local knowledge to break these cases."

There was something in the way he said it, a hint of condescension that he regarded Tucker's career change from FBI agent to private investigator as a step down.

"It's good to see you, too, David, but…" he glanced at Mallory, then continued, "We should be going. We still have loose ends to tie up."

"Actually," Lewis said, "I'd appreciate it if you'd stick around. Your insights could be valuable to our investigation, especially given your history with this case."

Tucker caught the subtle emphasis on the word "history." Was it a subtle reminder of the Marsha Cline case, of Tucker's resignation, of the bad blood between them?

"We've provided statements to Captain Reynolds," Tucker replied. "Everything we know is in the reports."

David smiled thinly. "Of course. Well, if you remember anything else, you know how to reach me."

As they walked to their SUV, Mallory glanced back at Lewis. "He seems nice enough," she said. "A bit of an improvement since the last time we saw him."

Tucker nodded once, his jaw tight. "He'll never change. Let's go see Tanya. I want to wrap this up and get back to Chattanooga."

They drove to the hospital in silence, Tucker lost in memories he'd rather forget, Mallory respecting his need for space. The case was essentially solved, the conspiracy exposed, but personal ghosts were harder to lay to rest than the cold case murders.

19

MALLORY WATCHED TUCKER AS THEY MADE THEIR WAY THROUGH THE hospital corridors toward Tanya Broadbent's room. His encounter with former FBI supervisor David Lewis had left him tense, his jaw set in the way she recognized as his defense mechanism against unwelcome emotions. She knew better than to press him about it, and that Tucker would talk when he was ready to, or more likely, he wouldn't talk about it at all.

Two state police officers stood outside Tanya's room, confirming Reynolds' promise of protection. They nodded at Tucker and Mallory, recognizing them from the events at the Parsons farm.

"Ms. Broadbent's awake," one of the officers informed them. "Captain Reynolds said you might be stopping by. You can go on in."

"Thanks," Tucker said with a nod of his head, then grabbed the door handle, pushed the door open, and stepped inside.

Tanya was sitting up in bed, looking much better than when they'd last seen her being rushed away from the farmhouse. The bruises on her face had darkened, but her eyes were clear and alert. She was wearing a hospital gown and had an IV in one arm, but otherwise appeared ready to leave.

"Hah! The investigators," she said by way of greeting. "I was wondering if you'd come back."

"We have a few more questions," Tucker replied, pulling up a chair. "If you're feeling up to it."

Tanya gestured to the TV mounted on the wall, which was showing news coverage of the raid on the Parsons farm. "I've been watching. Quite the show you two kicked off."

"It hardly begins to cover it," Mallory said, taking the other chair. "Tanya, we need to understand your role in all this. Specifically, your relationships with Terry Fisher and Malik Williams."

Tanya's expression sobered. "I wondered when you'd ask about that." She sighed, adjusting her position in the bed. "I dated Terry briefly in high school. Nothing serious, just teenage stuff. We stayed friends afterward, even when he got together with Tiffany."

"And Malik?" Tucker prompted.

"That was years later. I'd been away from Duckwood for a while, living in Memphis, trying to escape this place." A shadow crossed her face. "Malik was from here, but I met him there. We dated for about a year before he got a job offer back here in Duckwood. I came back with him, thinking maybe the town had changed."

"But it hadn't," Mallory guessed.

"No. It was the same old Duckwood, just with different paint." Tanya ran a hand through her tangled hair. "Malik was working construction. Good money, steady work. Then one day, he overheard Parsons and the pastor talking about a shipment. He didn't know what it meant at first, but he mentioned it to me."

"And you recognized it as suspicious because of what happened to Terry," Tucker said, watching her closely.

Tanya nodded. "Terry had told me things, back when we were friends. Not much, really. Just that he'd gotten himself into a mess and wanted out, and that he was going to talk to Pastor Pearcy about it."

"But instead, Pearcy turned him over to Parsons," Mallory said.

"I sort of figured that out later, after Terry was killed. But from what I've learned since, I think it was Pearcy that killed him, not Parsons. At the time, it just seemed like a random tragedy. But when

Malik mentioned the conversation he'd overheard..." Tanya's voice tightened. "I warned him to keep his mouth shut. I was afraid. But Malik was a righteous man. He thought he should report it to the police."

"To Winson," Tucker said.

"Yes. And he did, and three days later, Malik was dead. Same as Terry—two shots to the back of the head." Tanya's eyes glistened with tears she refused to let fall. "That's when I knew for sure. They were killing anyone who threatened to expose them."

"So you started collecting evidence," Mallory said.

Tanya nodded. "I did! Carefully. Slowly. I knew if they suspected me, I'd be next. So I got a job at the café. It was a good place to overhear things. I pretended to be a burnout that nobody needed to worry about."

"And Louis Fisher?" Tucker asked. "The waitress said you two were friendly."

A brittle laugh escaped Tanya. "Louis thought he was recruiting me. After Malik died, Louis approached me, acting sympathetic. Said he could get me 'work' if I needed money. Small jobs at first delivering packages, picking up cash. I played along, documenting everything."

"You were building a case," Mallory said, impressed by Tanya's courage and persistence.

"I was getting justice for Malik. And Terry. And the others." Tanya's expression hardened. "For a while, Louis thought I was just another useful idiot. Then he started trusting me with more information, thinking I was fully on board."

"How deeply was Louis involved?" Tucker asked.

"He was essential," Tanya replied without hesitation. "He was the money man. Parsons and Pearcy handled the hardware operations and connections, but Louis managed the finances. He set up shell companies, laundered the profits through legitimate businesses. He was good with numbers, and nobody suspected the quiet guy at the hardware store."

"And Tiffany?" Mallory asked, remembering Pearcy's words at the storage unit. "Did she know?"

Tanya shook her head. "I don't think she did. I think Louis kept her in the dark. She was his respectability, his cover, the grieving fiancée who found comfort with her dead boyfriend's cousin. Who would question that story?"

Mallory exchanged a glance with Tucker. They'd both wondered about Tiffany's involvement, given her quick relationship with Louis after Terry's murder.

"What was in the evidence you collected?" Tucker inquired. "Reynolds mentioned documents, but he wasn't specific."

"Everything," Tanya said with a hint of pride. "Photos of meetings between Parsons, Pearcy, and the buyers. Financial records Louis didn't know I'd photographed. Names, dates, locations of shipments. Recordings of conversations for years I'd gathered bit by bit."

"That was a dangerous game you were playing," Mallory observed. "What made you decide to use it now?"

Tanya's expression darkened. "I overheard Parsons and Pearcy discussing a major expansion. They were bringing in partners from out of state, planning to increase shipments through Duckwood. More guns, more money… and inevitably, more deaths to keep it quiet. I couldn't let that happen."

"So you were going to expose them?" Tucker asked.

"I'd arranged to meet a journalist from Nashville on Tuesday," Tanya confirmed. "But they found out somehow. Monday night, after my shift at the café, Parsons and his son were waiting at my house."

She described her captivity briefly, how they'd questioned her about the evidence, moved her from location to location as they searched her home, and finally brought her to the shed when Tucker and Mallory appeared and the state police began closing in.

"So, what happens now?" she asked when she'd finished. "Reynolds mentioned witness protection."

"It's the safest option," Tucker said. "The operation may have been centered in Duckwood, but there are likely connections to larger criminal organizations. People who might want to silence you."

"Plus, Louis and Tiffany are still out there," Mallory added. "They fled before the raid."

Tanya nodded, “I’m not surprised,” she said. “Louis always had contingency plans. He called it his ‘insurance policy.’ I think he bought some property somewhere, and I know he had cash reserves.”

“He has property in Mexico,” Tucker said. “We found a deed at their house.”

“That makes sense. Louis spoke Spanish, and he had connections south of the border; his weapons source.” Tanya sighed. “So I just… disappear then? New name, new life, all that stuff you see on TV?”

“Until the trials are over, at least,” Mallory said gently. “It’s the only way to ensure your safety.”

A knock at the door interrupted them. A nurse entered, followed by a state police officer Mallory didn’t recognize.

“Ms. Broadbent needs rest,” the nurse announced firmly. “And her transport team has arrived.”

The officer nodded to Tucker and Mallory. “We’re moving her to a secure location for witness protection processing. Captain Reynolds sent me to let you know.”

Tucker nodded, then turned away and called Reynolds. “I have an officer here— Okay. That’s all I wanted to know.” He ended the call, turned to Mallory and Tanya and nodded. She officer smiled knowingly at him.

They stood to leave, but Tanya reached out, catching Mallory’s hand. “Thank you,” she said quietly. “For believing me. For stopping them.”

“You did most of the work,” Mallory replied with a smile. “We just helped finish it.”

Outside in the corridor, Tucker checked his watch. “It’s getting late. We should head back to the hotel, pack up, and leave for Chattanooga in the morning.”

Mallory nodded, suddenly realizing how exhausted she was. The adrenaline of the past few days was wearing off, leaving her drained. “Food first? I’m starving.”

They found a quiet diner away from the center of Duckwood, where they’d be less likely to encounter curious locals or news reporters. Over burgers and fries, they discussed what they'd learned from Tanya, filling in the final pieces of the conspiracy.

"It's impressive," Mallory said, stirring her milkshake with a straw. "What Tanya accomplished. Working alone for years, gathering evidence, risking her life."

"She was driven by personal loss," Tucker observed. "Sometimes that's the most powerful motivation."

"Like Gary Fisher," Mallory agreed. "Eleven years, and he never gave up on finding justice for his brother."

Tucker nodded, his expression distant. "I should call him, let him know what we've learned about Terry's murder. The official investigation will take time to process all the evidence."

"I'm sure he's been following the news coverage," Mallory said. "But yes, he deserves to hear it from us directly."

As they finished their meal, Mallory's phone rang. It was Jen, calling for the third time that day. With a grimace, Mallory answered.

"Before you ask, yes, I'm alive," she said.

"I can see that on the news!" Jen's voice was a mixture of relief and exasperation. "You and Tucker are all over every channel! 'Private investigators crack decade-old murder conspiracy.' Mom and Dad have been calling non-stop."

"Sorry," Mallory said, genuinely contrite. "Things happened quickly. We uncovered a gun running operation, and—"

"I know! It's all the reporters are talking about." Jen's tone softened. "Are you okay? I mean really okay?"

"We're fine. Tucker got a minor gunshot wound, but—"

"A gunshot wound? Oh…m'God!" Jen's voice rose sharply.

"It's just a graze," Mallory assured her, catching Tucker's amused glance across the table. "Just a few stitches. He's already out of the hospital. We're heading back to Chattanooga tomorrow."

"Thank God. Does that mean you'll make the dress appointment?"

Mallory had completely forgotten about the wedding plans amid the chaos of the past few days. "Yes, I'll be there. Promise."

After ending the call, she found Tucker watching her with a faint smile. "Wedding planning calls? Even after solving five murders and exposing a weapons trafficking ring?"

"Some things wait for nothing," Mallory replied with a rueful laugh. "Not even near-death experiences."

Back at the hotel, they found a note from Captain Reynolds slipped under their door, updating them on the investigation's progress. The evidence from Pearcy's storage unit had yielded a wealth of information, confirming much of what Tanya had told them. Louis and Tiffany Fisher were still at large, but border patrol had been alerted, and their financial accounts frozen, those they could find.

Tucker made a brief call to Gary Fisher, providing a simplified version of what they'd discovered. From Mallory's side of the conversation, she could tell Gary was emotional but grateful for finally having answers he and his parents needed.

As Tucker hung up, Mallory felt a familiar sense of closure that came with completing a troublesome case. Justice had been served, to the extent it could be for victims long dead. Conspirators had been exposed, an illegal operation dismantled.

"I think we did good, Tucker," she said, sitting on the edge of her bed.

Tucker nodded, checking the bandage on his arm. "And a dangerous operation has been shut down. Who knows how many lives that might save down the line."

"What do you think will happen to Winson and Parsons?" Mallory asked.

"Federal weapons charges, five counts of conspiracy to commit murder, obstruction of justice…" Tucker shrugged. "They'll never see the outside of a prison again."

"And Louis and Tiffany?"

"They'll be found, eventually. People on the run make mistakes, especially with children in tow."

Mallory nodded, considering this. "It's hard to believe Louis was involved in his own cousin's murder. That's… That's family betrayal at its worst."

"According to Pearcy, Louis didn't directly participate in Terry's murder," Tucker pointed out. "But he certainly benefited from it. He got Terry's fiancée, a position in the organization. And he helped cover it up for years. Say what you want. Louis Fisher is a badass."

"And all the while playing the supportive cousin who stepped in to help the grieving Tiffany." Mallory shook her head in disgust. "Some people can compartmentalize anything."

Tucker was quiet for a moment, his expression distant. "We all have our compartments, Mal. Ways of separating and hiding the parts of ourselves we don't want to face."

Mallory recognized this was as close as Tucker would come to discussing his reaction to seeing David Lewis again, so she decided on a gentle approach. "Tucker, I thought you two made up before he left after we closed out Vinny's case last year."

"We did," Tucker said, "but you know, there are some things you just can't easily dismiss. What he did is one of them, The Marsha Cline case… it's one of those things. She was only nineteen. It should never have happened. David never did take responsibility for it."

"So that's it?" she asked. "You're never going to be able to put it behind you?"

Tucker shrugged, then winced as pain shot through his injured arm. "One day, perhaps. In the meantime, I'll get along with him when I have to. Other than that…" he trailed off.

He fell silent, the memory clearly still painful despite the years that had passed since Marsha's death. Mallory didn't press him further.

"It wasn't your fault, Tucker," she said simply.

"I know that," Tucker replied. "But knowing something and feeling it are two entirely different things."

They lapsed into silence, Mallory respecting Tucker's need for space after sharing even that small piece of his past. Eventually, she stood and gathered her toiletries. "I'm going to shower. Early start tomorrow?"

Tucker nodded, seemingly grateful for the change of subject. "Yep!" he said, brightly. "Six o'clock. I want to write and deliver our final report for Gary Fisher before we start back to Chattanooga. I'd like to be on the road by eleven. That should get us back in time for lunch. I have a hankering for some decent Mexican."

In the shower, Mallory let the hot water wash away some of the tension and fatigue of the past few days. Her thoughts drifted to the dress appointment, to the wedding plans that had been put on hold during this investigation. The juxtaposition seemed almost surreal. Planning a celebration of life and partnership while dealing with murder and betrayal.

Yet perhaps it was fitting. Their work as investigators was all about seeking justice, restoring order from chaos. Marriage was another kind of order, a commitment to building something positive together despite the darkness they often encountered in their profession.

"Room for one more?" Tucker asked.

"Always," she said and stepped to one side to make room for him.

When she finally emerged from the bathroom, Tucker was sitting on his bed, a towel wrapped around his waist, making notes in his precise handwriting. Always documenting, always ensuring the details were preserved accurately. It was one of the many things she admired about him: his thoroughness, his dedication to getting things right.

"What are you thinking about?" he asked, noticing her thoughtful expression.

"Life. Death. Wedding dresses, moments together in the shower." Mallory smiled. "The usual post-case existential pondering."

Tucker's expression softened slightly. "That dress appointment is important to you and Jen, isn't it? You should definitely make it."

"I will." She sat across from him on her own bed. "And you should definitely have an opinion on what kind of cake we serve. That's your one wedding planning assignment."

"I can handle cake decisions," he agreed with a rare smile. "As long as it's not during an active murder investigation."

"Deal." Mallory yawned, the exhaustion finally catching up with her. "I think I'm going to crash now. Wake me when it's time to leave?"

"Don't I always?" Tucker replied, returning to his notes.

As Mallory drifted toward sleep, images from the past few days flashed through her mind: Terry Fisher's autopsy photos, Tanya's determined face as she escaped her captors, Pastor Pearcy's storage unit filled with weapons and secrets, the fear in Winson's eyes as he realized his crimes had been exposed.

But these were gradually replaced by more pleasant thoughts: Tucker's steady presence throughout the investigation, the satisfaction of bringing closure, the wedding plans waiting for her in Chattanooga, and the beautiful, gentle moment in the shower. And finally, life continuing, as it always did, even after confronting the darkest aspects of human nature.

Tomorrow they would return home, file their reports, and close this chapter. But tonight, she would rest, knowing they had done what they set out to do: uncover the truth about Terry Fisher's murder. She smiled to herself as she drifted away. *And a whole... lot...... more...*

It was at that moment Tucker's phone buzzed, showing an unfamiliar number with a Washington, D.C. area code.

20

"TUCKER RANDALL," HE ANSWERED CAUTIOUSLY.

"Agent Randall. Or should I say, Mr. Randall now?"

Tucker stiffened, recognizing the voice immediately. "Director Hargrove. It's been a while."

FBI Director Alan Hargrove had been Tucker's ultimate superior during his Bureau days, a man he'd respected but rarely interacted with directly.

"Indeed it has. I've been following your work in Duckwood. It was an impressive investigation."

"Thank you, sir," Tucker replied automatically, years of Bureau protocol kicking in. "But I'm not sure why that would warrant a call from the Director."

"Let's just say I take a personal interest when former agents distinguish themselves, especially in cases involving weapons trafficking across state lines." Hargrove's tone remained pleasant, but carried an underlying significance. "Agent Lewis speaks highly of your work."

Tucker nearly scoffed at that. To his knowledge, Lewis had never spoken highly of him, not even before the Marsha Cline incident. "That's... surprising to hear," he said.

"People change, Randall. Perspectives shift with time." Hargrove paused. "The Bureau is establishing a new task force focused on domestic weapons trafficking. We need experienced people who understand how these operations work. People who can think independently, who aren't afraid to pursue uncomfortable truths."

The implication was clear, and Tucker felt a momentary vertigo, as if the past few years had suddenly collapsed, offering a return to the career path he'd abandoned. "Sir, I appreciate the implied offer, but I'm settled in Chattanooga now. My partner and I have built something here."

"Your fiancée, Ms. Carver, would be an asset to the Bureau as well. Her background and intuition would bring a valuable perspective."

Tucker glanced at Mallory, who was now awake and watching him with a mixture of curiosity and concern, clearly able to hear only his side of the conversation. "That's not a decision I can make unilaterally, sir."

"Of course not," Hargrove agreed. "Just something to consider. The official offer will come through proper channels if you're interested. Take some time, discuss it with Ms. Carver. The task force doesn't begin operations for another month."

After ending the call, Tucker set his phone down carefully, feeling Mallory's questioning gaze.

"The FBI Director?" she asked. "What did he want?"

Tucker summarized the conversation, watching her expression shift from surprise to thoughtfulness. "He's offering us both positions with a new task force, the focus being nationwide weapons trafficking."

"Us?" Mallory repeated. "Both of us? Me, an FBI agent. Come on, Tucker. The FBI doesn't work that way. It's you they want and they're using me as bait."

"I dunno," he replied. "Hargrove doesn't always follow standard protocols." He leaned back in his chair, processing the unexpected development. "It's a significant opportunity."

"But?" Mallory prompted, hearing the reservation in his voice.

"But it would mean returning to a system I deliberately left. Working under superiors like Lewis again, following directives I might not agree with." He met her gaze directly. "And it would probably mean relocating, postponing the wedding, starting over somewhere new."

Mallory considered this. "Would it be worth it? Going back to the Bureau?"

Tucker didn't answer immediately, genuinely uncertain. His departure from the FBI had been a principled stand, a rejection of a system that had prioritized expediency over safety in the Marsha Cline case. But he couldn't deny that the resources and reach of the Bureau far exceeded what they could accomplish as private investigators.

"I don't know," he admitted finally. "It's not a decision we need to make tonight. Or even this week."

"Agreed," Mallory said, standing and gathering her things. "Let's go home, get some rest, and tackle this with clear heads later."

He nodded. "Go back to sleep, Mal. We have an early start tomorrow."

As he watched Mallory close her eyes, he considered the life they'd built together in Chattanooga. Their partnership, both professional and personal, had brought him more satisfaction than his years with the Bureau. They worked well together, balanced each other's strengths and weaknesses, and most importantly, made their own decisions about which cases to take and how to pursue them.

Would returning to the FBI—even with Mallory alongside him—provide the same fulfillment? Or would the bureaucracy and chain of command eventually become as frustrating as before?

These were the questions that haunted Tucker as he lay down to sleep.

21

It was just after nine the following morning when Tucker loaded their bags into the SUV. The morning air was crisp, carrying the scent of dew-covered grass and distant wood smoke. The town looked peaceful, almost innocent, as if the events of the past few days had been a collective nightmare rather than reality.

He checked his bandaged arm, finding it stiff but manageable. The injury was minor compared to what could have happened if those bullets had found more vital targets. A few inches difference, and Mallory might be driving back to Chattanooga alone.

Speaking of Mallory, she emerged from the hotel with their last bag and a cardboard tray holding two large coffee cups. “Ready to leave this charming town behind?” she asked, handing him a coffee.

“More than ready,” Tucker replied, taking a grateful sip. “Though I doubt Duckwood will forget us anytime soon.”

That was an understatement. Their investigation had exposed corruption at the highest levels of local authority. The small town would be dealing with the aftermath for years to come.

The Fisher home looked different in daylight than it had during their first visit. The morning sun cast a warm glow over the modest house, and the front yard was quiet, the children presumably at school. Tucker pulled into the driveway. "Ready?" he asked Mallory as he tucked the folder containing their final report securely under his arm.

She nodded, staring out through the windshield, noting the subtle signs of a house where there was sickness: a wheelchair ramp recently added to the side entrance, curtains drawn in what was likely the master bedroom, a medical supply company's delivery notice still taped to the door.

They exited the car and walked up onto the front porch. Gary opened the door before they could knock, as if he'd been watching for their arrival. His expression was a mixture of anticipation and trepidation, the look of a man both eager and afraid to hear final confirmation of long-suspected truths.

"Mr. Randall, Ms. Carver. Please, come in. My parents are in the living room."

They followed him through the hallway into a living room transformed into a makeshift bedroom. Bill Fisher sat in a recliner, oxygen tubes in his nostrils, a blanket across his legs despite the warm day. Beside him in a comfortable chair, Margaret Fisher, thin and frail but with alert eyes that assessed the visitors carefully. The familial resemblance to Terry was visible in both parents: Bill's strong jawline, Margaret's expressive eyes.

"Mom, Dad, these are the investigators I told you about," Gary said, gently.

"Thank you for coming," Bill Fisher said, his voice surprisingly strong despite his obvious physical weakness. "After all these years," he said. "I'd nearly given up hope of knowing the truth."

Tucker approached, shaking the old man's hand gently. His grip was surprisingly strong.

"Mr. Fisher. Mrs. Fisher," he said. "This is my partner, Mallory Carver. We're glad we could provide some answers, sir. We've prepared a complete report of our findings."

He handed the folder to Bill, who took it with trembling hands, but made no move to open it.

"Why don't you tell us in your own words," Margaret suggested, her voice soft but steady. "The report will be there when we're ready."

Tucker nodded, taking a seat across from the elderly couple while Mallory sat nearby.

"Your son Terry was murdered because he wanted to do the right thing. He got in with some bad people, and he wanted out," Tucker said. "He wanted a clean start and to marry Tiffany, and it got him killed. He didn't know what he was getting into, and as soon as he did… Well, he talked to Pastor Pearcy, not realizing the pastor's involvement, and he unknowingly signed his own death warrant."

Bill's hand sought his wife's, gripping it tightly as Tucker continued explaining the conspiracy, how Pearcy, Parsons, Winson and eventually Louis Fisher had operated the gun running operation, using Duckwood's isolated location as a transit hub for illegal weapons. He explained how over the years following Terry's death, the other victims had each stumbled upon different aspects of the operation, and how they'd been systematically eliminated to protect the conspiracy.

"So it was our own pastor pulled the trigger?" Margaret asked, her voice breaking slightly. "The man who conducted Terry's funeral was the one who killed him?"

"Yes," Mallory confirmed gently. "He admitted it just before he killed himself. He killed all five victims personally."

"And Louis?" Gary asked, his expression hardened at the mention of his cousin. "Was he involved in Terry's death?"

"According to Pearcy's confession, Louis wasn't directly involved in planning or carrying out Terry's murder," Tucker explained. "But he learned about it afterward and he helped cover it up. Later, he became more deeply involved, managing the financial affairs of the operation."

"And he married Tiffany," Bill said, his voice tight with anger. "My brother's boy married my son's fiancée, knowing all along…"

"The evidence suggests Tiffany didn't know anything about it, that she was kept in the dark," Mallory interjected softly. "She appears to have been an unwitting part of Louis's cover. When the operation was exposed, he fled with her and their children. We heard just before we arrived here that they've since been apprehended trying to cross into Mexico."

A heavy silence fell over the room as the Fisher family absorbed these revelations. Gary stood by the window, his back partly turned as he processed the confirmation of his cousin's betrayal. Bill stared at the folder in his lap, one gnarled finger tracing Terry's name on the cover.

"I knew it had to be something like this," Margaret finally said. "Terry was a good boy. Not perfect, but good-hearted. He wouldn't have been mixed up in anything sordid. I'm so glad you found out he died because he was trying to do the right thing."

"All the evidence points to that conclusion," Tucker agreed.

Bill looked up, his eyes suddenly fierce despite his frail body. "Will they pay for what they did? All of them?"

"Parsons and Winson are in federal custody, facing federal weapons charges and multiple counts of conspiracy to commit murder," Tucker assured him. "Louis will be extradited back to Tennessee and will face similar charges. The evidence against them is overwhelming, particularly with Tanya Broadbent's documentation and Pearcy's confession."

"Tanya," Gary said, turning from the window. "She dated Terry briefly in high school, didn't she?"

Mallory nodded. "And latershe dated Malik Williams, another victim. After Malik's murder, she spent years gathering evidence against the conspiracy, putting herself at considerable risk. Her testimony and documentation will be crucial in the prosecutions."

"We owe her a debt," Bill said quietly. "Her and you two. Eleven years we've waited, wondering, imagining the worst."

"Knowing is better," Margaret added, reaching for the folder. "Even the painful truth is better than the endless uncertainty."

She opened the report, and she and Bill leaned together as they began to read the detailed account of their son's final days. Gary stepped closer to Tucker and Mallory, gesturing toward the kitchen.

"Let's give them some privacy," he suggested, leading the investigators to the adjoining room.

In the kitchen, Gary poured coffee into three mugs with mechanical precision, his movements suggesting a man on autopilot. "I should feel relief," he said finally. "After all this time, knowing what happened, why it happened."

"But?" Mallory prompted gently.

"But I don't. I just feel… hollow." Gary passed them the mugs. "All these years searching for the truth, and now that I have it, nothing's changed. Terry's still gone. My parents are still dying. Louis, who I grew up with, who I trusted, still betrayed our family in the worst possible way."

"Closure isn't the same as healing," Tucker observed quietly. "One is knowing what happened. The other is learning to live with that knowledge."

Gary nodded slowly. "That makes sense. I suppose the healing part comes next, now that we have the closure."

"Your parents seem like strong people," Mallory said. "And so do you. You didn't give up on finding justice for Terry, even when it would have been easier to let it go."

"I couldn't let it go," Gary admitted. "Not while my parents were still alive, still hoping for answers. Now at least they can…" His voice caught, and he took a moment to compose himself. "At least they can go with that burden lifted."

They spoke a while longer, Gary asking detailed questions about the investigation that hadn't been covered in their brief phone conversations. Tucker answered each query patiently, providing as much clarity as possible without being unnecessarily graphic about Terry's final moments.

When they returned to the living room, Bill had the report open in his lap, but his eyes were closed, oxygen hissing softly through his tubes. Margaret looked up as they entered.

"He got tired," she explained softly. "But he read enough. We both did." Her gaze shifted to Tucker and Mallory. "Thank you for not giving up on our boy. For making sure those responsible will face justice."

"It was our privilege," Mallory replied sincerely.

As they prepared to leave, Margaret reached for Mallory's hand. "Terry would have been about your age now. Maybe married, with children of his own." Her eyes glistened with unshed tears. "I hope you two have a long, happy life together. Not everyone gets that chance."

The comment caught Mallory off guard. They hadn't mentioned their engagement to the Fisher family. Margaret smiled at her surprise.

"I notice things," she said simply. "The way you work together, the ring on your finger. Life is precious. Don't waste a moment of it."

Tucker nodded, looked at Mallory and said, "Time to go, I think."

She nodded. They said their goodbyes and, with more than a little reluctance, they left the Fisher family to their thoughts.

22

As they pulled away from the Fisher home, Tucker drove slowly along the main street, noticing how empty it seemed compared to when they'd arrived. State police vehicles were still visible near the municipal building, and a few news vans remained parked nearby, but the usual morning bustle of a small town was notably absent.

"It's like a ghost town," Mallory observed, echoing his thoughts.

"People are staying home, processing what happened. Finding out your police chief and pastor were criminal conspirators isn't an everyday occurrence."

Mallory sighed. "This place will never be the same."

"Yes, it will," Tucker said as he steered the SUV toward the highway that would take them back to Chattanooga. "Time is a great healer. They'll get over it."

They fell into a comfortable silence as they left Duckwood behind, both lost in their own thoughts. Tucker reviewed the case mentally, a habit from his FBI days, analyzing what they'd done right, what they could have done better, what lessons they could apply to future investigations.

They'd accomplished their primary objective: discovering who killed Terry Fisher and why and, in the process, they'd uncovered a conspiracy far larger than they'd initially suspected and provided closure for four other families as well.

"You know, I've been thinking about Detective Bradley," Mallory said suddenly, interrupting his thoughts. "How he tried to investigate the gun running angle eleven years ago and was shut down. I hope he finds some peace knowing he was right all along."

"We should visit him again before we leave the area," Tucker suggested. "Let him know how it all turned out. It shouldn't take bet ten minutes, or so."

Mallory checked her watch. "The nursing home should be open for visitors by the time we get there. It's on our way back to Chattanooga, anyway."

Tucker adjusted their route, taking the exit that would lead them to the Golden Years Retirement Home. Thirty minutes later, they pulled into the facility's parking lot, noting how peaceful it seemed compared to the chaos they'd left behind.

Inside, the receptionist recognized them from their previous visit. "You're here to see Mr. Bradley? He's having a good morning today. He actually mentioned that he hoped you might come back."

They found the retired detective in the same sunroom where they'd first interviewed him, but his appearance had changed subtly. He sat straighter in his wheelchair, his eyes clearer, as if a burden had been lifted from his shoulders.

"The dynamic duo returns," he greeted them with a small smile. "I've been watching the news. That's quite the hornet's nest you two stirred up."

"We thought you'd want to know how it ended," Tucker said, taking a seat across from him.

"Oh, I already know that," he said, perkily. "It's all anyone here has been talking about. Duckwood's biggest scandal in living memory." Bradley's expression grew more serious. "You confirmed what I suspected all those years ago. The gun running, Parsons' involvement, Winson looking the other way."

"You were right about everything," Mallory assured him. "Your initial investigation was on the right track. They derailed it deliberately."

"My 'accident,'" Bradley nodded. "Not so accidental after all, I'm guessing."

"Probably not," Tucker acknowledged. "Pearcy confessed before he died that they eliminated anyone who threatened to expose them."

"Pearcy." Bradley shook his head slowly. "I never would have suspected the pastor, even though the first body was found on his leased land. He hid behind that collar very effectively."

Tucker updated Bradley on the details they'd learned—how the operation worked, Louis Fisher's role in managing the finances, Tanya's years-long evidence gathering, the arrests, and Pearcy's suicide.

"You've given an old man some peace," Bradley said when Tucker finished. "I've spent eleven years wondering if I missed something, if I could have done more for those families."

"You did everything you could," Mallory assured him. "Against powerful people who were determined to stop you."

They spent another twenty minutes with Bradley, answering his questions about the investigation. Tucker was impressed by the old detective's sharp memory and insightful observations, despite his advancing age and health issues. The man had been a good investigator, stymied not by lack of skill but by corruption beyond his control.

As they prepared to leave, Bradley reached out, gripping Tucker's hand with surprising strength. "One piece of advice from someone who's been where you are. Don't let the job consume you." His gaze shifted meaningfully to Mallory. "There's more to life than catching the bad guys. Took me too long to learn that."

Tucker nodded, understanding the message. "We're working on that balance," he said, glancing at Mallory. "In fact, we're heading back to Chattanooga for a wedding dress appointment."

Bradley smiled. "Good. Hold onto that. The cases will always be there, but the people we care about won't."

Back in the car, Mallory gave Tucker a curious look. "Wedding dress appointment, huh? I didn't think you were keeping track of that schedule."

"Jen's called you three times about it," he replied. "It would be hard to miss," Tucker replied, starting the engine. "Besides, you deserve to focus on something positive after all that's happened."

"We both do," Mallory said, settling into her seat. "Maybe you could actually come to the appointment with me, give an opinion."

Tucker's expression must have betrayed his horror at the suggestion, because Mallory laughed. "I'm kidding. I know that's beyond your comfort zone. Focus on the cake decision like we agreed."

On the drive back to Chattanooga, Tucker was quieter than usual, his expression thoughtful.

"What's on your mind?" Mallory finally asked as the city skyline came into view.

"Margaret Fisher," he replied. "What she said about not wasting time. About Terry never getting the chance to build a life with someone he loved."

"It got to me too," Mallory admitted.

"Our work reminds us constantly of how fragile life is," Tucker continued. "How quickly it can be taken away. Maybe that's why I've been reconsidering Hargrove's offer after all."

"Oh, you have, have you?" she said, slightly concerned. "And?"

"Life is too short to make decisions based on old grudges or fears. If working with the Bureau in some capacity allows us to make a larger impact while still maintaining what matters to us…" He glanced at her briefly. "Well, maybe it's worth considering, don't you think?"

Mallory nodded, understanding what this admission cost him. For Tucker to even contemplate returning to the organization he'd left on principle showed significant personal change.

"We'll figure it out," she assured him. "Together. That's what partnerships are all about."

As they reached the city limits, Mallory felt a sense of one chapter closing and another beginning. The Fisher family had their answers after eleven years of uncertainty. Now it was time for her and Tucker to determine their own next steps, as private investigators and partners in every sense of the word, or to become part of something bigger, much bigger.

The drive to Chattanooga had taken just under an ninety minutes, the familiar skyline welcoming them back to normal life, or as normal as life ever got in their profession. Tucker drove directly to his home office to find it exactly as they'd left it four days earlier, though it felt like months had passed.

"We should call it a day," Mallory suggested, noticing the time. "Finish the report tomorrow. I'm exhausted, and you need rest with that arm."

Tucker was about to protest, but then decided she was right. Some decisions couldn't be rushed, especially those that would affect not just his future, but Mallory's as well.

23

Mallory smoothed down the satin of the fifth dress she'd tried on, studying her reflection in the three-way mirror. Bridal Elegance was everything the name suggested—elegant, upscale, and filled with more wedding dresses than she'd ever seen in one place. Jen sat on a plush velvet chair nearby, watching with a critical eye as Mallory turned slowly.

"That's the one," Jen declared, her expression softening. "You look beautiful, Mal."

Mallory had to admit; the dress was perfect. The A-line silhouette complemented her figure. The sweetheart neckline was flattering without being too revealing, and the delicate lace overlay added just enough detail without overwhelming her frame. Most importantly, she could imagine moving comfortably in it during an outdoor ceremony.

"It feels right," she agreed, swishing the skirt gently. "Not too formal for the botanical garden, but still special."

The bridal consultant beamed. "We can add a simple belt with a bit of sparkle to accentuate your waist. And a chapel-length veil would complement the train beautifully."

Jen stood, circling Mallory with a practiced eye. "She's right. A bit of sparkle at the waist would be perfect. What do you think?"

For a moment, Mallory's mind flashed to the events of the past week—crouching behind a tractor in a dark barn, fleeing armed men on a rural highway, watching Pastor Pearcy's psychological breakdown. The contrast between that reality and this moment of traditional feminine ritual was almost disorienting.

"Mal?" Jen prompted, noticing her distraction. "The belt?"

"Yes, let's see it," Mallory agreed, pulling her focus back to the present. This was important too, a different kind of important than solving murders and exposing conspiracies, but significant nonetheless.

The consultant returned with several belt options. As Mallory tried them against the dress, her phone vibrated in the robe pocket where she'd tucked it. She resisted the urge to check it immediately—Jen would kill her if she got distracted by work now—but her mind immediately wondered if it was Tucker, or perhaps Reynolds, with an update on the case.

"This one," Jen decided, pointing to a delicate crystal belt that caught the light beautifully. "It's perfect."

Mallory nodded her agreement, and the consultant began making notes about the necessary alterations. Jen snapped a few photos, 'for Mom,' before the consultant helped Mallory back to the dressing room to change.

Once alone, Mallory checked her phone. A text from Tucker: "Lewis called. Wants to meet. No pressure."

She frowned slightly. Tucker's former FBI supervisor had been a shadow hovering at the edges of the Duckwood case, a reminder of Tucker's past and the incident that had prompted his resignation from the Bureau. What could Lewis want now?

Then there was Director Hargrove's surprising job offer, which they'd barely discussed. The idea of joining the FBI—working together on a specialized task force—was both intriguing and unsettling. It would mean leaving behind the independence they'd built, the flexibility of choosing their own cases and methods and, most of all, her family.

But it would also mean greater resources, a wider reach, the ability to tackle larger criminal networks than they could as private investigators. And if they were both offered positions, they wouldn't have to sacrifice their partnership.

These thoughts followed Mallory as she changed back into her regular clothes and rejoined Jen in the boutique's sitting area to complete the paperwork for her dress order.

"You're a million miles away," Jen observed as they left the boutique. "What's going on in that head of yours?"

Mallory hesitated, then decided her sister deserved the truth. "Tucker got a job offer. From the FBI. For both of us, actually."

Jen's eyes widened. "The FBI? Like, moving to Washington?"

"Possibly. It's for a new task force focused on weapons trafficking. After the Duckwood case, we apparently got their attention."

"Wow." Jen processed this as they walked to their cars. "How do you feel about it?"

"Conflicted," Mallory admitted. "It's a tremendous opportunity, of course. But..."

"But you've built a life here," Jen finished the thought. "The agency with Tucker, the wedding plans, being close to your family."

Mallory nodded. "Exactly. And Tucker left the FBI for a good reason. Going back would mean sacrificing some of the independence we value," she said as she followed her sister out into the parking lot.

Jen leaned against her car, studying her sister thoughtfully. "You know, when you started working with Tucker, I worried it was just another of your phases, like that year you decided to become a professional rock climber, or the six months you spent trying to launch a food blog."

"Thanks for the vote of confidence," Mallory replied dryly.

"But this was different," Jen continued, ignoring the sarcasm. "You found something that challenged you, that used your natural curiosity and persistence for something meaningful. And you found a partner who loves you."

"That's what I'm afraid of losing," Mallory confessed. "The way we work together as equals. In the Bureau, there would be a chain of command, protocols, all the things Tucker left behind."

Jen considered this. "Maybe. But you'd still be you, and Tucker would still be Tucker. The circumstances might change, but the core of what makes your partnership work doesn't have to."

It was surprisingly insightful coming from Jen, who typically focused more on practical concerns like wedding arrangements and social calendars than existential questions about career paths.

"When did you get so wise about relationships?" Mallory asked with a small smile.

"Twenty-four years of marriage teaches you a few things," Jen replied. "Like the fact that the right partnership can withstand changes in circumstance. Jared and I have moved three times, changed careers, had children—the external stuff shifts, but what matters is how you face it together."

Mallory hugged her sister impulsively. "Thanks. For the dress help and the life advice."

"Anytime," Jen said, returning the embrace. "Just promise me one thing: if you do move to Washington, you'll stay in touch?"

"Deal," Mallory laughed. "Hey, of course I will."

After saying goodbye to Jen, Mallory drove directly to the office, her mind clearer than it had been that morning. She found Tucker at his desk, the completed Fisher report printed and ready in a professional folder.

"Dress mission accomplished?" he asked, looking up from his computer.

"Mission accomplished. Even found one I actually like." She set her purse down and perched on the edge of his desk. "Your text said Lewis called?"

Tucker nodded, his expression neutral. "Wants to meet for coffee. Says he has information relevant to Hargrove's offer."

"Are you going to go?"

"I thought we might go together," Tucker replied. "Since the offer concerns both of us."

Mallory studied him, noting the tension around his eyes. "Are you considering it? The FBI position?"

Tucker leaned back in his chair, his expression thoughtful. "I'm considering considering it. Which means at least I'll listen to what Lewis has to say."

"That's... surprisingly open-minded, coming from you," she said, her head tilted to one side.

"Yes, well. Detective Bradley said something yesterday that stuck with me," Tucker admitted. "About not letting the job consume everything else. About balance."

Mallory remembered the exchange at the nursing home, how the retired detective had looked meaningfully at her when giving Tucker advice about life priorities.

"You think rejoining the FBI would help with that balance?" she asked skeptically.

"Not necessarily. But making decisions based solely on old grudges might not be the best approach either." Tucker met her gaze directly. "What about you? You've been quiet about the offer."

Mallory considered her conversation with Jen. "I'm intrigued by the opportunity. But I don't want to lose what we've built here, as partners, as investigators who can choose our own path."

"I share that concern," Tucker acknowledged. "But I'm also thinking about impact. What we could accomplish with federal resources behind us."

"Like taking down larger criminal networks than we can reach as private investigators," she said.

"Exactly." Tucker stood, moving to the window that overlooked downtown Chattanooga. "The Duckwood case was bigger than we initially thought, a decades-and-a-half-long operation with connections to international weapons suppliers. And that was in a town of less than thirteen thousand people."

Mallory understood his point. Their work as private investigators was meaningful, but inherently limited in scope. "So we meet with Lewis, hear what he has to say. No commitments, just information gathering."

"Agreed. He suggested tomorrow morning at the coffee shop down the street."

"Works for me," Mallory said, then changed the subject. "Did you finish the Fisher report?"

Tucker nodded, handing her the folder. "Complete account of what we found, who was responsible for Terry's murder, and how it connected to the other victims. I've anonymized some of Tanya's contributions for her protection, but everything else is there."

Mallory scanned the report, impressed, as always, by Tucker's thorough documentation. Every detail was captured, from their initial meeting with Gary through the raid on the Parsons farm and the subsequent arrests.

"It's good work," she said.

"Thank you," Tucker said. "I also called Reynolds this morning. They've located the murder weapon used on Terry Fisher."

Mallory looked up sharply. "Where?"

"Pearcy's storage unit. Along with weapons used in the other murders. He kept them as some kind of twisted trophies."

"So Pearcy himself pulled the trigger? On all five victims?"

Tucker nodded grimly. "Ballistics confirmed it. He didn't just orchestrate the murders—he committed them personally."

Mallory processed this new information. "The mild-mannered pastor was actually the executioner," she said. "No wonder he had a psychological break when it all started coming apart."

"His confession at the storage unit makes more sense now. He talked about the victims as 'sinners' who needed to be eliminated for the greater good. In his mind, he was delivering judgment."

"Religious justification for cold-blooded murder," Mallory said, shaking her head. "People can rationalize anything."

They spent the next hour reviewing case notes and organizing their files, the routine work of closing an investigation. It felt almost anticlimactic after the intensity of the past week, but Mallory welcomed the return to normalcy.

Eventually, Tucker suggested they call it a day. "Dinner? I owe you a proper meal after all those burger dinners in Duckwood."

"I'd like that," Mallory agreed, gathering her things. "Somewhere with tablecloths and wine glasses."

"I know just the place," he replied.

They ended up at a small Italian restaurant overlooking the Tennessee River, with a view of the lights reflecting on the water as evening fell. Tucker had made a reservation, surprising Mallory with his foresight.

"Planning ahead?" she teased as they were seated at a window table.

"Occasionally," he replied with the hint of a smile. "Especially for important occasions."

"And what occasion is this?"

"The end of another case," he replied "Plus, you found a wedding dress today. That's worth celebrating, too."

Mallory laughed, feeling the tension of the past days finally easing. "When you put it that way, we definitely deserve wine."

Over dinner, they deliberately avoided discussing the FBI offer, focusing instead on lighter topics—the upcoming wedding, a film they'd been meaning to see, plans for a short honeymoon. It felt good to remember there was more to their relationship than work, more to life than investigations and danger.

As they finished dessert—a tiramisu they shared—Tucker reached across the table and took her hand in his. "Whatever we decide about Hargrove's offer, we decide together. As partners. That doesn't change."

"I know," Mallory said, squeezing his hand. "That's what matters most to me—that we face these choices as a team."

"Agreed." Tucker's expression softened in a way few people ever saw. "Detective Bradley was right about one thing—the cases will always be there. The people we care about should come first."

For Tucker, this was practically a declaration of love, and Mallory felt its significance. "Does this mean you'll actually have opinions about wedding details now?"

"Let's not get carried away," he replied dryly. "I'm still delegating most of that to you and Jen. But I'll make the decisions about cake."

"Fair enough." Mallory smiled, feeling a certainty settle over her. Whatever they decided about the FBI offer, whatever challenges came next, they would face them together. That was the partnership they'd built—one strong enough to weather changing circumstances while maintaining its essential balance.

Later that night, as they prepared for bed, Mallory found herself thinking about the contrast between the darkness they'd encountered in Duckwood and the light they were building in their own lives.

"You're quiet," Tucker observed as he set his alarm for the morning.

"I was just thinking about how we spend our days investigating the worst of humanity, then come home to this."

Tucker considered this. "Maybe that's what makes our partnership work. We've seen enough darkness to appreciate the light. To protect it."

"Is that what you think the FBI task force would be? Protecting the light by fighting larger shadows?"

"Potentially," Tucker acknowledged. "But there are many ways to make that kind of difference. We'll know more after talking to Lewis tomorrow."

Mallory nodded, setting aside the question for now.

Tucker turned off the bedside lamp and reached for her.

In the darkness, Mallory felt Tucker's hand find hers.

TUCKER AND MALLORY arrived at the coffee shop ten minutes early the following morning, a habit Tucker had developed during his FBI days. The small café near their office was busy with the morning rush, but they secured a corner table that offered some privacy while still allowing Tucker to observe the entrance.

"Are you sure you're okay with this?" Mallory asked, noting the tension in Tucker's shoulders. "Meeting with Lewis again?"

"I'm not too bothered about it," Tucker said. "He's a total... He's...

Well, avoiding him doesn't serve any purpose if we're seriously considering Hargrove's offer."

The door opened, and David Lewis entered the café. He hadn't changed much since Tucker had last worked with him. His hair was a little grayer at the temples, the lines around his eyes had deepened, but he still carried himself with the confident bearing of a senior FBI official. He spotted them immediately and approached after ordering a coffee at the counter.

"Tucker. Ms. Carver." Lewis nodded to each of them as he took the third seat at their table. "Thank you for agreeing to meet with me."

Tucker acknowledged him with a neutral nod, then dove right in. "You said you had some information about Director Hargrove's offer and the task force."

Lewis took a sip of his coffee before responding. "I do. I've been tasked with helping structure the operation. Hargrove wants it to function differently from traditional Bureau units. He wants it to be more flexible, less bureaucratic. Similar to how you two operate, actually."

"Why the sudden interest in our methods?" Mallory asked directly. "The Bureau isn't exactly known for embracing independent approaches."

Lewis's expression shifted to something Tucker hadn't seen often during their time working together, a genuine reflection.

"The landscape is changing, Ms. Carver. Traditional approaches haven't been effective against the cartels and their sophisticated weapons trafficking networks. What you accomplished in Duckwood in just a matter of days was impressive and something that's eluded federal task forces for years in similar situations."

"Because we weren't constrained by bureaucracy," Tucker pointed out.

"Exactly," Lewis agreed, surprising Tucker with his candor. "Which is why Hargrove wants to create a unit that operates with similar autonomy within the Bureau framework."

Tucker studied his former supervisor carefully. "And you're on board with this approach? You were never a fan of operational flexibility when we worked together."

Lewis set down his coffee cup, meeting Tucker's gaze directly. "People change, Tucker. Perspectives evolve. The Marsha Cline case... I know how it changed you..." He paused, then said, "It changed things for me too."

The mention of Cline's name hung in the air between them. Tucker remained silent, waiting.

"You were right," Lewis continued after a moment. "We moved too soon. I overruled your assessment because I was concerned about the optics, about how a delayed operation would look in the report. It was the wrong call, and it cost that young woman her life."

Mallory glanced at Tucker, sensing the significance of this admission. Tucker's expression remained neutral, but his posture had shifted slightly.

"Why tell me this now?" Tucker asked.

"Because if you're going to consider returning to the Bureau in any capacity, you deserve to know that lessons were learned from that incident." Lewis leaned forward slightly. "Your resignation prompted a review of tactical decision-making protocols. Changes were implemented. I was reassigned temporarily, required to undergo additional training before returning to a supervisory position."

Tucker hadn't known this. He'd left the Bureau immediately after the incident, cutting all ties. "I wasn't aware of that."

"You wouldn't have been," Lewis acknowledged. "The Bureau doesn't publicize its internal corrective measures. But your principled stand had an impact."

Mallory interjected, bringing the conversation back to the present. "What exactly would this new task force do? And what would our roles be?"

Lewis seemed grateful for the shift. "The task force would focus on identifying and dismantling domestic weapons trafficking operations, particularly those with connections to international suppliers, like the cartels. Your roles would be as lead field investigators, with authority to determine operational approaches within broad parameters."

"Reporting structure?" Tucker asked.

"Direct line to Deputy Director Kaminski, bypassing regional supervision," Lewis explained. "You'd have access to Bureau resources, intelligence, and tactical support when needed, but day-to-day operations would be at your discretion."

"And you?" Tucker asked bluntly. "Where do you fit in this hierarchy?"

Lewis met his gaze evenly. "I'd be a resource, not a supervisor. My role would be liaison between the task force and other Bureau departments. I wouldn't have operational authority over your investigations."

Tucker nodded, filing this information away. "Location?" he asked.

"Flexible. The task force would have a nominal headquarters in Washington, but field operations could be run from regional offices. You could potentially remain based at the Chattanooga field office, traveling as cases required."

Mallory leaned forward. "And my role specifically? I'm not former Bureau. I don't have the training Tucker does."

"That's precisely why Hargrove wants you," Lewis replied. "Your background, including your three years as a private investigator and Tucker's partner, brings a different perspective, different methods. The Bureau needs that fresh approach. You'd receive abbreviated tactical training, but you had a good teacher in Tucker. Your investigative skills are already proven."

They continued discussing operational details for another thirty minutes: budget allocations, personnel support, jurisdictional considerations. Lewis was surprisingly forthcoming, providing specific information rather than the vague assurances Tucker had expected.

As the meeting wound down, Lewis reached into his briefcase and withdrew two folders. "The official offers, with complete details. No pressure to decide immediately. Hargrove said to give you two weeks."

Tucker accepted the folders without opening them. "We'll review them carefully," he said.

Lewis stood to leave, then hesitated. "For what it's worth, Tucker, I hope you'll consider it. The Bureau needs people who stand by their principles, even when it's uncomfortable. Especially then."

After Lewis departed, Tucker and Mallory remained at the table, the folders between them.

"That was unexpected," Mallory said finally. "He actually admitted he was wrong about the Cline case."

Tucker nodded, still processing the conversation. "People can surprise you, sometimes."

"Are you considering it more seriously now?"

Tucker met her gaze. "I'm considering it with an open mind. Lewis's admission changes the context somewhat. But what matters is what we want for our future, not what the Bureau needs."

Mallory placed her hand over his. "Whatever we decide, we decide together."

Tucker nodded, picking up the folders. They had a lot to discuss.

EPILOGUE

SIX MONTHS LATER

THE CHATTANOOGA BOTANICAL Gardens in late April was a glorious cacophony of cherry blossoms and dogwoods creating a canopy of white and pink, azaleas adding splashes of vibrant color along the winding paths. A white tent had been erected in the central garden, rows of chairs arranged in neat semicircles facing an arch woven with fresh spring flowers.

Tucker stood beneath the arch, adjusting his cuffs for the third time in as many minutes. Nate, his brother, leaned closer, speaking in a low voice only Tucker could hear.

"Relax. You've faced armed criminals with less anxiety than this."

"Different kind of stress," Tucker replied, scanning the assembled guests. Ninety-five people—mostly Mallory's extended family and friends, with a smaller contingent from Tucker's side. His parents in the front row, his former FBI colleagues scattered throughout, even David Lewis sitting near the back.

The decision about Hargrove's offer had not been easy. Their meeting with Lewis had revealed more nuance than Tucker expected

—a restructuring at the Bureau, greater autonomy for specialized task forces, even an admission from Lewis that his call in the Marsha Cline case had been wrong. The conversation had opened a door to healing old wounds, though Tucker still carried the scars of that tragic outcome.

In the end, they'd surprised everyone, including themselves, by proposing an alternative: they would consult for the FBI task force from Chattanooga, maintaining their private agency while lending their expertise to specific weapons trafficking cases. Hargrove had eventually agreed, recognizing the value of their independence and local connections.

The arrangement had worked surprisingly well for the past five months. They still chose their own cases, but occasionally traveled to assist the task force with investigations that benefited from their specialized knowledge. It was the balance they'd sought; impact on a larger scale without sacrificing the partnership dynamic they'd built.

The string quartet began a new piece, signaling the ceremony was about to begin. Tucker straightened, his attention drawn to the garden path where the bridal party would appear. First came Jen, resplendent in a deep blue dress that complemented the spring setting, followed by Mallory's niece Jackie and two friends from college.

Then the music shifted, and the assembled guests rose. Tucker's breath caught as Mallory appeared on her father's arm.

She was radiant in a simple but elegant gown, her hair swept up with a few strategic curls framing her face. She carried a bouquet of spring flowers that matched the arch above Tucker's head. But it was her expression that held him transfixed; confident, joyful, her eyes finding his immediately across the distance.

As she approached, Tucker was struck by how this moment crystallized everything they'd built together.

Mallory reached the arch and her father placed her hand in Tucker's before stepping back. Up close, he could see the faint scar above her eyebrow from a case last year, the determined set of her jaw that had faced down criminals and bureaucrats alike, the intelligence and compassion in her eyes that made her such an effective investigator.

"You look beautiful," he whispered.

"You clean up pretty well yourself," she replied with a smile. "No ankle holster under those pants, I hope?"

"Nate made me leave it in the car," Tucker admitted, drawing a soft laugh from her.

"You sure you want to do this?" she whispered.

There was a moment of silence. She nudged him. "Hey, I was joking."

"I know you were," he muttered.

"Well?" she persisted.

"Of course I do."

The officiant began the ceremony, but Tucker found himself only partially attending to the words. His mind flashed through moments from their partnership: their first case together, the gradual shift from colleagues to something more, the Duckwood investigation that had tested and ultimately strengthened their bond.

When the time came for vows, they had opted for simple, traditional words rather than writing their own—neither of them comfortable with public displays of emotion. Yet the standard phrases carried deeper meaning given all they had faced together: for better or worse, in sickness and health, until death do us part.

They had already proven their commitment through gunfire, danger, and difficult choices. This ceremony merely formalized what had been true for some time. They were partners in every sense of the word, stronger together than apart.

The exchange of rings, the official pronouncement, the kiss that sealed their union, all passed in a blur of emotion Tucker hadn't fully anticipated. Then they were walking back down the aisle together, husband and wife, greeted by applause and smiling faces.

The reception unfolded beneath the white tent, now configured with round tables and a small dance floor. Tucker had indeed chosen the cake, a simple three-tier design with fresh flowers matching Mallory's bouquet. True to his nature, he had researched cake options methodically, even creating a spreadsheet comparing flavors, textures, and prices before making his selection.

As guests enjoyed dinner and drinks, Tucker found himself approached by Gary Fisher, who had traveled from Duckwood with his parents for the wedding.

"Mr. Randall, or should I say, Agent Randall now?" Gary extended his hand. "Congratulations."

"Thank you," Tucker replied, shaking his hand. "And it's still just Tucker. We're consultants, not agents."

"Consultant, investigator, whatever the title, I'm grateful for your work." Gary glanced toward his parents, seated at a nearby table. "Dad's holding steady. The doctors say he might have another year, maybe more. Having answers about Terry made a huge difference."

"I'm glad to hear that," Tucker said sincerely. "How is Duckwood recovering?"

Gary considered the question. "Slowly. Trust doesn't come back overnight. The new police chief is working hard to rebuild community relations. Pastor Williams at the Whitehaven Baptist church is too. He's young, energetic, and determined to heal the wounds Pearcy left."

"And Tanya?" Tucker asked, lowering his voice. "Any word?"

"Witness protection program," Gary replied quietly. "Reynolds says she's doing well in her new location. She testified against Parsons and Winson last month: airtight cases, both of them."

"Good. She deserves peace after everything she did to bring the truth to light."

The conversation shifted to lighter topics—Gary's children, Tucker's consulting work, the botanical garden setting. After Gary moved on to greet Mallory, Tucker found himself momentarily alone, watching the celebration unfold around him.

His gaze found Mallory at the far side of the tent, deep in conversation with his parents. She laughed at something his father said, her whole face lighting up. Tucker felt a profound gratitude in that moment, for the partnership they'd built, for the balance they maintained, for the simple fact that they had both survived the dangers their work entailed.

As if sensing his attention, Mallory looked up, meeting his eyes across the distance. A silent communication passed between them, the same wordless understanding that had served them so well in investigations now connecting them in this personal moment.

The band began playing a slow song, and Tucker crossed to where Mallory stood, extending his hand in invitation. She took it with a smile, allowing him to lead her to the dance floor for their first dance as husband and wife.

"Happy?" he asked as they moved together to the music.

"Very," she confirmed. "Though Jen is already asking when we're going to start thinking about children."

Tucker raised an eyebrow. "I assume you told her we're a bit busy now, consulting for the FBI and running a private investigation agency."

"Something like that," Mallory laughed. "I told her we're taking one major life change at a time."

They danced in comfortable silence for a moment before Tucker spoke again. "I received a letter from Marsha Cline's parents yesterday."

Mallory looked up in surprise. After the Duckwood case, Tucker had finally told her the full story of the hostage situation that had gone wrong, the eighteen-year-old victim who had died because of a premature breach, the guilt he had carried for years afterward. And, with her encouragement, he'd reached out to the victim's family.

"What did they say?" she asked gently.

"That they appreciated hearing from me after all this time. That they've found some measure of peace. That they're glad I've found the same." Tucker's voice was steady, but Mallory could feel the emotion beneath his words. "They're good people. They didn't have to respond so graciously."

"Some wounds heal with time and truth," Mallory said, resting her head against his shoulder. "Like the Fisher family. Like Duckwood, eventually."

"Like my own," Tucker acknowledged quietly.

The song ended, and other couples joined them on the dance floor. Mallory's father claimed her for the traditional father-daughter dance, while Tucker found himself partnered with his mother.

The celebration continued as evening fell, lights twinkling in the tent and throughout the gardens. Tucker and Mallory circulated among their guests, accepting congratulations and sharing moments with those who had traveled to witness their union.

As the reception began winding down, Tucker spotted Reynolds in conversation with Lewis near the cake table. The two men had developed an effective working relationship during the prosecution of the Duckwood conspirators, despite initial jurisdictional tensions.

"Admiring your cake selection?" Mallory asked, joining Tucker as he watched them.

"Monitoring potential interdepartmental conflict," he replied with a hint of humor. "Old habits."

"Always the investigator," she teased, taking his hand. "Even at our wedding."

"Occupational hazard." Tucker said and squeezed her hand gently. "Ready to make our exit soon? The hotel's sending a car in twenty minutes."

Mallory nodded. "Almost. There's just one more thing I need to do."

She slipped away, returning to the bridal suite briefly before reappearing with a small, wrapped package. She handed it to Tucker with a smile that held just a hint of mischief.

"What's this?" he asked, weighing the package in his hand.

"Open it and see."

Tucker unwrapped the gift carefully, revealing a leather-bound notebook similar to the ones he used for case notes, but of finer quality. Opening the cover, he found an inscription on the first page in Mallory's distinctive handwriting:

For our next chapter. The best partnerships evolve, but never lose their balance. All my love, Mallory.

Below the inscription was a photograph he'd never seen before. It was of the two of them at a crime scene early in their partnership, heads bent together over evidence, completely focused on the work but also unmistakably in sync. Tucker couldn't recall who had taken the picture, but it captured perfectly the foundation of their relationship.

"How did you get this?" he asked, genuinely surprised. Tucker was not easy to surprise.

"Nate had it. Apparently, one of the officers at that scene was his friend from the academy. He thought we made an interesting pair and snapped the photo. Nate held onto it, thinking it might be significant someday. And then he gave it to me."

"He has good instincts," Tucker said, carefully re-wrapping the gift and tucking it into his jacket pocket. "Thank you." And he leaned forward and kissed her.

The final hour of the reception passed quickly—the bouquet toss—caught by Jackie, to Jen's visible alarm—the cake cutting—executed with Tucker's typical precision—and finally, the sparkler send-off as they departed for their hotel.

In the quiet of the car, Mallory leaned against Tucker's shoulder, her expression peaceful. "We did it," she said simply.

"The wedding? Or the past six months of juggling FBI consultations, private cases, and wedding planning?"

"All of it," Mallory replied. "Every bit. We did it."

"We did," he agreed, his arm tightening around her shoulders. "And we'll keep doing it, whatever comes next."

Detective Bradley's words came back to Tucker as the car carried them away from the celebration: "The cases will always be there, but the people we care about won't." He had taken that wisdom to heart, finding a way to pursue justice while prioritizing what mattered most.

The balance they'd achieved wasn't perfect, and it would require constant attention to maintain. But as Tucker looked at Mallory beside him, he knew without a doubt that they would succeed.

"By the way," he said, turning to look at her, "what are we going to call the business now we're married? Randall & Mrs. Randall?"

She made a face, then said, "Randall & Carver will do just fine."

AUTHOR'S NOTE:

While this story is loosely based on actual happenings, it is a work of fiction. Duckwood, TN, doesn't exist. I set it in Cumberland County because it's a beautiful area and I know it quite well having played a lot of golf up there when I was a journalist.

As to Chattanooga: there are, of course, no botanical gardens, though I think there should be. So why set the wedding there? Well, because I thought it would be nice.

THANK you so much for reading, ***Evil Never Sleeps***, the third book in the Randall & Carver Mysteries series. I hope you enjoyed it! If you did and you'd like to continue reading this series you can find the fourth book, ***Never No More*** for sale now.

Turn the page to find a full list of Blair Howards Books.

Short Stories and Novellas

Buried Secrets(Harry Starke)

The Painted Lady(Kate Gazzara)

Stand Alone

Hunter's Moon(Kate & Harry)

Series

The Harry Starke Genesis Series

9 Books in Series as of 2026

The Harry Starke Series

27 Books in Series as of 2026

The Lt. Kate Gazzara Murder Files

24 Books in Series as of 2026

Randall And Carver Mysteries

6 Books in Series as of 2026

The Peacemaker Series

3 Books in Series as of 2026

The O'Sullivan Chronicles: Civil War Series

5 Books in Series as of 2026

Science Fiction From Blair C. Howard

The Sovereign Star Series

7 Books in Series as of 2026

also available in German

The Predecessors Series

The Last Station-Book One

The Infinity War-Book Two

Andromeda Rising-Book Three

Blair Howard is the international best-selling author of more than seventy novels that span the worlds of gritty detective fiction, espionage thrillers, sweeping historicals, and hard-science military space opera. A Royal Air Force veteran and former journalist, he draws upon a rich background of service and storytelling to breathe life into unforgettable characters such as ex-cop turned private eye Harry Starke, and the fiercely determined homicide detective Lt. Kate Gazzara, who breaks her own trail as the head of a serious-crimes unit.

Under his sci-fi pen name Blair C. Howard, he expands his reach into the cosmos with the Sovereign Stars saga—an epic journey born from his lifelong love of the heavens, and the Predecessors hard science fiction trilogy. Whether unraveling a brutal crime scene or commanding starships in interstellar conflict, his stories are propelled by relentless pacing, vivid realism, and a watchful eye for justice.

Visit www.blairhowardbooks.com.
Email: BlairHoward@BlairHowardBooks.com

You can also find Blair Howard on Social Media

www.ingramcontent.com/pod-product-compliance
Lightning Source LLC
LaVergne TN
LVHW020645110826
845149LV00012B/1919

* 9 7 9 8 9 9 4 1 5 5 0 4 2 *